Ray Brooking has been writing professionally ...

He learnt his craft through working on some of the country's most popular TV drama series: *The Bill, EastEnders, Doctors, Casualty, River City and WPC56.* He has been nominated for many awards, and in 2004 won 'Best Episode' at the Soap Awards.

Venus Sleeping is his first novel.

A RHIDIAN HOOK CRIME THRILLER

VENUS SLEEPING

RAY BROOKING

ACKNOWLEDGEMENTS

To the people who made this possible.

To my mother, who lit the candle.

To Terry, Gráinne and Dawn for making me the writer that I am today.

To Jan, Andy and Daniel for keeping the flame alive.

Many thanks to Bill Morris for his invaluable technical advice on police procedures.

Prologue

What happens in those moments just before you die? For some, time slows down. For others, their whole lives flash before them like some home video on fast forward. Some describe seeing a blinding white light; others, nothing but dark oblivion. All that Rhidian Hook could say was that in the face of death, he had never felt so alive. It was as if all his senses were working to their full potential for the very first time. He heard every jagged note of the screaming metal as they tore through the barrier. He saw every splinter of the shattering branches as the BMW crashed through the trees. He smelt the peaty water even before the headlights showed that they were rushing to meet its ink black surface.

The impact took his breath away.

After all the noise, peace, except for the windscreen wipers and that annoying squeak that he'd been meaning to fix. He tried to make sense of what had happened. He saw that his hands were still gripping the wheel, as if he could just drive away. He turned to his wife. She was staring straight ahead, trying to understand why there were bits of tree sticking out of the twisted mess of the bonnet.

'Bethan.'

She turned to him, but shock had stolen her ability to form any words. He saw the bruise on her forehead, a tiny ruby of blood already forming in its centre.

'You're hurt,' he said.

'What?'

He watched the red bubble burst into a trickle. He took the handkerchief from the breast pocket of his dinner jacket and gently caught the drip. He knew she would be upset if she ruined the evening gown. It had been her grandmother's. Ivory silk. Bethan had dieted for a fortnight to get into it.

‘Rhidian? What happened?’

‘You were sleeping.’

‘We’re in the river.’

‘We’re going to be all right.’

‘We’re in the river!’

‘We’ll be all right.’

He held her look until she believed him, but then the car lurched towards the passenger side as the undercurrent pulled them away from the bank and swept them downriver towards the muddy vastness of the Severn Estuary. She hadn’t cried out until then.

‘Bethan. Look at me. Bethan. We won’t sink. There’s too much air trapped inside. We’ll wait until the river narrows, then we’ll bail out. Okay?’

She took a couple of deep breaths and calmed down; returning to the practical woman he loved; the one who could deal with all the different aspects of his job, from his remoteness when immersed in a case, to him coming home with a bullet hole in his shoulder.

‘Bail out. Okay. Got it.’

They looked out through their side windows.

‘Anything your side?’ he asked.

‘It’s too dark. Can’t see a thing.’

The irritating squeak stopped as the wipers finally gave up the ghost. Rhidian realised why. The car was tilting forward under the weight of the engine. The swollen, murky water was already lapping at the bottom of the windscreen.

They both saw it at the same time; the bull's-eye pattern Bethan had made when her head had hit the glass. A dribble of water was working its way through a hole, no bigger than a pinprick. Tiny chips of glass broke away. The drip became a trickle.

Bethan turned to Rhidian. ‘I love you.’

Before he could answer, the windscreen shattered into a thousand pieces and the ice cold water hit them like a wall. The car filled rapidly, the water only levelling off once it had reached their chests. There was no time to comprehend what was happening, let alone put their fears into words before the bonnet dipped down once, twice, then they sank like a stone.

The headlights tried to pierce the darkness, picking out the twisted shapes of submerged tree trunks and the ghost of a shopping trolley. As the car hit the stony bottom, Bethan's door was ripped open. She wasn't wearing her seat belt. They'd argued about it earlier, but she wasn't going to risk damaging the delicate teal orchid corsage he'd bought to show off the blue of her eyes; eyes that now stared at him, full of fear. She tried to grab his outstretched hand, but the undercurrent caught her. One moment she was sitting next to him, the next she was torn from the car by the undeniable, invisible force.

Rhidian reached for his seat belt, but it was jammed. He tried to call her name, but the brackish water filled his mouth. He could see her long blonde hair glowing in the darkness as she was swept away. The last thing he saw was the flash of her wedding ring. He tried to shout her name but only sucked in more water. He saw the orchid floating in the space that she had left. He closed one hand around the delicate petals. It was getting harder to focus; to keep his eyes open. He could no longer feel his fingers. His pulse was slowing. He gave up fighting and closed his eyes. He would see her again on the other side. Rhidian Hook had never been a believer, but now he would cling onto any hope. The headlights went out. The darkness was complete. All he wanted was to sleep; sleep and dream of the first time he saw Bethan.

The exhibition was in a small private gallery. But for once it wasn't the canvasses that interested Rhidian. He needed to find the source of the heavenly music that floated around the two rooms. As he got closer, he caught glimpses of her through the crowd, caressing her Welsh harp as if it were part of her; oblivious to everything that was going on around her. He couldn't believe his luck when she agreed to have a meal with him. And when they kissed for the first time, he remembered thinking that he had never felt so alive.

1

Six months later

Seventy eight minutes gone. The scores were tied. The girls of the Dinas Powys Women's Rugby Club were knackered. These valiant part-timers, mostly office girls and P.E. teachers, had given their all to hold back the full might of the Combined Services rugby team. There was added grit to this match because the visitors had come from across the Severn Bridge. They were English, and even though this was a small council pitch and not the national stadium, this still counted as another skirmish in the age-old war of Celt versus Saxon. There might only have been a few spectators following the action, but the girls knew that they were fighting for their country as well as their town. They had battled bravely, but now, pegged back on their own ten metre line, it looked like it would take a miracle to stop the army and navy Amazons from scoring the winning try.

As the ref gave a final warning to a couple of six-foot props who had been taking lumps out of each other all through the match, the Welsh number eight, Anwen Jones, took a moment to catch her breath and scoop the rainwater out of her eyes.

Wales had been basking in a mini heatwave for the last few days. It had to end sometime, and of course, it had to be at the very moment that the two teams took to the pitch. A day's average rainfall fell in half an hour, turning what had been rock-hard ground into the Somme. But that was the way Anwen liked it. After all, rugby was a game of mud, blood and thunder, wasn't it?

The ref had finished her lecture. The props stomped back to take up their positions in the line-out. Anwen joined the end of her team's line. The opposition hooker, a weapons engineer on a Type 45 destroyer, tried to wipe the ball dry, but her shirt was already soaked. She pulled back her arm, aimed and threw. It was going to be long, heading for their second jumper at the back of the line-out. But as her teammates lifted the forward up, she fumbled and the ball went loose. Almost before she knew what was happening, the cold, slippery ball was in Anwen's hands. Her passing options were cut off. She had a split second to decide what to do. And then, like some Old Testament miracle, the opposition defensive line parted. Anwen put her head down, and ran.

Fending off a clawing flanker, then jumping over a diving forward, she powered on towards the opposition's goal posts, a white, rain-streaked blur in the distance. Crossing the halfway line, legs pumping, Anwen became aware of another noise above the sound of her own pounding heart. The high-pitched wailing of a car alarm. A glance to her left; a full back the size of a wardrobe was heading towards her. A glance to the right; a skinny figure in a hoody was breaking into a 4x4 in the car park. 'Come on, Jones. Focus!' she said to herself.

Only ten yards to go. The full back was closing fast to block her path. Anwen waited until she could smell the defender's cheap deodorant before she planted her right foot, skidded to a stop, then pushed off again, changing direction, slipping, sliding, but managing to keep her footing, leaving the full back sprawled on the grass with a mouthful of Welsh mud.

Now Anwen's route was clear. No one was going to catch her. She headed for the try line. Her only mistake was to glance across at the car park and recognise the scrawny figure helping himself to the contents of the glove compartment; stick-thin, rodent-featured, wearing knocked-off Nike joggers. Anwen had seconds to decide. She could win the match. It would be an historic victory. She would never have to buy her own pint ever again! But the car thief was on the move. 'Bugger!'

Anwen changed direction, hearing the bewildered cries of her teammates and the shrill repeat of the ref's whistle as she jumped the advertising boards, her boots crunching on the loose gravel of the car park.

The lad turned, stunned to see the mud-splattered rugby player bearing down on him. Dropping his booty, the CD cases shattering on the gravel, he picked up his push bike and mounted up. Anwen knew she was too far away. As soon as he'd got his balance he'd be off and she'd have no chance of catching him. There was only one thing for it. Anwen stopped, sized up the distance, pulled back her arm and launched the ball with all her strength. It was a beautiful arc, culminating in the rugby ball hitting the lad plumb on the back of the head.

Just as the dazed thief got to his feet, he was clattered by twelve stone of prime Welsh beef. Anwen winced as she heard the unmistakable sound of snapping bone and she knew that he wouldn't be getting up anytime soon. The lad turned his head, pieces of gravel imbedded in his acne-pocked cheek.

'What the hell! I ain't done nothing.'

'Time you got a better line, Darren Powers. How many times have I heard that one?'

Darren recognised the voice and groaned. 'Not you!'

'In the flesh and twice as ugly. And you are under arrest. Theft from a motor vehicle.'

'You've busted my chuffing wrist.'

'Maybe that'll teach you to leave other people's property alone. You do not have to say anything, but it may harm your defence, if...'

Darren Powers could recite the caution in his sleep. With his right wrist throbbing like a bastard, he wished he'd never bothered getting out of bed that afternoon.

Hearing the distant final whistle blow and a cheer go up from the visitors, Anwen knew that she'd soon have to face the wrath of her teammates. To add insult to injury, Anwen saw the rest of her morning off vanishing under a mountain of paperwork. Darren Powers would be bailed and back out on the street before she'd finished typing out her report. On the brighter side, he was still nursing his wrist. At least that might give the decent folk of Barry and Dinas a break from this one-scrote crime wave.

*

As the rain clouds cleared and the sun re-emerged for what might be its last hurrah before it faded into autumn mists, office workers left their umbrellas dripping dry under their desks and emerged, blinking, from their offices. Those who couldn't grab their favourite benches had to make do with putting their coats down on the still-damp grass. Here they donned sunglasses and laid back, pretending they were on a fortnight's holiday in Ibiza, rather than a forty-five minute lunch break in the centre of Cardiff.

Situated in the picturesque surroundings of Cathays Park, the Baroque edifice of Cardiff Crown Court has seen its fair share of notorious cases during its 120 years. From the number of press photographers milling around outside on the steps, you would think they were covering a mass murder, not a road traffic collision.

The police weren't expecting trouble, but half a dozen officers had been sent across the road from the police station, just in case it kicked off. The football season was only a few weeks old. Cardiff City were off to a flier, but they couldn't risk losing their star winger. Rhys Pryce had scored fifteen and assisted in another dozen goals last season. The few fans who had turned up were more interested in trying to bag an autograph than causing aggro, and with the ugly 1960s police station lurking only yards away, they'd be stupid to pick a fight. But then again, your average football fan wasn't renowned for being among the sharpest knives in the drawer.

The jaded paparazzi supped on takeaway lattes or drew on sneaky fags under the numerous 'No Smoking' signs. Only one young photographer was watching the bottle-blonde in the high heels and tight skirt who was covering the story for the local news. Ginnie Lane had also noticed the handsome newcomer. She thought that he had a touch of David Beckham about him, with his trendy flat cap, stubble and tattooed forearms. Always on the lookout for fresh conquests, she was pleased to note how his interest in her was more than just professional rivalry, but for now she had to put him out of her mind. She had bigger fish to fry.

Ginnie had no intention of blowing this opportunity. For two years she'd laughed at her producer's lewd jokes and ignored how he talked to her breasts, not her face. Finally she was reporting live to the nation. To her this wasn't just filler between the football scores and tomorrow's weather; this was her chance to shine. All she needed was one serious news producer to see this and she could be off the local sports desk for good. She looked straight into the camera and tried her best to channel the seriousness of Kate Adie.

'...The twenty-five-year old winger was arrested at his Cardiff home in the early hours. He initially denied being involved in the collision, but forensic evidence linked his limited edition Lamborghini to the crash scene. The driver of the other car, Doctor Loretta Swann, is still in a coma. The trial continues. This is Ginnie La...'

The man came out of nowhere. With his beer-filled belly stretching the nylon of his replica football shirt to its maximum tolerances, he waved a blue and white scarf and bellowed into the camera. 'Rhys Pryce is innocent. Rhys Pryce is innocent!' Then he bent over and pulled down his baggy jeans to reveal the barely recognisable portrait of the Cardiff City winger, tattooed onto his left buttock. The man's pimpled arse gave the impression that Rhys Pryce had a bad case of chicken pox.

The man only just had time to pull up his pants and turn to his mates to give them a big thumbs up when he was hit square on the jaw. He was unconscious before he hit the floor. Rubbing her bruised knuckles and marvelling over where that anger-fuelled strength had come from, Ginnie Lane was snapped out of her reverie by the sound of a camera clicking multiple exposures. She looked up to see that David Beckham's doppelganger had captured every frame of her moment of unprofessional madness. The images of nine-stone Ginnie Lane flooring a sixteen-stone football fan with one punch would be sold around the world. This wasn't the kind of exposure she'd been hoping for.

*

The end of Ginnie Lane's dreams were the last thing on the mind of Detective Chief Inspector Liz Devlin as she sat, ramrod straight in the public gallery of Number One Court. She had no direct involvement in this trial. The investigation had been carried out by the Roads Policing Unit. It was the defendant who had drawn her here. She wanted someone from CID there to witness him finally getting the just punishment that he deserved.

Devlin was wearing her usual dark-blue tailored trousers with a matching jacket and a crisp white blouse. Tall, gym-toned, her dark hair tied back in French plaits, Devlin usually commanded any room she was in, but today she was eclipsed by the ebony-skinned man in the horsehair wig and black gown who strutted like a peacock around the court's oak-panelled splendour.

In full flight, Darius Gull was an impressive sight. Standing at six foot four, he had the presence of a champion boxer, the sartorial elegance of a male model and the dreadlocks of a reggae star. After listening to three days of the prosecution's case, Gull knew that his moment had come. He looked over at the witness box, to make sure that his client was ready for his part in the performance to come.

Rhys Pryce's good looks meant that he earned as much from his activities off the pitch as he did from sport. His bleached white grin and floppy dark hair could be seen on TV ads, in gossip magazines and on the sides of buses, endorsing everything from lager to toothpaste. He even had his own brand of male toiletries, despite the advertising authorities making him tone down the promise that spraying some of his deodorant under your armpits gave you a better chance of scoring with the ladies. Rhys's barrister had advised him to dress smartly, but not flaunt his wealth to avoid alienating the jury, so Rhys had dug out a five-year-old Paul Smith suit from the back of the wardrobe. It had only cost £800 new, half of what he'd spent on his latest pair of trainers. Although he had been brought up by a hard-working single mum who had sometimes struggled to put food on the table, it hadn't taken him long to forget how normal people lived.

An academic underachiever, Pryce was just another of those hormonal boys who larked about at the back of the class. His teachers predicted a future of flipping burgers until they saw what he could do with a football.

His life changed when he was spotted by a talent scout from Wrexham A.F.C. First joining the youth team, he was soon being celebrated as the find of the year. Now he lived in an eight-bed mansion and owned a nightclub on St Mary Street which was a favourite haunt of his teammates and the groupies who followed them. He had bought his mum a nice little new build on the outskirts of Caerphilly. She would never want for anything again, but some nights, as she tried to sleep on the hand-crafted bed that cost more than her annual wage as a school cleaner, she couldn't help but wish that Rhys's talent with a football had never been discovered.

She loved him because he was her son, but she didn't like the selfish, arrogant womaniser he had become.

Darius Gull's voice was like thick honey as he addressed his client. 'Mr Pryce, we've heard the prosecution make a great deal of your actions after the collision. Can you tell the jury why you didn't stop or phone for an ambulance?'

'Because he was as pissed as a newt,' muttered Devlin under her breath.

'Didn't know I'd had a prang, did I?' said Pryce.

'But your car was badly damaged. Are you expecting the jury to believe that you knew nothing about this?'

'Yeah.'

'How is that possible?'

'It was my doctor who explained it.'

'Go on.'

'It was because of the other crash.'

'The accident that happened in March of this year?'

'That's it.'

'When you were trapped in your car for two hours until the fire brigade employed their jaws of life to cut you out?'

'I thought I was going to die.'

Devlin could tell that Rhys Pryce had been practising his act of befuddled victim in the mirror.

'And afterwards?'

'I kept having nightmares. Had to take stuff to help me sleep.'

'Medication?'

'Yeah.'

'So, when you were involved in this second accident…'

'It took me back.'

'Back to the horrors of being trapped in twisted wreckage, fearing for your life?'

'Objection!'

Up popped the prosecution barrister like a Jack-in-the-box. Although she was considered a rising star by her chambers, this was the first time that the ambitious young barrister had faced the infamous Darius Gull and she was not enjoying the experience. 'My learned friend is trying to put words into the defendant's mouth.'

'Then I will rephrase the question,' purred Gull, drawing a nod from the judge. The prosecution barrister sat back down. She knew she had scored a point, but hardly a fatal one. Gull turned back to his client.

'Did you need to seek any kind of medical treatment after the second accident?'

'Yeah, I had to go to my doctor.'

'And what conclusion was he able to come to?'

'He said I had the same thing that soldiers get. PTSD.'

Gull slowly turned to the jury, emphasising every word for effect.

'So your doctor's expert diagnosis was that you were suffering from previously undiagnosed post-traumatic stress disorder?'

'Yeah. It was 'cos of the shock that I didn't know what I was doing.'

Gull saw the prosecution barrister scrambling through her notes, desperately searching for something to counteract this bombshell. Gull allowed himself the tiniest of smirks. Devlin's heart sank. Her 'Shit!' was audible in the silent court, earning her a rebuking glare from the judge.

Emerging onto the court steps, Devlin slipped on sunglasses to cut out the glare of the late summer sun. But the dark lenses couldn't shut out the sight of Gull and Pryce laughing as they addressed the assembled press pack and cheering fans. In her nearly twenty years on the Force, Devlin had dealt with domestic abuse, armed robbery and rape, but it was mercenaries like Darius Gull who really turned her stomach.

Through success in several high-profile cases, Gull had become the go-to guy if you were rich, stupid and believed that having your face on the front of a few gossip mags gave you immunity from normal motoring laws. Just in the last year Gull had successfully defended a soap star who claimed that he needed to travel at 140 miles per hour down the M6 because he'd had a dodgy prawn korma the night before and needed to get to a toilet; and the lingerie model whose excuse for ploughing through the side of an old lady's bungalow was that she was being chased by the paparazzi. The funny thing was that none of the alleged photographers were there to snap the bimbo staggering out of the wreckage, or the old dear being given CPR to restart her heart.

'We were always confident that my client would be leaving this court a free man,' boomed Gull. 'Now he just wants to put all of this unpleasantness behind him and concentrate on his career.'

Gull stood shoulder to shoulder with his beaming client, already thinking about where he would hang the blown-up photo of his latest celebrity scalp. Perhaps between the reality TV star and the inebriated knight of the realm.

Devlin could feel her blood boiling. She knew she should walk away, but as the press dispersed to file their photos, she moved in, bitterness dripping from her words.

'Well done, Mr Gull. Another dangerous driver back on the streets.'

'I know it's vulgar to keep score, but I make that five-nil. Does that sound about right to you, Detective Chief Inspector?'

'How do you sleep at night?'

'I didn't write the laws.'

'But you're happy to exploit any loophole?'

‘I am not going to apologise for being excellent at my job. Perhaps if your officers were better at theirs, we wouldn't get to meet so often.’

Devlin could do nothing except watch the grinning Gull join his triumphant client, heading for the nearest restaurant that had a good stock of expensive champagne. While they were celebrating, Devlin would be trying to explain to the Chief Constable why they had suffered yet another defeat by ‘Mr Loophole’.

*

The coastal road from the town of Barry to the hamlet of Ogmore-by-Sea offers some of the finest views of what the Welsh call Môr Hafren, or the Severn Sea, and the English call the Bristol Channel. The golden beaches and rugged cliffs are magnets for holidaying families and thrill seekers. Many climbers enjoy the challenge of the ragged rock faces. The more romantically minded explore the many caves that are only exposed at low tide and wondered whether this was where the wreckers of local folklore hid their booty after luring another well-laden schooner onto the rocks with false lights.

Rhys Pryce wasn’t there to take in the scenery. He loved driving the narrow road at night because he could take down the roof and open up the sports car. Not that he would risk going one mile over the speed limit tonight, only hours after being found innocent in a court of law. He kept checking his mirrors, expecting to see flashing blue lights behind him. Well, they could pull him over if they wanted to waste their time. That smarmy bastard Gull had made sure that he stuck to soda water through their celebratory meal, knowing that the police would love to nail him after he’d made them look like muppets for a second time. Pumped full of confidence and arrogance, Pryce felt invincible. Like a god.

Pryce only saw the car lights coming towards him when they were five hundred yards away. There wasn't room for two cars to pass. One of them would have to pull over. It wasn't going to be Pryce. What was the other car anyway? Some cheap old banger. The footballer tapped his horn, but the other car didn't slow down. In fact, it seemed to speed up.

'So you want to play, do you?' Pryce grinned. An inveterate gambler who regularly risked thousands on the turn of a card or the bounce of a roulette ball, this was just the kind of buzz he needed to polish off his day. He would give this arsehole the scare of his life. Pryce turned the wheel so that he was straddling the centre of the road.

Only a hundred yards to go, but still the other car kept coming, then switched its headlights to full beam. Blinded, Pryce twisted the wheel to the right. The dry-stone boundary wall had stood solid for three hundred years against the worst storms that nature could throw at it. The Italian sports car hardly scratched it.

As Rhys Pryce slowly emerged from the blackness, the first thing he became aware of was a gentle creaking noise. For a moment his mind tricked him and he thought that he was lying out on the foredeck of his best mate's yacht, cruising the Med, but there was no sun warming his skin and that wasn't the sound of a sea breeze gently stirring the rigging. He tried his eyelids. They opened. At first he thought he had gone blind, but then he started to make out the pinpoints of light high above and he knew that they were stars. As his eyes adjusted to the darkness he realised what was creaking; it was the thick, green stalks of the maize that surrounded him, gently rubbing together in a gentle evening wind.

A giggle bubbled out of Rhys Pryce's mouth. He was alive. But why was he lying in a field? How long had he been here? He tried to stand, only for a stab of pain to erupt in his left hip. Something was wrong. He knew he shouldn't move.

It might only be a sprain, but he daren't risk causing any more damage. He needed to be fit for next Saturday's match. He would have to wait for help. But did anyone know where he was? Patting his pockets, he remembered that his phone was in the glove box. He looked around. He was surrounded by four-foot-high curtains of maize, the long stalks topped by the yellow ears of corn that were nearly ripe for harvesting. How did he get here? Then he heard it, the sound of something slowly pushing through the crop. Rhys nearly cried for joy when he saw the light of a torch searching towards him. The other driver! Thank God the bastard hadn't driven off.

'Over here,' he called.

A shadow emerged, black against the wall of emerald cereal. It stopped and looked down at Pryce. What was he waiting for?

'Here, you *twmffat.'*

As the figure slowly approached, something in Pryce's guts tightened. The figure was wearing something covering its head, some sort of hoody, even though it was a muggy night.

'Say something.'

But the figure only stared at Pryce.

'Do you know who am I?'

Pryce noticed that the figure was wearing blue, latex gloves, like the ones his physio wore on match days. Was it a paramedic? Where was their uniform?

'Either help me or phone for an ambulance.' Pryce struggled to keep the panic out of his voice.

The figure answered by slipping a free hand into one of the hoody's pockets and pulling out something that Pryce couldn't quite make out in the darkness. Then the torch beam caught the object; something as black as coal but with many small, sharp edges that glinted razor-sharp in the light. The figure moved towards him.

2

Of all the remote regions of Wales, the Black Mountain is one of the wildest. Straddling the boundary between Breconshire and Carmarthenshire, the bleak, scarcely inhabited landscape is dotted with evidence of man's pitiful attempts to tame the mountain's raw nature.

Nobody knows why it is called the Black Mountain. Yes, it can be stark and unwelcoming in the depths of winter, but its slopes can also be a carpet of verdant green or purple heather flowers in the summer.

Many of its high points are capped with impressive stone cairns, some dating from the Bronze Age. The remains of old limestone quarries have become deep, indigo pools. Only a few farmers still cling to the sandstone slopes. When they have gone, what will be left to remember them by? Will the remains of a field boundary wall or a derelict barn being sucked back into the earth be all that marks how this hardy bunch scraped a living from the cruel hills?

Rhidian Hook had loved the mountain since he first set eyes on it as a small child. His father Geraint had joined the police after ten years in the army. Having been stationed in the dusty sand bowls of the Middle East, he longed to return to the lush green hills and rain-swollen skies of his native land.

Although he never rose higher than the rank of sergeant, Geraint Hook lived a dream of a life. For ten months of the year he was stationed in Newport, dealing with lost children, pub brawls and stolen bicycles. Then for two months in the summer he left the town behind and decamped to a sprawl of old army huts in the shadow of the Black Mountain. Here he ran camps for young police cadets from all over England and Wales. There was orienteering, canoeing on the lakes and the final challenge of the camp's notorious obstacle course. For the last month, his children would join him.

Geraint's wife Lili taught art at a comprehensive school. Although she loved working with the children, she was also a frustrated artist. She spent all year looking forward to the long summer break when she could tie up her hair and slop around in her paint-splattered dungarees to finally commit to canvas all the half-formed ideas she had filled her sketchbooks with. The arrangement worked well. Lili got four weeks to indulge her creativity, then the roles swapped and she took responsibility for the children until it was time for them to return to school.

On the 31st of July every year, Rhidian and his sister Cerys would be packed off to the mountain and into their dad's care. The family stayed on a small farmstead owned by Geraint's older brother and his wife, while the cadets were billeted in the nearby spidery, tin-roofed Nissen huts left over after World War Two. Uncle Arty wasn't much of a talker. He could often be seen standing at the farm gate, looking out over the mountain, smoking his old briar. Sometimes he would be there for hours and Aunty Grace would warn the children to not bother him now. One night Rhidian had been going downstairs for some water when he overheard his mother and father talking about 'poor Arty'. Rhidian instantly forgot his thirst and pressed his ear to the lounge door in order to hear more. What he was later able to piece together was that Arty had only been a child when he had come across his dad, hanging from a rope in the barn. The pyres were still smouldering on the hill from where his prize flock of black Welsh mountain sheep had had to be culled after an outbreak of foot and mouth. He had raised them from lambs and could trace their line back twenty generations. Geraint had only been a toddler at the time, so although he always felt the hole left by his father, he never knew him well enough for the grief to haunt him as it did his brother Arty. After overhearing the dark family secret, Rhidian would never again complain about his uncle not wanting to play with him.

What Uncle Arty lacked in warmth, Aunty Grace more than made up for. She always seemed to be cooking. Rhidian would forever remember her with flour on her hands. She was the shape of a cooking apple and when she grabbed you up and pulled you into her generous bosom she always smelled like rice pudding or fresh bread.

This precious month on the mountain was the highlight of the children's year. They were taught how to fly fish, trap rabbits and build fires. By the time Rhidian was eight and Cerys a year younger, they would be sent out on two mountain ponies to rendezvous with their dad and the cadets who would be somewhere on the mountain, practising their orienteering. The pony's saddle bags would be stuffed with luncheon meat sandwiches, hard-boiled eggs and a flask of sweet tea for their lunch. Back then nobody worried about children being snatched by paedophile rings. There were no mobile phones in case they got into trouble, but the siblings had been well trained, and even though they only had an Ordnance Survey map and a compass to guide them, they never got lost.

Thirty years later, and Rhidian was once again following tracks that his dad had shown him, but which had been laid down by the more ancient feet of primitive hunters tracking their game. Rhidian always returned here when his soul had been bruised and needed healing. During his walks he would open all of his senses; sight, sound and smell, creating enough distractions to blot out any disturbing thoughts.

A plaintive cry echoed over the hills. Rhidian raised his head, pushed away the dark hair which always went curly when it got this long and screwed up eyes as grey as wet slate to search for the telltale silhouette. There! High in the cloudless blue sky, the red kite glided effortlessly; using just the twitch of a wing or the dip of its tail to steady itself as it let the early morning thermals lift it over the crags and gullies where its next meal of carrion or heedless hare might be found.

Rhidian could normally walk for the whole day and not see another living soul, except for the occasional wild pony, or the sheep that outnumbered humans ten to one. These were not the skipping, cotton wool lambs of children's songs, but tough, mountain beasts who objected to any invasion of their territory, so watched closely with keen, feral eyes for any opportunity to charge and butt.

What the area lacked in people, it made up for in its abundance of myths and legends. The Lady of the Lake was supposed to have risen from Llyn y Fan Fach (the 'lake of the small peak') to receive Excalibur from the dying King Arthur, and Geraint Hook had enjoyed scaring his cadets with campfire tales of claw-handed hitchhikers and devil hounds.

Distracted by watching the raptor, Rhidian strayed off the track and crushed some of the brittle gorse beneath his boots. The perfume of the acid-yellow flowers caught him unawares, sparking a memory as fresh as if it were yesterday.

He was ten years old again, lying face down on the mountainside. The only sound was the drone of heavily laden bumblebees as they collected the last sticky grains of pollen before heading back to their solitary nests. Although the gorse pricked at his knees and the sun was scorching the back of his neck, Rhidian knew that he couldn't move, not without spoiling his dad's shot.

Every summer Cerys fell in love with a different animal on Uncle Arty and Aunty Grace's farm. One year it was the lambs, the next the Welsh black pigs. That summer it was the chickens that Cerys had adopted. She'd given them all names and every morning bolted down her Rice Krispies so that she could head down to the coop to feed the birds with last night's kitchen scraps and collect the warm eggs. Rhidian was still in bed when he heard her screams. Tugging on his jeans and daps, he ran for the coop, only to find his sister sitting in the centre of a scene of carnage. As Cerys sobbed, Rhidian took in the details; the way the earth had been scraped away under one corner of the wire fence to let the killer in; the bloodied bodies scattered all over the pen, their throats torn open, eyes frozen in horror of the nightmare they couldn't escape.

Rhidian already understood that nature could be red in tooth and claw, but only one of the hens had been taken for food, the rest had been destroyed by an animal in the throes of a blood frenzy. While Cerys wept uncontrollably, Rhidian was enveloped by a sensory tsunami. He not only felt his sister's pain, but he couldn't stop his imagination from recreating the slaughter. He could hear the birds' panicked cries. He could feel their fear when they first spotted the fox. He was nearly overwhelmed by their blind panic as they desperately tried to escape the merciless snapping, tearing jaws. He would later understand that it was a surge of adrenaline coursing through his body that make him feel sick. All he knew at the time was that he would have revenge on the creature that had broken his sister's heart. A trail of dripped blood marked the butcher's escape route. He would follow it until he found the fox and made it pay.

Geraint took his son to one side and explained that it was no good rushing off up the mountain while his blood was still burning. To catch such a wily predator they needed to use all of their wits. They collected the rifle and ammunition from Uncle Arty and sandwiches and a flask from Aunty Grace.

For two days Geraint showed Rhidian how to track their prey, to spot the crushed bracken that marked where it had bedded down for the night; to identify its paw marks in the wet mud of the river bank and to estimate how many hours ahead their quarry was. Geraint explained that the trick was to get into the mind of your target, to think how they think in order to get one step ahead.

The old fox was lying in the shade of a derelict lime kiln, sheltering from the heat of the midday sun. Hidden in a small copse of stunted hazel and white beam trees, Geraint loaded the rifle and removed the cap from the scope. He offered the gun to his son, but Rhidian knew that it was enough that he had helped bring the killer to justice. He didn't need to fire the fatal shot himself.

A split second before his dad pulled the trigger, the fox turned and looked straight at them. Rhidian swore that in that instant, he knew what the fox was thinking; not fear, but an understanding that this was all part of the game. The hunter had to accept that one day it would become the hunted.

The red body jumped as the bullet struck. It was only after it had limply hit the ground that Rhidian heard the shot echo off the hills before fading away. His dad stood up, shaking the stiffness out of his bad knee, offering Rhidian his shovel of a hand.

Rhidian paused before taking the hand. He wanted to drink in every detail. Towering, virile, smiling; skin like leather polished golden by a summer in the hills; this was how he always wanted to remember his father.

The cry of the kite brought Rhidian back to the present. After he lost her he returned to the mountain because this place was pre-Bethan. She was a city girl and had little time for anywhere that was more than thirty minutes away from a skinny latte or a concert hall. It had taken hard work, but he had eventually persuaded her to spend a weekend at the cottage.

Her laugh when she saw that there was no running water.

Rhidian spun, trying to find the source of the laughter, thinking that he saw her standing in a thicket of yew trees, but it was just a trick of the light. He cursed himself for letting her back in. He knew from experience how this would go. Now that she'd got a foothold there would be no stopping her, her shade was too strong. He strode on, but it was no good; here she came again –

The sun shining through her hair.

Rhidian upped his pace, splashing through a puddle, the oil-black, peaty water covering his boots. But in the echo of the splash he saw –

Bethan, wild swimming naked in the lake, laughing as she splashed water at Rhidian watching from the shore.

He stumbled on blindly, straying away from the familiar track, not caring where he was going. He just needed to get away from -

The sigh she made as she sank into a hot bath.

Rhidian's feet slipped on a moss-covered rock.

The look of childish hope when she made a wish, then blew out the candles on her thirtieth birthday cake.

He tripped and nearly fell but pushed on as if he could outrun Bethan's echo.

Her last words before she vanished into black river waters. 'I love you.'

Loose stones rolled away beneath his feet. Too late, he realised that he'd strayed onto the lip of an old quarry. He started to slide. He had no control. There was no solid ground to stop his downward momentum. He grabbed a small bush but it tore out of the stony ground. He saw the blue of the lake, a hundred feet below. He just had enough time to calculate that there was no way he would survive the fall, before he saw the roots of an old rowan tree sticking out of the soil. He grabbed the gnarled lifeline, felt pain in his shoulder as he slammed hard against rock. His feet danced over thin air before they finally found solid purchase and he was able to drag himself back away from the edge. A few lose stones continued the trajectory he had been on. He counted the many seconds before they splashed into the water. He wondered how long it would have been before anyone would have found his body.

*

Rhidian was nearly home when he saw the car. Black, new, moving too fast for the potholed track. There was only one place it could be heading for, but Rhidian didn't increase his pace. There was only one person who knew where to find him, and they would wait.

By the time Rhidian arrived at the cottage, the Mercedes was parked up on the cobbled yard. There was no sign of the driver, but he knew that his guest would be making themselves at home. He never locked the cottage's ancient oak door, but couldn't decide whether this was a throwback to a more trusting time, or a sad reflection on how little he had that was worth stealing.

The cottage had always been in his family. There was one old photograph of his grandparents sitting outside the back door in their Sunday best, with a sullen-looking five-year-old Arty staring distrustingly at the lens, and Rhidian's dad, then a babe in arms, being held tightly by his proud mother. When Uncle Arty died and Aunty Grace moved to Swansea to be nearer to her sister, the farm passed to Geraint, then to Rhidian and Cerys. His sister had never got over the shock of that summer's slaughter and had vowed never to return. Even though Hooks had lived and worked on the Black Mountain for generations, the locals still regarded Rhidian himself as being 'from off'.

The cottage hadn't changed. The slate roof was still doing a sterling job of keeping out the Welsh rain. The plaster-covered walls still looked as impenetrable as they did when they were built; the blood-red paint as fresh as the day it was daubed on by Rhidian's superstitious forebears who believed that it would keep out evil spirits. And perhaps they were right. Whenever Rhidian had been away, it would only take one night sleeping back under the cross-beamed roof before he felt the tension drain from his bones.

Rhidian was outside the front door, using the old iron scraper to clean the worst of the mud from his boots when he heard the familiar voice call from the kitchen.

'The door was unlocked.'

Rhidian entered the flagstoned heart of the cottage to find Liz Devlin looking through the large charcoal drawings that were scattered around the cosy room. Although at first glance they seemed to be stark landscapes of mountains and moorland, if you looked closer you would see a suggestion of Bethan's face in the contours of a hill or her long hair woven into the branches of a tree.

'Make yourself at home why don't you,' said Rhidian, closing the door behind him with a clunk of the old metal latch. He took off his coat and hung it on a hook. Seeing a drying streak of mud on one sleeve, he half-heartedly attempted to brush it off.

On the cast iron range, a dented copper kettle started to whistle, a sound that had reverberated around these humble walls for generations. Devlin picked up a tea towel with a faded image celebrating the Queen's Silver Jubilee. She wrapped it around the handle of the steaming kettle and brought it to the old kitchen table.

'I couldn't find any milk,' she said.

'I can give you a bucket. There are cows a couple of fields over. You can help yourself,' said Rhidian sitting in one of the oak wheelback chairs. He watched Liz Devlin pour the boiling water onto the coffee granules in the bottom of the only unchipped mugs she could find. He realised that he had forgotten how striking she was, having inherited the raven hair and blue eyes of her Irish and Spanish ancestors.

She sat opposite him and picked up one of the many empty wine bottles dotted around the tabletop.

'Been having a party?'

'Oh yeah. Me, the sheep, couple of badgers from down the lane.'

Devlin read the wine bottle's label. 'Goes well with red meat and casseroles.' She put the bottle back with the others. 'Looks like you've been having a lot of casseroles.'

Rhidian scooped a spoonful of sugar out of the Tate & Lyle bag sitting on the table. As he stirred his coffee he felt Devlin's keen eyes appraising him. She was an expert in evaluating whether the beads of sweat on a stranger's brow were because he was a villain with something to hide, or a civilian who felt guilty because he was cheating on his wife. Rhidian knew that every tiny detail was being subjected to her forensic scan, including the tear in his trousers which revealed a fresh raw scrape from the fall.

'You've lost weight.'

'It's all this fresh air.'

'I like the stubble. Very Heathcliff.'

Rhidian ran a hand over his chin, trying to remember the last time he'd shaved.

'I ran out of razor blades.'

'I could have brought you some supplies.'

'I've got everything I need. What about you? You look tired.'

'You've only been gone six months. Have you already forgotten that this isn't a nine to five job?'

'Have you heard from him?'

Devlin should have known that she couldn't deflect Rhidian. 'He's in Australia.'

'That's not far enough.'

'He's got a new job. He's moving on with his life.' Even to Devlin, her words sounded hollow. She changed the subject. 'I don't know how you do it.'

'What's that?'

'No telly or internet access. No coffee shop for miles. I'd be climbing the walls within a week. No, make that two days.'

'Maybe it's the simple life that's kept me sane.'

There was an awkward silence. Both knew that 'sane' was pushing it.

'You can't hide here forever, Rhidian.'

'Who says I'm hiding?'

'You forget that I know you. You need to be engaged, to have something to focus on. You're like a whale. You've got to keep swimming.'

'It's a shark, and I think that's an urban myth.'

'Shark, whale. The point is, if you never want to pick up your warrant card again, fine. But don't try and tell me that living in the back of beyond is enough for you.' Devlin stopped. She knew he was still fragile. Had she gone too far?

Rhidian stood, taking his coffee to the window. He looked out onto the peace of the mountain. Was he ready to leave this sanctuary behind? Devlin knew that it was time to get to the point.

'Single vehicle fatal crash.'

'Sounds right up Alun Gunter's street.'

'It's like no RTC I've ever dealt with.'

Rhidian felt that familiar sensation. The first tingling of excitement building as synapses in his brain that had remained unused for six months started firing again.

'The body's been mutilated.'

Questions were forming thick and fast in Rhidian's head. He had to hold them back. Devlin could see that he was struggling to hide his growing curiosity, so gave him a final nudge.

'We know the victim's name.'

'So you're halfway there. You don't need me.'

'It's Rhys Pryce.'

Rhidian froze in the middle of sipping his coffee.

'The scene's still fresh. I need a decision.'

Rhidian walked over to a set of bookshelves that had been lovingly made by his grandfather. He looked at the items displayed on the top shelf. The shrine to his father was made up of his old police helmet, the badge always kept gleaming; a battle-scarred truncheon and a framed commendation for bravery signed by the Chief Constable. Rhidian turned his attention to the middle shelf containing a row of neatly stacked, identical, black leather notebooks. The books on the left-hand side were all used. Some were nearly bursting with extra notes which had been stuffed between their pages. There were titles written by hand down the spines; 'Purgatory Pit', 'Dark Heart of the Wood', 'The Red Maids'.

'You know there will be questions,' said Rhidian. 'Is it a conflict of interest? Is he the right man for the job? Is he stable enough?'

'You'll have my full backing.'

'And if I'm no good to you anymore?'

'At least we'll know, one way or the other.'

Rhidian considered, then picked a new notebook from the right hand of the row. He opened a long, thin mahogany box and pulled out a vintage fountain pen. Ritual completed, he rejoined Devlin at the table, turned to the first page of the virgin notebook, and waited, pen poised.

'Everything. From the beginning.'

Devlin knew that she had him hooked. She should have been relieved, but she couldn't dispel the nagging doubt that rather than save Rhidian Hook, she had cursed him.

3

The flashing blue lights of two police cars marked the spot where Rhys Pryce's car had come to rest, it's once sleek lines now crumpled into so much scrap metal, it's once gleaming Arctic white paintjob stained by an arterial spurt of black oil. Over the other side of the dry stone boundary wall, dog units slowly quartered the field of ripening maize. A white tent rose out of the sea of green. Inside, a flash fired intermittently as the forensic photographer captured every detail of Rhys Pryce's body. From the entrance to the tent, Anwen Jones watched on as the white-suited crime scene investigators went about their expert work.

Jones had scrubbed up pretty well. She wore her hair practically short, and rarely wore make-up. When she wasn't wearing her rugby kit, she was usually decked out as she was now, in black jeans, monkey boots and a sweatshirt. Jones was the first to see the black Merc parking behind the other police vehicles. She called back over her shoulder.

'Boss.'

A voice from deep in the maize. 'Not now, Sergeant.'

'It's the DCI.'

'Bollocks!'

Jones heard the sound of a zip being urgently pulled up and then Detective Inspector Alun Gunter emerged, brushing uselessly at the front of his trousers. Jones tried to ignore the dark stain spreading over the crotch of the Asda chinos his wife had bought in a desperate attempt to make him look a bit younger. Prematurely greying hair, beer-bellied, face like a dropped Clark's pie, Gunter raised a hand to shield his eyes from the glare of the low autumn sun. He recognised his boss, Liz Devlin, but who was the second figure? Jones was equally puzzled by the stranger.

'Who is that?' she asked.

Gunter frowned when he recognised the mop of wild, dark hair and the black duffle coat.

'That, Sergeant, is an effing ghost.'

By the time Devlin arrived at the clearing, Gunter was fuming. He glared back down the track made in the crop, watching Rhidian Hook's slow, considered progress.

A uniformed officer was waiting with a clipboard to sign the two new arrivals in. 'Detective Chief Inspector Devlin.' Jones took a couple of steps closer so that she could catch the man's name. 'Detective Inspector Rhidian Hook.' This was duly noted down.

Jones had heard so much about the newcomer; his reputation for cracking the more unusual cases and how the loss of his wife had led to station gossip that he was never coming back. This was her first chance to see him in action, but for the moment she was distracted. She had never seen her DI so furious.

'Since when has a simple RTC needed two inspectors?' Gunter barked.

Devlin had expected resistance. 'If you think this is simple, Alun, then you've answered your own question. Talk me through this.'

Jones stood to one side so that Gunter could lead Devlin towards the tent which covered the site where Rhys Pryce lay on his back. They paused in the entrance to take in the details. The crushed green maize beneath what was left of the striker's right leg had been stained crimson. Jones edged closer to catch the conversation.

'No question about the ID. It's Rhys Pryce all right,' said Gunter. 'My Rhiannon's got his posters all over her bedroom wall. She knows bugger all about football but she can't resist a pretty-faced bad boy. Probable cause of death, severe blood loss from the severing of his right foot.'

'And how did he end up in the middle of a field?' asked Devlin.

'Seat belt was undone, roof down. Damage to the car suggests he was going at a fair lick. Reckon that when he hit the wall, the impact shot him over here.'

'Dr Bloom?' asked Devlin.

'On his way,' said Gunter. 'Don't know why he's needed for a RTA.'

Rhidian Hook's full attention was on the crime scene investigators, leaving the tent carrying the aluminium flight cases containing their specialist equipment. Their work was done. Now it was time for the detectives to take over.

Rhidian led the way into the tent, careful only to step onto the metal plates that had been placed to protect the soft ground and any trace evidence. He took in the muddy stain on the front of Pryce's tailored Italian shirt, then crouched to examine the jagged end of the wound. Jones watched him pull a leather-bound notebook from a voluminous pocket in his duffle coat and start making notes. She could tell that Rhidian was struggling with the sight of the raw bone and shredded flesh, but he wouldn't look away until he had finished what he needed to do. Jones's attention snapped back to the conversation between Gunter and Devlin.

'How do you think he lost his foot?' asked Devlin.

'He'll have snagged it on the barbed wire when he came over the wall.' Devlin didn't look convinced. Gunter tried again. 'We've all seen freaky shit at traffic accidents. Anything can happen when sharp metal meets soft flesh while travelling at high speed.'

Rhidian finally spoke. 'Where's the foot?'

The newcomer's deep baritone reminded Jones of something she couldn't quite put her finger on, some vague, tribal memory of men with coal-dusted faces and coal-dusted lungs singing in the snug of a smoky pub up in the valleys.

Gunter didn't bother keeping the bitterness out of his voice. 'It'll be in the wheat somewhere. Dogs will sniff it out.'

'It's maize,' said Rhidian.

'Wheat, maize. What do I care? I'm a copper, not a farmer.'

'Who found the body?' asked Rhidian.

'Member of the public saw the car. Phoned it in. A Roads Policing Unit was sent to check that the road wasn't blocked. They saw that the keys were still in the ignition and went looking for the owner in case they needed medical attention. When they found the body, they called us in.'

'And this "member of the public", you've cleared them?' asked Devlin. 'Wouldn't be the first time that a suspect's hung around the crime scene.'

'It was the local vicar's wife, ma'am,' said Gunter. 'I've got her details if you want to follow it up.'

Devlin had half an eye on Rhidian, waiting for the fireworks that normally exploded when these two men had to deal with each other, but this time there was no ignition. Instead Rhidian went back to the entrance to the tent and looked down the trail of broken stalks, leading back to the boundary wall.

'The catastrophic blood loss occurred here, and yet the broken stalks show that he dragged himself ten metres from where you say his foot was torn off. Why crawl away from the road and any chance of help?'

'It was dark. There's a farmhouse on the other side of the field. He'd have seen the lights. Gone for help.' Gunter was also waiting for the inevitable conflict, but Rhidian remained calm, disengaged as he crouched down to visualise Pryce's eye line.

'He couldn't have seen any lights from down here.'

'He'd just had his foot ripped off,' said Gunter. 'He'd have been in shock, disoriented.'

'Or he was trying to get away from someone?'

Jones and Gunter saw Devlin's nod of agreement. Gunter snorted in derision. As Rhidian crouched to take a closer look at the overlapping footprints left in the soil, Gunter rounded on Devlin, not caring that she outranked him.

'You cannot be serious. You can't let him within a mile of this.'

'When I need your advice, Alun, I'll ask for it.' Jones didn't need to get too close; Gunter's voice could probably be heard in the next county.

'I get that he used to be the golden boy, but he's spent the last six months sitting on a mountain talking to the sheep. Find him something else to do. He can't be joint SIO on this.'

'You're right. This doesn't need two inspectors.'

Gunter's moment of triumph died the moment Devlin turned to Rhidian.

'Are you sure you're up to this?'

Rhidian nodded. Gunter was furious.

'But he knew the victim. It's a total conflict of interest.'

'It's not your place to question the rights and wrongs of my decision,' said Devlin.

'It's not me who's going to be questioning it though, is it? It's going to be the press and the general public.'

'And I'll tell them that in my judgement, the fact that Inspector Hook knew Rhys Pryce might actually help the investigation.'

'Yeah. Good luck with that,' said Gunter. 'I thought it was just canteen gossip, but now I see that there's no smoke without fire.'

Devlin's eyes blazed. She took a step closer to Gunter. 'Speak to me like that again and I will have your balls for a paperweight.'

Message understood, Gunter turned to Jones. 'Come on, Sergeant.'

Devlin wasn't finished. 'Sergeant Jones will be staying on the case.'

Jones was too shocked to respond. Gunter was about to protest, but one look at Devlin's expression shut him up. He decided to pick his battles and stormed off towards his car.

Rhidian turned to Devlin, seemingly oblivious to the fact that Jones was standing there.

'I work alone,' he said.

'Not this time.' Devlin kept her voice low, but Jones strained to pick up every word. 'It's not just your reputation if this backfires. So. Are you ready for this, because if you're not, turn around. Walk away. You've done your bit. You don't owe the Force any more.'

'I'm ready,' said Rhidian with a certainty he didn't feel.

Devlin looked at the shadow of the man she used to know so well and could only hope that she'd made the right decision. Only time would tell. 'Good luck, Inspector.' Devlin turned to follow Gunter. Rhidian didn't dwell. He was already pulling out his notebook to make more sketches of the site. He headed for the tent, then paused before entering to look back at Jones, as if seeing her for the first time.

'Name?'

'Anwen. Anwen Jones.' She waited for some response, but Rhidian just entered the tent, scribbling in his book, leaving Jones puzzled. She knew where she was with Alun Gunter. He was an arsehole, but she could deal with arseholes, whereas Rhidian Hook, well, he was clearly something else entirely.

4

Jones briefed her new boss as they crunched up the stone chip path towards the uninviting, squat, moss-covered limestone farmhouse.

'Inspector Gunter's already canvassed the area. There are only three people living within two miles, and none of them heard or saw anything.'

'Perhaps Inspector Gunter didn't ask the right questions,' said Rhidian, reaching for the old brass door knocker in the shape of a snarling dragon. The clunk of the knocker echoed through the old house, but there was no response; not even a curtain twitch. Rhidian was reaching for the knocker for another go when the door swung open, revealing an old woman wearing a holey, shapeless cardigan over a checked shirt. Wild white hair haloed around her head. Her face was like the old brass knocker turned flesh. Her mood only darkened when Jones flashed her warrant card.

'Mrs Merrick?'

'I've already had your lot here. I told them what I know about the man in my field, and that is bugger all.'

'Actually, I wanted to talk to you about the car park,' said Rhidian.

The women's scowl thawed, like the sun coming out from behind thunder clouds.

'Hallelujah! About time,' she said.

Rhidian's mouth formed into a smile that didn't reach his eyes. It had been too long. Jones was puzzled. What had a car park got to do with anything? But she kept her mouth shut as the old woman led the way back down the path.

The gravelled parking area was just off the coast road and was favoured by holidaymakers and locals alike who wanted to stop and take in the impressive views and perhaps eat their picnics before continuing on their journey. A laminated sign gave information about the different birds, insects and animals they might see if they were lucky. This included the European shag and the black-headed gull. The more keen-eyed might spot the shadow of one of the great basking sharks that had become a common sight during the peak of the jellyfish blooms of late summer.

The only current occupants of the car park were a middle-aged couple sitting in their Volvo listening to the hypnotic tones of the shipping forecast. 'Cromarty, Forth, Tyne, Dogger. Wind, north west, five to six, rain or squally showers. Moderate or good.' The driver had his head back, eyes closed, fast asleep. His wife was reading the *Echo* and nibbling on a Scotch egg. There was a bench not five yards from their car. Jones could never understand why people would drive to a spot like this and then just sit in their car, rather than get out and enjoy the fresh air. Her attention was drawn back to Mrs Merrick, still in the middle of her rant as she stalked the car park, occasionally pouncing, heron-like, on a scrap of plastic or cellophane.

'What do I pay my council tax for, that's what I want to know? This is their car park, yet I'm the silly sod who has to clean it up. I keep asking them to put a bin in, but all I hear is "budget cuts". Is the country going to go to the dogs for the price of a ruddy bin?'

'So you come down every day?' asked Rhidian.

'If I didn't it would soon be knee-deep in fast food wrappers.'

'And at night?' asked Rhidian, helpfully pointing out a beer bottle top that she'd missed.

'Nights are the worst. That's when the racer boys come out. I wouldn't care what they get up to if they'd only clean up their filth afterwards. But like I said to the other policeman, I didn't see any sports car.'

'What did you see?'

'Actually it was quiet. Just one car in, and I didn't have any reason to bother him cause he was sitting there, quiet as you like. None of that boom boom music going on. And no rubbish either.'

'But you couldn't know that he wasn't going to tip his ashtray out of the window as soon as you weren't looking?'

Mrs Merrick looked at Rhidian with growing admiration.

'You're not as green as you're cabbage-looking, are you?'

She pulled a spiral-bound notebook from her pocket. Although it was pink and decorated with kittens, it was clearly used for the most serious business.

'They're all in here. Dates. Times. Car registrations. Descriptions of any discarded rubbish.'

'So, last night?'

Mrs Merrick turned to a page filled with spidery scrawl. A grubby fingernail pointed at the last entry.

'KDA 352B. Renault Clio. Silver. No litter so he got a tick.'

Jones walked a few paces away, taking out her police radio to call the station. 'DS Jones to Central. Index check please.'

'How many in the car?' asked Rhidian.

'Just the driver.'

'Male or female?'

'Male.'

'Description?'

'Couldn't say.' Mrs Merrick saw Rhidian's disappointment. 'He kept the interior light off.'

Mrs Merrick darted off, distracted by a discarded dog-end.

Jones ended her radio call and approached Rhidian. 'Car's registered to one Matt Conway. Address comes back to a uni halls of residence.'

'A first year student?' Rhidian shook his head. 'No. Doesn't fit.'

Jones delivered the punchline. 'He reported the car stolen from outside the student union.'

Rhidian nodded. 'Fits.'

Jones saw how Rhidian's interest in Mrs Merrick instantly vanished. Determined, he headed away. Caught on the back foot, Jones followed. Rising from retrieving more rubbish, Mrs Merrick saw that her audience was leaving.

'Hang on.' She waved her notebook at them. 'What about the rest of them? I've got dozens in here you know.'

Rhidian called over his shoulder.

'Send your list to Cardiff Central Police Station. Address it to Detective Inspector Gunter. He'll be more than happy to help.'

Jones had to suppress a grin, but Rhidian's expression remained deadpan.

Dusk was closing in as Jones drove Rhidian back along the coast road towards Cardiff in her Audi S3. They travelled in silence; Rhidian's mind already working the case, Jones trying to weigh up her new senior officer.

'How did you know?' she asked.

'About Mrs Merrick's obsession with the car park?' said Rhidian. 'Seemed like a good bet.'

'She never said anything about it to Inspector Gunter.'

'Like I said, he didn't ask the right questions.'

'I'm sorry. Still don't get it,' said Jones.

'People who live in the countryside are often hyper sensitive to their environment being spoilt by the detritus of the city. They can't drive down a lane without seeing the fast food carton dumped in a hedge or the Coke can chucked in a ditch. They start looking for the culprits and hoping that one day one of us will take it seriously enough to do something about it.'

'Okay, but isn't it a bit of a leap thinking that this stolen car's linked to Pryce's death?'

'I know he likes to put his foot down, but ploughing into a wall on a straight road would be going it some, even for Rhys Pryce. Something forced him off the road and that car park's got a perfect view of the coast road. It would have been the perfect place to lie in wait for Pryce.'

Before Jones could reply, her radio crackled into life. 'DS Jones from Central?'

'Go ahead.'

'Re your stolen Clio. It's pinged an ANPR camera on the Barry Road, heading west. Units have been dispatched to intercept.'

'All received.' Jones turned to Rhidian for instructions.

'Well? What are you waiting for?'

Jones pressed down on the accelerator. The hedges became a blur. She was totally focused on her driving and the road ahead. As the speedo crept up past sixty, seventy, eighty miles per hour, she didn't register that Rhidian had not secured his seat belt.

*

Five miles away, the stolen car idled at a red traffic light. To the casual observer, it was like any other vehicle waiting calmly for the lights to change. Only the driver's eyes betrayed his heightened sense of alertness as they flicked from rear-view to side mirror, then back again. This was how he spotted the police car joining the queue of traffic, three vehicles back. Without turning his head, the driver shot a glance to his left. A second police car was cruising up to the junction from a side road. One might be a coincidence, two meant they were hunting, but how did they get onto him so quickly? No problem. He'd soon lose them.

With a squeal of burning rubber, the Clio sped off, straight through the red light. The two police cars pulled out after him, switching on their blues and twos. The chase was on.

One of the officers in the lead car relayed their progress back to the control room and any other units who were listening in. 'We've got a failing to stop. Turning right, right, right onto Ashcombe Avenue. Road conditions good. Traffic is light. Speed four zero.'

Jones listened to the pursuit on her radio as she used her knowledge of back street shortcuts to plot an intercept course.

'Suspect doing fifty in a thirty zone. One up. Straight through another red light onto Pen Y Turnpike. Accelerating to sixty. Wrong side of the carriageway.'

A new voice joined the chatter. A female officer, slightly breathless after hurrying to get in front of the pursuit. 'Stinger available. Junction of East Westra and St Andrew's Road.'

The traffic was thinning out. The fleeing driver sped up, but taking a bend too fast he nearly lost the back end. He had to drive into the skid to wrestle back control. Just as he was congratulating himself on his skills, he saw the copper emerge from her hiding place behind a parked car fifty yards in front of him. She was carrying something.

The driver realised what it was and cursed as the officer sent the strip of metal spikes snaking across the road, where they waited, hungry to shred some tyres. Over her radio, Jones heard the officer's excited cry: 'Stinger deployed! Stinger deployed!'

The Clio driver had a split second to react. He jerked the steering wheel sharp right, mounting the pavement, the car taking to the air momentarily, before landing again, the tyres trying to grip the grassy bank. The family run-around became a tank, ploughing through box hedges as if they were paper, before speeding into the shadows of a grove of oaks and ash trees. The driver turned his headlights off. He knew these woods like the back of his hand.

'Catch me now.' He laughed.

The pursuing officer continued the narration. 'Negative on the stinger. He's gone off-road. Pencoetre Wood.'

Hearing the news, Jones changed direction, shooting down a narrow alleyway, predicting what was coming next on the radio.

'We've lost him.'

Jones wasn't impressed. She became even more determined as she dodged around slow-moving traffic, wheelie bins and dopey pedestrians who were more interested in sending texts than protecting their own lives. Jones was in the zone; at one with her car. It was only when she had to slow down for a dozy plank who was doing a U-turn in the middle of the road that she had time to realise that Rhidian hadn't secured his seat belt.

'Do you want to belt up?'

'Just concentrate on your driving.'

'It's five hundred quid and three points on my licence if you get caught.'

Rhidian just nodded to tell Jones that the blockage was now out of the road. Jones was putting the car into first when a privet hedge twenty yards ahead of them exploded as the stolen Clio carved its own exit out of the woods, and skidded back onto the road.

Jones was off like a greyhound after a rabbit. Although joining CID had other advantages, there just weren't enough car chases as far as she was concerned. She missed the adrenaline kick; that buzz she got when all her nerve endings were tingling.

The driver of the stolen car seemed to sense that the unmarked car now following him was more of a threat. He knew that he'd have to get tricky if he was going to get away from this more dogged opponent. First out of the 'Manual of how to escape a cop car' was going round a roundabout the wrong way. Even having to face speeding traffic coming towards them didn't faze whoever was driving the cop car.

Next he opened the sun roof and started throwing the contents of the glove compartment out through the hatch.

A flying can of de-icer bounced off Jones's bonnet. A map fluttered over the windscreen, blocking her vision momentarily, followed by a hail of splintering CD's, but Jones had seen it all before. It was going to take more than that to make her abort the pursuit. She was getting closer. She could see the driver's eyes glaring back at her in the Clio's rear-view mirror. Ten yards. Five. She nearly had him. It was at that vital moment that she glanced again at her passenger. He still hadn't secured his seat belt. Jones moved her right foot from the accelerator and applied the brakes, bringing the car to a controlled stop.

'What are you doing?' asked Rhidian.

'Do you know how much paperwork I'll have to fill in if my DI goes though the windscreen?'

Rhidian reluctantly pulled the seat belt over his shoulder and clicked it into place. He looked down the road. There was no sign of the Clio.

'And now we've lost our suspect.'

'Not exactly,' said Jones.

Rhidian looked at her, puzzled.

'I recognised the driver. I know where he's heading.'

'We never got close enough. When did you see his face? '

'Didn't need to. I know his style. That stunt with the roundabout, then the sun roof... Driving styles can be as individual as fingerprints. Only if we want to get to the car while it's still in one piece, we'll need to get a shift on.'

Rhidian lost all sense of direction as Jones cut through the rabbit warren that was the Lovelock Park council estate, finally entering a road lined with graffiti-covered garages that ended in a cul-de-sac. Jones slowed to a crawl. Rhidian scanned the street but could only see the carcass of an abandoned settee and a fly-tipped avocado bath and toilet set. Jones sensed his disappointment, until her headlights picked out the stolen Clio, parked at the far end. Scorch marks on the road and nearby brick wall showed that this was the elephants' graveyard for stolen cars.

As they urgently got out of the car, Jones saw a tiny yellow flicker in the darkness. This became a brighter flame as the lighter was touched to the petrol-soaked rag sticking out of the end of a cider bottle. Jones was already running for the silhouette of a man illuminated by the flame, but she was too far away to stop him from lobbing the Molotov cocktail toward the open boot of the Clio. The bottle shattered. Flames spread like something alive, licking at interior of the boot, then reaching out for the back seats.

Just as Jones wrestled the fleeing driver to the ground, the petrol tank exploded, sending a spiralling plume of black smoke into the night sky and rousing a cheer from the small crowd of onlookers who had gathered for their usual evening's entertainment. Jones got to her feet, hauling up a familiar figure; Darren Powers, cocky that he hadn't been caught, even with one wrist in plaster.

'Thought it was you,' he said. 'Good chase that. A right buzz.'

There was nothing Rhidian could do but watch any hope of forensic evidence go up in smoke.

Jones joined Rhidian sitting on the bonnet of her car watching Darren Powers being 'cuffed and stuffed' into the back of a waiting police van and the fire service douse the still-burning shell of the Renault.

'How did you know that he'd dump it here?' asked Rhidian.

'I grew up on this estate. If I'd gone another way, it could have been me you were chasing tonight.' Jones was aware that Rhidian was studying her more closely.

'Your family?' he asked.

'Still live just around the corner. I don't see so much of them anymore. Just birthdays, Christmas. I don't talk about work; they don't bring out any of the presents that fell off the back of the lorry until after I've gone.'

They fell back into the silence, watching the locals drift back indoors for the start of *EastEnders*; as if they didn't already have enough misery in their lives. Rhidian pushed himself off the warm bonnet. 'Let's get to the station.'

Jones glanced at her watch.

'Have you got somewhere better to be?' asked Rhidian.

'Can't it wait until morning? Darren's not going anywhere.'

'But why give him the time to concoct a story?'

They got into her car, but Jones sat there, key in the ignition, the engine off. Rhidian looked at her. She looked pointedly at his seat belt. He got the message and reluctantly belted himself in. Jones turned the key, put the car into gear and drove slowly past the fire brigade who were turning off their hoses, their job done. Before they had reached the end of the street, Rhidian Hook's attention had already turned to what awaited them in the interview room.

5

Jones parked at the rear of the police station and used her electronic key card to unlock the steel door with a heavy clunk. Together they walked down the scuffed, windowless corridor, through more security doors, and finally into the heart of the Custody Suite which tonight was the usual human zoo. Down the corridor in cell five, a Chinese drunk was singing 'My Way' at the top of his fag-scarred lungs, much to the annoyance of his neighbour, a petty shoplifter with the mother of all migraines who was pleading with the Shanghai Sinatra to shut up.

At the counter a constable was trying to deal with a belligerent female law student who was so drunk that she had pissed herself. Her expensive Jimmi Choo goatskin shoes were sitting in a plastic bag because they were soaked in the owner's urine.

The bitter tang of stale sweat and fusty feet was such a pervasive odour that it seemed to have worked its way into the very walls. Adding to this background malodour this evening was the pool of half-digested spicy chicken wings that a young custody officer was trying to mop from the floor without breathing in through his nose.

Prisoners responded to being brought into Custody in a variety of ways. Some hard lads cried for their mums. Others tried to carry on fighting, right up to when their cell door was slammed shut on them. Old hands like Darren Powers knew the routine and understood that it didn't pay to kick off here where you were outnumbered five to one.

'I'll have my usual room. Cell three. And the lasagne. Only make sure it's hot this time,' Darren told the custody sergeant who sometimes felt that he saw more of Darren Powers than he did of his own kids.

'Okay, Darren. Phone call to mum?'

'No point. She'll be off her head by now.'

'Thought she was in rehab?'

'Walked out. Couldn't stick it.'

'I'm sorry to hear that.' The custody sergeant was too experienced to think that many of his customers would turn their lives around. He had hoped that Darren might have been one of the few, but not if his mum was back on the smack. He turned to one of his colleagues. 'Number three. And make sure he's got an extra blanket.'

Before the officer could escort Darren to his cell, Jones stepped up to the counter. 'Actually Sarge, we'd like to interview Mr Powers, before he's tucked away for the night.'

Darren groaned when he saw his nemesis. 'Can't I even have some grub without you getting on my case?'

'If you co-operate you'll be happily tucking into your pasta before you know it.'

The windowless interview room was bare and functional, with a plain table, bolted to the floor and four plastic chairs. A recording device was secured to the table, and the black domes of several video cameras were placed around the room to capture every angle of any interview. Rhidian had spent hundreds of hours in rooms like this, looking across the table into the eyes of killers, rapists and other serious criminals. Each interview was different. He had learnt how to quickly judge which approach would best open up his suspect. Tonight he was taking a back seat. Having witnessed Jones's familiarity with the young car thief, he let her lead the interview. Rhidian and Jones had strong coffees in takeaway cups in front of them. Darren had requested a coke.

'Are you sure you don't want anyone here, Darren?'

'Like who? My dad? Haven't seen him since last Christmas when he nicked our turkey and took it to his girlfriend's.'

'You don't want a duty solicitor?'

‘For what? A twoking?’

‘This is a bit more serious than taking a car without the owner’s consent,’ said Rhidian.

Darren eyed up Rhidian, then turned back to Jones. ‘Who’s he then?’

Anwen didn’t answer, but slid two DVDs into the recorder. After the two beeps told her that the machine was recording, she checked her watch.

‘The time is nineteen thirty-four on the twelfth of September. Present are Detective Sergeant Anwen Jones and...’

‘Detective Inspector Rhidian Hook.’

Anwen prompted Darren. ‘Full name for the recording please.’

‘Darren Rhodri Powers.’

‘Just to remind you, Darren, you are still under caution,’ continued Jones.

‘Can’t we get on with it?’ Darren yawned a little too dramatically, but Rhidian had to admit that he was putting on a good act of looking relaxed. Rhidian sat back to observe as Jones started the questioning.

‘Darren, you were arrested earlier this evening after setting alight a stolen car, namely, a Renault Clio, registration KDA 352B. Where did you get the car from?’

‘You’ve got the wrong person.’

‘I saw you torch it.’

‘That don’t mean I was driving the car. Maybe I just found it abandoned. Maybe I’ve got a screw loose and like setting fires. Yeah, that’s it. I’m a nut job, so you can’t even charge me ’cause I’m sick in the head.’

‘Where did you get the car from, Darren?’

‘Already told you. Wrong man.’ He took another sip from his can. ‘And this own brand stuff is shit. Can’t you afford the real thing?’

Rhidian knew he should let Jones do this her way, but he couldn't prevent his impatience from bursting out. 'That vehicle has been linked to a suspicious death.'

'A what?' Darren's cocky grin died on his face. 'I don't know nothing about that.'

'Prove it.'

'How?'

Now he had shaken Darren out of his comfort zone, Rhidian was happy to let Jones continue. 'Tell us where you got the car.' She gave Darren time to calculate his options. It didn't take long for him to see that, in this case, for once, honesty was the best policy.

'It was just parked there.'

'Where?'

'Caddoxon train station. In the car park.'

'Did you see anyone in or near the car?'

'No. It was just sitting there, begging to be jacked.'

'How do you mean?'

'Driver's window had already been smashed.'

'Were the keys in it?'

'No, but it had been hotwired. The tank was half full. I thought all my birthdays had come at once. So I took it. Course I did. That's what I do. But what, a suspicions death? You know that's not me.'

Rhidian and Jones watched Darren being led to his cell for the night.

'So. Just a case of him being in the wrong place at the wrong time?' asked Jones.

'It's a good way to get rid of any evidence,' said Rhidian. 'Why do your own dirty work when there are plenty of unwitting accomplices out there?'

'Everyone knows that the train station is a favourite spot for teenagers to hang around in.'

'So you leave the car there, knowing the local joyriders are going to rag it around the city before torching it.'

'Disposing of any forensics that might link you to the murder.'

'And wasting our time because we're looking at the wrong suspects.' He glanced at her. 'It's lucky you know the lad or he could have been in real trouble.'

Jones knew that it was probably a waste of time, but she wouldn't be able to live with herself if she didn't have one more go at trying to persuade Darren Powers to turn his life around.

Anwen Jones opened the wicket in the cell door and looked in at the young man sitting on the crude bed, shoulders hunched, poking at his lukewarm lasagne with a plastic fork.

'You've had a good run, Darren, but now the shit's got serious. You're eighteen. You're running out of slaps on the wrist. Next time you're sent down it won't be juvenile detention; you'll be going to an adult prison.'

'Cai and Mal say it's easy.'

'And your brothers are idiots. You're smarter than them. Isn't it about time you started acting like it?'

Darren scooped another lump of minced meat and pasta into his mouth, not because he was hungry but to avoid answering Jones's difficult questions.

'Look, Darren. If you want to crash your future into a brick wall at sixty miles per hour, well, it's your life. But don't think that nobody cares, because we do, even if we are on opposite sides of a cell door.'

Closing the wicket, Jones had no idea whether she had got through to him or not, but she wasn't his social worker. Darren Powers would have to sort his own life out. Her focus needed to be on whoever had used the young chancer as their useful idiot.

6

It was only as Jones drove him towards the city centre that Rhidian realised he had nowhere to stay. He couldn't go back to the cottage every night, it was too far away. There was always the city centre apartment that he and Bethan had bought soon after their marriage, but he couldn't face that, even after all this time.

'What about friends? Family?' asked Jones.

Bethan's parents flashed into Rhidian's mind, but were quickly dismissed. On the rare occasions that they spoke, Bethan's mother tried to be civil, but her husband didn't bother with such polite niceties. He made no secret of how he blamed Rhidian for the death of his precious daughter. Rhidian's own mother now lived in a retirement complex. She would have given up her own bed for him in an instant but she had suffered enough through spending her married life living with a policeman. It was kinder to spare her any extra stress.

'Just stop at the first hotel that doesn't have sticky carpets,' he said.

As she watched the figure of Rhidian Hook recede in her rear-view mirror, Jones couldn't help but be struck by how lonely he looked.

Anwen Jones used her bum to push open the front door of her Victorian mid-terraced house because her hands were full with two bags of Chinese takeaway. Heading for the kitchen she called out, 'Are you in?' She wasn't surprised when there was no reply. She and Sam both worked long hours so it was always a bit hit and miss who got home first.

When they met, Sam was staying in a guest house behind Cardiff Central train station. He had not been in

Wales long and was waiting for his business to pick up before renting or buying a flat. Anwen couldn't believe it when she heard herself asking him to move in with her. They'd only been going out for a couple of months, but it felt so right, so why wait?

They had met on a dating app. Anwen had only been looking at it because she was bored. Well, bored and horny. She was tired of one-night stands. Yes, they scratched an itch, but she needed more. As soon as she loaded up her profile she was bombarded with messages from men. Some at least made an effort to get to know her. Others went straight to sending a dick pick. Where did they get the idea that a full-colour snap of an angry penis was the way to a woman's heart? She'd met up with a nice, but shy paramedic who couldn't get it up and then confessed that he had only gone with her to prove to himself that he wasn't gay. Then there was the retired fire fighter who had an impressive six-pack but who freaked out when she took charge by rolling him over and getting on top.

Sam was different. He didn't mind exposing his vulnerable side, admitting how lonely he'd been since moving from Bristol to try and establish his business. He explained that he needed a new start after a bad breakup with his long-term girlfriend. He wasn't sure that he was ready to get back into the dating game, until he met Anwen. She was prepared for another disappointment, but they instantly hit it off. She held off from admitting that she was a copper. She had learned from experience that at that point men either ran for the hills or asked if she would bring her handcuffs into the bedroom.

Anwen was turning the oven to low to keep the food warm when she heard the front door open, then slam shut. 'Boots!' she called.

Out in the hallway Sam Stokes knew the score and kicked off his dusty, steel-toed Cats and left them by the front door before joining Anwen in the kitchen. Even when he was covered in plaster dust and a hard day's sweat Anwen felt her heart skip a beat when she saw him. There was always a sparkle in his blue eyes and Sam had the strong, kind face that you trusted straight away.

Seeing the takeaway bags, Sam said, 'Great minds,' and held up his own takeaway bag.

'What did you get?' she asked.

'Indian. You?'

'Chinese.'

'Fusion night!'

The kitchen table was soon covered in plastic tubs. Each time a lid was popped another exotic aroma was released to mix with the spicy whiff of beef korma and the sticky notes of sweet and sour chicken. Anwen had remembered Sam's pork ribs and he hadn't forgotten to order her vindaloo, which was always too hot after just a few mouthfuls, but she still insisted on having it every time. They tucked in with relish as they talked about their days. Sam described the kitchen refit he was working on, but he could tell that Anwen had more exciting news to impart. 'Go on then. Tell me before you burst.'

'I've got a new DI and I'm on a murder case.'

'What? That's great. So who's the new boss?'

'Guy called Rhidian Hook. Bit of a legend by all accounts.'

'And who's been murdered?' He saw Anwen's hesitation. 'Sorry, you can't talk about it. I get it.'

'No. There's no point trying to keep it a secret. It'll be all over the papers tomorrow. It's Rhys Pryce.'

'The footballer?'

'Yeah. Looked like an accident, only we still haven't found his foot.' Anwen swallowed the last battered chicken ball. 'Sorry. Should have waited till we'd finished.'

Sam realised that he'd stopped eating his ribs and the sauce was dripping down his hand. He wiped it off with a napkin. 'I was just thinking. City are going to struggle without him.'

'Thought you didn't like football?' said Anwen. She eyed up the house special egg fried rice only to realise that she was well past full. 'What did you say on our first date? "Rugby's in my blood." Or did you only say that to get into my knickers?'

'Well it worked didn't it?' He knew she couldn't resist when he turned on that smile. 'Had enough?'

'Of the food, yeah.'

Sam leant over the table to kiss her. He tasted of hoisin sauce and Kingfisher beer. Anwen Jones had never tasted anything so good.

*

Liz Devlin returned home at the end of another long day. The lodge was surrounded by mature woodlands and had once been tenanted by staff who worked at the big house. When crippling death duties led to the estate being donated to the National Trust, some of the workers' homes were auctioned off in order to pay for the stately home to be adapted into a tourist attraction. The previous owners of the lodge had done a lot of work to bring the humble two-up two-down into the 21st century so when Liz and Peter moved in, all they had to do was redecorate to their personal tastes. Liz liked the oasis of calm offered by the solid little building.

She normally listened to music on her way home as part of her routine of decompressing between work and home. Tonight she was too distracted by doubts. Despite her strong defence of her decision to appoint DI Hook as the senior investigating officer, Devlin had to reluctantly accept that Alun Gunter was right. If the killer remained at large there would undoubtedly be an enquiry which would focus scrutiny on her decision, knowing full well that Rhidian had personal knowledge of one of the victims. If her judgement was called into question the Crime Commissioner might demand her resignation. Everything relied on Rhidian Hook catching the killer.

Opening the front door she was hit by a wall of heat. 'Not again.' Shrugging off her coat, she picked up her post from the hall mat and headed straight to the lounge where the remote control to the central heating system sat on a sideboard. She checked the programme details. It was still set to cut off when it reached 21 degrees, but the reading of the house's ambient temperature told her it was at 26. She switched the controls to manual to reduce the temperature, and then went around opening windows to clear the muggy air.

On her way to the kitchen Liz kicked off her flat, black shoes and reached for a business card: *'Dave Chapman – Central Heating Engineer'*, which was stuck to the fridge by a magnet in the shape of a police helmet; a present from her niece. She dialled the number into her mobile then headed upstairs, speaking once she heard the bleep. 'Dave. Liz Devlin. Sorry. You must be getting sick of me, only it's on the fritz again. Can you ring me back when you've got a minute? Thanks.'

Liz hung up, tossed her phone onto her bed then stripped off her clothes before climbing into a pair of old jogging shorts and a paint-splattered T-shirt, a souvenir from their honeymoon; featuring an image of the Eiffel Tower and the words '*J'aime Paris'*. She headed for the lounge.

She had been redecorating for weeks. Yes, it was extra work at the end of a busy, stressful day, but she had discovered that this rather mindless task was a good way to wind down. She also knew that it was about reclaiming the house as her own. She had established a little routine. First catch up with *The Archers* on the radio, then switch to music until it was time for the nine o'clock BBC news.

She sprayed the wallpaper with water, let it soak in, then got busy with the scraper. The wallpaper was only two years old, but it had been Peter's choice. She still hadn't decided on what to replace it with. All that mattered was that it was new. After finishing stripping the longest wall she turned her attention to the chimney breast. First she had to unhook a painting of the Gower Peninsula that they had picked up in an antiques shop in Chepstow. Lifting the painting away from the wall she paused, stunned. How could she have forgotten? They had been halfway through decorating when Peter got down on one knee and proposed to her. They were so happy that they had written their names alongside the date on the wallpaper behind the painting. He said it would be a lasting reminder of their love. It took her only two passes of the scraper to remove it forever.

*

As Anwen put the empty beer bottles into the recycling her thoughts returned to her new DI. The consensus was that his success rate more than made up for his unusual working methods. But good cops crash and burn every day. It came with the job. Many ended up running private detective agencies or retired to run pubs in the valleys. Was Rhidian Hook going to be another sad ex-copper leaning on the bar, boring his customers with old war stories?

'We've got enough here for another two meals,' said Sam as he scooped the leftovers into a plastic tub then slid it into the fridge. 'Maybe I should take some for my lunch.' Anwen was a million miles away. 'Hello? Earth to Anwen?'

'What? Sorry.'

'It's okay. You've had a big day. Lots to process.'

Anwen could only manage a weak smile.

'You'll be fine,' said Sam. 'You've been on murders before, haven't you?

'It's not the case that I'm worried about.'

'Then what? Your new boss?'

'I've heard tales about him since I was in uniform. Anything out of the ordinary, anything freaky, it always went to Rhidian Hook.'

'What's he got that makes him so special?'

'As soon as I find out, I'll tell you.'

'If he's so good, what are you worried about?'

'He's only just come back from sick leave.'

'What happened?'

'Something to do with his wife.'

'Messy divorce?'

'I think she died.'

'Shit.'

'Then he had some kind of breakdown.'

'And you don't think he's up to the job anymore?'

`Maybe his time is over. The question is, what damage will it do to my career if I'm associated with Rhidian Hook's first failure?'

'Come here.' Sam enveloped her in his arms. 'You're going to be okay.'

'Wish I had your confidence,' she replied, her face buried in his chest. They held each other tightly until Sam sniffed at his armpits.

'I need a shower.'

'Go for it. I'll finish up here.'

Sam held her gaze. Was she sure she was okay? She untangled herself from his embrace and playfully pushed him away.

'Go on, you stink.'

Sam kissed her on the forehead and headed upstairs. Anwen piled up the dirty dinner plates and carried the rattling stack to the old Belfast sink where she squirted them with a splash of Fairy Liquid. Hearing the boiler fire up as the shower activated, all thoughts of work and Rhidian Hook quickly vanished. Anwen said 'Bugger it' and left the dishes soaking as she headed upstairs, stripping off layers of clothing as she went.

Rhidian knew there would be little rest for him that night. He hadn't ventured out from the familiar comforts of the cottage for months. Generations of memories had seeped into the oak beams and flagstones. The stains of a thousand pots of tea marked the old kitchen table. He felt safe there, held in the warm embrace of his ancestors. It couldn't be more of a contrast to the sterility of the hotel room where all evidence of the stranger who had been sleeping in the bed the night before had been expertly expunged by the Latvian cleaners.

It had been so long since he'd been in the centre of the city that he'd forgotten how noisy it was. He could tune out the constant drone of the traffic, but not the giggles of girls and the incessant shouting, tuneless singing and smashing bottles as bands of young men roamed the streets, getting increasingly louder the more Jagerbombs they downed.

Standing in the window, he looked out on a scene from Brueghel's worst nightmares; one hen party, all dressed as Bunny Girls, had started a fight with another group kitted out as slutty angels. It could have looked like a Warner Brothers cartoon come to life if it weren't for the foul language, hair pulling and the blood spurting out of one matron of honour's busted nose. The bunny bride-to-be missed most of the action because she was too busy squatting in an alleyway expelling the two bottles of blue vodka she'd necked. Rhidian wasn't disgusted or even amused. He felt nothing but the familiar deep, heavy darkness inside him that drained his energy. He looked at his watch and realised he'd been standing motionless in the window for over an hour. He knew he wouldn't sleep, but he had to do something; he had to move if the darkness wasn't to engulf him completely.

The hotel reception desk was empty. He emerged onto the street just as the cacophony of kicking out time reached a peak and the night air was filled with drunken laughter, sirens, and the swish of the street sweeping machine on its nightly chore of clearing the gutters of empty bottles and nitrous oxide canisters. Rhidian Hook pulled the hood of his coat over his head and walked out into the night.

It didn't matter whether it was over barren moorland or the concrete and tarmac of a busy city. Long before lifestyle gurus started preaching about the benefits of 'walking therapy' Rhidian had discovered how the simple act of putting one foot in front of another helped to banish the extraneous noise from his head so that he could focus on whatever case he was involved in at the time.

Tonight's walk had a different purpose. Liz Devlin might have overcome her doubts about bringing him back, but Rhidian needed to test himself. If he wasn't up to the job he would need to stand aside and let someone else take over.

The private gallery was in a side street in the Cathays area of the city, handy for students from Cardiff University and the patrons of the City Museum. It was past closing time and through the picture window Rhidian could see the staff preparing the space for a forthcoming exhibition of modern abstract art. He closed his eyes and remembered that stormy winter evening several years ago when he had headed towards the gallery's bright lights and their offer of curative distraction.

The opening night had attracted the great and the good of the Cardiff arts scene. There was an excited buzz as the invited guests milled around the two rooms where the bold, impressionist landscapes of James Dickson Innes had been gathered together from private collections around the UK. Many of the paintings showed the artist's fascination with the Arenig Fawr Mountain in Snowdonia.

At first nobody took much notice of the latecomer who walked past the waiting staff without taking the proffered glass of red or white wine. The leather-coated figure didn't seem to have made any effort to dress for the occasion, but then again, art connoisseurs come in many forms so who was to say that the dishevelled, red-eyed man wasn't a rich, eccentric collector?

Rhidian had come straight from work. In the middle of a gory case he needed to seek out life and beauty to try and counter the dark pictures and imaginings that filled his head. He was drawn to one particular canvas; a large landscape capturing the mountain with a storm gathering over its peak. In the foreground was a lake, the wind rippling its surface into small waves. Although it was recognisable as North Wales, the colour palette of purples and blues gave it an exotic, foreign quality that put Rhidian in mind of the Tahitian paintings of Paul Gauguin. Rhidian tried to concentrate on the details of the painting, but he struggled against the all-pervasive memories from his day.

The flash of a crime scene photographer's camera burned the image of a derelict farmhouse into his memory.

Rhidian tried to concentrate on how the artist had captured the mountain's rough slopes.

Another flash captured the old barn with its sagging roof and the rutted tractor tracks leading to its moss-covered wooden doors, secured by a heavy chain.

Rhidian moved closer to examine the brush work.

Inside, rusty eight-inch hooks hung from ancient oak rafters.

Rhidian concentrated on how the artist had rendered the sun, breaking through the rain-pregnant clouds to illuminate the tops of the peaks.

Clotting blood dripped thickly off the hooks onto the dirt floor.

Rhidian focused on the detail of a flight of birds lifting off from the lake. Were they rooks? Crows? Finally the flashbacks were banished. The muscles in his back unknotted. He became aware of the other art lovers and how they were keeping their distance. He realised how disturbing his appearance must be. He hadn't slept for days. Paper sutures had been used to close a cut on his forehead. There was half an inch of red farm mud on his boots. Just as he was thinking that he should leave, he heard the heavenly harp music coming from the other room. He couldn't leave until he had located the source.

The second, larger room was more crowded as the gallery owner was in the middle of giving a talk about the exhibition. Rhidian was only interested in following the siren call of the Welsh harp. As he got closer he caught glimpses of the young woman wearing a simple but stunning crimson evening dress. Slipping through the crowd, Rhidian finally got his first unobstructed view of the woman who caressed her instrument, eyes closed, oblivious of everything that was going on around her.

He had never heard anything more restful. He had never seen anyone more beautiful. Sensing his attention, her eyes opened and locked on his. They were ice blue but not cold. She continued to pluck delicately at the strings. Rhidian was surprised and intrigued that she didn't look away when faced by this wild-looking man.

Rhidian was jolted from his reverie when the gallery staff turned off the lights, preparing to lock up. He was reassured that he had been able to control the urge to head to the nearest pub to try and drown the pain of the loss. He knew that he would never totally exorcise Bethan's ghost; she would always be with him, especially on these streets where they had spent so many happy hours, but he needed to ensure that her shade wouldn't distract him from his work. Although satisfied that he had survived the test, he was also reassured that the pain was still there. He dreaded the day when he woke up and didn't miss her. Rhidian turned away and headed back to the hotel.

Across the city, a young woman was sleeping. Her long auburn hair was spread out over the thin hospital pillows. Eyes closed, her coral lips were slightly parted, as if ready to laugh. Delicate alabaster hands rested by her sides, each fingernail perfect, as if she were newborn. Beneath the finest emerald silk, her chest gently rose and fell, rose and fell.

To one side of her bed a tiny light glowed on and off to the rhythm of her breathing. It was red, shaped like a child's drawing of a heart. Beside it, green numbers showed that her blood pressure was 110 over 70; well within healthy parameters. Apart from the transparent mask feeding her oxygen, she appeared to be perfect and yet something deep inside was broken, something that had baffled the finest doctors and the most sophisticated scanning machines. She looked as if a single breath upon her cheek would rouse her, but no kiss, even from a prince, would wake this sleeping beauty.

*

On the other side of the Channel a faint glow hung over the city of Bristol while pinpricks of light picked out the smaller settlements along the coast. This was the best time of day as far as Evan Evans was concerned; the hour between darkest night and true dawn. A long-distance lorry driver by trade, nobody would ever call Evan Evans a romantic, especially not his wife who was, at that moment, sleeping alone in their bed. But tonight, this middle-aged trucker couldn't help but feel that there was a magical quality to the atmosphere.

This was his favourite spot, a couple of miles down the coast from Lavernock Point. Because the nearest parking was half a mile away and nobody liked lugging their gear that far, it wasn't popular with the other anglers. This was just the way Evan liked it. He didn't want to make small talk about women or rugby or cars. He just liked to sit with his flask of thick, warming lamb cawl and let his mind drift like his fishing floats, bobbing gently out there on the black, velvet water.

He had two lines out. He was usually baited up for salmon or sea trout, but the season for landing fish closed last week. He wouldn't let this put him off. It was only fishing that got him through his daily grind so he was out, as usual, even if the only thing he was permitted to catch out of season were eels.

The only problem with eeling was the hooks they forced you to use. Evan would rather not use the barbaric half-inch gapes, but if a bailiff caught you using anything else, he'd have your licence off you before you could say 'stupid damned regulations'.

He hadn't had much luck tonight, but if angling taught you anything, it was patience, and how to cope with disappointment. Just as Evan was thinking about calling it a day, he saw the furthest float dip once, twice. He gently laid one scarred, grease-stained fingertip onto the line and tried to gauge through the vibrations what was nibbling at the bait. If he'd inadvertently snared a fish he would feel a pull; but this was a jag, jag, jag. Yes! Eel.

As Evan gently took the rod out of its stand, he could feel that this was a big boy. Must weigh ten pounds at least. He might even get his photo in the *Angling Times*. First he had to land the monster that was in danger of snapping his rod.

Slipping his net under his arm, Evan advanced into the surf to meet his quarry in its own element. Although aware that the cold of the water was creeping up his waterproofs, all he could hear was the thump thump of his heart as his excitement grew. Slowly reeling in, Evan was surprised when the catch finally broke the surface; not one eel, but a seething ball of long, grey and silver bodies.

Scooping the net under the mass, Evan strained under the weight. He prayed that his trusty old net would hold as he hauled his catch back to the shore. As soon as they realised they were out of water, the eels' feeding frenzy was replaced by the more urgent imperative to escape. The eels untied themselves, revealing what they had been fighting over; something white. It couldn't be a fish… there were hairs... and...were those nails? Recognising the object, Evan Evans staggered backwards. His leg slipped on the rocks and he went down on his backside, into the surf, dropping the net. The eels poured out, zigzagging back towards the safety of the water, revealing what remained of a man's severed foot.

7

Anwen and Sam left for work at the same time most mornings. Anwen was able to park her car on the hard standing in front of her house but Sam couldn't get his Transit van into the tight space, so had to park on the street.

As Sam did up the buttons of his overalls he flexed his shoulder, grimacing at the twinge of pain that jolted down his arm.

'Think I pulled something last night,' he said.

'And whose fault is that?' asked Anwen, smiling at the memory. 'You were the one who wanted to go for round two.'

Sam could see that behind her smile something was troubling her. 'You'll be fine. You're ready for this.'

'And if my new DI cocks up?'

'Keep your head down. Do the best you can. If the shit hits the fan, you just say that they shouldn't have brought him back.'

As Sam headed for his van, Anwen wasn't sure that she was comforted by his words.

*

Jones was waiting in the hotel car park, listening to the local news on her car radio.

'...South Wales Police are appealing for anyone who might have witnessed the collision to contact them. Cardiff City fans have been gathering outside Rhys Pryce's home ever since the news of his death broke.'

Jones saw movement in her rear-view mirror, a duffle-coated figure exiting the hotel. She turned off the radio and watched Rhidian Hook, hair like a rook's nest, dark circles under his eyes, step over the sad jumble of crumpled bunny ears and torn angel wings, and slip into the passenger seat, where he found a plastic bag from Boots the chemist waiting for him.

'Just a few things you might need,' Jones explained.

Rhidian looked inside and saw a disposable razor, shaving foam, toothpaste and a toothbrush. He couldn't prevent his anger from bubbling up. 'I don't need a carer.'

'And I'm not being funny, but I don't need to be stuck in a car all day with a bad case of halitosis.'

Jones's plain speaking soothed his irritation.

'Fair point.'

'And while we're at it, I'm only going to say this once, all right, but I'm not a babysitter and I'm not interested in office politics. I just want to do my job. If you'll let me.'

Jones waited for a response. The longer he was silent the louder the voice inside her head became, telling her she was a stupid cow and should have kept her mouth shut. Finally, he pulled out his wallet.

'How much do I owe you?'

'Nothing. Got it out of petty cash.' Jones waited until Rhidian had secured his seat belt then started the engine. 'Where to first? Check in at the station?'

'No. The mortuary.'

Jones was puzzled. 'They aren't going to have any results yet, not unless they worked all night.'

Rhidian was amused. 'I take it that you haven't met our esteemed pathologist then?'

'No.'

'He's a workaholic. Rumours are that when he does sleep, it's in one of his own fridges.'

Jones pulled out of the car park. She was amused to see, out of the corner of her eye, Rhidian surreptitiously checking his breath.

*

The National Health Service has undergone many reorganisations over its seventy-year history. Super hospitals were the current flavour of the month; huge facilities with state of the art emergency departments and each one specialising in a different area like paediatrics or cardiac operations. Their rise had led to the closure of many cottage hospitals and other local facilities, much to the fury of the locals they served. There was, however, one facility that had never been on any hit list.

Too many people had fond memories of the Hopewell Infirmary; from the son of a coal miner turned Hollywood star who had been born there, to the Voice of the Valleys, whose life had been saved after being struck down by a mystery virus while entertaining the troops in Afghanistan. In the era of vast, shiny, characterless super hospitals 'The Hope', as it was known to the locals, was a living, working testament to how bigger is not always better.

Turning left off the main road, a long driveway took Rhidian and Jones through acres of mature gardens with well-maintained flower beds and a mix of mature maples, horse chestnuts and ash. The trees were just on the turn. Give them another few weeks and they would deliver a magnificent display of red and gold.

Clearing the avenue of trees, they came in sight of the long, two-storey building, built with love out of red Victorian brick. There was a feeling of peace here, as if you had left the urgency of the 21st century behind the moment you entered through the gates. You almost expected to see nurses in flapping navy cloaks and huge, starched white hats hurrying around the grounds.

On the first floor newborn babies were placed in the beefy, tattooed arms of crying fathers, while on the floor below, life-saving treatments were administered and sad farewells were whispered to the dying in the small A&E department. While the main building was all about maintaining life, the basement was dedicated to those whose sparks had gone out.

The entrance to the mortuary was hidden around the back of the building and could only be accessed after identifying yourself via an intercom. The door was opened by a young man wearing a disposable plastic apron over green scrubs. He had pleasant, open features and spiky blond hair. Jones thought that he would look more at home in a boy band than in a mortuary. 'Can I help you?' he asked.

Rhidian flashed his warrant card. 'Detective Inspector Hook. This is Sergeant Jones. And you are?'

'Jac Mundy.'

'Are you new?'

'Started last week,' said Jac with a nervous smile.

'Are you going to let us in, Jac?'

'Er, yes, sorry, of course.'

He stood aside to let Rhidian and Jones enter.

Jac Mundy led Rhidian and Jones into a nether world of echoing corridors, unsympathetic strip lighting and pungent chemical smells that clung to your clothes for days. Although all three were aware of the awkward silence as they walked, the reputation and the starkly functional architecture hardly lent itself to flippant small talk. Finally Jac opened the twin swing doors to the autopsy room and the two detectives stepped into the subterranean kingdom of Doctor Augustus Bloom.

In his early sixties but looking twenty years older, you could be forgiven for thinking that he'd just risen from one of his own trolleys. Wispy white hair still clung hopefully to a dome of a skull. Thin, dry skin was stretched taut over angular bone. Despite seeing first-hand the damage it did to the human body, he smoked like a chimney and drank the finest whiskey. It was if his body had been preserved; tanned by the mix of tobacco and single malt.

His hands looked disproportionately large compared to the rest of his body. He had the long fingers of a pianist and he used these to wield a scalpel with both dexterity and strength, the muscles having been built up over years of cutting through resistant muscle, cartilage and bone.

Six foot something, Bloom had lost a few inches over the years as his back developed a slight curvature, so it was hard to dispel the impression of a white-coated praying mantis looming over the corpse on the autopsy trolley. Bloom had seen every way of dying come through this place. This peerless experience was currently being directed towards the mortal remains of Rhys Pryce.

As his latex gloved fingers worked, Bloom applied just the right amount of pressure needed to pierce the resistance of the first skin flap. Once the hole was made, the rest of the long, curved surgical needle slid through, trailing its tail of suture twine. Guiding the needle as if it were an extension of his fingers, Bloom then plunged it back into the pale, washed flesh on the other side of the incision. Powerful twin lights occasionally flared off the silver crescent of the needle as it performed its dance, until, with a final tug, Bloom pulled the crisscrossed twine, drawing together the two flaps of skin to close the red raw Y incision that ran from both shoulders, joined over the sternum, then continued down to the pubic bone.

In life Rhys Pryce had been poetry in motion, running into space to receive a pass, then skipping effortlessly past defenders to deliver a forty-yard cross with pinpoint accuracy. Laid out on the autopsy table, he looked smaller. The muscle tone was still there, along with the black swirls of Celtic tattoos snaking down his shoulders and arms, but without the power of animation, he could have been reduced to twelve stones of inert meat. This was not the way that Augustus Bloom viewed the unfortunate souls who crossed his path. Although he needed to know about each subject's life in order to better understand their death, Bloom never judged. He left that to a higher authority. He treated the wife beater, the suicide and the car crash victim with equal reverence. Bloom considered himself to be part of the last chapter in the book of life, a story begun by the midwife who first held the new life in her hands and wondered about the myriad possibilities that stretched out in front of it. Bloom provided the final reckoning. Had those potentials been achieved? Did fate, genetics, bad luck or villainy intercept the person's path to bring their life to an untimely end? When the body left Bloom's care, it would have given up all of its secrets, except for the one that Bloom could not answer; was death the final chapter? Momentarily distracted by his musings, Bloom belatedly realised that there were two figures watching from the doorway.

'Well well. Rhidian Hook.' Bloom's mouth broke into a broad smile, his yellowed teeth putting Jones in mind of a graveyard full of tumbled tombstones.

'Have you come to make sure he's actually dead?'

'I'm the SIO.'

Jones saw Bloom raise a shaggy eyebrow in surprise. This added to her growing list of questions.

'You're back. That's all that matters,' said Bloom. 'That philistine Alun Gunter is no substitute. I once tried engaging him on the subject of Wagner's *Ring* cycle. He thought I was talking about some disease of the bowel.'

Bloom turned his attention to Jones. 'And you have a new partner?'

When she realised that Rhidian wasn't going to introduce her, Jones did the job herself. 'Sergeant Jones.'

'Pleased to meet you, Sergeant. And if you're working with DI Hook, this won't be the last time that our paths cross.'

As Bloom and Rhidian caught up, Jones took in the details of the large, circular, windowless room; a scientific temple of white tile and stainless steel. In the centre of the room were several examination tables. Running along the sides of the wall were shelves used as preparation areas. Here organs could be dissected, the samples placed in small glass dishes, ready for examination under a microscope. Stainless steel doors led to the walk-in refrigerator that could store up to a dozen bodies, each on an individual roll-out shelf. Jones found this all fascinating, but had to return her attention to the centre of the room and the table that had been slightly tilted, so that the blood and other bodily fluids ran away from the body and into a drain.

'Formal identification was carried out by his mother,' said Bloom.

'Not his wife?' Rhidian was surprised.

'Perhaps she thought it would draw too much attention?' suggested Jones.

While Bloom summarised his findings, Rhidian jotted them down in his notebook.

'Preliminary findings. Well, we have a very fit young man, as befits a professional athlete. No sign of any underlying disease. Blood and toxicology reports won't be ready until tomorrow at the earliest. He suffered a fractured hip which is consistent with the impact of a high-speed collision; however, the actual cause of death was exsanguination through the plantar and dorsal arteries.'

'In English please?' asked Rhidian.

'He bled to death when his foot was cut off,' said Bloom with a smile. 'Simple enough for you?'

'How long would it have taken him to die?'

'Thirty minutes?'

'How long would he have been conscious?'

'For half that time perhaps.'

'So, for fifteen long minutes he would have known he was going to die?'

'Let's hope that he was unconscious throughout,' said Bloom.

This did little to reassure Rhidian. Where Bloom was fascinated by the intricacies of the human machine and what could stop it from working, Rhidian could never see a body as a mere shell that once held a human soul. If he saw laugh lines he wondered who had helped create them. White marks on a ring finger meant a grieving wife or husband, stretch marks suggested children, now turned into orphans; rough hands conjured up images of workers toasting their lost comrade. Although this hyper sensitivity was one of the keys to his success, it came with a cost. It was hard, sometimes impossible to turn off.

'It's actually a fascinating wound.' Bloom gestured for Rhidian to use the hinge-mounted magnifying lens to take a closer look. Rhidian didn't move. Bloom's eyes smiled. He was well aware of Rhidian's squeamishness, but the pathologist could see that the new DS was keen. Bloom gestured for Jones to step forward, positioning the lens so she could examine the jagged wound.

'As you can see, the foot was separated from the tibia and fibula, just above the talus bone.'

'And it wasn't an accident?' Jones asked.

'No. And it would have taken some effort, even for a skilled surgeon or a butcher.'

Rhidian tried to stop the graphic images that were forming in his head. 'So, we're not talking about a woman?' he asked.

Bloom looked at Jones, weighing her up. 'Oh I don't know. I'm sure that your colleague here would be up to the task.'

Jones wasn't sure whether to take that as a compliment.

'What kind of tool was used?'

'Tools plural. Something with a small cutting edge to slice through the skin and sinew, then something far more interesting to saw though the bone.'

'Interesting?' asked Rhidian.

'The marks don't match anything in my database which, as you know, is extensive.'

‘So not something you’d pick up from a DIY store?’ asked Jones.

‘Definitely not,’ said Bloom. ‘If I had to make an informed guess, I would say that this wasn’t a metal saw at all.’

‘Then what?’

Bloom looked at the stump again, then shrugged his bony shoulders. ‘All I can say is that it’s something I haven’t seen before, which is about as rare as teeth in a hen.’ That graveyard grin again.

‘Whatever they used, it would have taken some time?’ asked Rhidian.

‘Undoubtedly. Note the bruising to the centre of the chest.’

Rhidian examined the purple-blue bruise that matched where Rhys Pryce’s shirt had been stained with mud when he saw him in the maize field. ‘He was held down,’ said Rhidian.

Bloom used a ruler to measure the spread of the bruise. ‘A size ten shoe or boot I’d say, but there’s not enough definition to get any idea of what kind of footwear.’

‘But the killer didn’t rush? Didn’t panic?’

‘All reasonable assumptions,’ said Bloom, turning to nod to Jac Mundy, who wheeled a trolley over to the table. Together they transferred the body across.

‘I take it that the foot still hasn’t been recovered?’ asked Bloom.

Rhidian shook his head.

‘Shame. I don’t expect it to tell us any more than we already know, but it would be nice to send Mr Pryce on his forward journey, complete.’

Rhidian looked away as Jac used a small power hose to wash away some sticky blood that had pooled on the table.

‘So. Is this revenge? Professional jealousy?’ Rhidian asked.

‘Motive is your territory, not mine,’ said Bloom.

'It can't be a coincidence when someone removes the foot of a professional footballer?'

Jones piped up. 'If that was the motive, they've made a balls-up.'

'Explain.'

'Rhys Pryce was a left winger. Famous for it. So why take his right foot?'

Bloom was amused by Rhidian's discomfort at having missed something so obvious. Bloom turned to Jones. 'Inspector Hook is no lover of the beautiful game.'

As Rhidian puzzled over this conundrum, Bloom took a fresh, folded white sheet, unfurled it, then gently laid it over Rhys Pryce's body. Before he raised the last few inches, Bloom whispered reassuringly, 'All over now. Rest.'

Jones cast a look at Rhidian, but he had clearly seen this before and thought nothing of it. Bloom pulled up the sheet to cover Pryce's face, then stood in respectful silence for a moment, before nodding to Jac who wheeled the trolley towards the fridge. The heavy door slammed shut on Rhys Pryce with the finality of a full stop.

As Jones and Rhidian retraced their steps through the white tiled labyrinth, Jones couldn't keep her curiosity to herself.

'What was all that about? I did just see a man talking to a corpse?'

'It's just his way of being respectful.'

'It's not like they can hear him.'

'Can anybody be sure that there isn't some spark left, even after death?'

'Didn't have you down as a God botherer.'

'I'm not. But there's nothing wrong with keeping an open mind. Maybe if you'd spent every day with the dead, you might find yourself talking to them as well.'

As if on cue, the opening bars of 'Delilah' rose up to serenade them on their way. You might expect a thin, reedy voice to be produced from such a dry husk, but Bloom was a rich, deep, pitch-perfect tenor.

8

You get all kinds of walk-ins when you're on reception duty at an inner city police station. Sometimes this is a blessing as the variety helps the time go quicker. Other times you wish that you were facing a baying mob who wanted your balls hanging off the end of their big sticks rather than face the horror of what lurked on the other side of the scratched Perspex divide; tax-paying members of the British public. It took a certain type of character to deal with them day in, day out. You either had to have a natural talent for it, or be useless at anything else. It was very much the latter with the officer who was on duty today.

He had always wanted to be a police officer. His parents couldn't have been prouder when he first showed them his new uniform. This was the only reason that he hadn't jacked it all in for a job stacking supermarket shelves years ago. Every premature line on his mournful face told a different tale of another incident that had led to his dream job becoming a living nightmare.

His shoulder epaulettes identified him as number 357. His police ID card named him as Constable Andy Floyd, but because of one unfortunate incident fifteen years ago, everyone in the station knew him as Floyd-the-Goat.

Andy Floyd had been a fresh-faced probationer, just two weeks out of training when the incident happened. With his brand new boots shining, and his shirt neatly ironed by his proud mammy, Floyd was being puppy walked around his new beat by a hoary old sergeant when they received a tip-off that an illegal Halal butcher's was operating out of the back of a two-up two-down in Butetown. While the sergeant went to the front of the suspect house, Floyd was sent round the back to block off any escape route. Positioned outside the locked back gate, when he heard a commotion coming from the other side of the wooden fence, the eager probationer feared that his sergeant was in trouble. Stepping back to give himself a decent run-up, Floyd launched himself at the gate. What he hadn't appreciated was that the rotten timbers were only held together by its accumulated coats of paint. Shattering the gate into a thousand splinters, Floyd's momentum carried him well into the small, cobbled rear yard. He had only seconds to take in the picture: a still warm sheep hanging upside down from the rotary clothes line, its neck sliced open, the blood congealing around the drain; and the very much alive, petrified goat that was staring at him with devilish eyes.

The goat had faster reactions than Floyd. Knowing what fate awaited him and seeing its chance of freedom, it made a bolt for the open gate. Floyd lunged to block its path but slipped in the sheep's blood. By the time the sergeant ambled out to see what all the noise was about, he found the unfortunate Floyd on his knees, bent over the backside of a braying goat. Not only would Floyd have to explain to his mammy how his pristine uniform came to be covered in sheep's blood and goat shit, but he would also have to learn to live with his new nickname.

He tried to repair his reputation by moving to another area of police work. He thought that the dog unit would be a fresh start. This optimism didn't last long. On his first night of active duty when he unleashed Spike, his German shepherd, to run after a fleeing burglar, the hound turned around and bit its handler in the balls. Floyd's transfer to traffic was a similarly brief affair after he was run over by his own car when he forgot to put the hand brake on. His colleagues soon had him marked down as some kind of shit magnet and it was decided that the safest place for him was behind the reception counter. He might have to deal with a lot of grief from the general public, but at least he was no longer a danger to himself or to his colleagues.

Fifteen years of dealing with the public later, and Floyd-the-Goat had mastered the art of remaining patient and professional at all times. However, today even he was cracking under the unceasing flow of complaints coming from the young black woman standing in front of the counter. He couldn't help wondering how her partner coped with the noise level as well as marvelling at how such a stick-thin girl could talk for so long without taking a breath.

'See, I like a chicken madras as much as the next person, but this has put me right off I can tell you, I mean it's not just once a week it's every night that stink comes out of their flat, and then there's the rubbish they leave out in the hallway, not in a bin or anything, just in plastic bags and there's all sorts in there, fish heads and chicken's feet, bits of animal I don't even want to look at too closely.'

For a blissful moment Floyd-the-Goat managed to tune the woman out. The only light at the end of his tunnel was that his shift ended in ten minutes, and then he would be off to the Harlech Arms. He didn't normally drink during the day, but this harridan was enough to turn any man to the hard stuff. She must have raised her voice by a few decibels because it suddenly cut through his daydream about pies and pints.

'I am telling you, it is rank, man. Rank. Do you get me?'

As if Floyd-the-Goat's day couldn't get any worse, in burst a middle-aged man wearing a dusty anorak and hi-vis tabard. He had a plastic lunch box tucked under his arm. The newcomer ignored the queue, heading straight to the reception window, much to the displeasure of those who'd been waiting, and winding up Miss Madras even more.

'Hey. Where do you think you're going?' she said.

Although he wanted to see an end to the great curry complaint, Floyd-the-Goat didn't want a riot starting on his watch. 'She's right, sir. Back of the queue, if you please.'

Evan Evans wouldn't be put off. 'I'm not even meant to be here. I should be picking up two ton of pig iron from Port Talbot. My rig's parked outside.'

'On double yellows? That'll be a sixty quid fine for starters,' said Floyd.

But Evan was already popping the lid from his lunch box.

'I didn't know what else to do. Keep it cold, that's what they say, isn't it?' Evan held the box up to the Perspex screen so that Floyd-the-Goat could see.

Miss Madras was too nosy to resist leaning over to see what all the fuss was about. At first her mind couldn't comprehend what she was seeing. It didn't make sense, but there was no denying it – she was looking at a man's foot, surrounded by rapidly thawing bricks of fish, covered in orange breadcrumbs. For once, she was rendered speechless.

While the hapless constable was coming to terms with the idea that from now on he was going to be known as Floyd-the-Fish-Finger, three floors above, Rhidian Hook and Anwen Jones were looking around what was laughingly called their new office. As the last, reluctant fluorescent tube finally stopped flickering and gave them the benefit of its sickly yellow light, it revealed the room in all its underwhelming glory. Fifteen foot square, it had clearly been used as a communal storeroom for every broken printer, redundant keyboard and out of date telephone directory in the station.

'I'm sure that if you had a word with the DCI you could get your old office back,' said Jones, only to get a reply from a smug voice behind them.

'No can do.'

Jones turned to see Alun Gunter leaning against the doorway.

'See, my team's settled in. Devlin's tasked us to identify the source of this high quality coke that's been turning up all over the city.' Gunter used the toe of his shoe to flip open an old takeaway box that still contained a triangle of green, mouldy pizza. 'Besides, I'm sure you'll soon have this place up and running. Of course even when you've cleared it out, you're going to need computers, phone lines, the works.'

'If you're offering to help, Alun...' said Rhidian.

Gunter laughed. 'Oh I'd love to.' He looked at Jones. 'If I wasn't a sergeant down...'

'If there's nothing else, we do have work to do,' said Rhidian.

'Which is why I'm here. Reception just phoned. Something about a human foot that's been fished out of the Channel. As you are not connected to the twenty-first century yet, I said I'd pass on the message.'

'Would that be the same foot that was supposedly torn off by barbed wire?' asked Rhidian.

Gunter's grin died. 'Good luck, Hook. And I mean that. If you mess this up, the shit's going to splash back on all of us.'

Gunter slammed the door as he left, causing an avalanche of dog-eared crime prevention leaflets to cascade onto the floor.

*

You could always tell when Sister Cindy Campbell was on duty. You only had to follow the sound of her throaty laugh. Cindy had followed a long line of women who had joined the NHS, starting with her gran, Charity, who had answered Enoch Powell's call to travel from her home in the West Indies to the UK on the *Empire Windrush*, and her mother,

Princess, who had risen to the position of matron. If you placed a photo of each of the women in a line, the only thing that would change is the style of their uniforms. Each had been cast from the same mould – wide hips, big shoulders and strong arms, and within their reassuring bulk nestled the gentlest of hearts, filled with an inexhaustible capacity to care. Even though most of her colleagues preferred to wear the scrub-style trousers, Cindy liked the tradition of wearing a navy blue dress, even if infection controls meant that she could no longer wear the silver nurse's buckle that had been passed down the generations to her.

On Cindy's list of duties today was to bed wash the woman who had been transferred to a private room at The Hope once it became clear that she wasn't going to naturally wake from her coma. Cindy would normally have left such a task to a junior nurse or an HCA, but she had been on duty when the patient was transferred up from A&E. The textbooks tell you not to have favourites, but in practice it is impossible not to form attachments to some of the souls who come through the doors. As she washed the young woman's arms with a damp sponge, Cindy talked to her patient, 'just in case' she could hear. The theory was that hearing was the first sense to return and the last to go when someone died.

'Forecast says rain's on the way again. And me with a family barbecue to organise. Have you ever tried grilled red snapper?'

Some of Cindy's colleagues told her she was wasting her time; that her patient couldn't hear her. But who knew? Only the patient and the Good Lord. Cindy turned her attention to Loretta's hands, noticing how her nails had been expertly painted in bright red varnish.

'So, you have had a visitor then? I thought it was strange that a beauty like you did not have someone special in your life.'

Cindy hummed the song that her mother had sung to her on bath days, as she washed Loretta's neck and face. A change in the tone of the monitor made Cindy stop and check the machine's readings. The patient's blood pressure had gone up to 120 over 80 and her breathing had increased to sixteen breaths per minute. Small changes, but encouraging signs.

'You coming back to us are you, darling?' asked Cindy as she wrote down the readings on her patient's chart. But when she gently pulled back first one and then the other eyelid, her patient's stunning green eyes stared back vacantly. They might as well have been made of glass. There was no inner light in them.

'No. Too early to celebrate a miracle yet. But where there is life, there is hope.'

Cindy's humming returned to fill the room as she completed the bed bath. Even if Loretta Swann was able to feel her touch, she had no way to communicate the fact.

*

While Rhidian was downstairs following up on the fished out foot, Jones started cleaning. Her goal was to at least clear a desk and a couple of chairs so they had somewhere to work. She had just finished tying off a second bin liner stuffed with takeaway coffee cups and old newspapers when Alun Gunter shambled in.

'See he's got you straight on the glamour jobs then.'

Jones tried to ignore him.

'You've hitched your wagon to the wrong horse, Jones.'

'I didn't hitch anything. I was assigned. You were there.' Jones made to exit the office, only for Gunter to block her way.

'You could have refused.'

'On what grounds?'

'How about that you owe me?'

'Not sure that would have washed with DCI Devlin.' Jones said, putting the bin liners down.

'Has he started drinking yet?' asked Gunter. 'Or more to the point, has he stopped?'

'How's that any of my business?'

'I'm not talking about a friendly pint with the team after knocking off for the day, I'm talking about hip flasks, half bottles in coat pockets, little tot in his coffee. It was bad enough before his wife, but if he's mixing booze with anti-depressants…'

'I haven't seen anything like that.'

'But you'll tell me when you do.' Gunter didn't like her hesitation. 'You know he was pissed the night his wife died?'

'Then why wasn't he fired?'

'You or me, yeah, we'd have been thrown to the dogs, but not Devlin's favourite. You must have heard the talk that something went on between the two of them.'

'I don't listen to canteen gossip.' Jones said.

'How else do you explain why she's risking her own career to bring him back?'

'What's any of that got to do with me?'

'You're going to be my eyes and ears. First sign that Hooky boy's losing it, you tell me, right?'

'I don't know that I can do that.'

'Do you want to go back to the valleys busting pot heads and joyriders?' Gunter leaned in. 'It was me who got you out of that shit hole, and don't you forget it.'

Jones was saved from any further intimidation by DS Mal Rogers sticking his head in through the doorway. 'Boss.'

'What?' snapped Gunter.

'Mrs Merrick's on the phone again. I tried putting her off, but she insists on talking to you.'

Gunter cursed under his breath and reluctantly followed Rogers to the CID office.

Jones picked up the bin bags and was dragging them down the corridor when the lift doors opened, revealing Rhidian Hook, absorbed, writing in his notebook.

'Car keys?' he asked.

Jones patted her jeans pocket. Felt the hard lump. 'Yeah...'

'Good. Get in.'

Jones nodded to the bin liners. 'I was just…'

'That'll wait. This won't.'

Jones left the bin liners in the corridor and stepped into the lift. Rhidian pressed the button for the ground floor and handed her Evan Evans' lunch box. She took a peek and wished she hadn't.

'We can drop this off with Bloom. The mortuary's on our way.'

'On our way where?' The lift doors closed on Jones's curiosity.

9

Lying just a few miles north of Cardiff centre, Llandaff is known as 'the city within a city'. This lofty status derives from the impressive 12th-century Llandaff Cathedral, which stands atop one of the oldest Christian sites in Britain. Recent excavations had revealed the presence of pagan burials under the western part of the cathedral. First occupied by the legions of Rome and later by the Normans, this quaint community of village greens, grand houses and ivy-covered medieval ruins was now being invaded by a very modern band of barbarians – the tabloid paparazzi who were camped outside Rhys Pryce's gated mansion.

Many of them were the same faces who had been waiting for Rhys Pryce's exit from the court building, only now they had a bigger story to get their teeth into – the death of a local hero – and so the local hacks had been joined by stringers from national newspapers and TV news. Several outside broadcast vans were parked up, their satellite dishes ready to beam live images into the homes of millions of viewers. An enterprising local had brought his snack van to this unfamiliar territory, anticipating a busy day dishing out hot drinks and bacon baps to the hungry journos and the dozens of football fans and celeb watchers who were making their pilgrimages to lay floral tributes to their lost star.

Ginnie Lane sucked greedily on a lipstick-tipped cigarette as she bemoaned her lot to her balding, beer-bellied cameraman. She hated smoking; the expense, the smell it left on her clothes and the damage it was undoubtedly doing to her insides, but it did help keep her weight down. She would give up the fags as soon as she was finally famous.

'It's even worse if you're pretty.' she moaned. 'Nobody sees past your tits and teeth.'

The cameraman nodded when he was supposed to, but he had heard the same complaint from many eager female reporters over the years. He was just as aware as Ginnie was that her shelf life was limited. If she didn't make a quick move up from the local station there were plenty of younger, brighter, hungrier girls coming up behind her. He wasn't unsympathetic to Ginnie Lane's situation, but he couldn't help being distracted by the stomach-rumbling aromas coming from the snack van.

'One chance to prove that I'm not just Kate Moss with a microphone. Is that too much to ask?' moaned Ginnie.

The cameraman was only interested in a more pressing question; bacon and egg or double sausage?

Ginnie sensed the ripple of interest spread through the press pack and turned to see what had got the snappers reaching for their cameras. A volley of flashes greeted the arrival of Jones's car, until the press pack realised that she wasn't a famous sports personality or D list celebrity and their interest quickly withered.

Jones had to stop the car when faced by what looked like a ten-foot wall made up of dozens of bouquets of petrol-station flowers, interwoven with blue and white football scarves. Two moonlighting nightclub bouncers loomed forward, puffing up their steroid-enhanced muscles, ready for a ruck. They visibly deflated when Rhidian pressed his warrant card to the passenger window. One heavy got straight onto his mobile to get instructions.

Spying the familiar shaggy mop of dark hair and trademark duffle coat in the passenger seat, Ginnie was transformed into a tornado of sharp elbows and stamping stilettos. Dragging her clueless cameraman in her wake, she hacked her way through the press pack to lean down to Rhidian's window, microphone poised.

'Detective Inspector Hook. Why are you here? I thought that Rhys Pryce's death was an accident? Why are CID involved? Any comment? Inspector?'

Jones drowned out Ginnie's next question by leaning on the horn to remind the heavy to hurry up. But it was too late. Blood was in the water now and the sharks were moving in for the kill. The photographers crowded in to try to get that money shot of the copper who'd provided some juicy front pages six months ago.

Ginnie found herself being brushed aside by old hands even more feral than she was. Three of her perfectly pedicured toes were crushed under a size eleven boot and a zoom lens was dug painfully into her ribs, reminding her that she was just a girl playing by big boys' rules.

Camera lenses were pressed against the car windows. The strobing flashes were blinding. Crushing bodies blocked out the light. The shouts were deafening.

'When can we expect an official statement?'

'You back on duty now, Inspector?'

'Are you sorry he's dead?'

Rhidian felt panic rising. A cold sweat broke out on his brow. It was becoming difficult to breathe. He turned the air con up to maximum but even the inrush of cool air didn't help. His logic was being overwhelmed by the memory of being trapped, fearing he was going to drown. Aware of his discomfort, Jones nudged the car forward, but there was no dislodging the human hyenas now that they had latched their jaws onto their prey. Rhidian tried closing his eyes. That only made things worse. Jones was relieved to see the wall of tributes finally crack down the middle as the electronic gates slowly opened. As soon as the gap was wide enough, Jones shot through, leaving the hired heavies to stop the horde of reporters from breaching the gates.

Limping because of her crushed toes, Ginnie was surprised when a firm grip took hold of one of her arms and helped to steer her away to safety. Thinking it was one of the photographers using the chaos to cop a feel, she was about to spin and slap the man, only for her scowl to turn into a broad smile when she saw that it was the handsome photographer from the courts who was her unlikely knight in shining armour. The pain in her toes was instantly forgotten.

Rhidian needed a moment to recover before climbing out of the car and joining Jones who was standing, stunned by her first sight of the brick and glass testament to what you can achieve when you have too much money and not enough taste.

The original architects must be turning in their graves. What they had designed as a perfectly proportioned Regency town house had been butchered. It was as if someone had given a five-year-old a box of crayons and told them to design their fantasy home. The centre of the courtyard was dominated by a faux baroque fountain where jets of water cascaded out of the open mouths of leaping dolphins. The once formal hedging had been hacked into the shape of cartoon characters; Rhidian recognised Mickey Mouse, but he was blissfully ignorant of who or what a Pokémon was. Jones, however, was impressed.

'Triple garage. Jacuzzi. Bet there's a games room and a home gym. This is lush!'

'No, Sergeant, this is an abomination.'

An Eastern European housekeeper led them to the main drawing room, where the grieving widow was waiting. Lowri Lewis and Rhys Pryce had been marketed as Wales' own Posh and Becks. He was the handsome but not too bright athlete; she was the successful but not too bright pop star. When they fell in love on a reality TV show, it was a relationship made in PR heaven.

Every tasteless detail of their wedding had been captured in a twelve-page spread in *OK!* magazine. The guest list was a D to Z of celebrity royalty. The bride stepped out of her gold and white Cinderella pumpkin coach to reveal a silk train thirty feet long. Although some cynics suggested that Pryce was only getting married to dispel his image as a serial cheater, surely only the coldest hearts couldn't fail to be melted by his romantic gesture of splashing out on a new tattoo to mark the solemnity of the occasion - '*Lowri Forever*' written in Arabic script down his left arm.

Within a month, Lowri announced their plans to start a family, in another exclusive twelve-page photo spread. While she was busy nest-building, Pryce seemed in no hurry to settle down and play happy families. No matter how many times Pryce was papped staggering out of a nightclub with a couple of young women on his arm, the long-suffering Lowri followed Tammy Wynette's advice to stand by her man.

After the aesthetic horrors of the exterior, Rhidian was prepared for whatever challenges to good taste awaited inside. The oak-panelled walls and original floors had thankfully been kept, but the Regency furniture had been replaced by the kind of fixtures and fittings that are so expensive that they look cheap.

This was the part of his job that Rhidian hated the most. Facing a loved one's raw grief was often harder to deal with than the actual violence that had torn their life apart. But he knew that talking to the bereaved about a sudden death should never be easy. If it ever became so, you weren't doing it right. Rhidian believed that mourning was a time for quiet reflection, so he was unprepared for the Hogarthian nightmare that greeted him and Jones in 'the play room'.

Lowri Pryce was standing in the middle of the room, on top of a leopard print pouf, being fitted for her funeral dress by 'Andre of St Mellons', an overexcited designer who kept pricking himself with his pins because he was daydreaming about how this was going to be his big break. Another stylist was dipping into a Louis Vuitton suitcase to lift out a selection of tissue-wrapped designer shoes. As each gaudy creation was unwrapped, they were rejected by a dismissive wave of Lowri's spray-tanned hand. In her other hand Lowri was holding a highball glass containing something shockingly pink, which she took big slurps of as she watched a slide show of images from '*OK*! Magazine's Wedding of the Century' being played on the home cinema screen mounted on one wall. From the way she was wobbling on her perch, this wasn't her first drink of the day.

Over by the bone-white, baby grand piano, which seemed to be a piece of set decoration rather than a working instrument, Lowri's anaconda of a manager was doing her dance of the three telephones as she pitted different competitors off against each other in order to get the best deal. Down the first phone she hissed, '...but this is gold. Pure gold. You've got ten seconds or I'm taking it to Sky.' Into the second phone: 'Amazon Prime are gagging for it, but I came to you first out of loyalty.' Into the third phone: 'You know I wouldn't go to Channel 5, not after the way they ripped us off on "Christmas with the Pryces".

Rhidian tried to tune the manager out and focus on the grieving widow. 'Mrs Pryce?'

Lowri didn't even look in their direction. She was too distracted by the giant image of Rhys holding her hand as she cut into the five-tier wedding cake.

'Are you the flower people? You're supposed to deliver round the back.'

'I'm Detective Inspector Hook. This is Detective Sergeant Jones.'

Lowri turned, taking in the officers for the first time with red-rimmed eyes. The room fell silent. A pin dropped from the mouth of Andre of St Mellons and bounced off the parquet floor. Then the manager found her voice again and the hubbub returned. 'Working title, 'Life After Rhys', six parts, fly on the wall, access all areas, no holds barred look at the daily struggles of a grieving showbiz widow. Yes, you'll get exclusive access to the funeral.'

Rhidian continued. 'We need to ask you some questions about your husband. In private.'

‘What? Yes. Of course.’ Lowri’s entourage got the message and drifted away to the other side of the ballroom-sized space. Her manager didn’t pause from earning her seventeen per cent.

‘Elton’s already confirmed... No, I don’t know if he’s going to play. We thought that Lowri could visit some other widows; soldiers’ wives and the like. Share the pain, yeah? It is deffo BAFTA territory.’

No one had thought to help Lowri down from her perch, so Rhidian stepped forward to offer her a hand. Lowri’s years of partying was demonstrated by her ability to climb down without spilling a drop of her drink.

‘Won’t you sit?’ she offered, plumping down onto one of the matching white leather settees that could have seated the whole of the Welsh rugby team, including the substitutes.

Jones had never seen the ‘Lark of Llandaff’ without her make-up, false eyelashes and hair extensions. She was surprised to see that she had the fresh, naturally pretty features of a healthy valley girl once the mascara and foundation had been scraped away.

‘He was my soulmate.’ Lowri’s voice broke. ‘My everything.’

Rhidian had his notebook out. Jones perched uncomfortably on the edge of the settee, her attention distracted by the massive faux Warhol prints of Lowri and Rhys Pryce’s faces that dominated the walls.

‘I’m afraid I have some bad news for you.’ Rhidian lowered his voice, not wanting to share this with the agent. ‘It looks as if your husband’s death wasn’t an accident.’

A crease formed in Lowri’s perfect brow. ‘I don’t understand...’

‘We believe that he was murdered.’

Lowri froze. Only her eyes betrayed the internal struggle as she tried to absorb this new, devastating information. No matter how sympathetic he might be, Rhidian couldn’t give her a chance to recover, knowing that this was an unrepeatable opportunity to get unguarded information from her.

'Do you know anyone who might want to harm your husband?'

'No.'

'Had he received any threatening phone calls? Emails, online messages?'

Lowri could only shake her head. Rhidian had to press on. 'A man in his position must have made enemies?'

'You saw the gates...the flowers. Everyone loved him.'

'But he had everything; the big house, the glittering career, the beautiful wife. People can get jealous of someone who has so much.'

'Jealous, yes... but enough to... to kill him... No.'

Jones didn't understand why Rhidian wasn't calling Lowri out on her lies.

'Have you noticed anyone suspicious hanging around in the street? Cars you didn't recognise?'

Lowri shook her head. 'I don't know anyone who'd want to hurt him.'

Jones couldn't hold back any longer. 'He treated you like shit.'

'What? '

'It was all over the papers,' Jones persisted.

'He loved me.'

'He shagged your sister on your wedding day.'

Fearing Rhidian's admonishing glare, Jones avoided making eye contact with him. Now she had released the elephant into the room, Jones couldn't stop. She took a folded page from a gossip magazine out of her pocket and opened it up to read: 'You said, and I quote, "I'll cut his balls off if I catch him with another tart." A week later he was photographed falling out of a taxi with Miss Swansea.'

Lowri's eyes glistened. 'Do you think I care about that now? I'd let him sleep with whoever he wants if he'd only walk through that door now with that soppy grin on his stupid face.'

Three pregnant tears rolled, dropped and splashed onto the black organza. Rhidian gently took over. 'Mrs Pryce, I have to ask. Where were you two nights ago, between the hours of eight and eleven PM?'

There was no outrage from Lowri, just a sad admission. 'I was here. Watching the clock. Waiting for him to come home. Like I do every night.'

In the background Rhidian could hear the agent, still trying to sell her client's privacy for a few quid. Rhidian felt pity for this young woman whose grief was about to become public property. Lowri looked at Rhidian with pleading, tear-filled eyes, desperately hoping that he had an answer where no one else had.

'What will I do without him?' One hand went automatically to her belly where a slight bump was starting to show. 'What will we do?'

Rhidian realised he'd been absently stroking the gold band of his wedding ring. He knew better than most that there was no answer.

'We won't take up any more of your time.' he said as he stood.

Jones followed his lead. Lowri looked closer at Rhidian, as if seeing him properly for the first time.

'You're that policeman. Your wife...' Rhidian nodded. Nothing more needed to be said. For a moment the two were joined in their mutual pain. They both understood the regret of words they had always meant to say, but now never could. Lowri could see, etched into the shadows around Rhidian's eyes, memories of all the dreadful mornings when he had woken up and, for the sweetest of brief moments, had forgotten that his wife was gone; only to then suffer the pain of her loss all over again, as fresh and raw as it had been six months ago.

Rhidian had one last question that he needed to ask. 'You haven't been to see him?'

'I wanted to.' Lowri looked over at her agent. 'I was advised that it would be too upsetting.'

'You need to see him.' Rhidian knew the pain of not being able to say goodbye. 'You'll be assigned a family liaison officer who will support you through the weeks ahead. They will accompany you if you want to see your husband, and keep you informed about how the investigation is going.'

'Can't it be you?'

'That wouldn't be appropriate.' Rhidian saw the desperation in her eyes. He opened his notebook, wrote down a phone number, tore out the page and gave it to Lowri. 'If you need anything. Anything at all.'

She nodded her thanks. As Rhidian and Jones turned to leave, Lowri reached for a bottle of vodka with shaking hands. Rhidian stepped forward to gently take it from her. He poured her a generous double. Pressing the drink into her hands, he gently offered, 'It helps. For a while'.

Lowri nodded and raised the glass to her lips. Remembering Gunter's instructions, Jones made a mental note of the moment and hated herself for it.

As Jones bleeped open the car's central locking, she waited for the bollocking to start. Instead, Rhidian said, 'You were right to push her. I couldn't.'

'She didn't do it, did she?'

'Pumped up with rage, maybe she could have killed him. But Dr Bloom thinks the killer was calm; took their time.'

'She could have had an accomplice?'

'Her shock seemed genuine, and she clearly still loved her husband, no matter what humiliations he put her through. No, we've got to look elsewhere.'

As she watched Jones drive back out through the tribute-festooned gates, Ginnie Lane smiled and urged her cameraman to get his gear stowed away. Let the rest of the pack hang around here if they wanted to, she knew that the real story was elsewhere. Getting into the passenger seat of the works Volvo, Ginnie took out her mobile, looked up a number and then considered, how best to tackle this?

*

Liz Devlin had just got off the phone after delivering a progress report to the Chief Constable who was having kittens after getting confirmation that Rhys Pryce's death was murder. Devlin had reassured her boss that she had put her best man on the job, but had deliberately not named Rhidian Hook. Her hope was that he would make some progress on the case before the CC discovered who the senior investigating officer was. Her phone started ringing. Devlin was only half concentrating when she picked up the receiver.

'Devlin.'

'Hello, Detective Chief Inspector. Can you confirm that Rhidian Hook is back on duty?'

'Who is this?'

'Ginnie Lane, Cymru TV.'

'You need to refer your questions to our press office.'

'But as I have you on the line now, surely you can tell me why CID are investigating a single vehicle car crash?'

'We treat every death with the utmost seriousness,' was all that Devlin could manage.

'Was it your decision to assign DI Hook to the investigation?'

'Yes.'

'But wasn't there some question of a mental breakdown...'

'I don't comment about my staff's private medical records.'

'But you are confident that he is fit to return to work?'

'Inspector Hook is one of our most experienced detectives. Having him available again is a boon to any investigation.'

'And if that turns out to be a mistake, would you see that as a resigning matter, Chief Inspector?'

'Goodbye, Miss Lane.'

Devlin hung up. She took a moment to recover. Of course she had known this would happen. She had just hoped that focusing on writing Pryce's obituary would have distracted the press from the return of Rhidian Hook for at least a bit longer.

10

The room was small, plain, white and non-denominational. In its centre was a wheeled trolley, covered in a white cloth. Here lay Rhys Pryce, covered up to his neck with another white sheet. Apart from his face, only his left hand had been left uncovered so that his wife could hold his frigid fingers. Rhidian and Jones stayed in the doorway, not wanting to intrude on such a personal moment. Rhidian thought that he might be jealous that Lowri Pryce was getting what he never did; a chance to say goodbye. But would it really have helped him to see his wife's body laid out so lifeless?

'He's so cold,' said Lowri. 'He's never cold. I used to tell him, he was like my personal hot water bottle.'

Rhidian had seen enough bodies to know what she was feeling. Sometimes death left the corpse looking empty, so much like a husk that it was hard to imagine that it had ever been alive. In other cases, it looked as though the departed was merely sleeping and that one good shake would wake them up.

Lowri realised that something was wrong. At the bottom of the table, the sheet lay limp over the bottom of his right leg.

'You said it was murder.'

'Yes.'

'How?'

Rhidian hesitated.

'Do you really need to know the details?'

'I didn't, but now. Yes, I do.'

'He died from loss of blood after his foot was amputated.'

'I don't understand.'

'Whoever did this, removed your husband's foot.'

'Have you found it?'

‘We have.’

‘And it wasn’t an accident?’

‘No.’

‘Who would do such a thing?’

‘As soon as we know, you will know. I’m sorry. That’s all I can tell you for now.’

‘When will they give him back to me?’ Lowri asked.

‘That’s down to the coroner.’

‘I need to make arrangements. His club want to set up a trophy in his name; something to remember him by. Then there are all his fans; his family...’

‘It will probably be a couple of weeks, but it could be longer,’ said Rhidian.

Lowri nodded her gratitude. ‘I can’t believe how kind you’ve been. After what Rhys did to you.’

‘I’m doing this for you, not him.’

She wanted to kiss her husband goodbye. It took three attempts before she could bring her lips to his, but once she had made contact, she didn’t want to pull away, knowing that it would be their last kiss.

The solemn moment was interrupted by Darius Gull bursting into the room, followed by the mortified Jac Mundy.

‘Sorry Inspector,’ said Jac. ‘I tried to tell him this was a private viewing.’

‘I can confirm that he did his best to impede me. You can leave us now.’ Gull glowered at the technician who blushed scarlet with shame and left. Gull turned his glare onto Rhidian and Jones. ‘I didn’t want to believe it. When my clerk told me, I said “There is no way that Detective Inspector Hook would be allowed to investigate Rhys Pryce’s death.” And yet, here you are, alone with his widow.’

Gull turned to Lowri. ‘From now on, you say nothing unless it is in my presence, is that understood?’ Gull didn’t wait for a reply, but turned his attention back to Rhidian. ‘And the first thing I’ll be doing is making a formal complaint to get you removed from this case.’

‘That’s not what I want,’ said Lowri.

Gull smiled at her. ‘You’re distressed. Not in your right mind. That’s why you need someone who can make decisions for you.’

‘He’s been good to me,’ said Lowri, her voice nearly a whisper.

‘And how do we know that he isn’t responsible for your husband’s death?’

‘That’s low, even for you, Gull,’ said Rhidian.

‘But it’s public knowledge that there was no love lost between you and Rhys Pryce.’

‘This isn’t the place for grandstanding, Gull.’

‘I’ve only just been informed that my client’s death was suspicious. Why the delay? Was that your doing?’

‘Why don’t we talk about this outside?’ said Rhidian.

‘I’d rather do this in front of witnesses,’ said Gull.

‘Shut up!’ Lowri’s voice was loud in the small room as she turned on Gull. ‘If it wasn’t for you getting Rhys off so many times he would have been banned from driving. He would never have been on that road that night. He wouldn’t be lying here now.’

‘This must be a very emotional time for you...’ Gull stumbled.

‘Emotional? What do you know about being emotional? It’s all just a game to you, but you’re playing with people’s lives.’ Lowri’s eyes flared at the barrister. ‘And if I want legal representation, I’ll find it myself. So as you weren’t invited here I suggest that you fuck off before I get these officers to remove you.’

Tail between his legs, Gull’s quiet exit couldn’t have been more of a contrast to his exuberant entrance. Lowri had clearly been left shaken by her confrontation with Gull, but Rhidian was reassured by the knowledge that this was the last time she was going to be used by anyone.

*

Anwen Jones sat on the bonnet of her car, watching D.I. Hook escort Lowri Pryce back to her electric Mini Cooper. The singer had left her trademark pink Humvee at home because everyone knew whose car it was and this wasn't the time to draw attention to herself. There were a dozen questions buzzing around Jones's head. As Lowri Pryce drove away and Rhidian joined Jones at her car, she could bite her tongue no longer.

'Do you think that was a good idea? I mean, I get that she deserves our sympathy and all that...' said Jones.

'But?'

'But sharing details about the case? The fact that the foot was amputated by the killer. We haven't released that to the press.'

'I'd rather she heard the facts from us, rather than have to read unreliable speculation in the tabloids.'

'And if some gossip mag offers her big bucks for her story?'

'I'm sure she wouldn't do that.'

'Why not? Nothing's been off limits so far. Her engagement, the wedding; they even had a photographer with them when they went for the first baby scan.'

Rhidian realised that this was something he hadn't considered. All he had been concerned about was helping someone else whose heart had also been broken. He remembered the pressure that the press had put on him to tell his story, but there was no way that he was going to share his private grief with the world, and he believed that, no matter what the temptation, Lowri Pryce would now be just as determined.

'I trust her,' he said.

Jones thought about it, then accepted his point, but there was something else nagging at her.

'What was Gull referring to? About you having a history with Rhys Pryce?'

'That's got nothing to do with this case.'

'But you'd tell me if it did?'

Rhidian cut off her questions by getting into the car, but Jones hadn't got to be a detective sergeant without being able to tell when someone was being less than honest with her. The question was, what exactly was Rhidian Hook keeping from her, and why?

As Jones drove away, neither she nor Rhidian was aware that their every move was being watched and photographed by Ginnie Lane from her hiding place behind a plane tree. Although pleased that her instincts to follow DI Hook had been correct, Ginnie was disappointed that she still didn't have her scoop, not yet, but she knew it was coming, and when it did, she wouldn't care who she had to trample over to realise her dreams.

11

Augustus Bloom waved good night to the security guard and headed for the car park. Unlike Rhidian, he was able to switch off from his work. As soon as he peeled off his scrubs, he was off duty. Tonight he was looking forward to some fresh rigatoni and a few games of online poker, where he was known by the username - 'Sawbones'. Remembering the pain of going out of last night's cash tournament to a set of twos when he was holding pocket aces, Bloom didn't even notice the figure heading towards the hospital's public entrance, being careful to stay out of the car park lights and keeping their face hidden behind an impressive bunch of flowers. When asked about it later, all that Bloom could remember was the large bouquet of white lilies. He couldn't even recall whether they were being carried by a man or a woman.

*

Anwen Jones had decided to cook for a change. She never pretended to be Nigella Lawson, but she could knock up a passable spag bol.

'Something smells good,' said Sam, coming in from work.

'Hope you're hungry, only I think I've overdone it with the spaghetti,' said Anwen. She didn't have any parmesan so was grating some cheddar to sprinkle on the dish. 'If you want to help, you can lay the table.'

Suddenly Sam was behind her, his hands slipping around her, stroking her hips, his breath in her ear. 'It's not the table I want to lay.'

'Promises, promises.' Anwen pushed back against him.

'I've been thinking about this all day.' Sam reached up to cup her breasts.

Anwen moaned. 'I'm going to burn the bolognaise.'

'Bollocks to the bolognaise,' said Sam, kissing her neck.

Anwen tried to stir the frying pan containing the mince and tomato ragu, but horniness was taking over from hunger. The moment was spoiled when Sam snaked a hand around Anwen's body, to pinch a lump of cheese and pop it into his mouth.

'Hey!' Anwen rapped him over the knuckles with the wooden spoon. Sam laughed and licked the tomato sauce off the back of his hand.

'I thought you were horny?' she teased.

'I'm also starving. And you know I perform better when I've been fed.'

'In that case, it'll be ready in ten minutes,' said Anwen, turning up the heat on the frying pan.

Sam turned to the cutlery drawer and started laying the table as Anwen plucked a strand of spaghetti out of the boiling pot and bit into it to see if it was ready.

'How was your day?' asked Sam.

'Okay.'

'So you haven't put in for a transfer yet?'

Anwen laughed. 'Not yet.'

'I read about Rhys Pryce in the *Echo*,' said Sam.

'I said they'd be all over it.'

'So it's official; it's murder?'

'It was bound to come out sooner rather than later,' said Anwen.

'But the article didn't say anything about who might want him dead, or why?'

'That's 'cause we don't know.'

'I thought your new boss was meant to be something special?'

‘Tell the truth, most of the time I don’t know what’s going on in his head and he’s rubbish at keeping me in the loop. But I think I could learn a lot from him.’ The spaghetti was ready so Anwen fetched the sieve. Sam opened the fridge.

‘Beer or wine?’

‘You choose.’

Sam went for a bottle of Ozzie Chardonnay. As she strained the pasta, Anwen couldn’t help but wonder, what was her D.I. doing tonight?

*

Rhidian Hook stood in the window of his anonymous hotel room and looked out on the busy Friday night streets of Cardiff city centre. It must have been opening night at the opera as a stream of taxis dropped off men in dinner jackets and women in glittery evening gowns. He couldn’t hold back the memories from six months ago.

It had been a perfect night. The performance of *Tosca* by the Welsh National was faultless. Bethan had never looked more beautiful in her grandmother’s antique dress. Rhidian had been aware of men casting sly glances at her, but he had only felt blessed that she was on his arm, not theirs. There was only light traffic on the country roads as they drove home to the cottage, still basking in the afterglow of the performance.

It had come out of nowhere. One moment the rear-view mirror was black and empty. The next, full beam headlights blinded Rhidian. He only had time to get a vague impression of the vehicle – something big and dark – before the impact knocked his car off the road and into the river as if it were a toy. The other driver would walk away with only cuts and bruises, but Rhidian Hook’s nightmare was only just beginning.

It felt only just that it should rain on the day of the service. Not a light drizzle or a scattered shower, but a prolonged cloud burst that turned the skies ash grey, filled gutters to overflowing and kept all cats indoors.

The rain drummed off two dozen raven-black umbrellas, threatening to drown out the vicar's words. Rhidian stood unprotected. He wanted the rain to run into his eyes. He prayed for anything that would blur the sight of Bethan's distraught friends and family; her weeping mother who had to be held up by her granite slab of a husband. He was doing a good job of being strong for his wife, but when he did glare his way, Rhidian saw the unmistakable burn of accusation in his eyes. Not that he needed anyone to tell him that this was his fault. He should have insisted that Bethan wore her seat belt. Maybe if he hadn't had that second glass of wine his reactions would have been sharper? Could he have avoided the crash? Could he have grabbed her before the water snatched her away?

Rhidian was soaked to his bones, but felt nothing. He became aware of Liz Devlin's black leather-gloved hand squeezing his when it came to the moment for him to step forward to plant the rowan tree. Her parents had chosen it because in Celtic mythology it was known as the Tree of Life. He went along with their decision, but thought it perverse. He understood their need to have a focus; somewhere to come on the anniversary of her death or Bethan's birthday. He couldn't think of anything worse than revisiting this living calendar. Every foot the tree grew would just remind him of the time that he had been without her.

They had delayed holding any kind of ritual for as long as possible, hoping that her body would be found and they could have a proper burial, but eventually her parents insisted on some kind of closure. Would it have been any easier to bear if he'd been able to say goodbye properly? He would never know.

In the hotel window, Rhidian dragged his mind back to the present. He cursed the way that he could remember every moment of that dreadful day, yet treasured memories like their wedding were fading away like photographs left out in the sun. Being back in Cardiff was always going to be a challenge. He knew that being around the places where they had spent happy times together would risk inviting Bethan's ghost in, and he had to keep her at bay if he was going to be able to focus on the job. Needing to distract himself, Rhidian scooped up his room key and headed out into the night.

*

Sitting on her bed, Liz Devlin stared at the large brown envelope that had arrived with the morning post. As soon as she saw her solicitor's name and address stamped on the back, she knew what it was. It seemed as if she had been waiting forever for this day, so why was she hesitating? What was preventing her from opening it? Perhaps it was the fear that something had gone wrong, even at this late stage. Knowing that she couldn't put it off any longer, Liz tore open the envelope and slid out the slim document which contained such huge implications. She scanned the text, double checked that it had been signed in all the right places. It was only then that she could relax, knowing that the marriage was finally, officially over.

She couldn't help thinking of Rhidian Hook. Two marriages that had been so full of promise were now over, one ended by tragedy, the other by decree absolute. She reached for her mobile and speed dialled his number. Liz listened to the automated voice tell her that the number she was trying to reach was switched off. She terminated the call. She had already tried Rhidian's hotel but there had been no answer to his room phone. She tried to convince herself that she only wanted to check in on the welfare of an officer who had recently been off on sick leave, but she also wanted to find out where they stood on a personal level, now that both of them were single again.

They had met four years ago when she had been seconded from Avon and Somerset Police to liaise on a cross-border investigation. She already knew something of the man she would be working so closely with. Word of Detective Inspector Hook's successes had crossed the Bristol Channel. The police service is a huge blue family. Non team players don't normally last that long, but what every cop wants is villains off the street, and that's what Rhidian delivered.

Although her police record listed dozens of serious crimes that she had helped resolve, it was this one case that helped her rise to the rank of detective chief inspector. A murderous fire starter has been using ever more ingenious ways to kill using fire, creating an atmosphere of terror in the principality. During the early stages of the investigation his motives could only be half glimpsed, but Rhidian Hook believed that he was using the cleansing power of fire for revenge.

The press demanded action; the Chief Constable wanted results, and all that Liz Devlin had to rely on was the beautiful mess of a mind that belonged to Rhidian Hook. Liz lost count of how many times she'd come to work to find Rhidian asleep in his office, crashed out after his body had finally given up trying to keep up with his overworked mind.

After several months in his close company, Liz began to think that she knew Rhidian as well as anyone ever had. She in turn felt able to reveal some of her vulnerable side to the man she had come to implicitly trust. It was only natural for the two of them to wind down at the end of a stressful, frustrating day with a few drinks at the local. On one evening, even that wasn't enough.

Detective Inspector Alun Gunter thought he'd made a breakthrough by finally tracking the killer to his hideout.

Rhidian thought that Gunter had uncovered the location too easily. So far the killer had played a clever game. Why would he make such a stupid mistake now? Devlin had little choice but to send in a specialist entry team to raid the building.

Two groups of officers entered the back and front of the building simultaneously. They would later understand that breaching the doors was what triggered the pressure switches which clicked on to fill the air with an aerosol of homemade napalm which was undetected by the mask-wearing officers. The droplets fell like the finest rain onto their uniforms, their helmets, their gloved hands. Unlike rain, this tacky liquid stuck to any surface it touched. Here it waited.

Finding a locked door to the basement, the team forced entry with the steel battering ram, known as 'the big red key'. This triggered the small flame which instantly ignited the napalm. The fireball and pall of black smoke it sent up into the air could be seen from miles away. The fire destroyed all evidence linking the suspect to the crimes and put five police officers in hospital. One, whose mask had melted onto her face, would never see again. Considering the extent of her other injuries, that might have been a blessing.

Rhidian and Liz knew that they wouldn't get any sleep that night, so when the landlord rang the bell for last orders, Liz suggested going back to hers.

It was somewhere between the first and second bottle of Bordeaux that she realised that getting pissed wasn't going to do it that night. In the face of so much death, she needed something to remind her that she was alive. She needed to touch and be touched. She craved for someone to hold her, to whisper in her ear that she was safe; that everything would be all right. She knew that Rhidian was taking too much of the darkness into himself in order to try and understand and stop the killer. They both needed something, some one.

She made the first move. They were in the hallway. She was meant to be seeing him out, but found herself pushing him up against the door and telling him to stay. He started to tell her why that wasn't a good idea but she smothered his protests with a kiss. His hands reached for her waist and pulled her in tight. She ran her fingers through his hair and felt him harden against her.

It was only her phone ringing that stopped them from going further. She thought it was work, but it was only her mother who had forgotten the code for her house alarm – again. But the moment was gone. Rhidian got into his taxi. Liz went up to her empty, cold bed.

Liz and Rhidian never spoke of that night ever again, but neither had forgotten it. A week later, Rhidian met Bethan. From then on he had eyes for nobody else. After completing a permanent transfer to South Wales Police, Liz was introduced to Peter when his company was awarded the contract to upgrade the Force's IT. Within six months they were married.

Tonight, what concerned Liz was how Rhidian was coping with the stresses of trying to track down another killer when he no longer had Bethan to anchor him. She dialled Rhidian's hotel again. She let it ring for five minutes before she hung up, wondering where he was.

*

Rhidian walked aimlessly, trying to keep his mind wrapped in the case, but there were too many reminders of Bethan around every corner; the coffee shop that served the Portuguese tarts she loved and her favourite second-hand bookshop where she could lose herself for hours among the dusty shelves of undiscovered treasures. Rhidian found himself standing outside the tiny Italian where they'd celebrated so many special evenings. It was closed and dark on Sunday nights, but in his imagination the lights came on, a wave of happy voices bubbled out from inside the busy, bijou restaurant and the air was filled with the aroma of fried garlic and freshly baked bread. He was transported back to their first date.

Bethan had booked her favourite table at the back of the restaurant, right next to the kitchen. Others might have chosen somewhere quieter, but she had known the owners for years and always enjoyed chatting to the chef, Antonio every time he came to the serving hatch to deliver another order of food. Tonight Antonio could see that she was on a date, so he gave her some privacy; not that it looked like it was going too well. Bethan's natural beauty was only emphasised by the soft candlelight. By contrast the man sitting opposite looked, as Antonio's mother would have said, like something the cat had dragged in.

Rhidian had come straight from work because he had been running late. His scuffed leather coat was hanging from the back of his chair. He couldn't hide how tired he was and he wished that he'd had time for a shower.

There were two empty bottles of wine on the table. Bethan was enjoying a last forkful of melt-in-the-mouth sea bass. Rhidian had hardly touched his steak and was pushing some asparagus tips around his plate. They sat in an awkward silence. It had been like that for most of the meal. Bethan patiently waited for Rhidian to find something to say. Eventually he came up with something.

'Does it take a long time?'

'What?'

'Learning to play the harp. What is it they say? You need to put in ten thousand hours to be able to master an instrument?'

'I've been playing since I was thirteen,' said Bethan. 'I don't want to work out how many hours that is.'

Embarrassed by the stupidity of his question, Rhidian finished his red wine and automatically filled his glass, only belatedly noticing that hers was empty.

'Sorry. Where are my manners?'

But when he went to pour for her, the bottle was empty.

'I'll order another.'

Rhidian looked around, trying to catch the waiter's eye.

'I'm fine,' said Bethan.

'Merlot again?'

'Really. One glass was enough for me.'

Rhidian looked at the empty bottles and his full glass and realised how much of the wine he had actually drunk.

'Do you get to go on many second dates?' she asked.

'Not lately.'

He didn't see the twinkle in her eye that showed how much she was enjoying teasing him. 'Any idea why that might be?'

'I've never been much good at small talk.'

'Then tell me about your work.'

'You don't want to hear about that.'

She wasn't going to let it go now that she had finally got him talking. 'The missing child that's been all over the news. What's his name?'

'Dylan Shaw,' said Rhidian.

'You were on that case?'

'I was the SIO. That's the Senior Investigating Officer.'

'So you were the one who found him?'

Rhidian nodded.

'How did you know it was his mum?' she asked. 'The press were all behind her. There was that "Where's Dylan?" campaign; the armies of volunteers searching every scrap of forest and moorland, the fundraising sites. I even donated myself.'

'You weren't the only one taken in by her crocodile tears.'

'How is he?'

'Kids are resilient. I'd be more worried about him later, when he's a young adult and he has to ask himself what was his mother going to do with him? Hiding him in her dad's loft was one thing. But after all the publicity, she couldn't risk him being found alive.'

'How did she think she was going to get away with it?'

'She wasn't planning that far ahead. She was desperate to save her marriage. And it worked for a while; the shared anxiety of a missing child pushed her and her husband back together. It was never going to last.' He stopped himself. This wasn't the kind of conversation for a date. 'I hope the fish was okay.'

'Delicious.'

'So it hasn't been a total waste of an evening then?'

'Not at all.'

'Anyone else would have run for the hills after the starter.'

'Maybe I'm not like anyone else?'

'I'll get the bill and find you a taxi.'

Rhidian caught the waiter's eye and signalled for the bill.

'Can't wait to get away?' asked Bethan.

'What? No. I thought...'

'You're not getting off that lightly.' She smiled. 'You've told me all about your job. Next time it'll be your turn to listen to me, not that my work is anywhere near as interesting as yours.'

Puzzled, Rhidian waved the waiter away. He liked Bethan's spirit. If only he had met her at some other time. He had thought that he was ready to try dating again, but now that he had spent time with her he realised that this was just a fantasy. Men like him didn't get to have relationships with beautiful, talented women. They didn't get to have ordinary lives. It would be kinder to let her go now.

'This was a mistake,' he said.

'The choice of restaurant?'

'No.'

'Wrong dinner companion?'

'Not at all, said Rhidian. There was that teasing glint in her eye again. 'Look. Police work can take a heavy toll on a relationship. You'd be better off hooking up with a nice, safe doctor or maybe a bank manager.'

'A bank manager!'

'Someone who's job means that you know what time they're coming home and you're not left waiting for the phone to ring, fearing that it's bad news. You need –'

Bethan silenced Rhidian by leaning forward to kiss him, smothering his words with her soft lips, before sitting back, taking a sip of his wine, then passing him a menu.

'I hope you've left room for a dessert,' she said. 'The tiramisu is to die for.'

They would return to the same restaurant, same table many times and they always ordered the tiramisu.

A passing ambulance siren tore Rhidian from his memories. He found himself standing outside the closed restaurant, shocked by the pale image in the dark window; the reflection of a hollow-eyed, dark-jowled figure he hardly recognised. He backed away, but his spectre stared back at him.

He walked blindly down a side street and stumbled through the doors of the first pub he came to. He was relieved to be greeted by a wall of sound. Just what he needed to drown out his memories.

Rhidian headed for the bar, passing the quiz machine that bleeped and flashed, trying to tempt punters to feed pound coins into its slot. He edged around the score of football fans cheering on their teams on the TV mounted on the wall. The mix of red and blue shirts denoted their tribal allegiances, but for the moment their rivalry was mellowed, both by the many pints they'd downed and the fact that it was well into extra time and the match was still tied. Rhidian ordered four pints of the guest ale. He estimated that three wouldn't be enough and five too many.

He draped his coat over the back of a chair then lined up the four pints on the table in front of him. He pulled out his notebook and placed it in front of the drinks. He lifted the first pint to his lips, took a deep sip, replaced it in the row, then opened the notebook. He started to review the case from the beginning, with the sketches and scribbles he'd written down at the site where Rhys Pryce's body had been found. As well as the notes and sketches he'd jotted down directly onto the pages, also stuffed between the notebook's covers were a collection of thoughts he'd had when the notebook wasn't to hand. These he spread out on the table in front of him. On a scrap of newspaper he'd scrawled himself a note – '*Bloom – tool marks?*' On a coffee shop napkin he'd made a list of possible motives for killing Rhys Pryce. *Revenge? Jealousy? Spurned lover? Money?*

Once he'd re-read all of his notes he knew that he couldn't put it off any longer. He focused on the first sketch he had made while standing on the road, looking at the wall of maize and the beginnings of the path that had been driven through it. Another sup and he began.

It was always the same pattern. He needed a certain amount of alcohol to be able to detach himself from his own humanity so that he could try and enter the mind of the killer. He let his eyes defocus. He tuned out the sounds of the cheering football fans. The walls of the pub became less solid. He felt the wind ruffle his hair. It would have been exposed on the coast. He could hear the creaking of the crashed car as its torn metal settled moments after the crash. The pub's flock wallpaper became a curtain of maize that stirred gently in a sea breeze as he walked along its length, pausing when he saw where the uniformity had been breached, just like it was in his sketch. It was no longer his eyes that he was looking through, but the eyes of the killer. Calmly, in no hurry at all, he entered the maize, following the path of broken stalks. After he had walked in ten paces, he paused to look around. He could no longer see the coast road. He felt his mouth form into a smile. He heard a voice inside his head that was not his.

'Nobody can see you. You have all the time in the world.'

He continued down the freshly made path of broken stalks, noting the trail of blood, bright red against the green. Over the gentle rustle of wind through maize he picked up a new sound. A whimpering. Something in pain. He felt his pulse quicken. Knowing that he was closing in on his quarry he had to fight the urge to move faster. His blood might be hot, but his head needed to remain cool. The voice in his head reassured him.

'Don't rush. That's how mistakes get made.'

In the pub, Rhidian took another big gulp, hardly tasting the beer at all.

Deep in the maize he got his first glimpse of his prey, lying on his back, trying to crawl away from the doom that was steadily approaching. Rhidian felt something in his hand; reassuringly heavy, but perfectly balanced. When he looked down he couldn't get a clear picture of what the object was. It kept flickering; first it was a jagged hunting dagger, then a butcher's boning knife, a machete then a surgeon's scalpel. But none of the objects fitted the facts. Unable to stabilise the image, he refocused on Rhys Pryce. It was clear from the terror on the footballer's face that he knew what was coming. Rhidian could smell his sweat. He could feel his fear.

Rhidian's fingers felt for his glass and found it empty. He reached for the next pint.

His shadow fell over the prone form of Rhys Pryce. Despite the obvious pain from his broken hip, Pryce knew that if he didn't move he was dead. He cried out in pain as he tried to rise to his feet, but Rhidian placed a heavy boot on his chest and pressed him to the ground. Before Pryce could register what was happening the first cut had been made.

Deliberate. No hesitation. The blade sliced straight through the skin and muscle of his lower leg, right down to the bone. It was then that the screaming started.

The smell of ripening maize was overwhelmed by the metallic tang of fresh blood. He remembered to stand to one side to avoid the worst of the spray from the severed artery. The fight went out of his victim as shock took over. Rhidian looked at his hands that were red and slick with blood. He turned them over and wondered whether he felt any revulsion.

Suddenly there was a bag by Rhidian's feet. A sport's bag, then an old-fashioned doctor's medical bag; finally a plain old supermarket carrier. This was one detail that was unimportant for the moment. From out of the bag he brought a saw, something solid but lightweight; a cross between what a DIYer and a surgeon might use. Again the image of the object was hazy. What was all too clear was the effect that its razor-sharp teeth had on Rhys Pryce's foot.

He could feel the vibration of the bone's resistance as he sawed. He had to pause to wipe the sweat from his eyes. This was more effort than he had imagined. His hands were soon covered in the finest bone dust, white stained scarlet. There was a smell in the air; something both animal and meaty. This got worse when he hit the marrow.

Rhidian downed half a pint in one gulp, but it wasn't enough to get rid of the smell and taste that clung to the back of his throat. He had to see this through. He closed his eyes tight and tried to imagine what he would feel as he watched the last of his life pump out of Rhys Pryce's body.

A sudden smash shattered his train of thought, and instead of the faceless killer, it was Rhidian Hook who found himself, bloody-handed, standing over the body of Rhys Pryce. Looking down at what he had done, bile bubbled up, burning his throat.

It took a moment to realise that he was back in the pub and that it had been the barmaid dropping his empty pint glasses that had crashed him out of his dream state.

The landlord's daughter had been watching the stranger from behind the bar, curious about what he'd been so engrossed in. So when it came time to clear away his empties she couldn't resist a look at his open notebook. What she saw were graphic, anatomically accurate sketches of Rhys Pryce's raw stump of a leg.

Rhidian snapped the book shut but the damage was done. His muttered apology couldn't calm the girl's hysterics or stop the landlord from bearing down on him, angrily spluttering something about how he wouldn't stand for having his daughter upset. Rhidian tried to stand, but his balance had gone. He should have had something to eat before he started drinking. He tried to explain, but the right words eluded him. By now a couple of the beered-up football fans had also taken it upon themselves to come to defend the barmaid's honour and each grabbed one of Rhidian's arms.

'If you'll let me explain...'

But there was no reasoning with them. Rhidian managed to scoop his notebook off the table before he was frogmarched to the back door and unceremoniously dumped in an alleyway with a warning about what would happen to him if he ever crossed their paths again. Rhidian's coat was thrown out after him, landing in a pothole full of rain water, stale beer and piss. Still reeling from being dragged so violently from his imaginings, when he retrieved his coat, Rhidian couldn't dispel the image that his hands were covered in thick, cloying blood. He staggered to the wall and threw up a stomach full of beer.

*

A dozen fresh white lilies stood in silent watch over Loretta Swann's bed. The visitor knew the staffs shift patterns by heart. Visiting time had ended hours ago. The night shift had finished their rounds and left the woman in Room 3 alone to her dreams. They were confident that their special time wouldn't be interrupted.

The heady aroma of newly applied perfume hung in the air. Dido's first album was playing quietly on a portable CD player. She had once confessed to this guilty pleasure, and so it had duly been noted down in 'The Book Of All Things Her'.

An ornate, silver-backed brush glided through the woman's hair. Reassuring whispers were poured into her ear. If only the sleeper could answer; if only the room could have been filled by her voice and laughter. As cautious fingers felt the razor-sharp edges of the object held deep in a coat pocket, the whispers promised that this unbearable situation would not be allowed to stand.

A single strand of russet hair was left in the soft bristles of the brush. The visitor gently plucked it free but it felt sacrilegious to throw something so precious into the bin where it would mingle with used tissues and medical detritus. Holding the hair up to the light, the stranger opened their mouth and placed the strand onto the tip of their tongue. The visitor's eyes closed as they savoured taking part of Her inside.

12

Darius Gull was relaxing at the end of another golden day. Dressed in a black silk kimono with a golden tiger sprawled down its back, he stood proud on the balcony of his Cardiff Bay penthouse like a captain on the bridge of a ship. Eyes closed, he let the warm evening breeze wafting in off the bay play across his face as he sipped the perfectly chilled Pinot Grigio.

The confrontation at the mortuary had cast a brief shadow over his day. He had initially been vexed by Lowri Pryce's defiance, but once he had calmed down, with the help of some good wine and some even better sex, he was able to reassure himself that he would have no trouble in talking Lowri around to letting him represent her. There would be plenty of opportunities for Gull to earn some fat fees, including legal complications over Rhys Pryce's estate and rights issues over the use of the dead sportsman's image. First thing tomorrow he would set one of his juniors on the task of examining whether he could sue Rhidian Hook and the South Wales Police over whether their hounding of his client had led to his death.

Gull mused over whether to spend the predicted extra money on the thirty-foot yacht he'd had his eye on, or should he add to his portfolio of low-quality, high-yield student flats. He was jolted from his avaricious dreams by the chimes of his doorbell.

Gull frowned. It couldn't be the boy. If he'd returned thinking that this was the beginning of a beautiful relationship, he'd have to put him straight. He was a mere intern. If he wanted a leg up, and to continue sampling Gull's superior quality cocaine, he would need to understand that it was Gull who told the boy when his presence was required.

Heading for the door, Gull put his wine glass down on the dining table, but then remembered that he didn't want to leave a ring on the antique mahogany. As he moved the glass, the doorbell rang again and Gull's mood darkened. The boy was pretty and impressively endowed, but nobody was allowed to be in control, except for Darius Gull.

Gull flung the door open, but his scathing admonishments died on his lips in the face of the vision that greeted him; a figure dressed in what appeared to be a toga, only it was blood red and had a hood covering the head.

Gull laughed. 'What is this? Cos play? Okay. I'm game. So who are you meant to be? Only if it's a character from *Game of Thrones*, I've never seen it.'

Gull's smile faded as the figure reached into the toga and pulled out what could only be described as a large pair of shears. Gull had seen similar simple devices being used by shepherds; the two blades joined at the end by a spring. However, these weren't the crude utilitarian tools wielded by Ozzy sheep shearers at agricultural shows, but an ornate device cast from solid silver and decorated with images of Egyptian gods. On one tip was a stylised dog; on the other, a sphinx-like cat.

'Top marks for the prop. Looks very realistic.'

The figure calmly stepped into the room and closed the door. Gull found himself backing up. 'Well. Say something.'

The figure locked the door. Gull couldn't remember the last time he had felt so powerless. He made his living from twisting words until they served his purpose, but now that skill had been snatched away from him. He could think of no words to come to his aid; no clever argument to prevent whatever was to come. All he could do was stumble backwards into his pristine apartment, clutching the exquisitely thin kimono tight around his body as if that was going to be any kind of defence against the vicious-looking blades that advanced towards him. The figure squeezed the spring. The blades moved effortlessly. As the tips of the two blades met, the engraved figures of the cat and dog looked like they were kissing. Even as he knew that they would soon be slicing through his flesh, Gull couldn't help but admire the exquisite craftsmanship.

13

As she chewed on a slab of butter-smeared toast, Anwen glanced at the kitchen clock and realised that, not for the first time, she and Sam were running late. Fed up with her temperamental shower, Anwen hoped that Sam would offer to have a go at fixing it, but he wouldn't touch it.

'That's a job for a plumber,' he said.

'I just need to know, can it be repaired or do I need a new one?'

They were still talking about it when Anwen locked the front door behind them and they split off, heading for their own vehicles. Before Anwen could unlock her car she heard a 'Shit and fuck!' from Sam. She joined him at the back of his Transit van. One of the back doors was slightly open. You didn't need to be a trained crime scene investigator to see that it had been pried open with a crowbar. The tool marks scratched into the paintwork and the twisted lock were clear to see.

'Don't touch anything. Wait for forensics,' she said, but Sam ignored her and climbed into the back.

'Sam!'

She followed him in to find him standing in the centre of a near empty van.

'What did they take?' she asked.

'Everything. Power tools, couple of reels of electrical wire, my generator… Fuck!' He banged the side of the van, leaving a fist-sized dent. All that the thieves had left were some stepladders and some old dust sheets piled in one corner. Then Sam saw that something was under the sheets. He urgently pulled them back, revealing half a dozen pots of paint. Anwen could tell from the drips on the sides of the tins that they had already been used. She was surprised to see how Sam's mood lifted as he counted the pots and was satisfied that none were missing. Seeing Anwen's puzzled expression, he explained.

'It's for the job I'm on. Had to get it mixed specially. It would have set the whole project back if they'd taken that.'

'But your tools...'

'It's my fault. Shouldn't have left them in overnight.'

'Make a list of what they've taken. If I get it circulated quickly there's a chance we could get some of it back.'

'It's not worth it.'

'We just need to hit the second-hand shops. Cash Convertors...'

'They were old. Probably time I replaced them anyway.'

'You'll still need to fill in a report to get a crime number for your insurance.'

'I'm not going to claim.'

'Why not?'

'They'll only whack my premiums up next time. And to be honest, I'm getting paid so well for this job that it'll easily pay for a new set of tools.'

'Your choice. But if you change your mind...'

'You're going to be late for work,' said Sam, but he could tell that Anwen was still perplexed. 'Look, I get that you want to help, but this is just an occupational hazard. I'm lucky they didn't take the whole van, then I would have been really stuffed.'

Anwen knew there would be no shifting him, so she kissed him and jumped off the back of the van, heading for her car. She was impressed that he was taking it so well. She wasn't sure she would have been so calm in the circumstances.

Sitting in her car parked outside the Marriott Hotel, Jones was wondering whether to ask her colleagues in the Crime Analysis Department if the theft from Sam's van was part of a pattern. She'd loved to surprise Sam by finding and returning all his tools to him. After all, what's the point in going out with a police officer if they can't pull a few strings? The passenger door opened and Rhidian Hook slipped into the passenger seat.

'Morning, boss.'

'Sergeant.'

Rhidian saw Jones's nose wrinkle as a bitter aroma stung her nostrils. She knew that smell all too well from when her stepfather had come home legless and she and her mother had to put him to bed. She pressed the button to lower her window, put the car into gear and pulled away. Rhidian had a sniff of his duffle coat and realised that this was the source of the odour. He cracked his own window, grateful for Jones's discretion.

At the police station, Anwen Jones was well chuffed to see the welcome screen light up on the computer. For once IT had delivered in good time. Before she got on with her work there was something else she needed to do. What was the cause of the personal grit between Rhidian Hook and Darius Gull? And then there was the way that Lowri Pryce had recognised the DI's name. What connected them? On her way to the office she had called in at the files room. It hadn't taken long to find what she was looking for among the discontinued cases.

Like most official police reports, it sounded dry when laid out in black and white, but she had written enough of them herself to be able to read between the lines. As she turned the pages, she was so engrossed in the story that she didn't realise she had company until a shadow fell over the screen.

'You only had to ask,' said Rhidian.

Jones automatically tried to close the report, but she knew it was too late.

'I've heard the rumours. I wanted to check the actual facts,' she said.

'Which are?'

'It doesn't matter.'

'I've always found that it's best to get these things out in the open,' said Rhidian.

Jones reluctantly recalled what she had read. 'March the tenth. Just after midnight, Emergency Control received a nine nine nine call reporting a two-vehicle RTC. One of the cars had been shunted into the Taff. By the time the first patrol reached the scene a passer-by had pulled the driver out of the submerged car. Despite an extensive search of the river, the body of his passenger was never found.' Jones paused. Rhidian gave her the nod to carry on. 'The driver of the second vehicle was Rhys Pryce.'

'Haven't you missed something out?'

'Don't think so.'

'The driver of the first vehicle was found to be over the drink drive limit.'

'Marginally.'

'He failed the roadside test.'

'But by the time they got you onto the intoximeter at the station your blood alcohol reading was below the level needed for a criminal prosecution.'

'That doesn't mean that I wasn't responsible.'

'You were driven off the road.'

'But could I have done more to avoid the collision?'

'You'll never know for sure.'

'And where there's doubt, there's guilt.'

'Rhys Pryce was responsible for your wife's death.'

'The courts didn't think so. They didn't even take his licence off him.'

'How did he get away with that?'

'His barrister, Darius Gull. He somehow got hold of my confidential medical notes from after the Red Maids case.'

'That's when you lost your sergeant?'

'Not sure that "lost" covers what happened to him. But yes. After having to tell his parents that their son had been murdered and that they had to prepare themselves to read all the grisly details in the tabloids, I had to see the Force counsellor. Standard practice, but to hear Gull's spin on it you'd have thought I'd had a total meltdown.'

'But the judge wouldn't have let that enter as evidence?'

'She told the jury to dismiss it, but once the idea had been planted in their minds; a copper with mental health issues, that was enough doubt to undermine my evidence and let Pryce walk away an innocent man.'

Jones knew she should let it lie, but she never did know when to stop. 'Why did the DCI put you on this case? She must have known that it would open old wounds.'

'I think she hoped I'd get some kind of closure, so that I'd be able to get back to work. What else was I going to do, stuck on a mountain? Make artisan cheese?'

'Prefer a lump of Cheddar myself,' said Jones.

Rhidian took off his coat. Hanging it on the back of a chair he gave it a surreptitious sniff and was reassured that he had got rid of the stink by washing it in the Gents toilets. Only then did he take in how the office had been cleared of rubbish. There were also phones, two computers and new whiteboards.

'How did you do it?'

'Guy in office supplies owed me a favour after I helped his nephew sort out some bullies.'

Rhidian pulled on the cords of a set of blinds. After catching a few times, the plastic slats finally rose, revealing a large window with a magnificent view of the varied reds and golds of Cathay Park. He saw men and women on their way to work; an old woman feeding the pigeons and a young mother jog-pushing her baby in its buggy. He let the sun warm his face for a moment. Jones took in the new-look DI Hook. He'd had a shave. That was an improvement. The dark circles under his eyes were still there, but he was on the way to looking like a living person rather than an extra from a zombie film.

Rhidian became aware that he was being scrutinised, and was keen to deflect Jones's attention. 'Any word from Bloom?'

'Yeah.' Jones reached for a pad and read her notes. 'The foot is a match to Rhys Pryce, but still no idea of what tools were used.'

'So. No help from that quarter. Where are we with a motive?'

Before Jones could reply, one of the desk phones started ringing. Jones answered it. 'DS Jones.' she listened, then reached for her pad. 'When?' Rhidian noted the urgency in her voice. 'Give me the address.'

Rhidian was already putting his coat on before Jones could finish scrawling four words on a pad of paper – '*DARIUS GULL. FOUND DEAD.*'

Jones was speeding towards Cardiff docks, dodging in between slower moving traffic.

'You can slow down you know,' said Rhidian.

'But it's a suspicious death.'

'Exactly.'

'Boss?'

'What's the point of rushing to a corpse?'

Jones kept pushing, swerving around a cyclist with only inches to spare. Rhidian didn't blame her. He wanted his DS to be keen and not too compliant. He needed to be challenged sometimes, but he also hoped that she would still be open to listening and learning.

‘I was like you once,’ said Rhidian. ‘Rushing to the scene, foot to the floor, blood pumping. Then I realised that not only was it safer for other road users if I slowed down, but actually it gave me more time.’

‘Time for what?’

‘To think about what I was about to face. What would my first actions need to be? What other resources might I need to call in? It meant that when I arrived, I was calm, focused, not hyped up on adrenaline.’

Jones considered his words. Rhidian was pleased when she eased her foot off the accelerator and filtered back into the flow of traffic.

Pulling into the car park, Jones parked between an ambulance and a patrol car. She removed the magnetic blue light from the roof of her car and stowed it back in the glove compartment. Rhidian Hook passed her a pair of blue latex gloves then put on his own pair. They exited the car and headed for the entrance to the massive dockside warehouse that had been converted into luxury apartments. Rhidian’s attention was drawn to the penthouse that occupied the prime location overlooking the water. The development was so new that some of the apartments were still unoccupied, but Rhidian knew that soon this address would be added to the dark history of Cardiff; another black pin in his personal map of murder and pain.

‘The cleaner called it in,’ said Jones as they headed up in the lift. ‘She’s got her own keys so she let herself in. Dialled nine nine nine as soon as her hands had stopped shaking.’

‘Where is she now?’

‘Caretaker’s office. Still in shock. We might be able to interview her later.’

Rhidian and Jones exited the lift and headed for the door to Gull's apartment, where a white-faced young constable guarded the entrance.

'Were you first on the scene?' asked Rhidian.

'Yes, sir.' The memory brought bile up into the constable's mouth. He swallowed it back down. 'Sorry. Haven't seen a dead body before.'

'And how do you know he's dead?' asked Rhidian.

'All the blood…'

'Rule one. They're not dead until the pathologist says they are,' said Rhidian.

'Yes, sir.'

'Do you need to be relieved?'

'No. I'm good.'

Rhidian nodded. 'No one inside until I say so.'

'Yes, sir.'

'And if you need to throw up, do it away from my crime scene.'

Rhidian and Jones entered Gull's apartment. After an initial look at the scene, Rhidian and Jones went out onto the penthouse balcony to let the CSIs and Dr Bloom get to work.

Rhidian watched the hypnotic dance of half a dozen small sailing boats bobbing at anchor on the cobalt blue waters of the docks.

'No sign of forced entry,' said Jones. 'Did he let his killer in? Someone he knew?'

'Well he definitely had company some time during the evening,' said Rhidian. 'There are traces of white powder on the coffee table and two used wine glasses.'

'There's also a tube of K-Y Jelly on the bedside table. Cap's off. A party that went wrong?' asked Jones.

'Doesn't sound like any kind of party I've ever been invited to,' said Rhidian.

A white-suited CSI arrived at the French windows and spoke through her protective mask. 'We've cleared the body,' she said.

Rhidian nodded and led the way into the apartment to where Gull lay spread-eagled, face up on what was undoubtedly a very expensive antique Turkish rug. The blood that had seeped from his mouth had blended into the complicated weave of dark reds and blues. Although the area around the body had been photographed and tested, the rest of the room was busy with CSIs powdering surfaces for fingerprints and a forensic photographer documenting every inch of the scene.

'Well, Doctor?'

Augustus Bloom flamingo-stretched himself up to his full height, and pulled down his protective face mask.

'He died here. No question.'

'Cause of death?'

'I'll have to open him up to confirm it…'

'But your money would be on?'

'Drowning in his own blood after his tongue was severed at the root.'

'Lovely,' said Jones.

Rhidian had seen most things in his career, but this was new. 'Surely even a wound like that shouldn't have been fatal?'

'Indeed,' said Bloom. 'The proper pressure applied would have stemmed the bleeding until the blood clotted or he could have got help.'

Rhidian knew there was a 'but' coming.

'But there is fresh bruising on the victim's upper arms.' Bloom peeled back Gull's dressing down to reveal the purpling mottled marks.

'So his attacker sat on his chest, preventing him from getting up or attending to the wound,' said Rhidian.

'Which allowed the blood to fill his lungs. Game over.'

Rhidian didn't want to look again at the black red hole that was Gull's mouth. A trail of red splatters led down his chin, and across his smooth, shaved chest, as if left by some blood-bloated slug.

'Have you found the tongue?' asked Rhidian.

'Not yet. So it's just as well that Liz Devlin called you out of your self-imposed exile,' said Bloom. 'Mutilations. Missing body parts. Sounds right up your street.'

'If you haven't got anything else useful to contribute...' said Rhidian.

'I take it you noticed the white grains inside Mr Gull's nostrils,' said Bloom. 'No points for guessing what it might be.'

'And that matches the toxicology results from Rhys Pryce,' said Rhidian. 'He had traces of both cocaine and cannabis in his system.'

'Enough to suggest habitual use?' asked Bloom.

Rhidian nodded. 'Cocaine use isn't as rare as it once was.' He spotted a flat bulge in Gull's dressing gown pocket.

'Sergeant.'

Jones crouched down to the body and used gloved fingertips to carefully pull out the top-of-the-range mobile phone. She slipped it into an evidence bag, then pressed through the plastic to turn the phone on.

'It's locked.'

'Password protected?'

'Or you can use facial recognition,' said Jones.

'Perfect.'

Jones understood what he meant and held the bagged phone over Gull's face and pressed the button. She looked at the screen which now filled with icons telling her that it was unlocked.

'We're in.'

'Good. He must have a laptop as well. We'll take them both in.'

Jones nodded and moved off to search for Gull's laptop. Rhidian turned his attention to the body.

'The removal of the tongue. Was it the same tools that were used on Pryce?' Rhidian asked Bloom.

'I'll have to confirm it later, but no, I don't think so. Even to the naked eye I would say that Mr Gull's tongue was severed by two blades in a scissoring action.'

'But a killer doesn't change his MO.' Rhidian reluctantly looked at Gull's open mouth again. 'So our killer's behaving like a surgeon, bringing the right tools for the job?'

Bloom sounded a word of caution. 'Before you go around arresting anyone carrying a doctor's bag, I'd be surprised if I'll be able to match Mr Pryce's wounds with any widely used surgical instruments.'

Typical, thought Rhidian. Two steps forward, one step back. Just like every other investigation.

'Boss.'

The urgency of Jones's tone drew Rhidian and Bloom to join her at the large tropical fish tank that had been built into one wall of the lounge. Soft lighting falling upon golden sand, dancing emerald weeds and pink and white corals, created a convincing illusion that you were looking out through a porthole onto the bottom of a tropical sea. Neon fish darted around their mini universe, their colours so bright that you wouldn't be surprised to find that they were battery powered. Lovely and hypnotising though the setting was, it was the activity going on in one corner of the tank that had drawn Jones's eye.

A rainbow of fish was clustered around a slab of pink meat. Although the fish had been nipping at the alien invader into their world, it was still recognisable as a human tongue.

'Anyone got a net?' asked Bloom.

14

The black private ambulance carefully reversed up to the loading bay of the mortuary. As they opened the van's rear doors, the two black-suited funeral service operators were comparing who had had the worst call outs.

'She had to be twenty-five stone and there was just me and Pugh to try and get her off her bog, and he was moaning about his bad back. To this day I don't know how we got her out of there.'

'What about that double bagger I had last summer? Dead for two weeks during a heat wave? He'd rotted right into his armchair. And the stench...'

Their laughter died on their lips when the double doors swung open and Jac Mundy arrived, pushing a stainless steel trolley. Jac didn't admonish the men. Although he was new to the job, he already understood that black humour came with the territory. As long as it was never expressed in front of the public, especially the grieving relatives, it was accepted as a much-needed pressure release for people who had to spend so much time around the dead.

Jac pushed the trolley containing the black-bagged body down the long corridor and into the autopsy room where Dr Bloom was snapping on a fresh pair of gloves.

'Sorry to have to ask you to stay on, Jac, only it's another police job,' said Bloom.

'No problem, Doctor,' said Jac as he handed over the paperwork to Bloom and then moved to unzip the bag and peel the plastic away from the cadaver's face; which was when he froze.

'Can I have a fresh apron please, Jac?'

When he received no response, Bloom turned to the corpse and saw how the blood had drained from his assistant's face. Bloom wasn't unsympathetic. Although he was immune to the sight of death, he understood that this professional detachment took time to develop.

'Are you okay?'

Jac could only shake his head. His lips were too dry to answer. Jac couldn't understand what he was seeing. How could he be looking at the lifeless features of Darius Gull? Jac wanted to zip up the body bag, to shut out the nightmare vision, but his fingers wouldn't work. Although Gull's eyes were closed, any pretence of a peaceful end were dispelled by his lips, tinged blue and flecked with aspirated dried blood.

'Why don't you take the rest of the day off? I'll call Jane in.'

Jac managed a dry, whispered 'sorry' and stumbled out of the room, gasping for fresh air.

*

While the scenes of crime technicians continued to examine Gull's penthouse for evidence, Rhidian and Jones returned to their office to interrogate Gull's mobile phone and laptop for clues to who might want him dead.

'There's a lot of serious trolling on his social media,' said Jones as she scrolled through Gull's online accounts.

'Any credible death threats?'

'Does "Die slow in agony" count?'

'Is it anonymous?'

'Posted by someone called "Paul Logan". Could be a pseudonym.'

'No. His wife and daughter were killed in a head-on crash on the M4. We charged the other driver with causing death by dangerous driving. Gull got him off. Said he had dozed off at the wheel because of the side effects of his pain medication.'

'Do we add Logan to our list?'

‘We can’t rule him out. But this is going to be a very long list.’

As Jones added Logan’s name to her own laptop, Rhidian opened a file on Gull’s phone, labelled ‘amusements’.

‘There’s something else he wasn’t shy about.’ Rhidian showed Jones a photo of a semi-naked man, smiling at the phone’s camera lens as he drank something bright green from a cocktail glass. Rhidian swiped left, scrolling through more photos of other men. All were young, fit and in various states of undress. Some photos were selfies, showing Gull, lying in bed with men who were much younger than him.

‘I know this one,’ said Rhidian. ‘He was an intern at Gull’s chambers. Left with a very good reference, if I remember correctly.’

‘But which of them was sharing his bed last night?’

Rhidian swiped through more photos until he stopped.

‘We’ve got a problem.’

‘Boss?’

Rhidian showed her the picture of a young man snapped coming out of Gull’s wet room with a towel just about covering his modesty.

‘Shit!’ said Jones.

The semi-naked man was Jac Mundy.

Rhidian and Jones rushed to the shared terraced house. Their urgent knocks were answered by a sleepy male nurse. Jones identified themselves, then asked ‘Where’s Jac’s room?’

‘Er, upstairs. Second on the left.’

Anwen was first up the stairs with Rhidian right behind her. When they pushed open the door, they found Jac Mundy sitting on his bed, head bowed in resignation, a half packed sports bag on the bed next to him.

In the Custody Suite, Devlin and Rhidian watched from the doorway as Jones booked Jac Mundy in with the custody sergeant.

'He doesn't look like a killer,' said Devlin.

'They don't all have mad eyes and a swastika cut into their forehead.'

'Dissecting corpses would give him the expertise and the detachment to be able to remove a human foot and a tongue.'

'From what I understand, mortuary technicians only assist,' said Rhidian. 'Taking samples, cleaning the body; they don't get to do the dissection themselves.'

'He would have watched Dr Bloom at work; learned how to do it.'

'True. But he has access to the most efficient dissecting instruments known to man, why not use them? Why bring his own tools to the murder scenes?'

'You didn't find them at his room?' asked Devlin.

'No.'

'But he was getting ready to run?'

'There is an obvious link to Darius Gull, but what about Rhys Pryce?' said Rhidian.

'It will be worth looking into any mental instability. I mean, working so close to death all the time isn't most people's idea of a career,' said Devlin.

'I agree. He ticks a lot of boxes,' said Rhidian. 'But let's not count our chickens just yet.'

Devlin was obviously hoping for a more positive reaction. Before she could voice her displeasure there was a commotion at the rear doors as Alun Gunter and DS Mal Rogers bundled a prisoner in. He wasn't taking kindly to having a copper hanging onto each arm.

'Get your filthy pig hands off me.'

Although he was white and born and bred in South Wales, he was trying to sound like a Jamaican gangster, only he couldn't keep his Cardiff accent from slipping through every now and then.

'Seriously. I will mess you up, blood. You get me?'

'You can drop the hard man act now, Billy, there's none of your mates to see you here.'

The young man was wearing a lumberjack shirt over his T-shirt for a band that Gunter had never heard of. And, like most young men, he didn't seem to own a belt, so his jeans were falling down his arse, revealing his Tommy Hilfiger briefs. As the DS frogmarched the suspect up to the counter, Devlin called Gunter over.

'Alun. That your dealer?'

'No, he's a doorman at the Phoenix. Strictly low level, selling gram bags to clubbers. He's still on probation for a GBH so if we sweat him on that, maybe he'll give up his supplier.'

'Good work.'

'Thanks, ma'am.' But Alun Gunter couldn't just take his pat on the back and be satisfied with that. He turned to Rhidian. 'What's this I heard about you taking Pryce's missus to the mortuary?'

'She needed to say goodbye to her husband.'

Devlin's expression revealed that this was the first she had heard of this and she wasn't impressed. This encouraged Gunter. 'That's why we have family liaison officers. You're meant to be investigating his death, not going all candles and sandals like some bean-munching social worker.'

'Have you ever lost anyone, Alun?' asked Rhidian.

'My old man, but he was a bastard.'

'Anyone you cared about?'

'Stop trying to twist this onto me,' said Gunter. 'I'd have thought you'd have enough to get on with without having to hold the hand of a grieving widow.'

Pleased to have scored a few direct hits in front of their boss, Gunter joined his DS at the counter.

'He does have a point, Rhidian,' said Devlin. 'Let the FLO do their job. You'd be far more help to Mrs Pryce if you focus on catching her husband's killer.'

Rhidian didn't need reminding that he was yet to deliver on his promise to Lowri.

*

Jac Mundy had taken the option of having a duty solicitor present during the interview. Rhidian knew this wasn't necessarily a sign of guilt. The scrubbed-faced young woman who sat next to Mundy carefully watched everything through a pair of plain framed spectacles. She looked like a schoolgirl playing dress up in her mam's business suit.

The twin discs were recording; one copy for the police, the other for Jac's defence. The solicitor was typing into her laptop a record of every question asked by the officers and every answer given by her client. Jones was also keeping her own record, although her typing was a more clumsy, one finger at a time affair. Jac Mundy's clothes had been seized and retained for forensic tests, so he was wearing one of the sterile paper suits supplied by the custody office. His head was down, resting on his folded arms. He only looked up when Rhidian repeated his question.

'How did you know Darius Gull?'

Jac looked at his solicitor for advice. She shot him a stern look. He remembered her instructions and said 'No comment.' The solicitor might look young, but she knew her stuff.

'Did you meet him through your work?

'No comment.'

'Were you in a relationship with him?'

'No comment.'

'Were you at his apartment last night?'

'No comment.'

Jac sat a bit straighter. He placed his hands flat on the table in front of him, feeling more confident now that he had seen how easy it was to deflect any questions. What he didn't realise was that this was all part of Rhidian's plan. He needed the young man to be more relaxed so that he could get a base line reading on Mundy's reactions. This would help him to spot when he was telling the truth and when he was lying.

'Have you ever been to his apartment?'

'No comment.'

'We've recovered several sets of fingerprints from Mr Gull's lounge. His bathroom. Bedroom. Are any of them going to match your fingerprints, Jac?'

Rhidian saw one of Jac's hands twitch and knew that no matter how hard he was trying to stay in control, the young man couldn't conceal such telltale body language. His hands were open, too vulnerable. He was desperate to close them into a more defensive fist, but he knew that this would give him away.

'Officers are currently talking to Mr Gull's neighbours. Will any of them identify you as a regular visitor?'

'No comment.'

'Or perhaps there were so many young men going in and out that the neighbours might get confused.'

Another involuntary twitch.

'Did you think you were the only one?'

'No comment.' Weaker this time.

Rhidian knew it was time to strike. He opened a box file and picked out an evidence bagged exhibit. 'I am showing Mr Mundy exhibit RH3. An Apple phone belonging to Darius Gull. Do you recognise this, Jac?'

'No comment.'

Rhidian opened the gallery app.

'Is this you?' Rhidian showed Jac a photo of him and Gull at a nightclub, posing with a well-known drag artist. The memory clearly touched Jac who couldn't look away from the happy photograph.

'You look really happy there. Were you?'

Tears filled Jac's eyes.

Sensing danger, the solicitor tried to step in.

'My client needs a break.'

Rhidian ignored her, keeping his eyes locked on Jac Mundy's.

'He meant a lot to you?'

'Remember my advice,' said the solicitor. 'You are under no obligation to answer any of their questions.'

'Did you love him?'

The tears burst, rolled down Jac's cheeks and splashed off the coffee-stained table top.

'He was my life.'

Rhidian knew that he had his breakthrough. The solicitor knew it too and slumped a little in her chair.

'How did you meet?'

'Mary's.'

'Who's that?'

Jones chipped in. 'It's a cabaret bar.'

Jac sniffed up the tears and nodded.

'I used to help behind the bar at weekends. It was a good way to meet new people.'

'Was Darius Gull a regular?'

'I'd seen him there a few times. We'd exchanged a few words when I served him, but that was all. Then one night he gave me his number. Told me to give him a call.'

'When was this?'

'Valentine's Night.'

'And you've been in a relationship ever since?'

'He never lied to me. I always knew there were others.'

'But you were faithful to him?'

'Guess I hoped that one day he would want to settle down.'

'And you were at Darius Gull's apartment last night?'

'Yes.'

'What time did you arrive?'

'Just after seven.'

'Do you have your own key?'

'No. Darius buzzed me up.'

'So he was expecting you?'

'Yes. He was going to cook. Chicken carbonara.'

'Was there alcohol?'

'White wine.'

'How much?'

'He'd already opened a bottle before I got there. We finished that and opened another.'

'And after the meal?'

Jac hesitated.

'All we're interested in is finding Mr Gull's killer. Anything else that went on that evening is of no concern to us.'

Jac looked into Rhidian's eyes and decided that he could trust him.

'I'd never touched anything until I met him. Well, a bit of weed at uni, but that's all.'

'What did you take that night?'

'Coke. I only did one line, but Darius kept going back to it.'

'And Mr Gull supplied the cocaine?'

Jac nodded. 'I wouldn't even know how to get it.'

'So, you had a meal. You drank some wine. You took some cocaine. And then?'

'Then we went to bed.'

'Okay.'

'We made love. After an hour or so Darius said it was time for me to go. He had some important court case he had to prep for.'

'And you couldn't stay the night?'

'He never let me stay. Said he needed his own space.'

'So you just left?'

'Of course.'

'You didn't have a row?'

'I knew the rules.'

'But to be dismissed like that, must have made you angry?'

'I was used to it.'

'Did he taunt you about his other lovers?'

'Sometimes.'

'Did that make you jealous?'

'Yes.'

'He hurt you?'

'Yes.'

'You wanted to hurt him back?'

'No.'

'Is that why you killed him?'

'I didn't. I couldn't. Look, I know that he treated me like shit, but I didn't care because... I loved him.'

Rhidian gave Jac a moment to recover his composure. He already knew that Jac Mundy was no killer, but he still needed to tie up any loose ends.

'What time did you leave?'

'Half ten, maybe a quarter to.'

'Can anybody confirm that?'

'The Uber driver should remember me. I gave him five stars. He could tell I was upset and he was very kind.'

Rhidian caught Jones's eye. Did she have any other questions? She shook her head. Rhidian spoke for the benefit of the recording.

'Interview is terminated at eleven ten AM.' He pressed *stop* to end the recording.

'Thank you for your time, Mr Mundy.'

'I can go?'

'Yes.' Rhidian stood and picked up Gull's phone. He saw the photo of the barrister with Jac Mundy in happier times. 'I'm sorry for your loss.' Rhidian exited the room, leaving Jones to organise Jac Mundy's release.

*

Rhidian had rarely seen Detective Chief Inspector Liz Devlin in such a dark mood. Jones was wisely keeping quiet in a corner of the DCI's office, but most of the flak was coming Rhidian's way.

'I suppose there is one silver lining. At least Gull won't be making an official complaint against you anymore.'

'It's no secret that we didn't like each other,' said Rhidian. 'But I wouldn't have wished that on him.'

'You're sure that this mortuary technician is out of the frame?'

'The Uber driver confirmed the time he picked up Jac Mundy, and his housemates said he was having a bath at the estimated time that Gull was being killed.'

'What about the other young men in the photos on Gull's phone?'

'We've traced a few. Most were interns at Gull's law practice.'

'So, he was abusing his position?' asked Devlin.

'Hard to prove,' said Rhidian. 'Did Gull coerce them or did they just understand that engaging in a bit of extracurricular activity with the Head of Chambers would improve their career chances?'

'Both Gull and Pryce were cocaine users. Anything there?' asked Devlin.

'Two high-profile men using recreational drugs? Could just be a reflection of our modern society,' said Rhidian. 'But any coincidences need to be followed up of course.'

'Forensics any help?'

'The CSIs had a field day. There were fingerprints all over the place. We've eliminated Gull's, Jac Mundy's and the cleaner's, but there was one more set found on the doorknob, the doorframe and the fish tank.'

'That doesn't mean they belong to the killer,' said Devlin. 'Maybe he gets a neighbour to feed the fish when he's out?'

'And normally we wouldn't be placing so much hope in one set of unidentified prints,' said Rhidian. 'Only Gull must have had a touch of OCD. He had the cleaner come in daily and every surface had to be spotless.'

'You've run the prints through the database?'

Jones fielded this one. 'Yes, ma'am. No hits.'

'So he's a clean skin. No criminal record,' said Devlin.

'That's no real surprise,' said Rhidian. 'None of this feels like the actions of a career criminal. Feels like something more personal.'

'Seems a bit amateur to me,' said Jones. 'I mean, who doesn't know to wear gloves when you're going to murder someone? It's like he's not even taking the basic steps to avoid getting caught.'

'Yes, he doesn't bother wearing gloves, and yet he is a planner,' said Rhidian. 'He knew the route that Rhys Pryce was going to take home. He found out where Darius Gull lived. Gull often had company, yet his killer knew when he was going to be alone. He also knew how to avoid the CCTV cameras. The lifts are covered but the attacker must have taken the stairs. They are also adaptable. They don't feel the need to stick to the same MO. They attacked Pryce in the middle of nowhere and Gull in the centre of the city. They also changed the tools they used.'

'And they're strong,' said Jones. 'Able to subdue a professional athlete who would have been fighting for his life.'

'And Gull was well over six foot. He would have been no pushover,' said Devlin.

'I've checked the records. There's nothing like this on file,' said Rhidian. 'But if this really is their first time, they've shown one hell of a lot of self-control. That's why I think they're on a mission. We just can't see what it is yet.'

'That's a bit of a leap, isn't it?' said Devlin.

'I don't think so. Look. It doesn't matter how many times you might plan a murder in your head, you can never imagine the true brutality of the reality; the screams, the blood, the sheer physical effort needed to saw through muscle and bone. But in neither of these killings was there any evidence of panic on the part of the attacker.'

Devlin and Jones had to concede that he had a point.

'I take it there is no doubt that this is the same killer?'

'It's got to be,' said Rhidian. 'The victims knew each other. They've both had parts of their bodies removed. There could be some symbolism involved there; taking a foot from a famous footballer and a tongue from someone who earns his money with that particular organ.'

'A trophy hunter?' asked Devlin.

Rhidian wasn't convinced. 'The whole purpose of taking trophies is so that the killer can keep them close; to use them to relive the experience. But our killer is throwing the "trophies" away.'

'Why dispose of them so casually when they've made so much effort to get them in the first place?' agreed Devlin. 'So. Where do we go from here?'

'We need to focus on who would want both Pryce and Gull dead.'

'Apart from you?'

'*What?*'

'Pryce was responsible for your wife's death. Gull got him off any criminal charges.'

'You're not serious?'

'You were on your own at the cottage the night that Pryce was killed. What about last night? I rang your hotel. They said you weren't in. I tried your mobile. It was switched off.'

'I was walking.'

'Please tell me you have witnesses.'

'I had words with a lad who was urinating on Nye Bevan's statue,' said Rhidian.

'Don't suppose you got the name of this anonymous pisser?'

'No. I just gave him a friendly warning about anti-social behaviour and sent him on his way.'

'So you've got no alibi?'

Rhidian had no choice but to come clean. 'There was a bit of a misunderstanding with a pub landlord and some of his customers. He's not likely to forget me in a hurry.'

'Which pub?'

Rhidian shrugged. 'I'm sure I'd recognise it if I saw it again.'

'You don't exactly help yourself do you?'

'I didn't know I was going to be a suspect in my own murder inquiry.'

'I'm only asking the same questions that anyone else would,' said Devlin.

Jones tried to help. 'There is someone else who's connected to Pryce and Gull. The court case against Pryce that's just been dismissed. Some professor or other.'

'Loretta Swann?' said Devlin. 'Isn't she still in a coma?'

'Then she's got a better alibi than me,' said Rhidian.

'She might have friends, family who want revenge?' said Jones.

'Then find them, and quickly,' ordered Devlin. 'I don't want to have to tell the press that our strongest suspect in a double murder is the DI who's actually running the case.'

15

Jones returned to the station having interviewed another of Gull's conquests; one of the personal trainers at a gym where Gull was a member. She nodded a 'hello' to Floyd-the-Fish Finger who was writing a crafty text under the reception counter while things were quiet. Jones reached for the access card, on a lanyard around her neck, and tapped it on the door's code reader to give her access to the inner, secure area of the building.

Pushing through the twin doors she was surprised to see Rhidian Hook standing halfway down the corridor. She was about to tell him about her interview when something about his stillness made her stop. He was looking at a framed photo on the wall. Jones knew what this was; a gallery of the officers who had fallen in the line of duty. Rhidian must have sensed her presence because he addressed her without turning in her direction. 'Any luck?'

'No. Cast iron alibi for both murders.'

Jones joined Rhidian, confirming what she had already guessed, that he was contemplating the framed photo of Detective Sergeant Gough. Although she had never met him, she knew about Bryn Gough; everyone in the South Wales police did. The photo had been taken just after his graduation. Jones found it hard to look at that easy smile and the hopeful eyes that knew nothing of the horrific end that awaited him only ten years later.

'I'll support you one hundred per cent,' said Rhidian.

'Support me in what?'

'If you want a transfer back to DI Gunter's team.'

'Why would I want that?'

Rhidian never took his eyes off the photo.

'Because I know what's coming; you don't.'

'I've been on homicide cases.'

‘Not like this one. This isn’t a drunken bar fight that got out of hand, or a gangland grudge. People like the one we’re after, they are a different breed. Once they’ve got a taste for it, they don’t stop. And they won’t let anyone get in the way.’

‘I’m a big girl. I can look after myself.’

‘You didn’t choose this, but you can choose to step aside. Nobody would think any the less of you for it.’

‘I’m no quitter,’ said Jones, then tried to lighten the mood. ‘I play for a rugby team that’s come bottom of the league for three years running.’

Rhidian didn’t smile. ‘When you change your mind, let me know,’ he said and headed for the stairs.

Jones looked at the gallery of fallen heroes and remembered her own graduation photo. Yes, she had looked as hopeful as Bryn Gough; her eyes brimming with excitement at the thought of getting out there and making a difference. Okay, so she had put away her fair share of criminals, but had she made a difference? Weren’t there plenty more just waiting to take their places? At least with DI Hook she was going after the real predators. But she also didn’t want Floyd to be knocking another nail into the wall to hang her picture from it.

Rhidian stepped into the busy main CID office to find Alun Gunter standing in front of a map of Cardiff, picking at a shred of bacon fat caught between his teeth.

‘Alun. Can I have a word?’

Gunter raised his voice for the sake of his colleagues, dotted around the office at various desks. ‘Didn’t take long for you to come begging for help, did it?’

Rhidian ignored Gunter’s jibe. He was more interested in studying the various drug hotspots marked on the map with coloured pins.

‘He’s been a busy boy,’ said Rhidian.

'Yeah.'

'And you know it's all the same supplier because...?'

'The samples we've got our hands on have all tested the same. Eighty per cent pure coke.'

'Too pure for a student budget.'

'Yeah. Ninety quid a gram.' Gunter pointed to a pin that marked a nightclub on Mill Lane. 'First came across it a month or so back. A DJ stopped for speeding but then found to have a baggy stuffed down his boxers.'

'But you don't think he's the supplier?'

'No. He only had a few grams on him. He copped to possession for personal use but wouldn't give us anything about his dealer. Since then it's been popping up all over the city. Nightclubs, bars. All high-class joints.'

'What about that doorman you brought in? Did he give you anything?'

'No. Lawyered up then went "no comment".' He added suspiciously, 'What's your interest?'

'My two murder victims were both cocaine users who were too high profile to buy off street corners.'

'I'll add them to our database. But you don't think that our dealer is your killer?'

'It's not good business for drug suppliers to get rid of their clients, but I have to follow up every connection. You'll keep me informed of any progress?' asked Rhidian.

'Sure.' Gunter raised his voice again. 'Don't want you crying to the DCI that I'm not co-operating.'

As Rhidian Hook and Anwen Jones walked towards the main entrance of the Hopewell Infirmary, both were lost in their own thoughts. Anwen had always hated hospitals. She'd spent too many Saturday afternoons in A&E, the studs of her rugby boots click-clacking as she paced the waiting room, impatient to be treated for a suspected broken nose or fractured ribs, earning dark looks from the cleaners as she deposited another clump of mud and turf onto their just-cleaned floor. But it was an older memory which was always reawakened by the sight of paramedic green and the sharp tang of antiseptic.

Anwen's first trip in the back of an ambulance was when she was fifteen. She had been doing well at school; top in most of her classes, but her teachers had noticed a deterioration, both in her performance and school attendance. The cause was obvious; Craig Prosser. He was the kind of boy your parents always warned you about, but to a hormonal teenage girl, he was Eminem and Justin Timberlake all rolled into one.

Craig was a familiar sight on the estate, cruising around, always in a different car, baseball cap turned backwards, a can of Foster's wedged between his knees and ear-bleeding bass pounding out of the pumped-up stereo. It was a while before Anwen twigged that all the cars were nicked, but that only added to the appeal of the local bad boy with the crooked smile and the flashy trainers. Many different stories about Craig were swapped between giggling schoolgirls at the back of the bike sheds. One legend told of how he'd nicked three cars in one night; another whispered that he'd had a baby with a girl from Neath who he'd shagged in a toilet only ten minutes after meeting her on the Barry Island ghost train.

Craig didn't ask girls out. He just pulled up in his car, pushed open the passenger door and told them to get in. Everyone knew that this meant that you were his girlfriend, at least for that night. So when it was Anwen's turn to ride shotgun, she felt a pride that trumped any number of Grade A exam passes.

It didn't take long for Anwen to learn what being Craig Prosser's girlfriend actually meant. It meant nicking fags and booze for him and standing watch while he hotwired his wheels for the night. It also meant making all the right noises to make it sound like she was enjoying it when he gave her a quick one on the back seat. And it always was a quick one with Craig.

The night that Anwen's life was turned around started like any other. Craig had nicked a Fiesta from a pub car park and now the chosen ones were getting ready for their night of big laffs. Craig's brother Sean was the joker of the crew, always playing stupid practical jokes. They were all taking a toke on the spliff supplied by the newest member of Craig's inner circle. Anwen hated Rhiannon Matthews from the moment she set eyes on her ginormous breasts and bleached blonde hair. She wasn't even from the area, she was from Penarth! Rhiannon was supposed to be Sean's bird, but everyone could tell that Craig had the hots for her. Anwen had heard Rhiannon betting her mates that she'd 'have Craig Prosser' before the weekend was out. Not if Anwen could help it.

That night Anwen had never seen Craig so hyper. His pupils were like pinpricks. Was it just the booze and dope, or had he taken something else? Whatever was fuelling him, there was no stopping Craig. They were going to cruise around the city. Anwen couldn't say no. There was no way she was giving up her prized front seat for a slapper like Rhiannon, so the four of them piled into the car. Craig fired up the engine, stuck on some tunes full blast and promised that this was going to be the biggest raz ever.

Once they hit Cardiff they spent an hour tearing up and down the High Street, pulling donuts in car parks and generally showing off that the Lovelock Park Crew owned this city. But Craig wasn't satisfied. He wanted to see what the car could really do, so he headed for the dual carriageway.

Craig was soon pushing the car past the speed limit. Ninety, one hundred miles per hour. Anwen begged him to slow down, but she could tell from the way he kept turning to the back seat, that this was all about impressing Rhiannon.

They were flying at a hundred and ten when they saw the double lines of red tail lights ahead. Road works had brought traffic to a halt. There was no time to brake. The hard shoulder was their only option. Soon they were undertaking two lanes of stationary traffic at speed. Sean was laughing hysterically. Rhiannon started screaming. Anwen was the first to see the broken-down lorry that was blocking the hard shoulder. Craig slammed his foot on the brake. Black smoke streamed from the burning tyres. They were running out of road. In desperation, Craig jerked the wheel to the left, but they were still doing sixty. The car went into a spin, then started rolling. Once, twice, three times the car turned over, only coming to a stop when it crunched against the rear end of the lorry.

Anwen finally dared to open her eyes, unable to believe that she was still alive. She turned to her right. Craig was staring straight ahead, still white knuckling the steering wheel. There wasn't a scratch on him. A strange whimpering noise was coming from behind her. She looked in the rear-view mirror. Sean's eyes were wide, tears rolling down his cheeks, turning pink as they ran through a three-inch cut that had been sliced across his cheek by flying glass. There was no sign of Rhiannon. Her door was missing, torn off at the hinges.

Steam was billowing from under the crumpled bonnet. The smell of petrol stung her nose. Anwen reached down with trembling fingers to undo her seat belt. Her instincts told her she had to go; get out of the car, but when she tried to move her right leg she couldn't. She tried again, only to nearly faint when she was hit by the jag of pain shooting up from her foot. She didn't want to look, but she had to. She saw that the front of the car had been crushed by the impact. Her foot was tangled in the twisted metal. There was blood; a lot of blood. She turned to ask Craig to help her, only he was climbing out of the car, backing away. She called out to him, but he kept walking.

She kept drifting in and out of consciousness. She couldn't be sure how much time had passed since the crash. Once, she opened her eyes to see that people from other cars were reaching in to help take Sean out of the back. His legs wouldn't hold him. He had to be lifted onto the grass verge where he sat and put his head in his hands.

Later, a siren brought her back to consciousness. Her car door was opened and a dark shape crouched next to her. He said his name was Sergeant Chappell, but she could call him Paul. He told her there was nothing to worry about. He was going to stay with her until the fire fighters arrived to get her out. When she said she was cold, he took off his jacket and placed it over her. She remembered the way the blue flashing lights reflected off the shiny buttons. He took off his hat, sat on the tarmac and didn't let go of her hand for the next hour. He didn't stop talking. She couldn't remember much of what he said; she just let his words soothe over her.

Sean was taken to A&E to be checked over. Rhiannon hadn't been wearing her seat belt. The police would later find her body tangled among the scrubby trees, old tyres and used McDonald's cartons of the verge. She must have been thrown out of the car while it was rolling. Nearly every bone in her body was broken. Her pretty face was so smashed up that she had to be identified by her dental records.

Anwen's foot was a mess. There were still titanium pins inside it even now, and it gave her gyp whenever the weather turned cold and damp. She spent three weeks in hospital. Craig never visited or tried to get in touch. There were no grapes, no card wishing her to 'Get Well Soon'. After all the operations were finally over, she realised that what she really wanted to do was say 'thank you' to Craig. If it hadn't been for his reckless behaviour that night, she might be heading for a future that at best only contained a council flat, three brats by as many feckless fathers and a life on benefits.

Anwen occasionally saw Craig around the streets. He'd never been able to get into a car again without getting the shakes. He was now a pathetic sight, waiting at a bus stop in the rain. No one thought of him as the big man anymore. But the Lovelock specialised in breeding Craig Prossers. He was soon replaced by other no-hopers with bad skin, jeans hanging half way down their hips, and the same blank, dead eyes that only came alive when they were behind the wheel of someone else's car.

His mum and dad noted how Sean Prosser was unnaturally quiet after that night, but they were all as proud as punch when he told them he was joining the army. He looked the business in his brand new uniform. Everyone agreed that he had really turned his life around. But even the rigours of army training couldn't take away his nightmares about the crash. Early one morning, while Sean was on sentry duty, he watched the sun rise, took out a photo of Rhiannon Matthews, kissed it once, then braced the butt of his rifle against his boots, put the muzzle under his chin and pulled the trigger.

Anwen never forgot the kindness shown by Sergeant Chappell, who had made it his mission to help her, even after her physical injuries had healed. It was because of him that she joined the police. The only lingering side effect of the accident was that every time she came back into a hospital she had to fight back the metallic taste of bile that slid up the back of her throat.

Rhidian Hook had always been jealous of doctors. Yes, they had to deal with open wounds and blood, broken bones and cardiac arrests, but they didn't need to know why the pensioner had ended up with cigarette burns to his back, or why the teenage girl had thrown herself under a bus. The doctors treated the symptoms and sent them on their way. They were protected by their professional distance. Rhidian couldn't afford such luxury. If he was going to catch the sadistic care worker or the female pimp seducing underage girls into prostitution, he had to get into their minds; understand what drove them, what turned them on and got them off. A surgeon wore gloves and a mask; Rhidian had no protection. At the end of an operation they could wash their hands in sterilising agent, but for Rhidian nothing could cleanse him of having touched minds with sheer evil. No matter how hard he scrubbed, something of the darkness always stuck.

Rhidian looked down at the sleeping form of Loretta Swann as the doctor noted down her heart rate and other vital signs being monitored by a bank of reassuringly bleeping equipment. Although she was only twenty-eight, Dr Anna Moore looked thirty-five. Even while she had been working hard through medical school she had still managed to find time to keep fit; running, squeezing in a couple of visits to the gym every week. One by one, her healthy activities had fallen victim to her duties at The Hope.

As he listened to her describing her patient's condition, Rhidian took in Moore's mousey hair, scraped back into a limp ponytail; the chewed fingernails, the tired eyes.

'She came to us pretty much as you see her now. Oh, there were a few minor cuts and bumps, but they soon healed. She was on an oxygen mask until two days ago.'

'Is she ever likely to regain consciousness?' asked Jones.

Moore shrugged and adjusted the nasal cannula. 'She still needs help to keep her oxygen saturation up, but we never needed to ventilate her, which is a real plus in these situations.'

'If you didn't know better you could think she was just sleeping,' said Rhidian.

'Yes, but something's broken inside, something we can't diagnose or treat. It's up to her now. She'll come out of it, if and when she's ready.'

'What about playing her favourite songs, recording messages from her family?' asked Jones.

'We'd love to do that, but according to the ward clerk, we haven't been able to trace any relatives or anyone who was close to her,' explained Moore.

'Surely there must be loads of blokes buzzing round her?' said Jones, her words dripping with envy.

'You'd think so, wouldn't you? I'd do anything for a complexion like that,' agreed Moore. 'But if there is someone special in her life, he hasn't come forward yet.'

'What about the lilies; the CD player?' asked Rhidian. He pressed eject. There was no CD inside.

'Perhaps a work colleague brought them in?' suggested Moore.

'And nobody's seen any visitors?' said Rhidian.

'I don't know what goes on while I'm attending to my other patients.'

Now Rhidian saw it. Something in Moore's eyes; not just exhaustion, but a distant haunting. Realising that Rhidian was reading her, Moore changed the subject.

'There was actually some improvement this morning. Her latest MRI scan suggests increased brain activity. We've re-evaluated her Glasgow Coma Score up to eight. It's not enough to say that she is going to come out of this any time soon, but it's still a positive sign.'

'What about what she's wearing?' asked Jones. 'Can I?' Moore gave her a nod. Jones folded down the bedclothes just enough to reveal more of the silk pyjamas. Deepest purple today. 'Not exactly NHS issue is it?'

'As I said. You'll have to talk to the ward clerk.'

Jones pulled the covers up, aware of how Rhidian had respectfully turned away. He was a funny one. Most men would have jumped at the chance to get an eyeful of Loretta Swann's thinly clad curves.

'If there's nothing else,' said Moore. 'Only I am needed elsewhere.'

Rhidian had clearly lost interest as soon as he had obtained answers to his questions, so Jones had to step in. 'Thanks for your time, Doctor.'

Moore urgently left.

'How did Rhys Pryce get away with this one?' asked Jones.

'He claimed that her car swerved in front of him. That he couldn't avoid hitting her. There were no witnesses, no CCTV, so it would have been his word against hers. If she could have spoken.'

Rhidian frowned. Something distracted him. He moved closer to Loretta Swann, then leant down, closer to her face. Jones couldn't believe it. If he wanted to perv over an unconscious woman, he could at least wait until he was alone!

'*Boss?*'

Rhidian realised how sniffing a sleeping girl's hair must look. 'Are you wearing perfume?'

'*Me?* Never.'

'I thought it was Dr Moore, but it's still here.' He sniffed Loretta's neck, finally locating the source of the sweet tones leeching out from beneath the general aroma of bleach and alcohol hand rub. His eyes closed as the familiar notes hit him. 'Midnight Mist.' Rhidian moved aside to let Jones get closer.

Jones sniffed. 'Yeah. I've got it now. I thought that hospitals didn't like patients using perfume?'

'And she can hardly have applied it herself,' said Rhidian. 'See if you can find the bottle. It's about four inches tall. Shape of a crescent moon.'

As Jones searched the bedside locker, Rhidian couldn't resist leaning in to breathe in the heady scent again. In the dark days, when he had missed Bethan so much that he would have given anything to commune with her, even for a moment, he had searched their apartment for the items that she had used every day; her hair brush, lipstick and her bottle of Midnight Mist. He had sprayed the perfume onto her pillow, but it wasn't quite right. Now he understood what was missing. The fragrance needed to be applied to a warm body. It was this that subtly changed the scent and now brought back his wife to him.

Jones broke the spell. 'There's no bottle here.'

Rhidian nodded, then stood back to address Loretta Swann.

'So, you've got no family, no close friends. Yet someone's bringing you flowers, your favourite music, dressing you and spraying you with perfume. Who are you?'

16

The Mathias Museum had been founded in 1842 by Sir Thomas Mathias. He made his fortune from selling slate from his estates in Pembrokeshire during the years when Wales was said to have 'roofed the world'. Sir Thomas longed to see more of the world and its treasures. After two decades of expeditions to Egypt, the Middle East and South America, Mathias needed a suitable building to house his vast collection of ancient curios. A satisfactory site was found and from the foundations rose one of the finest examples of medieval Gothic revival in all of Wales. Employing the most talented craftsmen from all around Europe, Mathias' vision was all traceries and niches, carved bosses and turrets, and when finished, it towered like a fairytale castle over the surrounding buildings.

Although now dwarfed in scale by the National Museum situated not more than half a mile away, the Mathias was still internationally renowned for the range and quality of its artefacts.

When Sir Thomas died, his son inherited the slate quarries, the grand manor house and the museum collection. Unfortunately he didn't inherit his father's work ethic or his devotion to temperance. Within five short years Thomas Junior had blown most of the Mathias fortune on opium, whores and three-legged horses. The estate and quarries were sold off to pay his debts and he fled to Australia to escape the shame. He was later shot through the heart in an outback saloon after being caught with an extra ace tucked up his sleeve. Thankfully his father knew that his son was a weak man and had protected the museum in his will, leaving it and its contents to the good people of Cardiff, with a generous stipend to pay its running costs.

Careful investments by the Board meant that despite increasing costs, the museum always managed to keep its head above water. A café serving tempting cakes and well-filled sandwiches helped supplement the very reasonable entrance fees. Once the law was changed to allow wedding ceremonies to be held outside of churches and registry offices, the Trustees had been quick to cash in. Hundreds of newlyweds have since been photographed in the central courtyard, under the impressive statues of Zeus and the goddess Leda. Although it might seem perverse to want to pose your new wife next to a rendition of a woman being seduced by a god, a rumour had grown up that rubbing the fig leaf covering Zeus' godhood was an aid to pregnancy. So many eager hands had fallen for the superstition that the well-burnished fig leaf now shone like gold.

More recently, when the rights to a series of popular children's books were bought up by Hollywood, the Mathias Museum's grand entrance hall was selected as the perfect setting for the trainee wizards' Spell Room. This not only brought in generous location fees, but also attracted a new generation of visitors, even if they were more interested in seeing where their hero had practised his spells rather than in exploring the museum's unparalleled collection of Etruscan sarcophagi. This was a matter being lamented by the museum's curator, Professor Huw Llewellyn, as he gave Rhidian and Jones a guided tour.

'When I was a child I loved nothing more than wandering around the dinosaur bones and mummies,' Llewellyn wheezed, the short climb to the mezzanine level having taxed his breathing. 'Now they're welded to their phones or sitting like zombies in front of their computers.'

Jones was an Amazonian lass, but she felt dwarfed by Llewellyn's six foot three of doughy flesh, topped by a duck's egg of a head. Although he must have been in his early fifties, there wasn't a single line to help give any definition to his baby-smooth face. In the distant past, when he had possessed hair, it must have been very fair because you had to look closely to confirm that he even had eyebrows. Below them were pale eyes that you couldn't call brown; they were closer to the colour of milky tea. Jones couldn't shake off the image of a huge white pig. It was something to do with all that white flesh and the long, feminine eyelashes.

Rhidian and Jones joined Llewellyn on the balcony where they could take in a panoramic view of the main gallery. A life-sized model of one of daVinci's flying machines swooped over rows of glass exhibition cases. Two twelve-foot basalt pillars, carved into the shapes of roaring Abyssinian lions, greeted visitors. Several other displays caught the eye, including the black skeleton of an ancient coracle recovered from the silt of Milford Haven, and a diorama of a loin-clothed primitive man about to launch a stone-tipped spear at a rearing sabre-toothed tiger.

'The museum is spread over three floors,' said Llewellyn. 'We take the visitor on a journey through time, starting with our earliest Palaeolithic exhibits, then working up through the Neolithic period until we get to the earliest versions of what we might call true civilisation; Mesopotamia, ancient Rome...'

Rhidian was keen to get away from the history lesson and back onto more recent events. 'And Loretta Swann worked where?'

'*Professor* Swann worked in our Research and Conservation Department which is in the basement.'

'And what is your opinion of Professor Swann?'

'As a colleague, impeccable, an expert in her field.'

'Which is?'

'Ancient Rome. More specifically, Roman religion and myths.'

'The twelve great gods. Romulus and Remus?' asked Rhidian.

'Did you study Classics, Inspector?'

'I do a lot of crosswords and my wife likes...liked to watch *University Challenge*.' Rhidian was keen to get back on track. 'So, Professor Swann was well qualified, but what was she like to work with?'

'Excellent. Absolutely dedicated to her field. When I would leave of an evening, more often than not, her car would still be in the car park.'

'And outside of her work? Did she have many friends?'

'I don't know anything about her personal life.'

'We know she isn't married, but is there a boyfriend?'

'She never mentioned anyone special, but then our conversations were mostly work-related.'

'You never saw anyone pick her up after work?'

Llewellyn shook his head.

'She's never brought a date to any work parties?'

'Now you come to mention it, no, I don't think she has. She's actually quite shy. She doesn't really like dealing with the public. She prefers to be down among the archives, quietly getting on with her work, which is a shame. Being one of our brightest stars I invite her to our fund-raisers, but she always makes an excuse for why she can't come. Of course her current condition puts us in a very awkward position.'

'How so?'

'We've got far more artefacts that we can ever display at one time. Professor Swann was in the middle of updating the archive catalogue. She's uncovered all kinds of interesting finds; some objects that were wrongly attributed in the original catalogue and even several items that we didn't even know that we possessed. The Trustees will have to decide how long we can give it before we have to find someone to complete her work.' Llewellyn suddenly noticed the time. 'I'm sorry, Inspector. I did warn you about my three o'clock.'

'I need to see where she worked.'

‘Of course.’ Llewellyn looked around, frustrated when he couldn’t see any members of staff. Then he spotted a small, bespectacled man in a brown caretaker’s coat who was replacing a light bulb in a wall bracket.

‘Ah. Morris, just the man.’

The caretaker slipped the dead bulb into his coat pocket as he approached Llewellyn.

‘Could you show the officers here down to the basement?’

‘Of course, Professor. No problem.’ The caretaker turned to Rhidian and Jones. ‘Morris Palfrey, at your service.’ He wasn’t wearing a cap, but Rhidian was sure that, if he had been he would have doffed it to them.

‘Anything else I can help you with, don’t hesitate,’ said Llewellyn, offering a limp, clammy handshake before lumbering back down the marble steps.

Jones was relieved to see him go. He had been perfectly pleasant, but there was still something that disturbed her, almost on a primeval level. There was something fungal about him. Damp, white. As if he should be growing on the dead stump of a tree in the darkest corner of some ancient wood.

Morris wiped his dusty hands on an old rag. ‘If you’d like to follow me.’ Rhidian and Jones followed Palfrey through a door marked ‘Staff Only’, and down the back stairs towards the basement.

‘Do you know Professor Swann?’ Rhidian asked the shuffling caretaker.

‘I’ve been here twenty years now. Know all the staff, past and present.’

‘And what’s your opinion of her?’

‘It’s not my job to have opinions,’ chuckled Palfrey.

‘This won’t go any further. It’s just between the three of us,’ said Rhidian. This seemed to reassure the caretaker.

‘Well. You can tell that she loves her job. She’s always very enthusiastic. She’s often the first to arrive and the last to leave.’

‘That must cause you a few headaches,’ suggested Rhidian.

‘How do you mean?’

‘Having to hang around to lock up after her.’

‘I don’t mind that. See I live on site. Got a little flat in the back. And a place as old as this, well, there are always plenty of things need fixing, but some jobs I can’t do when the public are wandering around, so I’m often still working after we’re closed. Besides, Professor Swann, she’s given me a new appreciation of this place.’

Palfrey paused by a display case containing a humble, cracked bowl, ten inches in diameter, crudely formed out of thick, ruddy clay.

‘See that? Could be something out of a skip for all I knew. But Professor Swann, she took the time to explain why it was important; how a few bits of old pottery can tell the story of a whole civilisation. She helped me see the world in a different way. It was like, like I’d been sleepwalking through life until she opened my eyes. Yes, a real inspiration, that’s what she’s been.’

Palfrey continued on his way, the corridors getting narrower, the walls and wooden floors showing more signs of wear and tear, until they reached a locked door.

‘Can’t be too careful,’ explained Palfrey, tapping a five digit number into the code box. ‘Got some valuable stuff down here, by all accounts.’

With a reassuring clunk, the lock opened. Palfrey pulled the heavy door open.

‘I’ll leave you to it then. Got a blockage in the Gents to sort out.’ Morris left, calling over his shoulder. ‘Mr Calder’s in there somewhere. He’ll show you what’s what.’

Rhidian and Jones found themselves in a large, cool room with a vaulted brick ceiling. Sets of mahogany drawers had been built in. Each had an ivory drawer pull above a brass slot into which was slipped a rectangle of cardboard bearing a description of the drawer's contents. As they passed, Rhidian noted '*Stone beads. Anglesey*', '*Neolithic flints. Coygan Caves*' and '*Transverse arrowheads. Kidwelly'*, all written in delicate, copperplate style in black ink that had faded to blue over the decades. In the only space that was not filled with shelves stood a long refectory table. Several microscopes were stationed at one end, alongside computers and trays of tools used in the meticulous work of conserving rare antiquities; soft brushes, pointed picks and scalpels. At the far end of the table, a young man peered through a magnifying lens as he delicately removed dusty, brown paper wrappings from a battered Roundhead's helmet. He was so engrossed in his work that he didn't notice he had company until Jones loudly cleared her throat.

'How did you get in?' asked the man, trying to recover his composure. 'This area is staff only.'

Jones flashed her warrant card. 'Detective Sergeant Jones. This is Detective Inspector Hook. And you are?'

'Er, Calder. James Calder.'

Calder was late twenties, but his receding ginger hairline and heavy, black-framed spectacles made him look older. He was wearing jeans and a T-shirt with a cartoon image of an Egyptian mummy and the words '*Mummy's Boy'*. The T-shirt bulged a little over a stomach that suggested a love of beer or fast food. Rhidian stayed silent. Jones got the message. She was to lead the questioning so that he could observe Calder's reactions.

'And what do you do here, Mr Calder?' asked Jones.

'I'm the collections assistant.'

'So you work under Professor Swann?'

'That's right. Thought you'd turn up eventually.'

'Why's that?'

'Today's *Echo*. First Rhys Pryce and now his barrister's been found dead. Loretta could be a link, couldn't she?'

'She's one avenue of enquiry that we're following,' confirmed Jones. 'Do you drive, Mr Calder?'

'I've got a licence, but no car.'

'Why not?'

'I love working here, but the money's rubbish. It's hard enough paying the rent without running a car as well. Besides, my flat's only ten minutes away. It's easy to bike it.'

'Did you take Professor Swann any flowers?'

'Flowers?'

'White lilies.'

'No.'

'What about perfume?'

'Of course not.'

'You must have gone to see her in hospital?'

'No.'

'Why not?'

'How is any of this relevant?'

A sweat had broken out on Calder's brow. He tried to ignore it, but when it ran into his eyes he had to wipe it away with the back of his hand.

Rhidian finally spoke. 'Isn't it natural for one colleague to visit another when they're ill?'

Calder turned his attention to Rhidian. 'The truth is, I keep meaning to go, but...'

Rhidian said nothing, forcing Calder to fill the silence.

'We work all day surrounded by dusty relics of dead civilisations. But Loretta's so enthusiastic about her work that she brings the whole building to life. So I'm not sure I can stand to see her like that.'

'Would you say that she's good at her job?' asked Rhidian.

'The best.'

'Then why is she still here?'

'I don't get you.'

'Professor Llewellyn also spoke very highly of her. If she's as good as you both say there must be plenty of other museums who would want to employ her; places that can offer a bigger salary, better prospects.'

'But they don't have this,' said Calder, gesturing to the walls of drawers. 'The Mathias Collection is unique. We've been cataloguing it for two years and we're still not halfway through. Every time we open a new drawer we don't know what we're going to find. We're working from Thomas Mathias' original records, but they're not very accurate. Take this for example.'

Calder moved down the table and removed a white dust sheet to reveal a ten-inch-high clay vessel with a lid.

'This is what Loretta was working on before the accident. Thomas Mathias recorded it as a Roman urn for holding cremated remains, whereas we can use modern technology to carbon date the clay, which tells us that this is a much older, rarer example from Germany. So we now know that Anglo-Saxons were trading in South Wales two hundred years before the current estimates.' Calder caught himself, realising that he was getting too excited. 'Sorry. I've let the nerd out again, haven't I?' Calder looked at the ancient urn again. 'This should really be in the safe, but I didn't want to put it away.'

'Why not?' asked Jones. Rhidian already knew what Calder's answer would be.

'Because that would be like admitting that she's not coming back.'

As Rhidian and Jones exited the museum, Jones didn't hold back on her thoughts about Llewellyn.

'Didn't you feel it?' she asked.

'Feel what?'

'That there's something creepy about him?'

'Can you be more specific?'

'Not really. Maybe it's a woman thing, but some men are like that. The very thought of them touching you makes your flesh creep.'

'I wonder if Loretta felt the same,' pondered Rhidian. 'And what about Calder? He plays up his image as a nerd, but he's already made a possible connection between Pryce and Gull's murders.'

'Calder and Llewellyn said she's an amazing colleague, but then both claimed that they didn't visit her in hospital,' said Jones.

'And they say they know nothing about her personal life. Let's see if that's true,' said Rhidian.

They didn't notice the CCTV camera twist slowly on its mounting, its all-seeing eye following them off the premises.

17

Jones was driving towards Loretta Swann's flat when she was stopped by a red traffic light. Looking out of the window, Rhidian realised where they were.

'Take the North Road.'

'This is quicker.'

'Nevertheless.'

'And they'll be kicking out the schools your way.'

'Just do it.' He realised he'd been too sharp. 'Please. Could you just do as I ask?'

Jones couldn't let it go.

'What's the problem?'

'The Castle.'

'What about it?'

'It's where I proposed, and where we always celebrated our anniversary.'

Not knowing what to say, Jones was relieved when the light turned green. She indicated a left-hand turn and took the longer route.

Loretta Swann's one-bedroom flat was accessed via a side door between the Star of Madras restaurant and a Polish convenience shop selling exotic spicy sausage, unfamiliar beers and five different types of rye bread.

Rhidian unlocked the door with keys that were among her possessions locked up at the hospital. He paused on the threshold. He accepted the need to get to know the person whose life they were looking into, but at the same time it still felt intrusive. No one wants a stranger rooting around in every corner of your life. But this was different. Something twitched in his stomach; an irrational anticipation of finding out more about the elusive Loretta Swann. What if he discovered something that would disappoint him? Why was he even thinking like that? Disturbed by these conflicting feelings, Rhidian returned his focus onto the job.

'You take the bathroom. I'll do the kitchen,' he told Jones. Squeezing into latex gloves, they began their methodical search.

The kitchen was tired and crying out for refurbishment. Wood-effect Formica was peeling from the cupboards. Several tiles around the sink were cracked. Despite someone's best efforts, the build-up of grease around the oven hobs was refusing to budge. A touch of class had been added by a wall calendar showing images of the frescos of Pompeii. It was still turned to July, the month that Loretta's car had been hit by Rhys Pryce's. That month was illustrated by a faded wall painting of 'Baby Hercules and the Serpents'.

Rhidian examined the dish rack. He always believed that you could tell a lot from someone's washing up; not that he would want anybody to look too closely at his domestic arrangements. The dish rack contained one plate, one knife and fork, one wine glass and one mug with the museum's logo on it. Rhidian opened the fridge, revealing more pointers to someone who lived alone. There was a small container of milk and half a bottle of white wine stuck in the door. On the midle shelf was a ready meal for one and an egg box. There were only two eggs left, but the date stamp on the box told Rhidian that it had been bought two months ago. She mostly seemed to have a healthy diet. There was salad, low fat cottage cheese and rice crackers, although they were all well past their use-by date.

There was one photograph stuck to the fridge door with magnets; showing an overweight teenage girl with dull, mousey hair, her eyes screwed up against the sun behind the thick lenses of National Health spectacles as she looked up out of the trench of an archaeological dig. It was hard to date the photo. There was nothing distinctive about the clothes;

blue jeans and a woollen jumper. It could have been taken five or twenty-five years ago. Rhidian slipped the photo out from behind the magnets and tucked it into his notebook. He was entering the living room as Jones arrived from the bathroom to report back.

'Nothing of interest in there,' she said.

'What about the perfume?' asked Rhidian. Jones shook her head.

'Any signs of a boyfriend?'

'There's only one toothbrush. No man's razor or aftershave.' Jones was distracted by the smell of frying garlic and spices drifting up from the restaurant kitchens. 'It would be hell living here. My stomach would be rumbling all the time.'

Rhidian frowned. 'Surely she could have afforded something better. This is only one step up from student digs.'

'She certainly didn't spend her money on furniture,' agreed Jones. 'This looks like Ikea. Cheap but functional. And there's no home cinema system. No pile of Blu-rays.'

Rhidian had found a small sound system that could be switched between playing the radio and CDs. He turned it on. Melvyn Bragg's nasal tones instantly identified that it was tuned to Radio 4. Why was he so pleased? Would it have mattered if she preferred to listen to some pirate station playing hardcore grime? He shuffled through the small pile of CDs, noting that she had many of the same albums that were in Bethan's collection; songs that he could no longer bear to listen to. On top of the pile was Dido's first album. Rhidian opened the case, but it was empty. He pressed 'eject' to open the drawer of the CD player. The disc wasn't there either.

'You finish up here.' said Rhidian. 'Maybe the bedroom will give us some answers.'

*

Rhidian Hook stood on the threshold of Loretta Swann's bedroom, feeling all the anticipation of a lover who had been invited into this inner sanctum for the first time. Despite the late summer sun blazing outside, the room was in semi-darkness. The sleepy Loretta must have only half opened the curtains on her last morning of full consciousness. Rhidian stepped forward to complete the job. Disturbed dust motes danced in the sunlight that streamed in, fully illuminating the room.

The double bed dominated the square, twelve foot by twelve room. A duvet decorated in pale-blue cornflowers had been pulled aside; the plain white pillows were still askew from where Loretta must have risen on that last morning. He picked up a pillow and put it to his face and breathed in the lingering hint of Midnight Mist.

Rhidian crossed the bare floorboards to sit at the shabby chic dressing table. He opened the left-hand drawer and used his pen to stir through the contents; lipsticks in various shades; mascara, eye liner pencils. No bottle of Midnight Mist.

He opened the next drawer. It contained a spaghetti tangle of bangles and necklaces in a nest of scarves and gloves. The middle drawer contained winter woollens. Rhidian slid his hands between the soft layers, but the jumpers concealed nothing more interesting than a sachet of lavender to keep clothes moths at bay.

He paused before opening the bottom drawer, knowing what it was going to contain. He was right. Loretta's underwear. Why did he hesitate? This wasn't the first time he'd had to search through a stranger's most private things. He realised that Jones was watching from the doorway, clearly bemused by his discomfort.

'Do you want me to finish that?'

Rhidian nodded gratefully. 'Find anything interesting?' he asked.

'Well, I can confirm that she's not a natural redhead. There are several bottles of hair dye. Give it another week and her roots will be showing. Blonde I reckon.'

A question flickered in Rhidian's mind. Would that make her look more like Bethan? He quickly shut it down. 'Any luck with the perfume?'

'No. Maybe it's not hers?'

'The scent is still on her bedding.'

'So, a friend popped in? Picked up a few personal bits and pieces, including the perfume?'

'Her house keys have been at the hospital since the accident, and they said she hasn't had any visitors.'

'So someone forced their way in? You saw the lock. A ten-year-old could have sprung that and left no trace.'

'Why go to that much trouble just to take some perfume? Nothing else has been disturbed.'

Before he could untangle the puzzle any more, something in the oval dressing table mirror caught his eye. He looked at the reflection, knowing that this was the view that Loretta would have seen every day. Rhidian turned and walked over to take a closer look at the object that had drawn his attention.

A niche had been built into the wall next to the bed. This space had been filled by a two-foot-high white marble statue. Small red fairy lights had been strung around its base. Rhidian found the switch and turned the lights on, their ruby glow giving warmth to the ice-cold stone. The whole effect would have looked like a Catholic grotto, except that the statue wasn't of Mary, but something more classical; a female figure, draped in a thin shift which only emphasised her curves.

Rhidian called over his shoulder. 'Found anything?'

'Nothing that shouldn't be in a girl's knicker drawer. Like most women she's got one sexy bra and scanties; for special occasions. The rest is day-to-day stuff.'

'Expensive?'

'No. More Primark than Victoria's Secret.'

'But what she was wearing in the hospital looked like silk.'

'Could have been a present?'

'From whom?'

Absorbed in making a quick sketch of the statue in his notebook, Rhidian was unaware of Jones joining him.

'Do you think that's what she spent all her money on?' asked Jones.

'It does look like museum quality,' agreed Rhidian, until he touched the statue. Something wasn't right. He expected cold hardness from the marble, but it was room temperature, and there was a slight roughness beneath his fingertips. Rhidian took hold of the statue to judge its weight. He was surprised when it lifted easily. 'It's a fake. Resin or something similar. Convincing enough from a distance.'

As Rhidian went to replace the statue on its plinth, something shifted inside. He turned the statue over, revealing a hole in its base. He gave the statue several good shakes, dislodging the contents onto the floor. As he replaced the statue, Jones retrieved the fallen objects.

'What have you got?' asked Rhidian.

'Wales and West Building Society pass book, and some letters.'

Jones handed the letters to Rhidian and opened the passbook. Rhidian checked the postmarks. 'All dated within the last two months. Posted locally.' He opened the first of the letters and pulled out two pages of tiny spidery scrawl.

Jones flicked through the pages of the passbook. 'This explains where all her money went. Wish I could save like her. Regular amounts going in, seven hundred, nine hundred, two thousand.'

'What about money going out?'

'One big withdrawal, April last year. Twenty-three thousand. Another this May; fifteen grand and change. Both paid out in cheques. She's currently got a balance of eighteen K.'

'Get onto the building society. Find out where that money went.'

'Will do,' said Jones, tucking the passbook into an evidence bag as she looked over Rhidian's shoulder, trying to read the letters. 'So what are they? VAT demands or love letters?'

Rhidian read out a couple of excerpts. '"...Can't stop thinking about you... Can't wait till the weekend."' A bitter edge came into his voice as he read – '"I can still smell you on my fingers."'

'Doesn't sound like the tax man,' said Jones. Rhidian wasn't amused. He quickly scanned the last couple of letters. 'The rest are in the same vein.'

'I don't suppose our Romeo signed them?'

'Oh yes. He wasn't shy. Yours forever, J.C.'

'James Calder?'

'So much for there being no man in her life.' Rhidian pushed the letters towards Jones as if he wanted them out of his sight. She slipped them into an evidence bag.

'Let's bring him in,' said Rhidian. 'Find out what was really going on between him and Loretta Swann.'

They were too distracted to notice the figure that lurked outside the bedroom door, listening intently. By the time they had returned to the lounge, the figure had slipped away.

18

Although the world knew him by another name, in his heart, he was 'Felix'. It was the name She had given him, a name that only the two of them knew about. She explained that it meant 'someone who was in the favour of the Gods', someone who had achieved what the Romans called '*pax deorum*,' meaning that they were happy and full of nourishment.

There had been a few women in his life, but none had touched him so deeply. For most of his life he had been crippled by a loneliness that he tried to hide from the rest of the world, but somehow She could see his pain. He worried that their secret would come out because he was sure that he must glow whenever he was in Her presence. He couldn't believe that no one else could see it. He knew that he wasn't Her equal. He knew that other men lusted after Her. He could see their hungry eyes sliding over every inch of Her body when she walked past. But the love they shared was pure. He didn't need to possess Her. He only needed to serve.

One night, he had taken a needle, bathed its point in the cleansing yellow heart of a candle flame, then dipped it into jet black ink and slowly, painfully tattooed the letters F - E - L - I - X into the flesh above his heart. The pact was complete. He was Her devoted creature. He didn't know how he could repay Her for what She had given him... not until that dreadful day.

He had known that something awful was going to happen. The auguries had been dreadful. He had woken that morning to find a dead rook lying stiff and cloudy-eyed on his windowsill. Then when he opened the fridge, the milk that he had bought only yesterday had already congealed into rancid lumps. Before he could consult Her about what actions he should take to fend off whatever evil was clearly coming his way, he heard sirens in the distance and knew that he was too late.

He ran faster than he had ever run before. His breath came in ragged gasps as he saw the flashing blue lights at the end of the road and the crowd of the curious and morbid who were already gathering. As he got closer, he took in the details in vivid snapshots that would later come back to haunt him in his dreams; the flame-red sports car speeding away from the scene and the Mini that he knew so well, pushed into a lamppost, it's front crumpled like tin foil.

He tried to get closer, but the police pushed the crowd back to let the ambulance through. He moved to the other side of the street to get a better view of something he never wanted to see – Her lifeless body lying on the hard, cruel tarmac. Inside he was screaming that someone needed to support Her head; that She was cold! The paramedics were now in attendance and he had to trust them.

It seemed like an eternity before She was gently loaded onto the ambulance trolley. In all of that time She hadn't moved. He saw the look flash between the two paramedics. The tiny shake of a head. But they hadn't covered Her face, so that had to mean that there was still a chance.

He rushed home, mentally preparing himself for what he had to do. There was a dog in his street, a friendly little pug he always patted when he walked past. He loved dogs, but he loved Her more. He didn't have time to prepare everything properly. He knew he had to cover his head. He remembered to make a *precatio* or prayer to the gods or all of his efforts would be wasted. He ensured that the blade was sharp, but he didn't have enough towels. He hadn't expected there to be so much blood.

Seeing the 'Have You Seen Fifi?' posters going up on lampposts around the neighbourhood made him sad, but he had no regrets. He had no doubts that it was only his act of devotion that had kept Her from death that day. But he also knew that he would have to work harder if he was to bring Her back to life.

19

There was no answer at James Calder's Splott bedsit and no signs of life when they peered in through the net-curtained windows. Rhidian left Jones to locate the landlord while he raced to the city centre in a patrol car with a couple of uniformed officers.

*

The museum had closed to the public half an hour ago. Rhidian left the uniforms watching the main entrance while he went round the back and pulled on the long brass lever that rang an old bell deep in the bowels of the building. He noted the mountain bike chained to the railings. If it was Calder's, he would soon have his man.

Rhidian was just about to pull on the bell for a third time when the heavy door swung in on well-oiled hinges to reveal Morris Palfrey, wearing a puzzled expression and holding a potato masher.

'Inspector. Sorry. In the middle of making my tea.'

'James Calder. Is he still here?'

'I don't know. I locked up twenty minutes ago, but he could have let himself out.'

'Is that his bike?'

'Yes. But he often leaves it there if he's going into town for a few drinks after work.'

'Take me to the archive.'

'Of course.' Palfrey hesitated before stepping aside to let Rhidian in. 'Does Mr Llewellyn know you're here? Only I really should let him know.'

'You can do that after you've taken me to the basement,' said Rhidian, pushing past Palfrey and into the hallway.

Calder's landlord didn't need a second invitation from the police before rushing around from the taxi firm he managed, to let Jones into the bedsit.

The interior smelled stale; a mixture of old takeaways, sweaty feet and a hint of cannabis. Having been brought up with several brothers, it was an odour that Jones was all too familiar with.

She moved quickly but carefully around the humble two rooms that James Calder called home; the pokey bathroom with its mouldy grout and the remains of orange stubble sticking to the sides of the sink. She moved on to the slightly more generous kitchen / bedroom / living room. This search wasn't going to take long.

The living space was focused around the large, flat screen TV that hung on the widest wall. A dark patch had been worn into the headrest of the mock leather armchair that faced the TV. On one arm of the chair were lined up the TV remotes and games console. This told Jones that this was where James Calder spent a lot of his time.

'How long has he been a tenant, Mr Patel?'

'Two years. He has never been any trouble. Always pays on time. Never makes any noise. No, I have never received any complaints about him.'

'Does he have many girls stay overnight?'

'Girls? How would I know? That is none of my business. He is not in any trouble is he?'

Jones ignored the question as she rifled through a desk drawer, finally plucking a UK passport out of the jumble of bank statements, instruction booklets for electrical goods and a few top shelf lads' mags. She flipped to the back page, confirming that the passport was still valid and was the property of James Robert Calder. The photo was a few years old. He had more hair then, but was wearing the same glasses through which his eyes stared out blankly. Was this the face of a double killer?

Jones checked the wardrobe. There was a suitcase in the bottom. Empty. The clothes rails didn't look as if they had been stripped. Calder's toothbrush was still standing in the *Jurassic Park* glass on the bathroom sink, along with a fat new tube of toothpaste. It might not look like the home of a killer, but then Jones recalled how Fred West's Gloucestershire home seemed normal, until they started digging the bodies out of the basement.

*

Calder's workspace looked much the same as it did the last time Rhidian was in the archive. The helmet he had been working on was still on the table, next to a half-full mug of coffee and a jam donut with a single bite taken out of it. A black hoody hung over the back of the chair. Rhidian turned to Palfrey. 'Is there anywhere else he could be?'

'Not in the main museum. I put the alarms on, see. If he'd gone in any of the galleries he would have set them off.'

'Do you have security cameras?'

'Yes, you've got to have these days. You won't believe what people get up to. They'll nick anything that's not nailed down.'

'Can I look at your recordings?'

'For that you will need Professor Llewellyn's permission.'

'Five minutes?'

'I couldn't, even if I wanted to. The head of security's the only person who's got the key to the Monitor Room. Trevor Cassidy. He's the one you need to speak to, but he won't be in till tomorrow.'

'Can't he be called in?'

'Not likely. Lives with his mum. She's not well. Trevor clocks in at eight on the dot and out again on the stroke of six. We never get a minute's overtime out of him.'

Rhidian couldn't disguise his frustration. Looking at the table, Palfrey frowned. 'Not like Mr Calder to leave the place in such a mess; not like him at all.'

Rhidian touched the mug. It was still warm. Wherever Calder had gone, it was recently, and in a hurry.

In his office, Professor Llewellyn had little to contribute to the mystery of the whereabouts of James Calder. He had seen him in the museum café earlier in the day, but hadn't seen him leave. Llewellyn's irritation about having his evening interrupted drained away as the implications of Rhidian's questions started to sink in.

'How well do you really know your staff?' asked Rhidian.

'Well enough.'

'But you didn't know that Calder and Loretta Swann were in a relationship?'

'What? No. That's ridiculous. Loretta and.... No,' insisted Llewellyn. 'There was never any sign of any, any intimacy between them.'

'Would they have any reason to keep it a secret?'

'It wouldn't have been an issue for the Board of Trustees.'

'And for you personally?'

'I don't know what you're suggesting, Inspector.'

'Just that she's a very beautiful woman.'

'And I am a married man.'

A tinge of pink flushed Llewellyn's putty skin. Rhidian wondered – was it anger, jealousy, or perhaps a mixture of both?

'I assure you that my relationship with Professor Swann is purely professional.'

The arrival of Palfrey, bringing Jones to the archive gave Llewellyn the distraction he needed to withdraw. 'If you have any further questions, please, make an appointment with my secretary.'

Llewellyn turned away.

'Before you go, Professor...' Rhidian pulled out his notebook and turned to the sketches he'd made in Loretta's flat. 'Do you recognise this statue?'

Llewellyn was momentarily thrown by the change of direction. 'Yes, of course. It's in the Borghese Museum, Rome. The goddess Venus. It's attributed to a student of Bernini. How is that relevant to anything?'

'Thank you for your time.'

For a moment Llewellyn's professional interest was piqued, but this was quickly trumped by his desire to escape any further questioning. He loped off. Palfrey waited patiently in the doorway, absently playing with a large set of keys. Rhidian turned to Jones.

'Did you find anything at Calder's place?'

Jones held up the evidence-bagged passport. 'We know he hasn't left the country; not by any legal route anyway. I still don't get it though. King nerd and Loretta Swann? He was playing well out of his league.'

'And why keep it a secret? Why wasn't he shouting it from the rooftops?'

'But do you really think he's capable of murder? I mean, yeah, he lied to us, but can you imagine him cutting out someone's tongue and sawing off a foot?

'People have done stranger things for love,' said Rhidian.

In the doorway, Palfrey cleared his throat, reminding Rhidian that he was still waiting on his tea. Rhidian and Jones were heading for the door when Rhidian remembered something. He turned back. The hoody. He hadn't searched it. He reached into the pockets, pulling out a packet of chewing gum from the first pocket, and then, more surprisingly, a mobile phone from the second.

‘What young man leaves his phone behind?’ asked Rhidian.

‘One who’s just realised that the police are onto him?’ suggested Jones.

Rhidian passed the phone to her. ‘Names and addresses. Any friends or relatives he might run to. He’s on the back foot at the moment. Let’s find him before he’s had time to get organised.’

20

'Felix' strode down the hospital corridor, confident that the stolen scrubs he was wearing rendered him invisible. To the casual eye he was just another medic on his nightly rounds. It had been a stressful day, what with the police nosing around, asking questions. But his own personal discomfort was nothing compared to the greater goal. He was pleased that She was responding. There could be no doubt now that he was on the right path; that no matter how much it cost him, he was doing the right thing.

His heart quickened, as it always did when he entered Her corridor. Something was wrong. There were too many lights on and urgent voices coming from Her room; a man and a woman. Now he could hear the bleeping of a medical alarm.

'Oxygen's down to seventy-five per cent,' said the woman's voice.

'She needs intubation.'

Felix had to duck into an empty sluice room when a male nurse burst out of Loretta's side room, scanning up and down the corridor.

'Where the hell is Moore?'

'I paged her ten minutes ago,' came the voice from inside the room.

'Try again,' urged the male nurse, rejoining his colleague.

Anna Moore was floating. Weightless, carefree, she looked down and saw that she was hovering over her own body which was slumped against the toilet cubicle wall, one sleeve of her scrubs rolled up, the syringe still sticking out of her arm.

A single child born late after her parents had given up all hope, Anna was doted on by her father; local vicar and pillar of the community, and her mother; organiser supreme of all the good causes in their Cotswold village. Anna was sent to the finest private schools and wanted for nothing. Her perfect life only started to disintegrate when she left home to study medicine at St Bart's.

Used to being top of her class, she now shared lectures with many brighter minds than hers. She was unprepared for the heavy drinking, recreational drug use and casual sex that she was suddenly exposed to in Halls. Confused about her sexuality since she was ten, the only advice she had received from her mother was that 'the right boy will come along eventually'. When she finally did fall in love, she could hardly bring her first girlfriend back for afternoon tea with the folks. Failing several exams in her second year, she had sought help; just a little something to keep her going through the long hours that junior doctors were expected to work, and to ease the guilt that she felt every time she gave in to what her father called 'ungodly lusts'.

By the time she started working full time in A&E, she had a three hundred pound a week monkey on her back. She swore that as soon as the pressure eased, she would clean up her act. But then, during her first week of being in charge of the department, a case that she diagnosed as a migraine turned out to be a subarachnoid brain tumour. As she looked down at the still warm corpse, her consultant welcomed her to the club with the words, 'You're not a proper doctor until you've killed one.' His attempt at reassurance did little to ease the guilt, but a quarter gram of Mexican Brown did the job very nicely indeed.

Now, as she glided across the ceiling, she looked down at the shell of her body. She could see the new frown lines; the nails she had bitten down to the quick and the raw areas of scalp where she had scratched too hard. But for those blissful few moments she felt no pain, no guilt, nothing at all.

Across the corridor from where Anna Moore was enjoying her pharmaceutical escape, Felix was distraught. Something was wrong, but he was powerless to help. All he could do was watch through the crack of the sluice room door. It was then that he heard a distant pager going off. The sound became louder as the door to the Ladies toilets opened and Doctor Anna Moore crept out, clipping the pager back onto the pocket of her scrubs, then pulling her sleeve down; but not before Felix had spotted the telltale red bloom where she had injected herself.

Anna Moore took a moment to gather herself, then headed to Loretta Swann's room, only to be greeted by the sight of Cindy Campbell preparing an intubation kit.

'What's happening?' barked Moore.

'Respiratory failure.'

'Give me some room.' Anna Moore brushed Sister Campbell aside to tilt Loretta's head back to straighten the angle of her throat. She then snatched the intubation insertion tube from Cindy, who kept an eye on the monitor. 'Down to sixty-five.'

Anna Moore turned on the light at the end of the tube, opened Loretta's mouth and guided the curved end of the tube between her teeth, pushing her tongue to one side. Moore could now look directly into the patient's throat.

'I can't visualise the cords.'

'Sixty per cent,' warned Cindy Campbell.

Anna Moore tried to change her angle of view, but it was no good.

'Fifty-five,' said Cindy, struggling to keep the panic out of her voice.

Dr Moore moved the metal tube, sweat forming on her brow as she mouthed a silent prayer, and then, finally, she was able to move the epiglottis, exposing the opening to the larynx.

'Tube.'

Cindy Campbell slapped the plastic breathing tube into Moore's hand. She deftly threaded it down the guide sheath and into Loretta Swann's throat, then withdrew the sheath, leaving the breathing tube in place inside her patient's larynx. 'Okay. Bag her.'

The male nurse attached the plastic ventilator bag to the end of the breathing tube and started pumping it, sending precious air into Loretta Swann's lungs. Dr Moore used her stethoscope to check that the breathing tube was in the correct position. 'Saturation?' she asked.

'Coming up. Sixty-eight, seventy-two.'

Only now could Anna Moore try to calm the thumping in her own chest. 'Good.'

'We paged you three times.' said Cindy.

'I had another emergency,' said Anna Moore. Even she wasn't convinced by her own words.

Down the corridor, hanging onto every word, Felix realised that he was in pain. He looked down to see that he had been digging his fingernails into the tattoo on his chest so hard that he had drawn blood.

*

Turning the key in her front door, Anwen had never craved the comforting normality of her home more. It was a well-established ritual for coppers who had shared a mutual shock or tragedy to find the nearest pub to talk through the events over a pint or three. It was cheaper than therapy and meant that you didn't need to take the shit home to your families. She had asked DI Hook if he wanted to go for a drink. He said that he needed to be somewhere else.

She saw that Sam was in the back garden, having a rant at someone on his mobile. The double glazing prevented her from hearing what had got him so angry. She stood and watched because she'd never seen him like that before. He must have sensed that she was there, because he turned, saw her at the window and all the tension drained from his body. He raised a hand in greeting and mimed that he just needed two minutes.

By the time Anwen had changed out of her work clothes and into joggers and a sweatshirt, Sam was in the kitchen making a brew.

'What was all that about?' she asked. 'You were tamping fit to burst.'

'Just a job that's gone wrong. Sub-contractors, you know. I'll sort it in the morning.' He realised that Anwen was subdued. 'How was your day?'

'Put it this way, I don't think a cup of tea's going to do the job. How about a couple of pints down the Princess and a dirty burger on the way home?'

'Sounds like a plan,' said Sam. His smile evaporated when his phone started ringing and he checked the caller ID. 'Sorry. Got to take this.'

'I'll wait for you outside,' said Anwen. 'But don't be too long or I'll start without you.'

Sam waited until he heard the front door slam behind her before answering the call.

*

The old red brick building had originally been named after Princess Mary, the consort of King George V, but after the death of Diana in a Paris underpass, the owners had commissioned a new pub sign featuring 'the people's Princess'. It had once been a typical locals' pub, but with the influx of students into the area it had been remodelled to try and attract this younger crowd. Pool tables had been installed upstairs and the walls were now decorated with a deliberate mismatch of old, framed photographs from the 1950s. It was meant to be kitsch. Anwen and Sam didn't really care what the décor was like, as long as the beer was kept well. Anwen was halfway through her second pint of the guest ale before she finally started to open up about what was troubling her.

'Sometimes I feel like an imposter,' she said.

'How do you mean?'

'I can be standing in the middle of a crime scene, or interviewing a suspect and I suddenly think – yeah, I might look like I'm in control, but inside I'm shitting myself.'

'But you've been doing this for some time.'

'I know.'

'They wouldn't have put you on a murder case if they didn't think you were up to it.'

'That's what I keep trying to tell myself, but this case is so important. I'm scared of messing up.'

'Isn't there someone you can talk to?'

'At work? No way.'

'Your colleagues must have been through the same thing?'

'Nobody wants to look weak.'

'You know that I'm here for you. Yeah?'

Anwen couldn't believe that she had been so lucky to meet this man.

'Think you might be a keeper, Sam Stokes.'

Sam returned her smile. He hadn't been sure about settling in the capital, but then he hadn't planned on meeting someone like Anwen Jones.

The noise levels suddenly increased when the doors burst open and half a dozen students staggered in. From the state of them, they must have pre-loaded on cheap booze in their digs before coming out. There was no harm in them, but they were definitely going to make having a quiet conversation more difficult.

Sam looked at Anwen. 'Snug?'

'Good idea.'

Anwen gathered up their jackets. Sam picked up their drinks and they headed for the smaller bar. As hoped, the snug was quiet and sparsely occupied. Fitted out with comfy leather armchairs and wallpaper made to look like shelves full of old books, it pulled off a fair impression of a gentleman's library. Anwen couldn't believe their luck. A couple of old boys were just leaving the seats nearest to the real log fire. In her haste to nab the best seats in the house, she didn't see the figure sitting in an old wingback chair. It was Rhidian Hook, sipping a pint of bitter as he studied his notebook. Sam nearly bumped into Anwen as she stopped dead. Before she could back out, Rhidian looked up and saw the newcomers. All that Anwen could do was snap on a smile and carry on to the comfy chairs. Sam followed.

'You're a bit out of your way, aren't you?' said Anwen to Rhidian.

'I was looking for somewhere quiet,' said Rhidian as a great cheer roared up from the students in the other bar. 'This place has changed a bit since I was last here.'

Anwen saw that Rhidian was looking beyond her as Sam placed their drinks on the table.

'Sam. This is my boss, Rhidian Hook.'

'Pleased to meet you,' said Sam, offering his hand. 'Anwen's told me a lot about you.'

'Good to meet you too,' said Rhidian, hiding how uncomfortable he was. All three of them would rather be anywhere else, but they were trapped by politeness. Anwen and Sam turned their chairs so that they faced Rhidian. For a moment nobody knew what to say, until Rhidian felt the need to fill the silence.

'So, what is it that you do, Sam?'

'House renovation. Kitchens mostly, but I can turn my hand to most things.'

'Except plumbing,' said Anwen, just for something to say.

'Yeah, that is my least favourite job.'

'I'm trying to place your accent,' said Rhidian.

'Born in London but moved to Bristol halfway through comprehensive school. So, I guess I'm a kind of West Country Cockney.'

'What made you come over the bridge to Wales?'

'Work. I was in business with my brother, but we had a falling out. Decided to split the business; go our separate ways.'

'Must have been a bad falling out if you had to move to another country,' said Rhidian.

'I just wanted a fresh start.'

'But why Wales?'

'Used to come here for holidays when we were kids.'

'So you know Cardiff then?'

'More Barry Island. The Gower.'

'Do you think you'll ever patch it up with your brother?'

'Given time, maybe.'

Anwen was surprised that Rhidian had got more information out of Sam than she had in three months, but she could also see that Sam was getting uncomfortable.

'We're not in the interview room now,' she said.

'Sorry,' said Rhidian. 'One of the curses of the job; you're never off duty.'

'No problem,' said Sam.

Rhidian knew that he had to do something to try and repair the poor impression he'd made.

'My shout,' he said. 'What will you have?'

'IPA,' said Anwen.

'Same here,' said Sam.

As Rhidian headed for the bar, Sam was unable to conceal his relief that his interrogation was over.

'Sorry,' said Anwen.

'Any longer and I would have signed a full confession. Armed robbery. Sheep shagging. I would have copped for anything.'

'Now you know why he's got such a good reputation.'

'Yeah, and I don't want to cause any hassle at work, but do you think we could get away after the next drink?' said Sam. 'I wanted to spend the evening with you, not your boss.'

'No problem,' said Anwen, realising that she now had two men in her life.

*

Liz Devlin was back in her jogging shorts and Paris T-shirt. She unrolled the new wallpaper onto the pasting table and dipped the soft, wide brush into the paste, only for the flash of a memory to stop her. She was taken back to that Sunday morning when she and Peter had gone to the DIY store to buy that very same pasting table. She had lost him in the cavernous store, eventually finding him in the kitchen section looking at smart fridges. She told him that she had no need of a fridge that would send photos of its contents to her phone. He reminded her about the mouldy cucumber he'd found at the back of the vegetable drawer. She laughed and said that she'd rather put up with the odd bit of rotten food than have her life organised by a bloody fridge. They had been happy then.

She wished that she could find a way to stop such unwelcome memories from bubbling up at the slightest invitation. She had spent the last six months trying to avoid any thoughts about her marriage. It had already wasted too much of her time and energy. Then she looked at the coffee table where she could see the decree absolute and she felt safe to think about her now ex-husband without it overwhelming her.

When Liz and Peter first got married she had enjoyed the attention; the flowers, the chocolates. It was like being sixteen again. Every day there was another thoughtful gesture, another declaration of Peter's love for her. But it soon became cloying. Peter started working from home so that he would always be there the moment she returned at the end of the day. She would be at the hob, making dinner and feel his breath on the back of her neck. In the evening, as they sat watching the latest Scandi Noir thriller on the TV she would sense that his eyes were on her, not on the screen. When they went shopping he was always standing right behind her. She started staying later at work even when she wasn't needed. She tried talking to Peter about it, but he didn't seem to understand. All that he would say was that he had never loved anyone as much as he loved her. She convinced herself that once the honeymoon period had worn off he would calm down; give her more space.

The final straw was when she came back from work late one night and he asked about her day, as he always did. She had spent most of it with Rhidian Hook. A body had been discovered in one of the lime pits of an old tannery. The initial stages of the investigation were focused on trying to identify whether the drowning was an accident or homicide.

Liz had become aware of Peter's growing jealousy about the amount of time she was spending with Hook. She insisted that it was purely professional and Peter had said that he accepted this. As they ate their dinner, he said that he'd never been to the open-air museum where a town had been recreated by relocating forty buildings from various periods of Welsh history. But Liz hadn't mentioned that the suspicious death had happened at St Fagans. Peter tried to backtrack. Where else would there be an old tannery? Her stomach turned over. How could he have known where she had been?

As she filled the dishwasher she cast her mind back, remembering other occasions when Peter seemed to have known her movements while she was at work. There was only one answer. She challenged him, and eventually he had admitted that he had placed a tracker on her phone. He begged for forgiveness. Yes, he was jealous, but only because he loved her so much. It was only then that she realised how he had been slowly suffocating her. He pleaded for another chance. He would do anything. She had to be strong and tell him that it was over; that she wanted him to move out; that she would be filing for divorce. He rented a flat not half a mile away. He bombarded her with gifts. He would cry down the phone. He ignored her solicitor's letters to leave her alone. But that was all over now. She had the legal proof that their short, sad marriage was well and truly in the past.

Liz realised that it was seven o'clock. Time for *The Archers*. But as she was hanging the first strip of paper, the action from Ambridge was suddenly cut off by music; 'Can't Take My Eyes Off Of You' blared out at full volume.

Liz nearly fell off the stepladder in her rush to turn the music off. She cursed when she saw that she had spilled wallpaper paste on the floor. As she cleaned it up with an old rag, she admonished herself for over-reacting. It was just a song. Yes, it was the one that he had picked for their first dance at their wedding reception and which *he* declared was their song; but, sitting on the floor with the gluey rag in her hand, Liz had to laugh. If only her colleagues could see her now, the famously tough DCI freaked out by Andy Williams. She had to remind herself that Peter was on the other side of the world. He couldn't be more out of her life. She selected some music that Peter definitely wouldn't have liked – Adele's latest album – and went back to work.

*

The delivery driver rode his moped slowly down the residential street, passing the pollarded plane trees, looking for the address of the customer who had been struck by a case of the late-night munchies that could only be satisfied by a deep crust pepperoni pizza. The beam from his headlight swept over the dark windows of the ground floor bedsit, momentarily illuminating the outline of a man standing behind the thin, threadbare curtains, watching the street. As the biker continued down the road, Rhidian Hook stepped away from the window and back into the shadows of James Calder's bedsit to resume his vigil.

21

The next morning, still damp from the shower, Anwen sat at the kitchen table, finishing off a bowl of porridge. Sam had an early start so had left without any breakfast, saying he'd grab an egg and bacon bap from the van later.

Seeing Calder's phone sitting in the evidence bag, she decided to hit the floor running. Pressing through the plastic bag, she switched the phone on. Last night she had scrawled through the contacts. A few mates, his mother, numbers for takeaways, then Loretta Swann's mobile and Llewellyn's direct line at the museum. Nothing suspicious there. Now she went to the main menu and selected the video folder. There was one file. Big. Two gigabytes. She clicked on it. The images that came to life on the small screen stopped Jones mid-chew. DI Hook needed to see this.

*

Rhidian nudged open the door to his office with his elbow so that he wouldn't spill the two takeaway coffees. As the strip lights flickered into life, he took off his duffle coat, and was about to hang it up when he saw the odd, blue cotton that secured one of the buttons. The memories rushed, in as fresh as if they had happened yesterday.

It was three years ago. The morning of his birthday. He saw Bethan's anticipation as he opened his birthday present. Whatever he expected, it wasn't a black duffle coat. Sensing his disappointment, she had made him put it on and feel how warm it was. She demonstrated how the hood would keep him dry, even in the teeth of the penetrating Welsh rain and there was plenty of room in the pockets for his notebook.

And then he realised that this gift wasn't just about keeping him warm and dry, it was about reassuring her. She was worried about him from the moment he left the house in the morning, to the time that he put his key in the front door at the end of his day. He had to phone if he was going to be half an hour late or she would be standing at the window, fearing the worst.

Since then he had come in for a fair amount of stick from his colleagues for always wearing that coat, rain or shine, but he wouldn't change, not if it gave her some peace of mind.

Bethan had carried out many running repairs, even though she was no seamstress. He remembered coming into the kitchen one morning to find her reattaching the middle button that had been pulled off in a scuffle with a serial rapist. She apologised for having no black thread. He didn't mind that it didn't match.

His reverie was shattered by Jones bursting in.

'Latte. Two sugars,' said Rhidian, offering her one of the coffees.

'Video file,' said Jones, passing him Calder's phone. Her tone warned him this was serious.

The phone must have been propped up on a bedside table. The camera had a clear view of everything that took place on the bed. Jones confirmed that it was filmed in Calder's bedsit. Although a little grainy, there was no doubt that the two star performers were James Calder and Loretta Swann.

Calder was lying naked on the bed, stroking himself as he watched Loretta undress, taking her time to fold her clothes into a neat pile as if trying to delay the inevitable. There was no tease in this strip. Impatient, Calder rose from the bed and went to her, his urgent fingers clawed at her breasts, his rough lips smothering her mouth and nipples with kisses that turned into bites. He pulled her to the bed and clambered on top of her. He didn't wait for her to be ready, he just pushed her thighs apart and entered her. Calder was too obsessed by desire to register Loretta's discomfort, but her every grimace was captured by the unblinking eye of the phone camera.

When he had finished, Calder lay heavily on Loretta, staying inside her until he had gone soft. Finally pushing himself onto his elbows, he kissed her on the lips, as if, now his passion was spent, he remembered that this was supposed to be an act of love. He pulled himself away from her sticky thighs and padded, naked to the bathroom. Loretta didn't move, lying there like a puppet whose strings had been cut.

Jones stopped the recording. She and Rhidian sat in shocked silence for a moment before he spoke. 'You couldn't call it rape. Not technically.'

'That was nothing to do with love, or even being friends with benefits,' said Jones.

Rhidian had to agree. 'Now we know why nobody's seen them together outside of work and why there were no photos of Calder in Loretta Swann's flat.'

'Why would she let him treat her like that?'

'And then he had the gall to write her love letters. Some men make me ashamed of my sex,' said Rhidian through gritted teeth.

'That is not a man,' said Jones. 'I'll check with uniform. See if there's been any movement at his flat.'

'No need. He didn't come home last night.'

Jones belatedly saw how creased Rhidian's clothes were and remembered that he had been wearing the same shirt yesterday.

'You kept obs all night?'

Not wanting to explain why he knew that he wasn't going to sleep, Rhidian ignored her question. 'Anything else on Calder's phone?'

'I've already got uniforms chasing up his contacts.'

Rhidian was impressed by her initiative.

'Good. If they suspect that anyone's shielding him, bring them in. I'll go back to the museum, see if their CCTV system can shine any light on Calder's disappearance.'

As Jones was gathering her notes, the office phone rang. Rhidian answered it and engaged in a few short, sharp words before hanging up with a curse. '*Coc y gath!*'

'Boss?'

'That was the hospital. Loretta Swann's had some kind of relapse.'

He reached for his coat and left without a backwards glance. Jones called after him. 'I can take the security guy if you want?' But Rhidian was already gone. 'I'll take that as a yes then,' Jones said to herself. She wondered whether this was the usual way he worked, or had Loretta Swann got under his skin, like she seemed to have done with so many men?

*

Rhidian sat next to Loretta's hospital bed. The crisply folded sheets and Loretta Swann's peaceful repose gave no clue to the urgent activities of the previous night. Dr Moore checked the flow of the oxygen feed.

'How close was it?' asked Rhidian.

'I had everything under control,' said Anna Moore. Rhidian wasn't convinced, and she knew it.

'Has this affected her chances of recovery?'

'That's impossible to say.'

Rhidian noted how Dr Moore kept looking at the monitor. She had been avoiding eye contact since he'd arrived.

'It's not easy to establish exactly how well a coma patient is responding to treatment at the best of times, she said.

'Surely she's being monitored around the clock?'

'Of course.'

‘Then how did this happen?’

‘The important thing is that she’s stable now, said Moore. ‘Now if you don’t mind, I’ve only got seven hours before I’m on again, and I need to get some sleep.’ Moore had nearly made it out of the door, but Rhidian had one final question.

‘Who else was here last night?’

‘I was the on-call doctor.’

‘Nursing staff?’ asked Rhidian.

‘Nurse Kohli helped with the intubation.’

‘I’ll need to talk to him.’

‘He’s gone on leave for a week.’

Dr Moore started to push through the door. She wasn’t quite quick enough.

‘It can’t have just been the two of you on duty,’ said Rhidian.

Moore just wanted out of there. ‘Sister Cindy Campbell.’

‘Thank you.’

Watching the doctor urgently leave, Rhidian wondered what she was hiding. He hoped that Sister Campbell might be able to shine some light onto that.

*

As soon as Trevor Cassidy opened the security office door to her, Anwen thought – bulldog on steroids. Although he couldn’t have topped five foot seven, what he lacked in height he made up for in toned bulk. His head was a clean-shaven bullet. Gym-honed muscles strained at the seams of his white uniform shirt.

It was a tight fit, even for just two of them. Most of the space was taken up by the leather chair from which Cassidy monitored a large screen, which was itself split into nine smaller screens, each relaying a live feed from a different CCTV camera.

'Is this a typical set-up?' asked Jones.

'It does the job. Covers all the public areas.'

'But not the offices?'

'Nor the archives,' said Cassidy.

'And you record everything?'

'Onto a hard drive, yeah.'

'How long before you run out of space?'

'It usually manages two weeks' worth. Then I clean the hard drive, ready to start again. Of course if any incidents occur during that time, I can burn the footage onto a DVD.'

Cassidy belatedly realised that his quick tidy-up hadn't been a total success. A small pile of body building magazines were still poking out from a poorly closed filing cabinet. He kicked the drawer shut.

'So, what can you show me of James Calder's last day at work?' asked Jones.

'I've got it all lined up for you. I cut together the footage from the different cameras to give you a timeline.'

Cassidy used his mouse to fill the whole screen with one picture. Because Calder spent most of his time in the areas not covered by the cameras, he only showed up on the footage when he crossed the public areas; getting lunch in the café and checking on a visiting exhibition of Asian ceramics. Cassidy pressed pause, freezing on an image of Calder heading down the corridor towards the archives. Jones noted the time code: seventeen twenty.

'And that's the last sighting?' asked Jones.

'Yeah.'

'Then how did he leave without being picked up on a camera?'

'There's no coverage on the rear service door. He could have gone out that way.'

'So we have no idea when he actually left?'

'Sorry. What's he done? I mean, why are you looking for him?' asked Cassidy.

'I'm sorry, I can't disclose that.'

'We're in the same business.' said Cassidy.

'Even so. You know how it is.'

Cassidy nodded, friendly; like he was in the know; like they were sharing some professional understanding. Jones needed his co-operation so didn't correct his mistake of comparing a police officer to a private security guard. Jones was just about to leave when she had another thought.

'Professor Swann.'

'What about her?'

'What do you think of her?'

Cassidy shrugged. 'Nice enough. Some of the staff look down on the likes of me, but she was all right.'

Jones sensed that Cassidy had more to tell. She hoped that a bit of flattery might open him up. 'This would be the perfect job for me; watching people all day.'

'The novelty soon wears off,' said Cassidy, reaching for a can of energy drink and popping the ring pull.

'You must see things that others don't.'

'That is my job.'

'I'm not talking about kids taking selfies with the dinosaurs. I mean, after a while the staff must forget that everything they do is on camera.'

'My job is to watch out for visitors tampering with the displays or nicking stuff from the shop. What the staff gets up to is none of my business.'

Jones was relieved to get out of the tiny room and the cloying atmosphere of testosterone and the cheap deodorant favoured by teenage virgins. Out in the courtyard, breathing in lungfuls of fresh air, Jones was disappointed that she wasn't going to be able to report back with any new information. Wherever Calder had gone, they weren't going to get any help from Trevor Cassidy, wannabe detective.

*

Caryl Llewellyn stood in front of the walnut wardrobe that had once been her grandmother's pride and joy. She summoned up all her courage, reached for the little brass knob and pulled the door open, revealing her naked reflection in the full-length mirror on the inside of the door.

When she was younger she was considered attractive, in a natural, farmer's-daughter-next-door kind of way; all rosy cheeks, ample bosom and thick, flowing blonde locks. It had been a bit of a shock to realise that it had been ten, maybe fifteen years since she first started avoiding the detailed scrutiny that she was forcing herself to face this afternoon. The more frown lines and crow's feet that etched themselves into her face, the less time she spent in front of the merciless gaze of any mirror.

She tried to look objectively at her exposed body and bare face, to see what others would see. More specifically, what did her husband of nearly thirty years see? And why was this no longer as appealing to him as it had been when they first met and he hadn't been able to keep his hands off her?

There were a few things that stood out immediately. Her once corn-blonde hair was now more grey than golden and it had become thinner over the years. Her breasts weren't as pert as they used to be, and she was carrying an extra stone – okay, an extra two stone – spread across the gentle swell of her stomach and on her thighs and upper arms. All in all she didn't think that the woman staring back at her was in bad shape. After all, it wasn't as if her husband was still the lithe youth with the wild, thick hair who had first wooed her. But that was so many years ago.

They had met during the summer of '85. She was helping her parents run their B&B while trying to decide what to do with the rest of her life. He was in his second year at Cardiff University and had come to Anglesey with a party of students who were spending their summer break looking for archaeological evidence of Viking settlements. They were staying in tents in the five-acre field and would be looking after themselves as far as food was concerned. They needed to come to the house for fresh water every morning. That's when she first met him, standing on the doorstep outside the kitchen door with his arms full of empty water bottles.

She had dated a few island boys, but found them as dull as a wet Sunday. Here was a handsome, well-educated city boy full of dreams of seeing the Great Pyramids of Egypt and who was writing a thesis on the architects who had built ancient Rome. But he was also genuinely interesting in hearing about her thoughts, her dreams. When she went to sleep she dreamt of riding across a sea of sand dunes on the back of his camel, her arms clutched around his waist.

That summer was one of urgently stolen kisses, and then, on his final night, she gave herself to him in his tent while the other students were at the pub. She later realised from his nervous fumblings that it was his first time too.

The next morning, as she watched the minibus drive away towards the bridge, heading back to the mainland, Caryl had to accept that it was the last time she would see him. She would have to content herself with the memories of a wonderful summer romance that was now over.

A few weeks later, she was changing the sheets in room 3 when her mother called her downstairs. Caryl was stunned to see him standing in the middle of the kitchen, nervously clutching a bunch of flowers. She hardly recognised him out of his shorts and heavy metal T-shirts. He had clearly dressed up for the occasion in a poorly fitting suit that she later found out was reserved for interviews and weddings. The cause of her father's shocked expression and her mother's broad grin soon became apparent. He had come to ask her parents for her hand in marriage, like some character from a Jane Austen novel. Her father was impressed by his old-fashioned politeness. Her mother was already thinking about new hats and seating plans.

After the wedding they lived with her parents for a year while they saved up for a deposit on their first flat. He still had his studies to complete and she got an extra job in the pub to try and speed up their dreams of independence. Even though they were now man and wife it still felt like they had to sneak around, snatching any opportunity to make love when they were alone in the house.

It was remembering those heady, early days of carefree, easy lovemaking that had given her the idea of how to save their marriage.

She had never been to an Adult Shop before. She was pleasantly surprised to find that it wasn't full of seedy old men in dirty macs. Most of the customers were couples or women, including a giggling hen party that was filling a shopping basket with chocolate willies, edible panties and furry handcuffs. Caryl was no prude, but some of the objects on sale, well, it boggled the mind to think what their purpose might be. She moved on past the Rampant Rabbits and remote-controlled Love Eggs. Caryl wanted to keep it simple. She didn't want to 'frighten the horses' as her mother would say, so she finally selected some peppermint lubricant, (he always loved mint on his lamb chops), a pair of fishnet stockings and a black, mock-leather basque.

She had read enough women's magazines to know that most marriages went stale, but that didn't mean that she had to give in to the inevitable. However, some facts couldn't be ignored. He hardly touched her anymore. She couldn't remember the last time she saw any glimmer of lust in his eyes when he looked at her. He had even taken to sleeping in the spare room, claiming insomnia. He promised that once the stress of his work had eased, he would move back into the marital bed. She feared that if she didn't challenge this, it would become the status quo. She needed to take positive action to try and turn things around. Then, if the marriage did end, at least she could reassure herself that she had done all that she could have to save it.

She had spent all afternoon on the preparations, but it would be worth the effort if it brought them back to the intimate closeness that they had once shared. She thought that she was ready, but when she heard his key in the front door, her stomach filled with butterflies. He called from the hall, as he did every time.

'Home.'

She took the stairs with more caution than usual. She didn't want to stumble on the unfamiliar high heels. She found her husband standing in the middle of the kitchen, looking puzzled at the lack of cooking smells. 'Is the oven broken?' he asked. He was even more confused when he saw how different Caryl looked. She was wearing her hair up and had painted her face.

'Lipstick. At six o'clock?' he asked.

'You used to like it,' she said and tried a smile. When he didn't smile back, she opened her dressing gown to reveal the black net and leatherette. Huw Llewellyn's mouth gaped open. Was it shock, or lust? Caryl had come too far, she could only press on. She let the dressing gown slip from her shoulders and pool on the floor around her feet. She stepped out of it and remembered that when she walked towards him she needed to strut, deliberately placing one stockinged leg in front of the other, swaying her hips. She was halfway across the kitchen when he held up a hand, as if stopping traffic.

'What are you doing?' he asked.

'I thought we'd have a late dinner.' She tried a sultry voice, which cracked under her nervousness. 'After we've worked up an appetite.' She tried taking another step forward, but he stepped back. This wasn't going to plan at all.

'Do you know what you look like?' he said.

'I did it for you. For us.'

'Cover yourself up, woman. You look ridiculous.' Huw took off his coat and draped it over her shoulders, pulling the front closed to cover up any glimpse of flesh. 'I'm going out,' he said, heading for the hallway.

'Don't. Not tonight, Huw. Please.'

The only answer to her plea was the slamming of the front door.

Caryl was left standing there, feeling foolish, then ashamed. Had she made things worse? What else did she expect? Why would any man be attracted to such a fat frump? Slowly her shame turned into a burning anger. She couldn't ignore it any longer. There was some outside influence at work here. She had to find out who, or what was causing her husband to be so distracted. She buttoned up Huw's coat over her lingerie, and reached for her car keys.

*

At the police station, Jones sat in front of her computer with a bag of Haribo Tangfastics within easy reach to try and keep her awake. Alun Gunter's investigation still hadn't identified the new drug dealer in town, but DI Hook's theory was that anyone with a high public profile would need home delivery of their favourite vice. He didn't think that their dealer was the killer, but everything that connected the two victims had to be explored. So, whenever she had a spare moment Jones would watch another of the DVDs of footage captured by the council's CCTV cameras around Rhys Pryce's mansion and Darius Gull's penthouse. The coverage was not comprehensive, but it did cover most of the major roads in and out. Her aim was to try and spot any vehicles that visited both premises. It was a long shot, and, apart from the boredom, Jones didn't mind. The overtime was adding up nicely. The new wet room she'd been saving up for would soon be within her reach. Her fantasies about quarry tiles and sparkling chrome were cut off by the arrival of Alun Gunter.

'That's a job for a DC, not a sergeant.' he said.

'Somebody's got to do it,' said Jones, determined that he wasn't going to wind her up.

'So, where is your lord and master? Down the nearest boozer I bet.'

'Is there something I can help you with, Inspector?'

'I'm only thinking of you Jones. When Hook falls I don't want him to drag you down with him.'

'I need to get on.'

'I'm just saying. When my team nails this dealer, we'll all be up for commendations. It's not too late to jump ship; come back onto the winner's team.'

Gunter helped himself to fistful of Haribo and left. Even though he was a wanker, Jones had to accept that he had a point. Working on a high-profile murder case could do wonders for her career, but not if it all went tits up.

*

Water has always been vital to Cardiff. The need to transport coal down from the valleys and ship it around the world led to the construction of the impressive industrial docks in the 1800s. Seafarers from around the world were drawn to the port and made the city their home, making it one of the most cosmopolitan communities in the United Kingdom. By the 1980s the coal industry was dying. The docks became derelict ghosts of their former glory. It would take many years and millions of pounds to reshape the neglected wasteland into a thriving mix of new housing, leisure and business opportunities, as well as establishing a home for the Welsh Senedd.

The new marina overlooked a wetlands nature reserve. Dozens of sailing boats bobbed on the waters, a clear sign that South Wales was on the up. Anna Moore first spotted the *Nauti Girl* when on a long weekend in Amsterdam. The old barge had put in years of sterling service as a floating brothel, before being left to rust away in a disused canal basin. Maybe

Anna had been influenced by the mind-bending skunk she'd been smoking for two days, but as far as she was concerned, it was love at first sight for the newly qualified doctor. It cost Anna a small fortune to have the hulk brought to Cardiff on the back of a low loader, and it took a year to transform it from a rusting knocking shop into a cosy home.

Anna sat on the edge of her bed. She needed to rest but knew that the scare of nearly losing a patient meant that she wouldn't sleep, not without some pharmaceutical help. The brown stained liquid was already bubbling on the bowl of the old bent teaspoon. Anna was so intent on drawing the precious elixir into the syringe that she took no notice of the creaks coming from the aft gangplank. She dismissed it as a swell caused by a passing water taxi. She was tying the length of rubber tube around her bicep to encourage a vein to reveal itself, when she heard the scrape of the hatch being slid open and realised that she wasn't alone.

*

Cindy Campbell lived in a key worker flat in the hospital grounds. When she opened the door to him, Rhidian didn't have to bother flashing his warrant card.

'I know who you are. I have seen you in her room,' said Cindy, making no effort to invite him in. 'Didn't think it would take you long to come knocking.'

'Why?'

'Doctors are all the same. Watching their own backs. It's us nurses who get the blame for everything.'

'So. Something did go wrong last night?'

'I never said that.'

'A patient who was under your care nearly died.'

'And I am not having that put at my door. Right?'

'All I want is the truth.'

'No bullshit?'

'No bullshit.'

Cindy considered for a moment. Her three-year-old son appeared at her side, clinging to her legs, staring up at the stranger. 'I'm on my own. I can't afford to lose my job,' she said.

'This is between you and me. Your name won't even be mentioned. I promise.'

Cindy stepped aside to let Rhidian enter.

*

Anna Moore floated in the warm embrace of the heroin as it flowed around her body. She felt the rush of chemical changes in her brain and anticipated what was coming, moments before being bathed in an overwhelming sense of euphoria. All her worries faded away. Even if she had wanted to get off the bed, to try and flee, her limbs were no longer capable of following any instructions from her brain. Such were the anesthetising properties of the drug that she didn't feel it when the blade made its first incision at the midpoint between her breasts. When it sliced deeper, all that she was aware of was a slight pressure and then the release of moist warmth that trickled down her body and onto the sheets. 'That's my blood,' she thought, but with no alarm. Although somewhere in the furthest depths of her mind she knew what was happening to her, there was nothing she could do to stop it. She was surprised about how little pain there was, until the crude but efficient saw started to bite into her ribs. She tried to call out, to make it stop. All that she could manage was a groan, and it worked. For a moment the hewing on her chest paused. A latex-gloved hand reached for the syringe that was still sticking out of her arm and gentle fingers pressed down on the plunger, sending the last of the drug into her vein. She looked up at the ceiling and smiled, even as the saw started its rasping song again.

*

Jones couldn't believe her eyes when she spied a vacant space in the hospital car park. Her joy was short-lived. She hadn't even turned the engine off before the passenger door was tugged open and Rhidian Hook climbed into the passenger seat.

'Cardiff Bay Marina,' he said.

'What's happened?'

'This time you can put your foot down, Sergeant.'

Jones needed no second invitation, and was soon weaving through the evening rush hour traffic, shifting effortlessly through the gears.

'Any luck finding Calder?' asked Rhidian.

'His only living relative is an uncle in Sunderland. He says he hasn't heard from him in two years. I didn't take his word for it of course. Got the local boys to have a look around. They said the place was clean.'

'So he could still be in Cardiff?'

'Why would he risk it?' asked Jones.

'Because his work isn't finished?'

'His work?'

'Remember Calder's letters? If he is so delusional that he believes that Loretta Swann loves him, he could want revenge against the men who he sees have taken her away from him.'

'Gull and Pryce?'

'The motive fits.'

'And the marina?'

'The respiratory emergency that Loretta Swann suffered was caused by negligence, which could put Dr Moore right in Calder's crosshairs.'

Jones blasted her horn at a cyclist who was drifting all over the road, more interested in texting his mates than what was going on around him.

'He must know we're onto him. Surely he wouldn't risk going after the doctor?'

‘She was supposed to start her shift an hour ago but didn’t show, and she’s not answering her phone.’

Clearing the last of the inner city traffic, Jones accelerated. Pushed back in his seat, Rhidian hoped that for once, his instincts were wrong.

Following Rhidian down the weather-bleached wooden pontoon, Jones had to take a moment to get used to the swaying beneath her feet, as they headed for Anna Moore’s seventy-five- foot barge. A razor-beaked cormorant, startled by Rhidian’s approach, flapped its black wings and took to the air, landing back on the water twenty feet away, its jet button eyes keeping a wary watch on the newcomers.

Stepping onboard, Rhidian skirted the old tyres that had been turned into herb gardens and headed for the rear wheelhouse. Jones headed for the forward ramp, taking glances through the portholes as she went, but there was no movement inside.

A wind-tattered flag bearing a red dragon snapped in the wind on top of its broom handle flagpole. Bundles of firewood were stacked neatly on the flat roof. Nearing the wheelhouse, Rhidian noted the woodsmoke lazily coiling out of the aluminium chimney. Faint music could be heard playing below deck. He hoped that this meant they had got there in time. The door to the wheelhouse was propped open with a jolly, red-cheeked gnome wearing a white coat and a stethoscope. Rhidian paused at the top of the three wooden steps, and looked down into the dark of the body of the boat. Jones joined him.

‘Doctor Moore? It’s Detective Inspector Hook.’

No reply. They exchanged a look, then descended into the main cabin.

It took a moment for their eyes to adjust to the change of light. Rhidian had expected to find himself in a traditional houseboat. He was surprised to find that Moore’s tastes ran to the modern and minimalist. A 52-inch flat screen TV and state-of-the-art home cinema sound system had been recessed into one, pine-panelled wall. Simple, tubular chrome and white leather furniture was arranged around the central wood burner. There was not a single 'rose and castle' painted coal scuttle or horse brass to be seen.

Jones called over from the built-in bookshelves. 'Looks like she didn't mind a bit of self-prescribing.'

Rhidian joined Jones to examine the red leather make-up bag. Instead of lipstick and mascara, it contained a selection of syringe needles, a couple of disposable lighters, and a small plastic baggie containing a brown powder. There was no syringe.

'I knew there was something off about her,' said Rhidian. 'I put it down to stress and exhaustion.'

Jones slipped Anna Moore's shooting kit into an evidence bag before joining Rhidian in the galley which had equipment that would have put many restaurants to shame. It was when Rhidian pushed open the door to the sleeping quarters that everything changed.

At first Rhidian thought that it was the setting sun shining through the portholes that was staining the room red. But sunlight doesn't coagulate into sticky pools or drip thickly down the walls. Sunlight doesn't fill a room with the bitter tang of hot rust.

Rhidian hoped that Anna Moore was unconscious before the madman went to work. The young woman's medical knowledge would only have increased her suffering when she saw the tools that her killer was planning to use and imagined the pain they would cause when applied to her flesh, muscles and internal organs. Rhidian knew he couldn't look away. They would only get one chance to take in the crime scene while it was still fresh, while the smell of death still hung heavily in the air.

Before he moved closer, he took note of the bloody prints of naked feet leading from the body towards the shower. Rhidian crouched down to touch a tentative finger to the puddle of blood that spread from under her body, soaking into the planks. Even through the latex of his gloves he could feel that it was cold but turning sticky, still only in the early stages of coagulation. They must have only missed the killer by minutes.

It was some time before he could look at the dead woman's face. He was surprised to see that, although her eyes were open, there was no fear in them. But their brightness was already dulling over. It was Jones who answered this mystery by pointing out the syringe still sticking out of the dead woman's arm. This explained why, despite the terrible insults that had been inflicted upon her body, Anna Moore's dying expression had been one of bliss.

Rhidian's morbid imagination was already at work. He could hear the wet crunching of Anna Moore's ribcage being cut through. Even when he closed his eyes he could still see the arterial fountains of warm blood pumping over the walls. Knowing that he risked having his senses overwhelmed, he turned to his tried and trusted distraction technique. He took out his notebook and started to sketch the crime scene in as much gory detail as he could.

22

Being so close to the water transported Rhidian Hook back six months. It had been two weeks since the underwater search teams had completed their fingertip search of the Taff. Standing on the river bank, Rhidian could still see the raw wound where his car had crashed through the bushes and the two, deep ruts gorged into the shingle where his car had been dragged back out of the water. Liz Devlin knew that she'd find him here, but when she approached, he seemed unaware of her presence.

'Why do you keep torturing yourself?' she asked.

'It's the thought of her still being in there, somewhere in the cold.'

'We'll find her,' said Devlin.

'Like that lad who fell off Penarth Pier? We were never able to give him back to his parents, were we?'

'We'll never stop looking.'

'Yes we will. There are too many of the living who need us.'

Devlin knew he was right. She had stood in too many living rooms telling loved ones these same words.

'You know I'm here for you, Rhidian.'

Devlin laid a hand on his arm, but could he feel it? Rhidian stared at the meandering river. It looked placid now, but he remembered the strength it had the night it took his love from him.

The gently undulating Taff turned back into the still waters of the Cardiff Marina. Rhidian emerged from the shadow of his memories to find that he was on the deck of Anna Moore's barge and that darkness had closed in. After the nightmares down below, he was relieved to be out in the fresh air, but even the breeze off the bay couldn't blow away the images of Anna Moore's ribs, splayed open like something on a butcher's block.

Bloom and the CSI team were below decks, collecting their samples; measuring and logging. At first light an underwater team would be sent into the water to search for any discarded weapons.

Rhidian couldn't escape from the idea that this was his fault. Why hadn't he seen the signs that Moore was an addict? If he had been interviewing a burglar or a prostitute he would automatically have looked for the dilated pupils, the collapsed veins. Did he ignore the possibility because Moore was a professional, or because whenever he was in her company he had been distracted by Loretta Swann? If he had identified Moore as being a user, could he have prevented Loretta Swann from suffering her medical emergency? Could he have stopped Anna Moore's murder?

Jones sensed Rhidian's dark mood. 'At least there can't be any more doubts that this is all linked to Loretta Swann.' No reaction. 'And it's only a matter of time before we find Calder.'

'But you ran him through the computer.'

'And he's clean, so what?'

'So how did he go from law-abiding citizen to multiple killer without flagging up on our systems?'

'He's a clever bugger, that's all. I mean, he's got a First from Cambridge and a Masters from Durham.'

'Yes. Degrees in Archaeology, not butchery.'

Rhidian looked out over the water. Jones thought she was losing him again, that he was retreating into his own thoughts, until Rhidian looked up, his eyes shining. Before she could ask him what was up, he leaned over the side of the barge, studying the waterline. Jones tried to see what he was looking at, but there was nothing. Then Rhidian was moving quickly down the length of the boat, still looking down into the water.

‘What are we looking for?’

‘I’ll know it when I see it,’ said Rhidian. There was nothing on the port side of the boat, so he quickly crossed to starboard. Again he leaned over, scanning the water line, only this time he saw something. He moved five feet to his right to get a closer look. Jones joined him to see an orange nylon rope, hanging over the side of the boat and down into the murky water.

Rhidian used a finger to test the rope. It was taut. There was something heavy on the other end. He gave Jones the nod and she started pulling on the rope. Rhidian saw a vague shape emerging from the depths; something pale, no, white. A few more pulls, and Jones was landing her catch onto the deck; a water-swollen Tesco carrier bag. Half a dozen jagged holes had been slashed through the plastic to help it sink. Water poured out over Jones’s Doc Martens and Rhidian’s desert boots. Neither cared. Rhidian wanted to leave the bag for the CSI team to open. The last thing he wanted was to see what was inside. Not for the first time, he wondered why he chose to do a job where he kept having to expose himself to the cruellest things that one human being could do to another. But his need to try and understand the killer trumped his desire for self preservation. He untied the handles and opened the bag. At first he couldn’t make out what the blobs of pink, squishy sponge were. Then his brain joined the dots and his stomach churned. It was all he could do to not vomit on the spot.

*

It was well past midnight by the time Augustus Bloom completed his initial post mortem on the woman who had, only a few hours ago, been working in the hospital wards upstairs. Now she was lying cold, white and bloodless on the pathologist’s table, all of her sins exposed to a microscopic scrutiny. Rhidian made the mistake of looking into her still-open eyes, and now he struggled to break the milky orbed lock they had on him.

'The chest was cut open with something sharp and precise,' said Bloom. 'There are no hesitation marks. They went straight for it, slicing through the skin and muscle to expose the ribcage. Then they cut through the sternum using some kind of saw rather than the surgical shears that I would use. That's how these rough ends of the bone were created.' Bloom turned to Jones. 'Your killer could have opted for a power saw but I don't suppose he could guarantee that he would have access to an electrical supply.'

Rhidian noted that Bloom had a new assistant; a young woman with multiple facial piercings and purple-dyed hair. When Rhidian had asked how Jac Mundy was doing, Bloom confirmed that he had been reassigned because it was inappropriate that he should have any connection to the continuing investigation, considering his personal relationship with one of the victims.

'Brute force now came into play,' Bloom continued. 'The ribcage was pulled apart like opening a book. This would have taken some effort. The killer would have been covered in blood.'

'I think he stripped before he started work,' said Rhidian. 'Then he took a shower afterwards.'

Bloom nodded. That made sense.

'What about removing the lungs?' asked Rhidian.

'Not the neatest job I've ever seen,' said Bloom. 'Simply sliced through the trachea, releasing the lungs. They were then scooped out and presumably placed in the carrier bag as you found them.'

'Cause of death?'

'Technically, cardiac arrest. Your heart will tend to stop once your lungs have been removed,' said Bloom. 'But note the blue tinge to the lips and fingertips. Both signs I would expect to see in a death by opiate overdose. We'll have to wait for the tests on the syringe to come back, but I don't think I'd be making too wild a guess to say that if having her lungs removed hadn't killed her, the OD would have.'

'I don't get it,' said Jones. 'Why kill her twice?'

'Mercy,' said Rhidian. 'He didn't want her to suffer any more than she had to, so he let her shoot up first.'

'And are we definitely saying it's a man now?' asked Jones.

'Tearing open a ribcage? I'd say so, wouldn't you?' Rhidian looked to Bloom for confirmation and got a firm nod. 'And then there's the footprints in blood. They look to be a man's size nine, maybe a ten. The question is, who is this man who can deliver such violence, and yet show such compassion?'

*

Rhidian Hook couldn't sleep. It wasn't just that the plastic hospital chair was uncomfortable or that the drone of the floor polisher was keeping him awake. He could have been lying on the finest mattress, but still the conflicting thoughts running around inside his head would have kept him awake.

He knew what the problem was. This was the first time for many years that he'd had to try and deal with a case on his own. Before, when he had come home from a tough day, Bethan knew that he needed to be wrapped in a blanket of normality. Soaking in a hot bath washed away the physical aches from hours crammed into a police car on stakeout. Listening to her rehearsing for a concert helped banish the cries of a victim's grieving loved ones. Eventually she realised that to truly recover he needed the peace of the cottage on the mountain, so whenever neither of them was working, they would retreat there. She made sure there was always a list of physical chores to tire him out so that he got a good night's sleep. Fixing the roof, restoring an ancient stone wall. Rhidian knew what she was doing and loved her even more for it. When he returned to Cardiff he would be refreshed, ready to renew the fight. Now he had to consider, could he do this without her? Was it too late to tell Liz Devlin that he needed to go back to the mountain?

He stood, stretched and grimaced when the knot in his back triggered a stab of pain. He looked down on the sleeping form of Loretta Swann. The only time she moved was when the nurses came to turn her or to wash her pale, freckled skin with a damp sponge. He tried to tell himself that he only stayed by her bedside all night because he hoped that the killer might return. It had become clear to him that this was the same person who had been visiting Loretta, brushing her hair, reapplying her perfume and dressing her in expensive nightwear.

They had interviewed her neighbours, who all claimed not to have had any interaction with her, apart from the odd casual 'hello' as they passed in the communal corridor. Was that Loretta's choice, or just another symptom of the modern malaise of creeping loneliness that affects inner city living? Rhidian thought it tragic that many people didn't even know their neighbour's name, but were experts on the lives and loves of their favourite celebrity.

Rhidian was sure that Loretta Swann was not in any danger from whoever had been watching over her. By the same token, they were bound to have noticed Rhidian's bedside vigil so he wasn't going to be caught so easily. But if Rhidian wasn't there to protect her or to catch the killer, what kept drawing him back? An extraordinary event saved Rhidian from having to answer that question. A movement, out of the corner of his eye. Was it his imagination? Rhidian pressed the red button to summon the staff. He didn't take his eyes off Loretta for the eternity that it seemed to take for Cindy Campbell to arrive.

'What is it?' she asked.

'She moved.'

'Are you sure?'

'Right hand. Index finger.'

They both watched. Rhidian realised that he was holding his breath. But there was nothing. Cindy was sympathetic as she checked Loretta Swann's nasal oxygen tube.

'We all want her to improve, but sometimes your mind can play tricks on you.'

Then it happened again. No more than a twitch, but it was a definite movement.

'Could just be automatic. A reflex,' said Cindy, but the urgency with which she reached for the emergency button suggested otherwise.

Rhidian backed out of the room as it filled up with more nurses, then a junior doctor, and finally the department's senior consultant and he could only see glimpses of Loretta through the wall of scrubs. Rhidian Hook was not a religious man, but he did find himself mouthing a silent prayer.

23

Liz Devlin's office phone had been ringing all morning. She understood that journalists had a job to do, but why wouldn't Ginnie Lane take 'no comment' for an answer? Devlin had eventually blocked the journalist's number and this seemed to have worked, as the phone had gone quiet and Devlin was finally able to concentrate on her work. No sooner had she started trying to triage her email inbox into 'urgent', 'important' and 'bin', her mobile started ringing. It wasn't a number she recognised.

'DCI Devlin.'

'All I need are answers to a couple of simple questions.'

'How did you get this number, Miss Lane?' Devlin didn't bother concealing her irritation.

'Can you confirm that there is a connection between the deaths of Rhys Pryce, Darius Gull and Dr Anna—'

Devlin stabbed her finger at her phone, cutting off the call. Needing to clear her head she left her mobile on her desk and headed for the canteen.

*

Even after Anwen Jones had managed to get to sleep, her rest was plagued by the nightmare vision of Dr Anna Moore, lying on the mortuary table, her chest spread wide, her eyes open. In her nightmare Jones looked down and saw that she was holding Anna Moore's flaccid, wet lungs on the palms of her hands. Every instinct told her to drop the heavy, damp objects, but then the limp tissue started filling with air like a pair of grey balloons.

Sam had had to go to work early to oversee the delivery of some supplies, which meant that he wasn't there to rouse Jones when she slept through her alarm clock. Running late, she didn't have time to make even the simplest breakfast, but she knew that she could fill up at the police station's canteen.

South Wales Police Force was not immune to the many public health awareness campaigns championed by various celebrity chefs and then reluctantly adopted by the government. The population of the UK was getting fatter and this included police officers who were not shy when it came to calling at a kebab van in the middle of a night shift. This is why the staff canteen now offered a selection of healthy salads and fresh fruit alongside the usual fare of carbohydrate-heavy meals and snacks. Anwen Jones was very much of the 'lettuce is for rabbits' school. That was why she was busy tucking into a sausage bap with extra brown sauce and ruminating on her chosen career.

Most coppers are uncomplicated people. An investigation normally followed a simple pattern:

Take a crime report.

Identify your suspect.

Gather the evidence against them.

Hope that the CPS will let you charge them.

Cross your fingers that the twelve men and women of the jury will see through the defendant's lies and bang them up.

Top it all off with a session in the local to celebrate with your colleagues.

Move on to the next case.

Every copper has their pet hate. For some its domestic burglars and the way they defile the sanctity of the one place that you should be able to feel safe; your own home. Other officers make it their mission to get drunk drivers off the road. Anwen Jones hated county lines gangs from the big cities who groomed vulnerable local kids to push their drugs in small towns and villages. She had seen first-hand how a few hardcore offenders could blight whole communities.

Jones also knew that if your average copper spent their days and nights hunting jackals and hyenas, Rhidian Hook was after bigger game; the lions, the crocodiles, the great white sharks. Hook's targets were not driven by simple greed or a lust for power; they were fuelled by darker, more primeval desires. How did exposure to so many monsters not rub off? Rhidian Hook might have found ways of coping, but could she do the same? She remembered the last time she was on a case that had her waking in the middle of the night in a sweat. Was it really only eighteen months ago?

It was an A&E doctor who raised the alarm. A woman in her thirties had been rushed to hospital by her distraught brother who said he had no idea what had happened; he had just found her collapsed in the bathroom. The woman had lost a frightening amount of blood, PV (per vagina). An examination quickly established the cause, an internal haemorrhage. The doctor located the source of the bleed and repaired the damage. The woman's life was saved. The doctor's job should have been over, but something about the matter didn't sit right. He suspected, but couldn't prove, that the bleed had been caused by complications after a chaotic birth. Both the patient and her brother insisted that she had never been pregnant; that there was no baby. The doctor informed a contact in Social Services. They contacted the police. A constable from the nearest police station had been sent out to talk to the siblings, but he had been sent away with a promise that if he trespassed on their land again he'd get more than just a flea in his ear.

The country had been enjoying an unseasonably warm Easter as Anwen Jones drove DI Gunter out to the remote sheep farm, car windows down. Before confronting the brother and sister, they had stopped in the nearest village to gather some intel. The gossips confirmed that the siblings kept themselves to themselves. The whole Pritchard clan had always been the same, going back generations, and Mari and Elis had remained unsociable, even after the deaths of their parents. The thought that Mari had ever been pregnant was met with laughter and ridicule from the locals. Everyone agreed that Mari had never even had a boyfriend. The one young man who had shown an interest in her had been chased off the Pritchard land by her over-protective brother wielding an axe. Jones suggested contacting the local station for some uniformed backup, but Gunter didn't want to look weak in front of a bunch of yokels. Besides, if it all kicked off, he had his own little Rottweiler in DS Jones to take care of business.

The farm could only be accessed via a long, poorly-maintained dirt track. Luckily the weather had been dry for several days, so Jones didn't have too much trouble getting her Audi through the thick mud that had been churned up into stiff ridges by tractors and other heavy machinery.

'Hope they haven't got dogs,' said Gunter. 'I hate farm dogs. Vicious, mad bastards.'

Pulling into the farmyard, Jones skirted around stacks of old tyres, bails of rotting hay and a dead sheep splayed on its back in an old wheelbarrow. Jones and Gunter closed their windows in unison as the tang of sheep shit and general decay hit their nostrils. She parked between a quad bike and an ancient Land Rover that only seemed to be held together by rust and mud; its windscreen cracked and the one remaining wing mirror tied on with some twisted wire.

The sound of their unfamiliar engine must have alerted the occupants, as Elis and Mari Pritchard were waiting for them by the time they exited the car.

'Coppers is it?' asked Elis.

'What gave us away?' said Gunter, trying to keep the mood light, while nervously scanning the yard for dogs.

'Who else wears nice shoes on a farm?' said Elis.

Gunter looked down at his suede loafers and saw that they were already splattered with mud.

'You were either cops or social workers, and we don't like either.'

While Gunter was distracted by his ruined footwear, Jones focused on Mari, noting how she stayed in the shadow of the doorway.

'I've got work to do, so tell us what you want or piss off,' said Elis.

'What's with the language?' asked Gunter. 'Have I been disrespectful to you?'

'You're the ones who have rucked up here with no warning.'

'And we're not leaving until we've had a good look around,' said Gunter.

'No frigging chance!'

The farmer took a step towards them, rolling up his shirt sleeves to reveal an impressive set of muscles, forcing Gunter to step back. Jones pulled papers out of her back pocket and held them up.

'We've got a warrant, Mr Pritchard.'

This stopped Elis in his tracks.

'So how are we going to do this?' said Gunter. 'You going to co-operate, or do I need to call in the troops and take this whole place apart?'

Elis took a deep breath and his whole body relaxed, much to Jones's relief. 'Why are you here?'

'Concerns have been raised about your sister's health,' said Gunter.

'And there she is. Perfectly healthy, so what's the problem?'

'You recently took her to A&E?'

'So?'

Jones tried addressing Mari directly. 'What was wrong with you Miss Pritchard?'

Elis didn't give her a chance to answer. 'She was bleeding. Docs patched her up. End of story.'

'But why was she bleeding?' asked Gunter.

'I don't know. Women's troubles. What do you care? I thought you were cops, not social workers?'

'Where's the baby, Miss Pritchard?'

'Baby? said Elis. 'She hasn't even got a boyfriend.'

'Then what's that for?' Gunter pointed to the bulge in Elis's shirt pocket.

Elis pulled out a baby bottle, half filled with milk. 'You are joking?'

'Just take us to the baby. Let us see that it's okay,' said Gunter.

'If that'll get you off our backs, fine,' said Elis. He led the officers towards a corrugated tin-roofed barn.

'You keep the baby in here?' asked Gunter.

Elis didn't reply, he just pushed open the metal gate to reveal half a dozen tiny lambs that started bleating as soon as they saw the baby's bottle.

'Satisfied?' asked Elis, kneeling to feed the first hungry orphan.

Gunter wasn't going to let a farm boy get the better of him.

The search of the farm and land took several hours but didn't turn up any sign of a newborn baby, or its grave. Elis was indignant about this invasion of their privacy. Mari remained withdrawn. Jones tried to separate the siblings, to see if Mari might be more talkative away from her brother, but Elis was quickly onto the plan and instructed his sister that she didn't need to tell the police anything.

As Jones drove them away down the dirt track, Gunter fumed about 'Bloody do-gooders.'

'Who do you mean? The doctor or the social worker?'

'I'd do all of them for wasting police time. Look at my shoes. Ruined.' Gunter sniffed at his fingers then wrinkled his nose. 'And what is that stink? How can they live like that?'

Gunter nearly hit his head on the windscreen when Jones slammed on the brakes.

'What the f—?'

'I saw something,' said Jones, putting the car into reverse, and slowly backing up the track. 'There.'

Gunter saw what had caught her eye; something bright, only half visible through the thick tangle of brambles. 'This had better be worth it.' said Gunter, opening the passenger door.

To get to the spinney, Jones and Gunter had to step over a rusty barbed wire fence that was dotted by clumps of sheep's wool where the animals had snuck under the ramshackle defences to get to the greener grass on the other side.

As they approached they could see what had caused the flash of light; the sun, reflecting off the window of an old caravan. The vehicle must have looked stunning when it came out of the factory, the answer to every family's dreams of holidays in the sun. Now its once gleaming white paintwork was stained dull green by moss and mould. Its tyres were flat, its roof was peeling off and there were several holes in the bodywork that showed where someone had used it for target practice for their air rifle. One side window was rusted open. It was this that had caught the sunlight. A tarnished chrome sign denoted that this model was a 'Gadabout', but it had been many years since this sad hulk had looked out on any vista other than a small field, dotted with thistles and sheep dags.

Pushing through brambles and stingers, Gunter was first to reach the caravan's door. He tried the handle. It was stiff, but unlocked and the door opened with a creak of seized hinges. An old enamel bath that had once served as a water trough had been turned upside down and placed under the door to act as a step. Gunter used this to enter the caravan. Before Jones could join him, they heard the guttural approach of a 200cc engine.

Elis Pritchard jumped off the quad bike before it had even stopped moving and stormed towards the caravan.

‘What the hell do you think you’re doing?’

He must have been watching them from the farmhouse and saw them stop.

‘Our warrant covers the whole of the farm, Mr Pritchard, including any outbuildings.’

‘It’s a caravan.’

‘Which hasn’t moved in many a moon, so I call it an outbuilding,’ said Gunter. ‘What do you use it for?’

‘We used to put the visiting shearers in here back when we had a bigger flock and when the price of fleeces made it worth our while.’

‘So if there’s nothing in here, you won’t mind if we have a look, will you?’ said Gunter with a patronising smile.

Elis backed down. ‘Do what you want. Only the floor’s rotten, so don’t blame me if you break an ankle.’

Having seen the state of the exterior, Gunter had no doubt that Elis’ warning was genuine. He tentatively stepped into the caravan, his nervousness growing when he felt the floor shift beneath his feet. Jones joined him and got her first look around the sad interior.

What had once been a homely environment, lovingly installed by the finest craftsmen, was now a bombsite. The sink was still piled high with plates and cutlery from some long-forgotten meal. On the gas hob sat a rusty frying pan containing half an inch of black fat. There was a seating area built along one wall facing a yellow Formica-topped table scarred by burns from cigarettes and hot saucepans.

The sleeping area contained only a threadbare duvet covered in the bloom of many stains that didn’t invite further inspection. Someone had made curtains out of a pretty fabric decorated with daffodils, but these were now just the faded home for spiders and their cocooned prey, waiting for the bite that would put them out of their misery.

Elis stayed in the doorway, which Jones was pleased about. With the oppressive stale heat, the caravan already felt too crowded with her and Gunter, who took one look into the shower and quickly declared it 'clear'. He pulled aside the concertina door to the toilet. It was surprisingly clean, leading Gunter to speculate that even Ozzie sheep shearers appreciated having sanitary surroundings while taking a dump.

Jones crouched down to open a cupboard and took an involuntary step back when something small and dark darted away into the deeper shadows. She tried to reassure herself that it was a large mouse and not a rat. Gunter found a snail-nibbled copy of *Big Ones* magazine. He checked the date. June 2005. That and the crushed lager cans seemed to fit with Elis' story of bored sheep shearers relaxing after a hard day's work with a bit of soft porn and a few tinnies. It was a small space, so it didn't take long to search.

'Happy now?' asked Elis.

'I'm just doing my job, Mr Pritchard. I hope you understand.'

Gunter headed for the door. Jones was about to follow him when she looked again at her surroundings and was struck by an old memory.

'Hang on.'

'Come on, Jones, there's a pint with my name on it waiting for me.'

'I stayed in one of these. Place near Tenby, when I was a kid.'

'Fascinating I'm sure.'

'Me and my cousins played hide and seek.'

'Oh well. If you've had a nice trip down memory lane, then this wasn't such a wasted trip after all,' said Gunter sarcastically.

'They never found me because I had such a good place to hide.'

Now Gunter was interested.

'You've had your look, now it's time for you to go,' said Elis nervously, and Gunter and Jones knew that they were onto something.

‘Where?’ Gunter asked Jones.

She walked over to the Formica table. Taking hold of the top, she twisted it once, anti-clockwise, releasing the base from the floor bracket. She set the table to one side and looked more closely at the built-in seating area made of interlocked pine panels.

‘I’m telling you, it’s time to get lost,’ said Elis.

‘We’ll go when we’re good and ready,’ said Gunter, watching as Jones felt under the seat until her fingers located a catch. When she released it, the top of the padded seat sprung up half an inch. As Jones slipped her fingers into the gap, Elis lunged at her. His hands were around her throat before Gunter could react. Jones was pushed back onto the seat. She clawed at the farmer’s hands but their grip was solid as he squeezed all of his frustration into her neck. She tried to scratch at his face, but she was getting too weak. She knew she only had moments left if she couldn’t get a breath into her body. All she could hear was the blood pounding in her ears and Elis Pritchard’s grunting as he squeezed the life out of her. Then there was a shattering of glass and the pressure on her throat was released. Sucking in oxygen, Jones tried to understand what had happened. Elis Pritchard was on his knees, clutching the back of his head, trying to stem the blood that was pouring down his face and the neck. Gunter stood over him, holding the neck of the whiskey bottle he had whacked the farmer with. While Elis was still groggy, Gunter pulled his arms behind him and tried to cuff him. Even with an open head wound and possible concussion, Elis continued to resist. In the end it took Jones kneeling on the small of Elis’ back to subdue him enough for the cuffs to finally be snapped tight.

With Elis safely locked in the back of the CID car, Jones and Gunter were able to return to the caravan to see what the farmer had been so keen on protecting. Jones lifted the padded seat, revealing a space, two foot deep. It had been designed as a place to store clothes and bedding and there was something nearly filling the whole space. Gunter and Jones tried to make sense of the shapes. She counted half a dozen bundles wrapped in thick plastic bags that had once contained sheep feed. Each was tied off at the top by a length of orange bailing twine. Gunter found a bread knife in the sink, then used it to cut the twine on one of the bags and cautiously peel open the plastic. At first Jones thought it was a doll. But dolls don't have sallow, yellow skin stretched tightly over a tiny skull. Dolls don't still have umbilical cords attached and dolls don't reek of a dusty, desiccated death.

At the mortuary, the rest of the bags were carefully opened and unpacked of their macabre contents. Six perfect babies. Five had been mummified by the very special conditions of low humidity and lack of air. The other was only in the early stages of preservation so it was still soft and fresh. It looked as if it was sleeping.

Psychiatric reports would later paint a tragic picture of the lives of Mari and Elis Pritchard. They had been home schooled, before home schooling had become such a trendy, middle class choice. Their parents had made them work the land since the moment they could walk. Nobody visited the Pritchard farm, and the Pritchards only ever ventured into the village to get the few things that they were not self-sufficient in. The siblings had no friends and nobody else to turn to when their parents died. They knew nothing about birth control, so every time their 'special love' produced more physical evidence of their secret relationship, it had to be got rid of; hidden away; forgotten. They knew that if the authorities ever found out, they would be forced to separate. Their secret would have stayed safe if it hadn't been for the complications after the last birth and Elis' panic that he was about to lose the love of his life. It could not be proved which of the two had suffocated the newborns, so they both stood trial and were found guilty of the multiple homicides.

In the nightmares that still occasionally broke her sleep, Anwen was twelve again, playing hide and seek. She slipped into the tight space under the caravan seat. As she waited in the dark, she realised that she wasn't alone. Small bodies were moving in the darkness all around her. She could hear the rustle of plastic feed bags. She felt tiny, dry fingers moving up her legs and an icy cold breath on the back of her neck. Usually it was when the babies started crying that she woke from her nightmare with a scream of her own.

Back in the canteen, trying to shake off the bad memory, Jones knew that she would have to decide, would she be able to deal with walking in DI Hook's shadow, or would she sleep better chasing down the more common or garden villains? Before she could come to any conclusion, she was interrupted by the arrival of DCI Devlin.

'Sergeant Jones. Do you mind …?'

Jones nearly choked on her bap. 'No, ma'am. Please.'

Liz Devlin slipped into the plastic seat opposite Jones who was caught between the need to empty her mouth, and the thought that if she kept chewing she would have an excuse not to answer the questions that she knew were coming. Devlin cut straight to the chase.

'DI Hook. How's he doing?'

Jones chewed. Devlin filled in the silence.

'A freak RTC with enough mystery to get his brain firing again. That's all it was supposed to be,' said Devlin.

Jones chewed on, even though the bread had turned to mush.

'I just need to know. Is he coping, or did I bring him back too soon?'

Jones had no choice but to swallow. 'Not sure if I'm the best person to judge that.'

'You've been closest to him.'

Jones considered.

'I only have his best interests at heart,' said Devlin.

'Okay, so what it is, he's not exactly the easiest man to work with,' said Jones. 'He's not great on letting me in.'

'Tell me about it,' said Devlin, with feeling.

'I just wish he'd trust me more.'

'That's no reflection on you, Sergeant. He's never been much good at sharing.'

'Then if you'll forgive me, ma'am, why bring him back?'

'Because he needs this. It's what he does. If I'd left him up on that mountain... Have you seen any evidence that he's not coping?'

Jones was relieved when she was saved from having to answer by the arrival of an excited Alun Gunter.

'Ma'am.'

'What is it, Alun?'

'You might want to look at your news feed.'

Seeing how Gunter could barely contain his glee, Devlin and Jones knew that this could only be bad news for Rhidian Hook.

24

The small hospital shop was staffed by volunteers, mostly retired pensioners, so it was taking longer than necessary to pay for the packet of mints that Rhidian needed to freshen his breath after the night spent at Loretta Swann's bedside. A glance at his watch. Nine thirty. Jones would be wondering where he was. He knew that he should be at the office, but how could he, when just one floor up, Loretta Swann might be opening her eyes?

Finally it was Rhidian's turn to pay, but the old lady behind the counter wasn't giving him her full attention. She was distracted by something going on over his shoulder.

'I don't know what the world's coming to. We didn't have all this in my day. Oh we had punks with their spitting and before them the teddy boys slashing cinema seats, but we didn't have maniacs running round stealing your bits.'

Rhidian turned to see what she was talking about. The last thing he wanted to see after a sleepless night was a live report from Ginnie Lane, standing in front of the yellow police tape that was keeping the public away from Anna Moore's Dutch barge.

'Can you turn it up please,' he asked.

The old lady reached for the remote but couldn't find the right button. Rhidian impatiently took it from her and pointed it at the TV. Ginnie Lane's voice rose with the green bars.

'…the owner of the boat has been identified as Anna Moore, a doctor at the Hopewell Infirmary. A source close to South Wales Police has confirmed that body parts were removed from the victim. My source also says that body parts were taken from Cardiff City winger Rhys Pryce, and his barrister Darius Gull. We have tried to speak to Detective

Chief Inspector Devlin, but so far she has been unavailable for comment.'

Rhidian knew exactly what Liz Devlin's first question would be…

'Please, tell me the leak didn't come from us?' Devlin took her seat behind her desk. Knowing he was in for a dressing down, Rhidian remained standing.

'All I can say is that it didn't come from me or Sergeant Jones,' said Rhidian. 'The last thing I wanted was for this to become even more of a media circus than it already is. That's why we kept the details of the trophy-taking from the press.'

'Well, Ginnie Lane got her information from somewhere,' said Devlin.

'A high-profile case like this was bound to leak,' said Rhidian. 'It doesn't need to be anyone from our end.'

'So you don't think it's worth an internal enquiry?'

'I'd rather have everyone focused on the case.'

'Rhidian, the bodies are stacking up and you can't even find your main suspect. The Chief Constable's got every right to ask the question.'

'What question?'

'Have I got the right man on the job?'

'And you said?'

'Yes. One hundred per cent.'

Rhidian was surprised by the sense of relief. A few days ago he wasn't even sure that he wanted to come back to his job. Now he was positive that he didn't want to lose it.

'There is some good news,' said Rhidian. 'Loretta Swann. There's been a change in her condition.'

'She's awake?'

'No. But there are signs of improvement.'

'What good is that, if she can't explain why all of this is going on around her?' asked Devlin. 'I'm going to need more than that to lower the Commissioner's blood pressure.'

*

Jones returned to the office with a couple of coffees from the canteen. She was disappointed to see that the room was empty. She was used to working on her own initiative, but she expected to be kept informed about where her boss was, especially after Ginnie Lane's news report.

A voice behind her. 'He's really cocked it up this time.'

Jones turned to see Gunter leaning against the doorframe. Who else would gloat over another officer's misfortune?

'This has got nothing to do with DI Hook.'

'You sure of that? Only the way he's been since his wife died, I don't suppose even he knows what he's doing.'

'He wouldn't talk to the press.'

'Then why's he in the DCI's office, getting the old hairdryer treatment?' Gunter was pleased to see the flash of doubt cross Jones's features. He snatched one of the coffees from her hand. 'Hope you didn't forget the sugar.'

Gunter walked up to the nearly bare incident board. The only item displayed was a map of Cardiff with the crime scenes highlighted by a neon green marker pen, and photos of Rhys Pryce, Darius Gull and James Calder.

'Doesn't look like you're making much progress.'

'The DI doesn't like using the boards,' said Jones.

'Why's that then? Doesn't he trust you enough to share? Maybe he thinks you're the leak?'

Gunter was pleased to see how this struck home, but it was Rhidian who answered from the doorway. 'I know you love a whiteboard, Alun. Remind you of your school days does it?'

'There are ways of doing things, Hook.'

'We've already got enough leaks. Why display the inner workings of our investigation just to see it plastered all over tomorrow's *Echo*? Now, if there's nothing else...'

As Gunter passed on the way out, Rhidian snatched the coffee from him. 'Mine, I believe.'

They could hear Gunter chuntering curses under his breath as he disappeared down the corridor.

'The story didn't come from me,' said Jones.

'The thought never crossed my mind,' said Rhidian.

Jones was surprised to see that he was in such a good mood. 'I don't think I'd be so upbeat if I'd been summoned to see the DCI.'

'I've just come from the hospital,' said Rhidian. 'Loretta Swann moved.'

'But she's not able to talk?'

'Let's hope that it's only a matter of time. Any luck with the CCTV?'

'Not yet,' said Jones. 'And I've only got another twenty hours or so to sit through.'

'It was a long shot.'

'I have finally got an appointment with the manager of the Wales and West Building Society. Let's hope he'll co-operate,' said Jones.

'Have CSI filed their report yet?'

Jones turned to her computer. 'It's just come in.' She read from the summary. 'Only two sets of fingerprints found at the scene. Anna Moore's and another....'

'Which matches those found at Darius Gull's place?'

'Yep. Definitely the same person.'

'So we've got someone who's confident that his fingerprints aren't on file, and he's not concerned that we'll eventually ID him. He just doesn't want it to be any time soon. How about the underwater unit?'

'They recovered an old shotgun, a lump hammer and a suitcase full of whips and dildos, but nothing connected to our case.'

There was a knock on the door. It was Floyd-the-Fish Finger.

'Sorry to interrupt, only there's a young woman downstairs. Says she's got some information about your case.'

*

The woman who sat across the interview table from Rhidian no longer looked like the simple valley girl that she used to be. Josie Hughes' fake eyelashes and bleached teeth gave her the appearance of a doll, or a Japanese cartoon. At least her tan was natural, the result of having lived on the Costa del Sol for ten years, running a taverna with her Spanish husband.

'I met Carlos when we all went on a package holiday. Ninety nine quid, all in. A dozen horny Welsh girls out to grab themselves some sun, sea and sangria.'

'Did Loretta Swann come with you?' asked Rhidian.

'No. She wasn't into that kind of thing. She was shy, see. I shared a room with her, but I don't think I ever saw her naked. She always wore baggy jumpers and trousers that did nothing to show off her figure, not that she had a lot to show off to be fair. Some of the girls called her 'the ironing board' because she was so flat-chested. It was no wonder she never got laid in the whole three years she was at uni.'

'She didn't have a boyfriend?'

'We tried to set her up with a couple of lads, but as soon as they knew it was Velma we were talking about, they didn't want to know.'

'Velma?'

'You know. The speccy one off Scooby Doo. That's who she looked like.'

‘We are talking about the same Loretta Swann?’

‘That’s why I didn’t come forward earlier. I mean, the details are right; her age, where she went to uni and that; but the photos they keep printing in the paper, they’re nothing like the frigid virgin I knew.’

Rhidian opened his notebook and slipped out the old photo that he’d taken from Loretta’s fridge door.

‘Is this her?’

‘Yeah. That would be.... summer of eighty-five. College dig at Offa’s Dyke.’

‘Do you know anything about her family?’

‘She was an only child, and her parents both died when she was in her teens.’

‘Did they leave her a lot of money?’

‘Doubt it. From what I remember, her mum didn’t work and her dad was on the ferries. They lived in a council place in Fishguard. Loretta was always short of cash. Lived on boiled rice with a few veg chucked in. Are you sure we’re talking about the same woman?’

*

The small room was dark and warm. He liked it that way. It was intimate. Private. The only illumination came from the blue light of the laptop screen. As he watched her move, silent, ghostlike in the grainy, black and white images, he felt the same familiar stirrings that always grew when he was in her presence; the tightening in his trousers, the dryness of his mouth, the quickening of his pulse.

He had edited together the best bits from the hundreds of hours of recordings that he had made of Loretta Swann. He knew every nuance of her movements; the way she walked, the swish of her long hair as she turned her head; the rhythmic sway of her hips. He often zoomed in to study a favoured part of her body; the last two vertebrae of her neck, her teeth, as tiny and perfect as pearls; the valley between her breasts when she bent over to pick up papers she had dropped.

He sometimes froze one of his favourite images, the better to savour it; like that time last summer when she spilled coffee on her blouse and had to take it off to wash the stain out in the sink, or the moment when she looked straight into the camera and he had felt their souls touch. This wasn't as good as the real thing, but until she came back to him, it would have to do. He made sure that the door was locked, then released his belt and reached for his flies.

*

After being called down to reception, Jones was surprised to find Sam waiting for her on one of the plastic seats in the waiting area.

'This is a nice surprise.'

'I've got a break from the job,' he said. 'Waiting for the plaster to go off. Hoped you might have time to grab some lunch?'

'Wish I could, only we're snowed under.'

'Thought you'd say that,' said Sam, producing a paper bag. 'So I called in at the baker's.' He passed the bag to Jones who hungrily opened it and peered inside.

'There goes the diet!' She pulled out the chocolate-topped cream éclair, took a bite and closed her eyes in bliss. She offered the pastry to Sam who just smiled and shook his head. Jones took another bite, chewing the choux pastry.

'Do you like haggis?' asked Sam.

'Never had it.'

'What about tossing the caber?'

'What are you on about?' Jones laughed and licked cream from her lips.

'How do you fancy a long weekend in Glasgow?'

'I'd love it.'

'Next weekend?'

‘I’d be lucky to get a day off, let alone the whole weekend,’ said Jones sadly.

‘They’ve got to give you a break sometime.’

‘It’s a triple murder case. There won’t be any proper time off until it’s done. I’m sorry, Sam.’ Jones sensed that there was something deeper beneath his disappointment. ‘This isn’t just about a weekend away, is it?’

‘No.’

Jones looked around and was reassured that there was nobody within earshot. ‘Talk to me.’

‘It’s not really working out for me here,’ said Sam.

‘I thought you had loads of work?’

‘Yeah. But my heart’s not really in it anymore and I’ve been thinking, maybe it’s time for a change.’

‘Change your job?’

‘I don’t want to be that old boy who can’t even climb a stepladder ’cause his knees are shot.’

‘You’re twenty-eight!’

‘And if I’ve already had enough, what does that say?’

‘What do you fancy doing?’

‘I don’t know. Run a pub. Maybe open a café?’

‘That’s harder work than the building trade.’

‘I’m not afraid of a bit of graft.’

‘Okay. But what’s wrong with looking at opportunities in Cardiff?’

‘Nothing. I like it here, I just think, if I’m going to make a change, why not make it a big one?’

‘So this weekend in Scotland would be what? A research trip?’

‘And if we like it, we could go to some estate agents; see what’s available.’

‘You want me to move with you?’

‘Of course. You can get a transfer, can’t you?’

‘I suppose...’

‘And you’ve said you’re not sure about your new boss.’

'Yeah, but...'

'And it's not like you've got anything keeping you here. You don't get on with your family.'

'I've got my friends. My rugby team.'

'They play rugby in Scotland, don't they?' He could see that this didn't convince her. 'This could be a new start; a new life for both of us.' Sam could see that she was struggling. 'I'm sorry I sprung this on you.'

'I'm not saying no. But can you give me some time?'

'Of course.' Sam leaned over to kiss her. 'I'll let you get back to it. See you later, yeah?'

Sam headed for the exit. Jones realised that Floyd-the-Fish Finger was watching from behind the reception counter. He gave her a sympathetic look. He was too far away to have overheard their conversation, so she realised that her confusion must have been showing on her face. She nodded to Floyd and headed upstairs to CID.

*

Ginnie Lane and her cameraman joined the rest of the press pack camped outside the entrance to the police station. Still flushed from the excitement of her live broadcast from the scene of Anna Moore's murder, Ginnie was pleased to see the handsome photographer mime an appreciative clap when he saw her. Journalists could be a jealous, cynical bunch, but at least he appreciated that she had done a good job. As her cameraman cadged a fag off one of the other old hands, Ginnie approached the young photographer.

'Any word on a press conference?' she asked.

'They can't keep stonewalling us, especially after the kick in the balls you've just given them.'

'You're new aren't you?'

'I normally freelance in London, but now all the action's over here I thought I'd come home for a bit.'

'Home? You don't have a Welsh accent.'

‘I was born in the Rhondda. Parents moved us all to Devon when I was a kid. And you know what they say; you can take the boy out of the valley...’

‘I bet your wife’s missing you,’ probed Ginnie, with no pretence to subtlety.

The photographer held up his left hand, which was bare of any wedding band. ‘I’m footloose and fancy-free.’

Ginnie held up her own ringless left hand. ‘Snap.’ Before she could continue, her phone starting ringing. She checked the caller ID. ‘Sorry. Got to take this.’ She stepped away, out of earshot. She might fancy the pants off the snapper, but she wasn’t going to share a scoop with him. ‘Ginnie Lane.’

‘Well done, Miss Lane. Your bosses must be very pleased with you.’

She recognised the phlegmy, condescending voice instantly. ‘Are you going to give me your name this time?’ asked Ginnie.

‘I’m going to give you an address and you’re going to be there in half an hour, or I’ll start talking to one of your rivals, okay?’

‘I’m listening.’ She headed towards her car without even a backward glance at the bemused photographer, or her cameraman, who hadn’t even noticed she was leaving.

25

Anwen Jones felt about as comfortable as a vegan in a butcher's shop. After being shown in by the receptionist who looked and walked like a catwalk model, she had been left waiting a long twenty minutes during which she couldn't help but think about Sam's offer to relocate. Needing to stay focused on the job in hand, she tried to distract herself by looking around the stark, minimalist office.

Apart from the Danish-designed, blonde wood chairs, the rest of the office was all glass and mirrors. At first, all she could think about was how difficult it must be for the cleaners to get all the smears out of all those highly polished surfaces, but it was getting harder to resist looking into the mirrors to see her every line and blemish exposed by the merciless lighting. Was that...yes, there was even the beginning of a zit on her chin! She wondered if this was part of the Chrysalis Clinic's sales technique, leaving the self-conscious client waiting for so long staring at their huge conk or flabby bellies from a hundred different angles that by the time the main man made an appearance they'd have their credit card ready and waiting, begging him to start slicing and filling ASAP.

Anwen was confident enough in her appearance. She knew that she could make more of herself, but where would she find the time? She would rather have the extra half hour in her warm bed than waste it standing in front of the mirror applying mascara and lipstick. Bored enough to pick up a brochure, she flicked through a series of Before and After photos; great beaks of noses turned into rosebuds, flat chests transformed into twin pillows of silicon delight. There was even a section of pictures of men who'd had buttock implants to give their saggy backsides more definition.

Just as Anwen was wondering what they did with the litres of liposuctioned fat they must extract, the door opened and 'the man with the golden scalpel' as the gossip columns called him, swept in. Wearing a dark-blue bespoke suit that clearly cost more than Anwen's entire wardrobe, he offered his hand. Manicured nails. Gold cufflinks in the shape of butterflies.

'Alex Sumner. Pleased to meet you.'

Jones could feel his eyes scanning her up and down, not with any sexual desire, it was purely business. Satisfied that he had identified several thousands of pounds of potential income, Sumner took his seat behind the slab of smoked glass that served as a desk.

'Sorry for the wait, but if you had made an appointment…'

'It was good of you to fit me in.'

Sumner searched his diary on the laptop. He might have frowned. It was hard to tell with the amount of Botox he must have injected into his forehead.

'Sorry. My PA didn't make a note of your name.'

'Jones.'

'I understand,' beamed Sumner, his teeth so white and perfect that they gave the illusion of being made out of glowing plastic. 'There's no need to hide behind a pseudonym here. Our records are kept in the strictest confidence. So. What brings you here today? Not breast enlargement. Nature has been most bountiful there I see. Unless it's a reduction that you are wanting.'

Jones looked at her chest. 'I only had bee stings till I was sixteen, so there's no way I'm getting rid of these now.'

'Of course. But as for the rest. We do have some very popular packages that might be of interest.' Sumner turned to the pricing information at the back of his glossy brochure. 'A tummy tuck and eye bag removal are on sale this month.' Sumner leant forward to tuck Anwen's hair to one side to get a better look at her ears. 'Or we have a two for one on ear corrections.'

'I'm not here as a client.'

'Oh?' Sumner tried to look puzzled.

Jones flashed her warrant card.

'Detective Sergeant Jones. South Wales CID'.

'If it's about those parking fines…'

'No, Mr Sumner. I'm here about Loretta Swann. She was one of your clients?'

'I couldn't possibly comment.'

Sumner flashed that plastic smile again. Anwen tried to wipe it off his face by spreading a statement from Loretta Swann's Building Society on the desk in front of him.

'We have evidence of multiple payments to the Chrysalis Clinic, spread over the last three years. All I need from you is confirmation of what the payments were for?'

'If you want to go rooting around in my files, you'll need a warrant, and I doubt if any judge will grant you one; not when several of their wives are repeat customers.'

Sumner rose.

'I'm sorry that you've wasted your time, Sergeant.'

Sumner waited for Anwen to leave and was clearly frustrated when she stayed glued to her chair. She couldn't go back to Hook with nothing. Just as importantly, she couldn't let this smarmy bastard win. It was then that she saw the copy of that morning's *Echo* on the side of Sumner's desk, with the headline '*Body Parts Taken from Murder Victims*'.

'You're probably right to be cautious,' she said, reaching for the newspaper. 'Details about this case are leaking like a busted toilet. I wouldn't want to see your name splashed all over tomorrow's front pages. "*Plastic surgeon helps police with their enquiries.*" Don't want your clients choking on their cornflakes.'

'Are you threatening me?'

'I couldn't possibly comment,' said Anwen.

She let her words stew. It didn't need long. Sumner's confident smile faded as his resolve cracked like a cheap facemask. He turned to his computer and tapped in the password to open his patients' files. He hesitated, before clicking on the Icon labelled *Swann L.*

'What do you want to know?'

'What has she had done?'

'It would be easier to list the areas that I haven't transformed. I plumped up her lips, reshaped her cheek bones, shaved her nose, enlarged her breasts and reduced her stomach. I even removed a couple of ribs so that she could achieve that hourglass figure.'

'How sad is that?'

'Sad? She's one of my finest creations.'

'She's a person, not an object.'

'All I know is, that she always left here happy.'

'And came back for more?'

'The client is always right.'

'How much money are we talking about?'

'Ball park? Seventy thousand.'

Jones whistled.

'That's way beyond her income. So where did the money come from?'

'I am paid to work miracles, not do accounts. Now, I do have work to attend to.'

'Just one last question. Where were you last Friday, between the hours of six and ten PM?'

'Why?'

'Because that's when Darius Gull was murdered.'

'Now you've gone too far.'

'We are looking for someone who's handy with a knife. Know anyone who fits that description?'

Sumner's fake tan went from Caribbean fudge to paper white in a matter of seconds.

*

Rhidian Hook was sitting in the chair, pulled up next to Loretta Swann's hospital bed. Watching the numbers on the monitor became hypnotic as her heartbeat danced somewhere between seventy and ninety beats per minute. Sister Campbell had reassured him that this was stable, and that the fact that she no longer needed the oxygen feed was a positive sign. There had been more movement; a few twitches, and she now responded to external stimulus. At one point her eyes suddenly opened, but they just stared vacantly ahead. There was no spark of consciousness in their green depths.

Although there was plenty of noise going on outside the private room, Rhidian felt strangely at peace. And then he realised why. He had been here before, or at least in another room, with a bed and a sleeping woman and a growing sense that he was in a place of safety and healing.

Life had been simpler when he was single. It was his work that drove him. There was always another twisted predator out there and it had become his mission to stop them all. He went home as little as he could get away with, but sometimes he needed to seek out a bit of 'normality' to remind himself why he put himself through all of this. He would turn up on his sister's doorstep, clutching a bunch of wilting garage flowers and a bottle of wine. She got to recognise the haunted look in his eyes and would always invite him in. But it became increasingly difficult for him to remember the small niceties that went with maintaining healthy relationships. He lost the art of making small talk about the weather or asking how the kids were getting on at school. It all came to a head at a bank holiday barbecue when the smell of burning meat triggered a flashback of the murder of a local politician whose body had been hidden inside a community bonfire. Rhidian thought that he had put the horrors behind him, but the sweet stench of crisping flesh and the sizzle of rendering fat took him straight back to the crime scene. He could see the charcoaled face of the victim, his mouth still held shut by the melting tape that had smothered his cries. It was only the sobs of his niece that brought Rhidian back into the summer garden and to the realisation that he had kicked over the barbecue before throwing up, all over the burger buns. Cerys reluctantly told her brother that she couldn't have him around her children. She knew that he didn't mean to, but he just couldn't help bringing the blackness of his work with him.

Searching for ways to purge himself, Rhidian went back to his old love of art, and rediscovered its healing properties. Listening to music or spending an afternoon in an art gallery could dispel some of the darkness of his daily world, if only temporarily.

When he met Bethan he knew that he had to change or he would risk losing this precious thing that he had found, so he committed himself to keeping his two lives separate, compartmentalised from each other. The job was always left outside the front door. He refused to bring the poison of what he had to deal with every day into the sanctity of their home. But sometimes it wasn't so easy to turn off at the end of a working day, so he would wait until Bethan was asleep, then he would sit on the floor with his back to the bed and he would tell her all about his day; the evil he had faced; the victims he had comforted, the shattered lives that he had tried to bring peace to. Sometimes this act of catharsis would lead to a breakthrough, the untangling of another knot in some twisted case. Mostly it was just a matter of unburdening his daily trials to someone who could not hear.

Normally he would have shut down any shadow of Bethan before it could form, but here, in the hospital room, it felt safe; that he could risk letting some memories in without them overwhelming him. He looked down on the dreaming woman, conscious of the hints of familiarity with Bethan; the same pale complexion, the delicate bone structure, the full lips and long neck. He wondered what Loretta's voice would sound like, or her laugh. How would her smile animate that sleeping face?

'Where are your friends?' he asked her. 'Are you lonely? Why isn't there someone to listen to how your day went?'

Rhidian had to wonder; was he speculating about Loretta Swann's life, or talking about his own? Was he any better than this comatose woman, hovering somewhere between life and death? Yes, if they wired him up to a monitor it would show that his heart was beating, that he had a pulse and a reasonable blood pressure, but it couldn't show how hollow he felt. There was no machine capable of measuring the weight of the loss which had, in his darkest moments, drained him of all desire to carry on. No scanner could visualise the hole left in his soul. He looked at the sleeping woman and was touched by jealously.

'At least you have the chance to wake up and pick up where you left off,' he told her.

Belatedly Rhidian realised that Jones was standing in the doorway.

'I've been trying to ring you,' she said.

Rhidian pulled his mobile out of his coat pocket.

'Turned it off. Hospital rules.'

'It's not like it's going to wake her,' said Jones.

'How did you know I was here?'

'Call it a lucky guess.' Rhidian heard the sarcasm in Jones's tone and wondered how much she had heard of his one-sided conversation with Loretta Swann.

'I take it you have news?' said Rhidian.

'Yeah. Think I've found where all her money went.'

'Cosmetic surgery,' said Rhidian.

Jones deflated like a pricked balloon.

'How did you know?'

Rhidian showed her the old 'Velma' photo then compared it to the sleeping woman that Loretta Swann had become.

‘Ugly ducklings don’t turn into swans overnight without at least a little help.’

Back at the station, Jones loaded the newly-acquired coffee machine with a fresh pod of Smooth Americano as Rhidian looked through the slim file of A4 sheets that she had persuaded Sumner to print off.

‘And you’re sure it’s watertight?’ he asked.

‘I double checked. Alex Sumner was definitely in Paris at the time of Darius Gull’s murder. He was key speaker at a conference. It’s all on YouTube.’

‘So we can scrub him off our list of suspects?’

‘He’s a vain, patronising arse, but that’s all.’

‘What I don’t understand is how Loretta Swann could undergo so many physical changes without any of her colleagues noticing,’ said Rhidian.

‘Men aren’t always that observant. And some of the changes would have been easy to explain away. Take the laser eye surgery that corrected her need to wear specs. She could have just said that she’d swapped to contact lenses.’

‘The breast enhancement? The liposuction?’

‘Miracle diet? She’d joined a gym?’

Rhidian agreed with a nod. ‘Have you accounted for all of the money taken from her building society?’

Jones produced Loretta Swann’s passbook and showed how it matched the invoices from the Chrysalis Clinic.

‘Each withdrawal matches one of her surgical procedures. All we need to do now, is work out where she got the money from,’ said Jones, filling a second mug with steaming coffee.

When Rhidian didn’t reply, Jones saw that he was staring at the clinic’s Before and After photographs of Loretta Swann. She was naked in both pictures, captured against a plain white background. Rhidian seemed to be most interested in the After photo, the one showing the new

Loretta Swann with her slimmed-down stomach and enlarged breasts.

'I can get them framed if you want,' said Jones sarcastically.

Rhidian didn't hear her. He was too distracted, reaching for his notebook; eagerly looking for a particular page. Jones moved closer as Rhidian stopped at the sketch he had made of the Venus statue found in Loretta Swann's bedroom, and compared it to her After photo.

'I knew there was something. See. It's the same lips, identical cheek bones.'

Now Jones could see the striking resemblance between the statue and Loretta Swann's remodelled face and body. It was as if the ancient sculptor had captured Loretta Swann's image thousands of years ago. The statue's lips were slightly curled into a knowing smile, as if enjoying Rhidian's surprise.

'It can't be a coincidence,' agreed Jones.

'The statue isn't just an ornament,' said Rhidian. 'It's a template for her transformation.'

*

When Felix awoke and saw the sunlight spearing through a gap in the curtains, he was overtaken by a surge of panic. He had no sense of what time it was. It had been the same each time. After the act it was all he could do to drag himself home, strip off his clothes then drop, exhausted, onto his bed. He tried to sit up, but every muscle, every tendon in his body was on fire. He was used to moderate levels of exercise, not the rigours of extreme physical labour.

Naked, his skin sheened by dried-up sweat from yesterday's efforts, he stumbled the few yards to his bathroom and turned on the shower, the tightness in his legs easing slightly with the movement. While he waited for the water to get hot, he padded to the kitchen sink. There, drying on the cutlery rack were the tools he had used. He must have washed them when he returned home and they had been left to dry next to his favourite tea mug.

Felix stood under the shower, feeling his fingertips prune under the hot water as he massaged the stiffness from his biceps, shoulders and thighs. His body was being used in ways he could never have imagined, but by contrast, during these bursts of exertion, his mind turned itself off. He was self-aware enough to realise that this was some kind of inner defence mechanism to enable him to carry out his work without any distractions. He was, during those moments, a machine made of flesh and muscle, being guided by a greater hand. To do what he had to do, he had to shed every vestige of civilisation to call upon something instinctual, primeval. But now he couldn't stop the memories of his gory task from coming back to him.

He had cut his nails as short as he could manage, but the image of sticky, pink matter wriggling under his fingers kept returning, so he reached for the kitchen scouring pad again. Even after using up a whole bottle of bleach, he could still smell the blood. He knew that it was just in his mind, but it was getting harder to shut out the cries, the whimpers, the crunching of bones.

What surprised him the most was that he felt no guilt, but then, he was working to a greater cause. For the first time his life had true meaning, a purpose, and he had no doubt that he was doing the right thing. On many occasions he had questioned why he hadn't achieved more. It had felt as if his life had as much direction as a leaf blowing in the wind. Now he understood that he was being saved for this one moment. He knew that he was blessed to have been chosen for this sacred task, but had he reached his limit? He didn't want to fail before his work was completed. He scrubbed at his fingers, then up his arms; almost breaking the skin in his efforts to cleanse himself.

As he towelled himself dry, he refocused. The police must be close to catching him now. He didn't need much more time. One more benefaction should do it. Just one more…

26

It seemed to Sara Bowen as if she had been waiting for this day for an eternity. The reality was, that she had only set eyes on History teacher Dillwyn Thomas the previous September when she joined the staff of St David's Academy to provide maternity cover for Miss Prothero who was off having her third baby in five years. Sara had listened to her best friend talk about how George Clooney always made her go weak at the knees. She had never experienced this sensation until that fateful lunch break when the delectable Dillwyn sat opposite her in the school canteen. She didn't know what it was that made her temperature rise every time she saw him; was it his smouldering, coal-dark eyes or his strong, square jaw? Whatever it was, she felt a burning desire for him that she had never felt for anyone before.

She had spent countless hours working out what she would say to him if they were ever alone. She would be witty and bright and a little bit flirty. But when her moment came and they were both on playground duty together, her mouth dried up, her tongue felt that it had swollen to the size of an aubergine and she couldn't string two intelligent words together.

She had tried to put him out of her mind, but would often find herself making up some excuse for why she had to pass his classroom. She would press her ear to the door, listening to the deep boom of his voice vibrating through the wood. If he was lecturing about the Crusades, she saw Dillwyn Thomas mounted proud upon a great steed, clad in armour, his mailed fist clasped around the thick hilt of a massive sword. If the subject was the Vikings, it was his buff body she saw jumping off the dragon ship into the surf, while she was the trembling maiden waiting to be pillaged.

She had waited and kept her lustful thoughts hidden, and now, finally, she would be spending the day alone with him. What that meant in practice was that she and the delicious Dillwyn were the only two adults. The rest of the party on the trip to the Mathias Museum was made up of the fifteen members of year ten who needed all the help they could get if they were going to do well in their History mocks.

The girls were only interested in checking out any tasty totty; the boys were instinctively drawn to the grossest exhibits, crowding around the exhibition case of tiny shrunken heads with cries of 'See that one. That's your mum that is.'

Sara didn't care whether year 10 were learning anything or not, as long as she could have these precious hours with the definitely shaggable Mr Thomas. What she hadn't reckoned on was a ball of snot, spots and specs, with an unquenchable curiosity. He had always been a curious child, but exposing Billy Reubin to the wonders of the museum threatened to send his brain into meltdown. He was a question machine; firing off the next before she had even finished answering the previous query.

'Could I swim faster than a turtle, miss?'

'Who would win a fight; a crocodile or a bear?'

'Miss. Where do slugs go in the winter?'

Just as Sara was about to snap, he hit her with –

'Why are those flies coming out of that sarcophagus?'

*

In the warm womb of his dark office Trevor Cassidy was master of his domain; a spider with a dozen electronic eyes watching every corner of his world, always vigilant, always hungry for a tasty titbit to stray into his web.

He had been following the pair all afternoon, predicting their moves, always one step ahead; the next camera ready to pick them up as they entered its range. The girl was sixteen, seventeen max. The boy was a similar age. She was Asian. Pretty. The boy was white. Handsome enough with his trendy, buzz cut hair and peach-fuzzed cheeks. They were with a party from a local school. It was obvious to Trevor that they had no interest in any of the exhibits. They had arrived separately. The boy with his bunch of friends, the girl with hers. It was the way that they so obviously avoided looking at each other that first set Trevor's web twitching. After getting instructions from their teacher, the kids drifted off into smaller groups, clutching clipboards. However, the boy and girl hung back as if they were actually interested in reading the information boards that told the history of the museum. As soon as the rest of the school party were out of sight, the pair headed off in the opposite direction.

Trevor tracked them through the recreation of a Neanderthal's cave and straight past the small display of dinosaur skeletons. When they didn't stop at the gift shop, Trevor knew that this was going to be good. He loosened the collar of his shirt. It was suddenly hot in the windowless room.

The boy and girl finally slowed down in the geology section. They looked around, confirming that they were alone. They had chosen well. Few people came to look at the rock samples. It might have been the finest collection outside of a national museum, but to the untrained eye it just looked like a few cabinets filled with lumps of different-coloured rock.

They were nervous at first. Perhaps this was the first time they'd dared give in to their feelings. Trevor zoomed in until he could pick out the individual buttons on the girl's white school blouse. Trevor's mouth had gone dry. He leaned closer to the screens.

The girl seemed to be in charge. She showed the boy where she liked to be touched. He was a quick learner. Soon his eager mouth was all over her neck, her lips; his hand groping for her breasts as she placed one hand on his thigh, feeling his heat through the cotton of his trousers.

Trevor was so engrossed that he nearly missed what was happening on the other monitors. Eventually the movement on monitor 3 demanded his attention. Something was going on in the Egyptian Pavilion. A crowd of kids had gathered around one of the sarcophagus exhibitions, pressing against the glass. There were too many of them. That glass was old. If it broke! Why now? Frustrated, Trevor stood and reached for his uniform jacket. Before he left, he allowed himself one more look at monitor 2. Yes, the young lovers were really going for it now as she guided his eager hand up, under her skirt. Trevor checked that the red record light was still lit on the CD burner. It was a shame that he was going to miss out on the delicious added thrill of watching the action live, but he'd come back and enjoy the recording later. Yes. Definitely one for the collection.

*

By the time Rhidian and Jones arrived at the museum, Morris Palfrey had roped off the sarcophagus to keep the public back, not that this stopped year ten from their excited speculation about what was going on.

'It'll be a mummy. Come back to life 'cos of a curse.'

'Yeah, I saw that in a film. You gotta cut their heads off to kill 'em.'

'That's zombies, you numb nuts.'

Their excitement rose when they saw the police officers approaching with Llewellyn in tow, holding up a cluster of keys of various shapes and sizes, trying to select the one that would open the glass door and give them access to the sarcophagus. Rhidian wasn't pleased to see that they were going to have an audience.

'Why haven't you closed?' he asked Llewellyn.

'Over a few flies? I'm sorry Inspector, but don't you think that this is getting just a little hysterical?'

Rhidian looked into the display. It was hard to count the flies. There must have been dozens of them. Some were walking up the inside of the glass, while others flew around in lazy circles. Whatever patience Rhidian had for the stressed Llewellyn was just about used up. 'How do you explain how they got inside an airtight cabinet?'

'Yes, that is odd,' agreed the curator. 'There's nothing organic in there to attract an insect in the first place.'

'What about the mummy?' asked Jones.

'Nothing but dust wrapped in linen. The tomb had been robbed out a hundred years ago. They tore the remains to pieces, just in case any precious jewels were hidden inside. Vandalism. Pure vandalism.'

Llewellyn finally found the correct key. As soon as he had the door of the display open, many of the bloated bluebottles took their opportunity to buzz to freedom, causing much shrieking from the teenage girls as they brushed past their faces or caught in their hair. The reinforced glass box was just large enough for all three of them to enter. Rhidian and Jones crouched to take a closer look at the heavy limestone sarcophagus lid. Carved into it was a representation of what the inhabitant of the tomb must have looked like in life. The decoration didn't have the gold leaf splendour of one of the great pharaohs, but the refined features of the young man had clearly been carved and painted by reverent, skilled hands.

Now they could see that there was a gap between the lid and the base, as if the lid had been moved and not replaced exactly into its original position, and when Rhidian leant closer to the gap, he could hear the unmistakable dull buzzing of more flies inside. He nodded to Jones. They took up their positions at the head of the long-dead prince, braced themselves and then started pushing. The lid was heavier than expected. At first it didn't budge. Then Jones really put her shoulder into it, as if she were trying to push back an opposing team in a scrum. With a grating rasp the lid started to move, inch by hard-won grinding inch until at last they had exposed a gap wide enough to look into. Several of Year 10 stepped over the ropes, ignoring Palfrey's protests, to press spotty faces up against the glass, desperate for a look at whatever horrors lay inside.

Rhidian reached into a coat pocket and pulled out a small, silver torch. Switching it on, he directed the narrow beam into the black depths of the ancient tomb. At first it looked like there was nothing there. Then the blackness moved; the light flickering off hundreds of obsidian wings as the mass of gorged flies took to the air. Jones stepped back as they buzzed past her face, but Rhidian kept the torch beam steady, to reveal what the flies had been feasting on; the death mask face of James Calder.

Rhidian played the light down the archivist's body. He was lying, hands crossed over his chest as if he were some deity from ancient times, the weight of his body crushing the more ancient corpse beneath. Only Calder's wide, fish-slab-clouded eyes and his mouth, stretched into a scream showed that this was no peaceful lying in state. A last, tardy, bloated fly crawled out onto the corpse's blue lips and rested for a moment to recover from the effort of laying hundreds of eggs somewhere deep, dark and damp.

Rhidian was only shaken from his shock when he realised that he was still surrounded by fifteen goggle-eyed teenagers, taking photos of the corpse on their phone cameras. Rhidian snapped off his torch, while Jones quickly left the glass box to begin confiscating the mobiles.

Devlin might be pleased that they had answered one mystery. Yes, they had found James Calder, but this only raised a bigger question. If he wasn't their killer, who was?

27

The last time that Rhidian had seen James Calder's body animated by life, it had been on the phone-camera footage of him using Loretta Swann as some kind of living sex doll. Seeing Calder now, lying on the mortuary table, the ragged Y scar vivid across his chest and abdomen a reminder of how Bloom had explored every inch of his body with bone shears and razor-sharp blades, it was hard not to feel some pity for him.

'What we have here is a thirty-five-year-old male. Average health. A little overweight,' said Bloom. 'His last meal was a meatball sub. No salad.'

'Cause of death?' asked Rhidian.

'Blunt trauma to the back of the head did the job,' said Bloom, gently turning Calder's head to reveal where a three by three-inch section of hair had been neatly shaved off to reveal the white of the skull, crazed around the impact site.

'Before you ask, no I can't tell you yet what the weapon was. Something with a curved end to it. That's the best I can do.'

'Some kind of specialist hammer?' asked Rhidian.

'No. This was something longer. Thinner. More of a blunt blade than a hammer head. If you find it, I'll be able to tell you, one way or the other.'

Bloom respectfully turned Calder's head back.

'What about the tattoo?' asked Rhidian. He had spotted the design on Calder's left shoulder on the home video, but the quality of the phone images hadn't been good enough to show it as anything more than just a dark blur. 'This whole thing doesn't feel like gangs...'

Rhidian saw the look of amusement play between Jones and Bloom.

'Okay. What am I missing?' he asked.

'You're not a Trekkie then, boss?'

'A what?'

'It's the symbol of the Klingon empire,' said Bloom.

'Which marks him out as a geek, not a gang banger,' said Jones.

Rhidian covered his embarrassment. 'Can we be sure that it's the same killer? Calder's body is clearly intact.'

Bloom smiled. Rhidian had fallen into his trap. Now it was the pathologist's turn to pull the proverbial rabbit out of the hat.

'The clue's in the nose. See those scratch marks? There. Inside the nostrils.'

Rhidian saw the tiny tool marks and understood the implications immediately. 'You found it? The killer would have left it somewhere close.'

'Found what?' asked Jones.

With a conjuror's flourish, Bloom turned to a bench and picked up a transparent evidence bag, containing a large yoghurt pot; peach and mango flavour. Bloom held the pot up in front of one of the spotlights. With the bright light shining through the plastic, Rhidian and Jones could see that the container was two thirds full of thin liquid.

'Water?' asked Rhidian.

'Common or garden tap water,' confirmed Bloom.

This confirmed Rhidian's theory.

'And the jelly stuff in the bottom?' asked Jones, fearing that she already knew the answer.

'James Calder's brains. Scrambled inside his skull using some kind of sharp probe, then pulled out with a hook.'

'The same technique used on the pharaohs when preparing them for mummification,' said Rhidian. 'But why? Is the killer playing games, or is this all part of some ritual that he feels driven to observe?'

Rhidian focused on the remnants of black powder on the yoghurt pot. He turned to Jones.

'Prints?'

'One very clean set. The fingerprint bureau is processing them now,' said Jones.

'They'll match the ones we've already lifted from Gull's place and Anna Moore's boat,' Rhidian said, much to the pathologist's surprise.

'So we've got a killer who comes with their own excerebration kit, but then doesn't bother hiding his fingerprints?' said Bloom.

'They must know that their prints aren't on our records,' said Rhidian. 'So for the moment they are free to carry on with, whatever this is. Revenge? Jealousy? Power? We're still in the dark as far as motive goes.'

'Well, all I can tell you is that they did a very efficient job. Do you want to see, Inspector?' Bloom offered the yoghurt pot to Rhidian for a closer look. Rhidian clearly didn't want to handle it, so Bloom passed the pot to Jones, who showed none of Rhidian's queasiness and was fascinated to test the weight of a human brain.

'This can't be a whole brain,' said Jones.

'No, indeed. One presumes that only a sample is needed for his purposes,' said Bloom.

'Where was it found?' asked Rhidian.

'Staff kitchen of the museum. In the fridge.' Bloom turned the pot around to show where *'James'* had been written on it with a thick, black felt pen. 'It was lucky that nobody felt peckish.'

'Don't think I'm going to be rushing to have a yoghurt for a while,' said Jones.

'How long has he been dead?' asked Rhidian.

'I'm still waiting on a few tests to be absolutely sure…'

'Your best guess is?'

'Seventy-two hours.'

'Which gives him the perfect alibi for the Anna Moore killing,' said Jones.

'He could hardly have been carving her up if he was already dead,' agreed Bloom.

'And the flies?' asked Rhidian.

'The killer must have dispatched his victim, then not have been able to get him into the airtight cabinet straight away. That's how the flies got to him.'

'Calder could have been attacked while the museum was still open; but then the killer had to wait until it was closed before he could move him into the sarcophagus,' said Rhidian. 'We've been scouring the country for Calder, yet he was right under our noses all the time.'

'Being passed by hundreds of members of the public who didn't know what they were looking at,' said Bloom.

With a practised movement Rhidian slipped his notebook out of his pocket. Opening it at the sketch he'd done of Rhys Pryce's body, he looked at Calder's body again. Jones was learning what Bloom already knew, that the DI needed time to get his thoughts into order. She watched Rhidian flip through the notebook to a sketch he'd made of Darius Gull's corpse; and then Anna Moore's. Finally he turned to the last drawing of the sarcophagus after he and Jones had pushed back the lid.

'The other bodies.' Rhidian excitedly showed the sequence of drawings to Jones and Bloom. 'Pryce, Gull, Moore. They were all left in plain sight. So why hide Calder?'

'Because the killer wanted us to think that Calder was the prime suspect?' suggested Jones.

'So they could buy more time? Maybe. But why? And what about the removal of the body parts. Why are they always left in water? Pryce's foot thrown into the sea...'

'Mr Gull's tongue in the fish tank,' said Bloom.

'Anna Moore's lungs left dangling in the docks,' said Jones.

'And now this. Brain matter placed in tap water,' said Rhidian looking at Calder's putty-coloured corpse. 'This isn't about sadism or torture. There's a plan here. We have all the pieces. Only the killer knows how they all fit together.'

Returning to the station, Rhidian and Jones continued their debate about the relevance of the body parts being found in water.

'You don't think it's just a coincidence?' asked Jones.

'No. Whoever's behind this is a meticulous planner. He's taken great care to harvest the trophies. He wouldn't just cast them away without a thought.'

'Who knows what goes on in the minds of these sick bastards? Perhaps he's so screwed up that he doesn't know why he's doing it?'

'Yes. It could be someone driven by inner demons that they don't understand. But wouldn't they have come to our attention before this? There are well-established red flags. Cruelty to animals as a child; arson; poor impulse control.'

'Could be drugs?' said Jones. 'There are loads of dodgy synthetics out there with pretty scary side effects.'

'Could someone high on drugs evade us so effectively while they carry out four murders?'

Jones had to accept his point.

'No. There's something more calculated going on here,' said Rhidian. 'As for the water connection, there is something… back of my mind.'

Rhidian's musings were cut off when he opened the door to their office and saw Devlin and Gunter standing in front of the nearly bare whiteboards.

'Alun. You seem to spend more time here than in your own office,' said Rhidian.

Gunter bit his tongue. Why bark back when he had the boss to do that for him?

'DI Gunter was concerned about your lack of progress,' said Devlin.

'Perhaps if DI Gunter spent less time worrying about what I'm up to he'd have his drug supplier safely locked up by now.'

'He's not the only one with concerns,' said Devlin. 'I've had complaints. Alex Sumner says that Sergeant Jones harassed him.'

'*What?*' said Jones.

'He was obstructing a murder investigation,' said Rhidian.

'I've also received a formal complaint from Lowri Pryce's agent. She claims that her client has turned to the bottle, thanks to you.'

'All I said was that it could take the edge off the pain.'

'They're threatening to sue if their TV deal collapses.'

'I hope it does,' said Rhidian. 'The loss of a loved one isn't something that should be exploited for the sake of ratings.'

Gunter couldn't resist stirring the pot. 'People are dying and you've wasted time looking for the wrong suspect, who's now turned up dead himself. You really have lost it, Hook.' Gunter turned to Devlin. 'Give me the case, before he makes the whole Force look like idiots.'

Devlin was reluctantly having to consider this, when Jones chipped in. 'We've made progress.'

'Go on,' said Devlin.

'The murders are all connected to Loretta Swann,' said Jones. Seeing that she had Devlin's attention, Jones turned to Rhidian for him to expand. All that she got for her troubles was a flash of anger fired in her direction before Rhidian reluctantly turned to Devlin.

'We believe that the killer is out for revenge against the people he thinks have harmed her,' said Rhidian. Seeing that Devlin wanted more, he continued. 'Rhys Pryce caused the accident that put her in a coma. Darius Gull made sure that his client avoided any blame. Anna Moore's negligence led to Professor Swann going into respiratory failure.'

'And James Calder?' asked Devlin.

'He'd been coercing her into having sex with him,' said Jones.

'Coerced, how?'

'We don't know yet,' said Rhidian.

Gunter's face was going redder by the minute as he tried to contain his frustration. 'There are four bodies. How many more need to rack up before you realise that you've got the wrong man on this job?'

Devlin had made her mind up. 'If there's anything you need, Rhidian.'

'Just the space to do our jobs.' He didn't need to look at Gunter to make his point.

As soon as Devlin and Gunter had left, Rhidian turned on Jones.

'I didn't need your help.'

'What?'

'You shouldn't have volunteered information that I hadn't cleared.'

'Devlin needed to hear that we were getting somewhere.'

'Not your choice to make. I am the senior investigating officer.'

'And you would have been investigating diddly squat if she'd taken you off the job.'

Rhidian grudgingly had to accept this. 'I didn't want to lay our whole case out in front of Alun Gunter. So next time, follow my lead. Right?'

Not trusting what she might say in reply, Jones just nodded.

'Let's get back to the Mathias. See if we can't find out how one of their staff ended up as an exhibit without anyone noticing.'

28

They drove in the direction of the Mathias Museum in silence, the argument hanging over them like a cloud. Jones had just driven over the Llandaff Bridge when Rhidian shouted 'Stop!' Jones stamped on the brakes, then had to wrestle with the steering wheel to stop going into a skid on the wet tarmac. Before she could ask what was wrong, Rhidian was out of the car, running back down the road before jumping the low metal barrier and disappearing into the trees. Jones pulled off the road, put her hazard warning lights on, then jumped out to follow.

Jones pushed through bushes and brambles that snagged at her jeans and leather jacket, finally bursting out of the thicket to find herself on the stony bank of the Taff to see Rhidian Hook wading out into the rain-swollen river. The water was already up to his knees. He was struggling against the strong flow but kept on going.

'What the hell?' muttered Jones. 'Boss!' she called over the gushing noise of water over rocks. Whether he heard her or not, Rhidian just kept pushing forward. The water was now up to his thighs. Jones cursed under her breath. 'This is not what I signed up for.' She followed him into the river.

It took a few steps before she got used to keeping her balance on the slick, weed-covered stones that formed the riverbed. By then the waterproofing of her boots had been breached and her toes were already going numb from the cold.

By the time she got to him, Rhidian had stopped dead, the water up to his waist, and he was staring at the opposite bank where something off-white in colour had been caught in overhanging blackberry brambles.

'What is it?'

It was as if her words woke him from a dream. Now that he could tell that it was only an old piece of plastic sheeting blown in off one of the neighbouring farms Rhidian let Jones take his arm and help him back to the riverbank.

In the car, Jones turned the heating up to max. From the boot she had produced two brown blankets and luminous police tabards which they put on to prevent hypothermia from setting in. For several minutes only the drone of the heater filled the awkward silence. Jones could bite her tongue no longer.

'If you want to top yourself, that's your business. But how about doing it when I'm not around so I don't have to get my chuff wet trying to save you?'

'If I wanted to end it all, don't you think I would have come up with a better idea than trying to drown myself in the Taff?'

'So, what? You just fancied a paddle?'

'I thought I saw something.'

'Like what?'

Rhidian had seen enough of his new sergeant's curiosity to know that she wasn't going to let this go until he gave her an answer. He reached into his pocket. Relieved to see that the water hadn't reached his notebook, he flipped through the pages until he came to a dog-eared photo he had taken the night of their fateful car crash. Bethan had looked radiant when she came out of the bedroom. The light bounced off the ivory dress, making her skin glow and putting a sparkle into her eyes. Rhidian begged her not to move, then fetched the camera. Just as he pressed the shutter she put on a Marilyn Monroe pout which made him laugh. If only he'd known that it was the last picture he would ever take of her…

Jones now understood how, in the dimpsey light, the off-white plastic caught in the brambles could have been mistaken for an ivory dress.

'They must have searched the river?' she said.

'They had teams out for days, but it was in flood. If she got as far as Cardiff Bay, the tide would have taken her out into the estuary. It's no wonder they never found her.'

'But you haven't given up hope?'

'I know she's gone. Most of the time.'

Rhidian closed the notebook and put it away in his pocket. Pleased that he had been so open with her, Jones decided that there was no need to share any of this with Alun Gunter.

In the Egyptian Pavilion, Jones slipped on a fresh pair of nitrile gloves as Rhidian questioned Cassidy about the CCTV camera covering the sarcophagus, which was still cordoned off with police tape.

'It's been down for two days,' said Cassidy. 'I did tell Llewellyn.'

'How long does it take him to get something like that fixed?'

'Depends on how much budget he's got.'

'Do the cameras malfunction often?'

'It has been an issue. Some of them are pretty old. Bound to have the odd glitch.'

'And this "glitch" just happened to take place at the same time that a body was being disposed of?'

Morris Palfrey arrived with a stepladder. Jones climbed the steps to examine the camera while Rhidian took the opportunity to question the caretaker.

'The body must have been put there while the museum was closed. How come you didn't hear anything?'

'My flat's on the other side of the building,' said Palfrey. 'And I like to have my opera cranked up loud. Once

I've got my Verdi on, a bomb could go off and I wouldn't hear it.'

'And there's been no sign of forced entry to the museum?'

'Not as far as I can tell.'

'How many sets of keys are there?'

'All the staff have keys to the rear entrance. Only myself, Mr Cassidy and Professor Llewellyn have keys to the front entrance and all the other internal locks.'

Rhidian made a mental note to check Loretta Swann's effects to see if her key to the museum was still among them, or had her secret visitor been making use of her access to the museum?

'There are the skylights of course,' said Cassidy. 'It would be tricky, shimmying up one of the drainpipes then coming over the roof, but not impossible.'

'Have you had trouble with intruders before?' asked Rhidian.

'No. I have mentioned the roof to Professor Llewellyn, warned him that it might be a weak spot. See, it's not just thieves you've got to worry about these days. You've also got the repatriation brigade to consider. You know, people who think that ancient artefacts should be returned to their home country. Some of them are pretty militant. They wouldn't shy away from a bit of breaking and entering if it achieved their aims.'

Jones called down from the ladder. 'The lead's been disconnected.'

'Could it have fallen out?' asked Rhidian.

'No. It's a bayonet connection. Had to have been done deliberately.'

'Okay. Leave it for CSI.'

Jones climbed down the ladder. Rhidian turned to Cassidy. 'We'll let you know if we have any more questions.'

Cassidy nodded and left. Rhidian and Jones waited until Palfrey had folded up the ladder and carried it away.

'He played it cool,' said Jones.

'Cassidy? But if he had done it, wouldn't he have just reconnected the lead?' said Rhidian.

'I liked the way he tried to muddy the waters with all that guff about someone using the skylights. Forensics have already checked the roof. There's no sign that anyone's been up there for years.'

'So. Llewellyn or Cassidy. Who's your money on?' asked Rhidian.

'Both of them make my flesh creep.'

'Unfortunately we can't take your instinctive revulsion to the CPS.'

'I'd like to take a closer look into Professor Llewellyn's life,' said Jones.

'Good idea. I'll get straight onto it.'

'And what am I going to be doing? Trawling through more CCTV footage I suppose?'

'You're going to concentrate on Cassidy.'

'Oh. Right. Tidy.'

'Unless you need me to hold your hand?' asked Rhidian, amused by her surprise.

'No. I've got it.'

'Good.'

Rhidian walked away. Jones was reminded of the tatty feral cat that came into her garden. It took months to earn his trust. She remembered her satisfaction the first time he took a slice of cooked ham out of her hand. They were never going to be best pals, but at least he didn't try and scratch her anymore.

*

Anwen Jones always felt a growing sense of pride when she approached the seat of the Welsh Parliament, or the Senedd as it had been renamed. As the impressive undulating roof of steel and timber loomed into view like some giant manta ray soaring out of the bay to spread its protective wings over the glass frontage, she remembered her school trip to see the construction of the skeleton of the building that would come to symbolise so much for so many proud Welsh men and women.

Okay, so the leaders sometimes made poor decisions, but at least they were *their* decisions, and weren't imposed upon them by an English Parliament. And yes, they didn't have full autonomy to run the country as they would like, but most agreed that it was at least a start along the long road to eventual full and true independence.

Climbing the steps to the main entrance, Jones had to remind herself that this wasn't the time to enjoy the award-winning architecture. She headed through 'The Hall' and approached the impressive slate and glass reception desk. She had phoned ahead, so Human Resources were expecting her. Jones was hoping for a cup of tea and a Welsh cake in the café. Instead, she was directed to an office on the second floor where she soon found herself sitting opposite a young woman who seemed to be proof that life-like androids had infiltrated society; or at least the HR department of the Welsh government.

'Trevor Cassidy,' said Jones.

The woman tapped some buttons on her laptop, calling up a file that Jones couldn't see because the screen was deliberately turned away from her.

'He worked here for six years. In 2016 he was promoted to Deputy Head of Security,' said the woman in a surprisingly human voice.

'Why did he leave?'

'His file just says that he gave a month's notice and left our employ.'

'So he wasn't sacked?'

'No.'

'He wasn't asked to leave?'

'He was given a glowing reference.'

'May I see it?'

'That's confidential I'm afraid.' Her mouth formed into the shape of a smile but there was no warmth in it. It was just a well-practised manipulation of certain muscles.

'Can I speak to Mr Cassidy's boss?'

'Sorry.' That robotic smile again. 'Annual leave.'

Jones wondered if the woman's fixed grin hurt her face or were the muscles so used to that inane expression that it came naturally now?

'Don't you think it's strange?' asked Jones.

The woman just blinked. Her eyes were cold and blue. It was like looking into ice cubes.

'Why would he go from a position of authority, here in the heart of the Welsh government, to working in a private museum?' asked Jones.

'Perhaps he fancied a change?'

Jones knew that she wasn't going to get anything more out of this interview. But if she couldn't get any joy through going down the official channels, the only option was to seek out the people who really knew what was what.

Jones found the smokers and vapers in a huddle around the back of the building. She didn't beat about the bush. Either they would know why Trevor Cassidy left or they wouldn't. Tucked out of sight they would be free to talk. There was no all-seeing-HR Terminator to eavesdrop on them here.

'Cassidy. Yeah. I remember him,' said a data inputter who seemed to have grown his floppy hair long to cover the acne that dotted his brow. 'He was always on your case. Threatened to report you if you didn't have your security pass visible at all times.'

'He gave me the creeps,' said a girl with pink hair whose uniform identified her as one of the café staff.

'In what way?' asked Jones.

'He was always there, always watching.'

'He was a security guard,' said Jones, playing devil's advocate.

'Yeah, but this was more than being professional,' said the girl. 'One time, right, the café had closed for the day and I was in the kitchen on my own when suddenly I felt this breath on the back of my neck and it was him, Cassidy. I asked him what he was doing there, and he said that he knew that I was hanging about, waiting for him, so that we could be alone.'

'Did he try to touch you?' asked Jones.

'He didn't get a chance 'cause one of the other girls came in. If she hadn't....' The girl shuddered.

'I know why he left,' piped up a Goth who was in her late fifties, but it was a good look for her. She pursed her black painted lips and blew out a cloud of cherry-flavoured smoke. 'He was obsessed with one of the PAs.'

'Go on,' said Jones.

'I can't remember her full name. Ruth something. Pretty little thing. She was engaged to a paramedic. I remember her showing us the ring. Only that didn't stop Cassidy from chasing after her.'

'What did he do?'

'Oh there were bunches of flowers left on her desk. Boxes of chocolates. Even a giant teddy bear once.'

'And you're sure it was Cassidy?'

'Oh he didn't make any secret of it. He said they were meant to be together. That they were soulmates.'

'And he wouldn't take no for an answer?'

'At first she was too kind. Tried to let him down easy, you know. Maybe that encouraged him. Being in security, he always had an excuse to look in her bag or escort her to the car park. In the end her fiancé threatened to come down and sort him out, only Ruth was worried that she would be the one who got fired or that her bloke would end up getting arrested.'

'What happened?'

'She had no choice. Had to make an official complaint. That same evening when she went to go home she found that her car had been vandalised. Every tyre slashed; threats scratched into the paintwork.'

'How did they know it was Cassidy?'

'They couldn't prove it, but by then there was more than enough evidence of his "improper conduct". Nobody wanted a scandal, so it was agreed that they would hush it all up. Ruth was compensated for the damage to her car.'

'And Cassidy?'

'Way I heard it, they told him he could resign with a good reference, or they'd sack him and he'd struggle to get another job.'

'Does Ruth still work here?' asked Jones.

'No. She left not long after Cassidy. Said she needed a fresh start. Last I heard she'd moved to Norfolk. Think she wanted to put as much distance between her and that creep as she could.' The woman took a big suck on her electronic cigarette.

Jones was left wondering whether Loretta Swann had also become the object of Trevor Cassidy's unrequited lusts, and what he was capable of doing to anyone who got in the way of them.

29

Huw Llewellyn wasn't at work, so Rhidian headed for his 1930s semi, just off the high street in Dinas Powys, a pleasant village five miles outside of Cardiff. Although a lot of new houses had been built in recent years, the heart of the old village remained largely unspoiled and was still a traditional mix of small, independent shops, pubs and restaurants. Rhidian hadn't phoned ahead, preferring the element of surprise.

Caryl Llewellyn had never entertained a police officer in her lounge before. She offered him tea. It was only when she came to pour it that she realised she hadn't put any bags in the pot. Was her nervousness middle-class embarrassment at having a detective inspector on her settee, or was it because she was hiding her husband's guilty secret?

'He'll be working late,' she said.

'And if I told you that he wasn't at the museum?'

Caryl considered, then nodded, resigned. Rhidian got a sense that, beneath the appearance of calm that she was trying to project, she was as fragile as one of the bone china tea cups that he was sure only came out for special guests.

'Is he often late home?'

'Twice, maybe three times a week.'

'What do you think he's doing?'

'All I know is that money's been going missing from our joint account.'

'And you have no idea what he's been spending it on?'

'Well, it's not me, that's for sure. I can't remember the last time he took me out. We haven't had a proper holiday for years. Sometimes, when he comes back, there's a smell clinging to his clothes.'

'Perfume?'

'Not exactly. Something, I don't know. Like spices?'

‘How long has this been going on?’ asked Rhidian.

‘Six months. Maybe more.’

‘And you think he’s having an affair?’

‘That’s normally why a man changes his behaviour, isn’t it?’

Rhidian didn’t disagree.

‘Why are you so interested?’ asked Caryl. ‘It’s a private matter.’

‘Who do you think he’s been seeing?’

‘If you’d have asked me last month, I would have said it was her, the “wonderful Professor Swann”. When she joined the museum she was all he could talk about. How brilliant she was. How talented. But then she had that car accident and he’s still staying out, so he can’t have been carrying on with her, can he?’

‘And you’ve never challenged him?’

‘I’ve got my book club, choir, the WI.’

‘And has keeping busy stopped all of your questions?’

Her hesitation told Rhidian to give her another nudge. ‘Isn’t it time to find out, once and for all?’

Caryl busied herself with tidying away the tea things. Rhidian gave her the space to decide whether her need for answers outweighed her embarrassment. His patience was rewarded.

‘I’m not proud of it, but the other night, I followed him. I was going to ask her why she had to steal someone else’s husband. I was going to tell him that he had to choose; her or me. In the end, I turned around and drove home.’

Rhidian understood. ‘You were too frightened of his answer?’

‘What if he chose her? I couldn’t risk it. I couldn’t just throw away thirty years.’

Caryl put the tea cups on the tray and took them to the kitchen. Rhidian thought that he’d got as much as he was going to get out of her, until she returned to give him a Post-it note with an address written on it.

‘Whatever you find out, I don’t want to know,’ she said, handing over the note.

*

Jones put her hood up as she turned the corner and entered the street where Trevor Cassidy lived. One of her uncles and some cousins lived across the road. She didn’t want them to see that she was on duty and kick off. The Cassidys were at number five, the last in a short row of Housing Authority bungalows built for the less mobile. Jones looked down the road, checking that her backup was ready. A flash of the headlights from the unmarked car told her they were in position. She felt the reassuring weight of the police radio in her pocket. One word or a click on the emergency button would have three big CID constables running to her aid, should she need them.

Jones rang the doorbell, and, when she saw a shadowy shape approach through the frosted glass, pushed the hood back away from her face.

‘Mrs Cassidy?’ Jones asked the instantly suspicious woman who opened the door. ‘Is Trevor home?’

‘No.’

‘Any idea when he might be back?’

‘Who’s asking?’ said the woman who must have been halfway through a home dye job as she had a stained towel over her shoulders and her hair was slick with a sticky crimson colourant. Her features might have been pleasant, if it didn’t look like they had been set in concrete by a life full of woes. She shuffled her slippered feet closer to better take in Jones. Then her scowl thawed, taking ten years off her age.

‘Well I never. What’s your name, butt?’

‘Anwen Jones.’

Before she could pull out her warrant card, Mrs Cassidy ushered her in.

'Don't stand there getting cold. Come in. Come in.' Jones was pleasantly surprised. The police didn't normally get such a warm welcome on the estate.

The living room was a decent size, but was made to look smaller because of the many glass cabinets filled with trophies. Jones leaned in for a closer look. All had been awarded to Trevor for weightlifting or bodybuilding. The dates showed that he'd been collecting them ever since he'd left school.

'Where's he been hiding you then?' asked Mrs Cassidy. 'I knew it was only a matter of time. Leaving it a bit late if you ask me, but there's still time to make me a grandma.'

Belatedly Jones realised that she was on the wrong end of a misunderstanding.

'Mrs Cassidy, I'm a policewoman. A detective sergeant.'

'That's no surprise to me, dear.'

'It isn't?'

'Trevor's wanted to be a copper since he was a tot. He was so disappointed when his application was rejected. But now he's gone and bagged himself a detective sergeant no less.'

Jones knew she was treading on thin ice as far as correct procedure went, but could she really turn down this chance to search for potential evidence of murder without having to obtain a warrant?

'I wonder, might I have a look around his bedroom?' she asked.

'It does need a feminine touch. First thing I'd do; get rid of that mattress. The springs won't be up to taking the two of you.' Mrs Cassidy winked like a saucy character from a *Carry On* film.

The bedroom was a strange jumble of adult and teenager. A basic metal shelving unit displayed a collection of hand-painted orcs and dragons alongside large tubs of weight gain supplement. A dogfight of model planes was suspended from the ceiling in a miniature recreation of the Battle of Britain, with Airfix Spitfires taking on the German Messerschmitts. The RAF was winning of course. One wall was dominated by a full-length mirror, flanked by posters of a young Arnold Schwarzenegger in his Mr Universe days on one side, and a collection of reproduction weapons on the other. This included a samurai sword, a WW2 bayonet and a vicious, multiple-edged weapon that Jones thought came under the classification of 'zombie knife'. Was she looking at potential murder weapons? There were no obvious signs of blood on any of the blades, but only a forensic examination would tell.

The whole room was as messy as a fifteen-year-old's. Clothes were strewn over the floor. Empty energy drink cans dotted every surface. There was a box of man-sized tissues next to the bed that she definitely wouldn't be getting too close to. Then something struck her. Why was one corner so neat? She stepped over dirty socks and a misplaced size nine trainer to look more closely at the set of shelves on which were neatly arranged dozens of DVD cases. These weren't the action movies she had expected, but plain DVDs burnt off on a home computer, labelled down the spines with a date which she presumed referred to when they had been recorded. She selected one at random. The disc itself was plain, except for the initials *'L.S.'* written on it in black felt pen. Jones turned on the desktop computer and inserted the disc into the carriage.

She found herself watching images taken from the Mathias Museum's CCTV system. The focus of the images was Loretta Swann. The cameras followed her, cutting from one to the next as she moved through the public areas. When she stopped, the camera zoomed in, focusing on a flash of cleavage or her skirt tightening as she bent over.

Jones looked at some of the other DVD cases, confirming that they were also marked *'L.S.'* Before she could decide what to do with this new information, she heard the front door open and close, then Trevor's voice from the other room.

'Hi mam. Got your medicine.'

'Ta, love. And have you got something to tell me?'

'Like what?'

'No need to be shy. She seems like a nice girl. And a policewoman as well.'

'What are you on about?'

Jones opened the bedroom door to see the puzzled Trevor Cassidy standing in the middle of the lounge, still clutching his mum's medicine; a litre bottle of supermarket own label gin.

'Hello, Trevor,' said Jones.

'What are you doing in there?'

'I think we've got a few things to talk about, don't you?' said Jones.

'Don't go having a lovers' tiff already,' chided Mrs Cassidy, turning to Jones. 'Are you staying for tea?'

Jones didn't want to upset Mrs Cassidy any more than she had to, so was happy to play along with her delusion, for now.

'Should we take a little ride in my car first, Trevor?' she said.

Trevor was looking past her; clocking how some of his meticulously organised DVDs were out of sequence. Seeing the growing rage on his face, Jones reached around to her back pocket where she had stuffed a pair of handcuffs, just in case. Trevor was bearing down on her, fast. Jones instinctively stepped back, into the bedroom. He followed her in and pushed the door closed behind him with his foot.

'You shouldn't have touched them.'

A Lancaster bomber exploded into plastic splinters as Cassidy swung the gin bottle. Jones jumped back to avoid the blow and pulled out her radio to press the emergency button to summon help, only for it to be knocked out of her hand and sent flying across the room by a backhanded swing of the bottle. Jones wished she had brought some CS spray. Then she spotted the can of Rhys Pryce's *Back of the Net* deodorant. She snatched it off the shelf, flipped off the lid, and held it out at arm's length, making sure that the nozzle was pointing at Trevor.

'Calm down or I will spray you.'

'Go on then. Do it!' shouted Trevor, spittle flying from his mouth. As he lunged forward, Jones covered her nose and mouth and hit the trigger. The cloying, sweet musky aerosol sprayed into Trevor's eyes. A direct hit. But the spray soon fizzled out. She realised that the can was too light. It must have been down to its last few CCs. She dropped the empty can, hoping that this had taken the fight out of Trevor, but he just glared at her through his screwed-up, hate-filled eyes and Jones knew that it was time for plan B; negotiation.

'Okay, Trevor. This hasn't gone too far…yet. Why don't you put the bottle down, then we can talk.'

Cassidy only took a firmer grip on the neck of the bottle.

'This is my personal space.'

Jones couldn't stop herself. 'You didn't worry much about Loretta's Swann's personal space, did you?'

'You had no right!'

Cassidy's face was turning purple with rage. Jones had a split second to decide. Make a move for the radio, or try tacking him head on? He had a weight advantage over her, but Jones calculated that, like many gym bunnies, he was all bulk. It would be a case of his muscle versus her agility. Jones reckoned that she could stay out of range of his gin-bottle-club. It was essential that she stayed between him and the wall full of knives. If this was going to work, she had to make him mad enough to make a mistake.

‘What’s the matter, Trevor? Can’t you get a real woman?’

Seeing Cassidy’s eyes blaze, she knew that her words had done the trick. When he lunged for her, Jones neatly sidestepped. In the same movement she stamped with all of her strength onto the sensitive spot on the top of his foot. Cassidy howled in pain. She hoped he would drop the bottle. Instead he looked for the nearest hard object – the corner of a chest of drawers, smashed the bottle, then held up the jagged bottle neck, pointing it at Jones’s face. She had to stop this, now. Scanning the room she saw what she needed. As Cassidy brought his arm back, ready to swipe at her with the broken bottle, she reached for a tub of bodybuilder’s protein powder, ripped off the lid and flung the contents into his face. Cassidy took in lungfuls of powder before he could shut his mouth. More went into his eyes. Jones used his temporary blindness to make a move for her radio, but Cassidy felt the movement in the air and reached out to grab her. She twisted away, and in doing so, Cassidy lost his balance, tripped over his Playstation 4, and fell with a sickening clunk of skull meeting five-kilo dumb bell. It couldn’t be a worse time for the door to open and Mrs Cassidy to arrive. She had quickly rinsed out her hair and was carrying a tray of tea and biscuits.

‘I hope you like a chocolate digestives. They’re Pound Shop, but taste just like the real thing.’

Mrs Cassidy’s smile faded as she took in the sight of her son prone on the floor with blood pooling under his head.

‘Nine nine nine,’ said Jones.

‘What have you done to my baby?’

‘Ambulance. Now!’

Stirred from her shock, Mrs Cassidy and the rattling tea tray headed for the phone. Jones crouched to touch Trevor’s neck. He had a pulse. She rolled him into the recovery position, but she wouldn’t relax until the paramedics got there.

*

Rhidian was surprised to find that the address given to him by Mrs Llewellyn led not to some swanky hotel, lap dancing club or massage parlour, but to a trading estate on the Newport road. Not the most romantic setting for an affair. Unit 5 was set between a discount tyre fitter's and a wholesale Chinese supermarket. There was no sign to identify what services were supplied out of Unit 5. There was just a plain door and a bell which Rhidian pressed, then waited, wondering what could bring a museum curator here, two or three times a week? His question was answered when the door was opened by a middle-aged woman wearing gold sandals and a white toga. Her dark hair was piled up high and her eyes were heavily kohled. However, the image of an ancient Roman woman was somewhat spoiled by the cigarette hanging out of the corner of her mouth and her broad Cardiff accent.

'All right or what?' she said.

'I'm looking for Huw Llewellyn,' said Rhidian.

'Think you're in the wrong place, darling.'

She was just about to close the door when Rhidian held up his warrant card.

'Detective Inspector Hook.'

'There's nothing illegal going on here.'

'I know he's in there,' said Rhidian. The woman just took another drag on her cigarette. 'I'm not going anywhere until I've spoken to him.'

The woman blew out a perfect smoke ring, then retreated inside, leaving the door open for Rhidian to follow.

Inside, the unit looked like any other. The front door led into an area that was bare except for a few cheap plastic chairs which suggested a reception area. However, the magnolia-painted partition walls were bare. There were no posters, no corporate logos or framed photographs of 'Employee of the Month' to give any hint as to what went on within these four walls.

Rhidian's eye was drawn to a trail of sand spilt on the floor, and then he felt the heat coming from the other side of an inner door. The woman dropped her cigarette in the sand, rubbed it out with a sandalled foot and opened the door. Rhidian followed and stepped straight back into ancient Rome.

The whole space had been transformed into the interior of a Roman villa, complete with Doric columns, a tinkling fountain and statues of assorted deities. Rhidian thought that he recognised Vulcan, god of the underworld, and Diana with her bow and hunting dog at her feet. He tapped on one of the walls. Although it was painted to look like marble, it was plasterboard; the statues were fibreglass. The plants and sand were real, but the mosaic floor tiles depicting Neptune surrounded by dolphins was very cleverly printed lino. Large lights mounted high up on a gantry that ran around the edge of the ceiling mimicked the light and heat of an Italian summer. In the centre of the room was a raised dais covered in large, red silk pillows, in the middle of which lounged Huw Llewellyn, resplendent in a gold-trimmed toga and with a laurel leaf wreath circling his bird's egg of a head. Eyes blissfully closed, Llewellyn held out a silver goblet.

'Cassia. More wine. *Cito. Festina.*'

Before the woman could act, Rhidian stepped forward, picked up the ewer and poured wine into the professor's goblet. It was only when the liquid overflowed down his fingers that Llewellyn opened his eyes, and nearly spilt the rest of the wine when he saw Rhidian standing over him.

'What! How? You can't be here.' The last vestiges of the image of all powerful emperor faded fast.

'He's a copper,' said 'Cassia'.

'You didn't have to let him in, you plebeian.'

'Talk to me like that again and that'll be the last grape I peel for you, emperor or no emperor.' Cassia turned and flounced away, leaving the embarrassed Llewellyn to face Rhidian alone.

'It's not what you think,' said Llewellyn.

'And what do I think?'

'It's not about sex.'

'Then what is it about?'

Llewellyn didn't hold out much hope that a mere policeman would understand, but he had to try. 'Do you ever feel that you were born in the wrong age, Inspector?'

'I can't say that I've ever given it much thought.'

'The twenty-first century just isn't for me. The noise, the incessant pace of life. Is it so wrong to want to live in simpler times?'

'So you decided to turn one small part of Cardiff into ancient Cambria?'

'It's no different from people who dress up as Cavaliers and Roundheads. Only rather than rolling around in muddy fields we stage debates and hold bacchanalia,' said Llewellyn. 'Oh I know this is just a fantasy, but a few hours here and all my stress evaporates. And with everything that's been going on... this place has saved me.'

Llewellyn looked around his mock villa. The thought of losing it was too much. 'Surely you don't need to tell anyone else about this.'

'Frankly, I have no interest in what you get up to in your spare time, as long as it's not the murder and mutilation of one of your employees, among others.'

'You cannot be serious, Inspector.'

'Do you want to change first, or do you want to go to the police station dressed like that?'

Llewellyn looked at his toga and sandals and decided that full co-operation was his best option. 'Do you know when James Calder was killed?' he asked.

'Somewhere between seven PM and eleven last Saturday.'

'Then I've got an alibi. I was here.'

'Witnesses?'

‘Plenty. We had the whole senate here that night. All respectable members of society.’

‘So you can supply me with a list of names?’

‘Is that really necessary?’

‘This is a murder investigation.’

‘Some of our regulars like to keep a low profile.’

‘I think you’ve already wasted enough of my time, don’t you, Professor?’

Rhidian passed over his notebook and fountain pen. As he watched Llewellyn start his list of names, Rhidian wondered how Mrs Llewellyn was going to take the news that her husband hadn’t spent their money on a mistress but on indulging a fantasy life that had no place for her. He couldn’t help wondering whether their marriage wouldn’t be healthier if he’d only asked his wife to peel his grapes.

Rhidian understood that murder investigations often took him into unfamiliar worlds. This was definitely one of the strangest. If Rhidian needed anything to confirm his suspicions that the museum curator was not a killer, it was the sight of the pale-fleshed man perched on the edge of a chaise, using the sleeve of his toga to wipe sweat from his brow as his soft, fat fingers forced the pen to give up the names of the other sad men who struggled to live in the modern world.

30

Rhidian crossed over the road. Passing the Welsh Craft Shop selling love spoons and souvenir tea towels featuring maps of the country or women in traditional dress playing harps, he approached the familiar black beams and white plaster façade of the hundred-year-old Goat Major pub.

Pushing through the main doors, he paused on the threshold to take in the familiar sight of the long, curved bar built of lovingly-polished dark wood and gleaming brass foot and hand rails, the latter being attached to the bar by the curling trunks of elephant heads. It was all as he remembered it. The floor was made of original red, black and cream tiles. The walls were adorned with framed photos of regimental mascots through the years.

The pub's name was taken from the soldier in charge of the mascot of the Royal Welsh Regiment. The tradition of having a goat as a regimental mascot dated back to the Crimean War. The goat, resplendent with his curled horns tipped by silver, was a regular visitor to the pub before he went on his ceremonial duties at international rugby matches where he led the army band and the national team onto the pitch.

Rhidian was reassured to see that the pub hadn't changed since the first time his dad brought the family here to celebrate how well Rhidian had done in his GCSE exams and Cerys' success at being chosen to play Juliet for her school's annual production.

Taking his beer to one of the green leather booths, Rhidian settled down, supped his pint and tuned out the modern noises of an inner city pub to let his thoughts slip back into the past.

At his comprehensive school, Rhidian had shone. He was blessed with a natural talent for art, but he was also top of his class in anything that involved lateral thinking. Despite his obvious talents, Rhidian's form tutor became concerned that having too many potential career paths meant that the boy was struggling to decide what to do next. His mother knew that he was good enough to secure a place at even the most prestigious art school, so she helped him put together a portfolio of work to support his application. She encouraged him to aim high. Why not The Slade or St Martin's? She was looking forward to visiting so they could spend time going around the London galleries together.

Unlike many of his classmates who spent their spare time reading the adventures of Spiderman or Batman, Rhidian devoured books on the lives of Pablo Picasso and Edvard Munch. But even the works of the great artists weren't enough to distract him from his other interest. At night, he would go to the coat rack where his dad's uniform jacket always hung. He would take out his police notebook and pore over the details of the day's operations that Sergeant Hook had been involved in. The last time he did this, several pages were taken up by the search for Pauline Jackson, a nine-year-old girl who had gone missing on the way to school. On the next page were details of a prolific shoplifter who was back to her old tricks, stealing tinned ham from Woolworths, and the description of a VW campervan that had failed to stop when a beat officer tried waving it down because of a broken headlamp.

Lili knew that Geraint wanted his son to follow in his footsteps and join the police force. However, as Rhidian grew older, Geraint's enthusiasm cooled. Lili finally asked him about it one night as they got ready for bed. Geraint had to admit that although he would be the proudest man alive to see Rhidian pass out from the Cwmbran Police Training Centre, he had reluctantly come to the conclusion that his son had too much of his mother in him. He was just too sensitive. Whatever path Rhidian chose, Geraint would support him all the way.

Rhidian would never forget the day that he was called out of school in the middle of double history. One of their neighbours, Mrs Lewis, was waiting in the headmaster's office to take him home. She wouldn't say what was going on, but she smiled too much, and for some reason that made him nervous. As they walked up the front path to his house, Rhidian could hear the cries of his mother coming from inside. All that Mrs Lewis would tell him was that Cerys was spending the night with her best friend. Because Rhidian didn't have any close friends, they had no choice but to bring him home.

Even though the door to the lounge was closed, he could hear hushed male voices from within between his mother's sobs. He couldn't make out what they were saying, but the soothing tones suggested that they were trying to calm his mother. Mrs Lewis flapped about. Did Rhidian want something to drink? Was he hungry? Did he want her to do him a pop tart?

After an hour or two, his mother's crying ceased and Rhidian watched two grim-faced police officers leave the house. The man that he recognised as the Chief Superintendent put a leather-gloved hand on Rhidian's shoulder and told him to look after his mother.

Rhidian's mother was too devastated to tell him many details of what had happened, so Rhidian took to going to the newsagent's every day to read the full story as it was gradually revealed in local and national newspapers over the next few days. Sergeant Geraint Hook had been on routine patrol when he spotted a VW campervan that had been mentioned in the previous day's morning briefing. The vehicle was parked on derelict land behind a gas holder that was due for demolition to make way for a new shopping centre. Sergeant Hook called it in and then approached the van to see if he could identify the owner. Because of the isolated nature of the area there were no witnesses to what happened next, but the evidence gathered by the forensics team formed the scenario that was presented in court and which led to a life sentence for Gary Speers, thirty-eight, of no fixed abode.

The prosecution case was that when Sergeant Hook first saw him, Speers was burning something on a small bonfire. Speers' defence was that it was just a pair of jeans he had spilt oil on while repairing the van. This was undermined by tests on the charred remains that identified one of the items as a pencil case with the words *'I love Take That'* written in felt pen still discernible. Sergeant Hook must have been in the middle of writing Speers' name into his notebook. He only got as far as *Gary Sp....* The fact that Sergeant Hook hadn't had time to call for help on his radio testified to the speed and surprise nature of the attack.

The jury didn't believe Speers' claim that 'I panicked. The spanner was in my hand and I must have just lashed out.' The autopsy, carried out by the newly-appointed pathologist, Dr Augustus Bloom, revealed three separate blows to the head. The first, delivered from behind, put Sergeant Hook onto the ground and would probably have been enough to kill him. There was no need for the two extra, skull-cracking blows delivered while he was powerless to defend himself.

It was only after Sergeant Hook failed to answer his radio that a patrol was sent out. They found his police car next to the abandoned campervan with the traumatised, nine-year-old Pauline Jackson tied up and gagged in the back. After a nationwide manhunt Gary Speers was found by a police dog, hiding in a barn in Cwmbran.

On the day of the funeral, Rhidian and Cerys rode with their mother in the back of the undertaker's limo, following the hearse to the Cathay Cemetery. They were stunned to see how the streets were lined with people wanting to pay their last respects. A guard of honour made up of the last cadets to attend Geraint's summer camp waited with flags which they slowly lowered as the funeral cortège passed. Rhidian had never felt prouder of his dad, nor missed him so much.

The next day, when Lili went into Rhidian's bedroom to sort out his washing, she found his portfolio of art shoved under his bed and she knew that he had finally chosen which path he was going to take.

Rhidian's painful remembrance was interrupted by the arrival of Anwen Jones. She had been surprised when Hook suggested that they carry out their debrief, not at the station, but in the pub. She couldn't help wondering about his motives. Was this some clumsy attempt at bonding, or was he just keen to get away from the prying eyes of Devlin and Gunter? She phoned Sam to warn him that she was running late. He was cool about it. He sometimes had to call in on a client after work to give a quote, so both accepted that neither of their jobs was strictly nine to five. If she was going to drink, she needed something to line her stomach, so she had plucked a menu off the bar on her way to the booth where Rhidian was waiting.

'Have you ordered?' she asked. 'I'm going for a pie. It's just a case of whether it's lamb or the beef and ale.'

'You go ahead, I'm all right,' said Rhidian.

Jones ordered a lamb and redcurrant pie with chunky chips and peas, hoping that the sight of it might tempt her boss into eating something, but he seemed content with his third pint of Brain's bitter. She realised that in the week since she'd started working with him she hadn't seen him eat anything. He seemed to live on black coffee and beer. While waiting for her food, Rhidian told her all about his discovery of Llewellyn's fantasy version of ancient Rome, lovingly recreated on a Cardiff trading estate.

'So you don't think he's a suspect anymore?' asked Jones.

'His alibi for two of the murders was backed up by one GP, a bank manager and two city councillors,' said Rhidian.

'What about Cassidy?'

‘He’s got the physical strength to cut through sinew and bone. Has he got the dexterity, the finesse to remove a tongue with such surgical precision?’

‘And don’t forget that his mam says he was with her, but then, she is his mam,’ said Jones. ‘Reckon she’d swear that the sky was purple to protect her precious boy.’

‘Any news on when we can interview him?’

‘Still unconscious. Fractured skull. Docs don’t know when he’ll be back with us,’ said Jones.

‘Remind me to never get on your bad side.’

‘It was an accident.’ Jones didn’t know Rhidian well enough to tell if he was teasing or not. ‘The labs have examined his collection of weapons. There’s no evidence that they’ve ever been used. Looks like they were just for display.’

‘What about his private DVD collection?’

‘I’ve gone through about half of them. Seventy per cent are of Loretta Swann.’

‘And the other thirty per cent?’

‘Other young women who visited the museum. Some are just teenagers.’

‘So he’s a voyeur. Is he also a killer?’

Rhidian drained the last of his pint. The empty glass joined the row of others. Rhidian pulled out his wallet as he stood.

‘Another?’ he asked Jones.

‘No. I’m fine ta.’ She had hardly touched her drink.

‘Have a half.’

‘I’m driving.’

‘Okay,’ said Rhidian. As he gathered his empties to take to the bar, he caught her critical look and instantly knew what it meant.

‘Gunter or Devlin?’

‘What?’

‘Which of them asked you to keep an eye on my drinking?’

Jones tried to look innocent, but under the probing gaze of his grey eyes, quickly gave up.

'DI Gunter.'

'Thought so,' said Rhidian, slumping back onto the bench seat. 'So, what are you doing, keeping score in your notebook? Or maybe you've got it on a spreadsheet so he can see exactly how many units I'm having each day.'

'I haven't said anything to him,' said Jones.

'You can tell him what you like. I've got nothing to hide. It's no secret that I like a drink.

'Alun Gunter says it affects your work.'

'And he's right, only not in the way he thinks.' Rhidian could see that Jones wasn't going to settle for that. 'Alcohol helps me to touch the minds of the wicked; to put myself into their heads. To hunt down a devil, sometimes I need to engage my own demons.'

Seeing that Jones was hanging off every word, Rhidian wondered if the beer had loosened his tongue too much. Jones was pleased that he had finally opened up to her, but she had a hundred questions. Before she could give voice to them, they were interrupted by the arrival of her dinner. Rhidian used the distraction to head to the bar. Jones was sprinkling her chips with vinegar when she realised that he'd left his precious notebook on the table. She looked at the bar. There was quite a queue. It would be a while before he got served. She knew that she shouldn't, but, as usual, her curiosity got the better of her and she reached for the notebook.

The book had become so thick that it now had to be held closed by a thick rubber band. She slipped this off and the pages sprung open. Jones saw that he had not only filled many pages with notes and sketches; he'd also crammed in odd thoughts scribbled on various scraps of paper and even on the back of a beer mat. She could see that where he had had time to consider, his writing was neat, easily readable. Then there were pages filled with illegible scrawl, as if his pen couldn't keep up with his thoughts. She found the pages where Rhidian had sketched the horror of Rhys Pryce's death. Although they were factually accurate and therefore useful as an aide memoire, Rhidian had also captured the look of terror on Pryce's face. Somehow, the drawing caught more of the horror than any scene of crime photo could.

As she turned another page, something slipped out of the book and onto the floor. Jones stooped to pick it up. It was a dried flower. Delicate. A pale blue, faded by time. An orchid? Surely this was nothing to do with the case? She was so distracted by her speculations that she didn't realise that Rhidian had returned from the bar and was watching her with unconcealed disappointment. He put his pint on the table and held out his hand. Jones handed him first the notebook, and then the flower. Seeing the hurt in his eyes, Jones realised that she had not only broken a professional trust; she had also intruded into his personal life.

As Rhidian sat, Jones knew that she had to come up with some kind of explanation. 'It's that question isn't it?' she said. 'Why did you join up? I know the answer that everyone expects you to give, "I wanted to help people," or "I needed to give something back to my community."'

'Not in your case?' Rhidian's tone suggested that he really didn't care what her answer was.

'No. I just wanted to drive fast cars and have an excuse to nose about in other people's lives. What I'm trying to say is, I'm sorry, that was totally inexcusable. Won't happen again.'

Rhidian gave a small nod. Jones hoped this was a sign that she hadn't totally cocked things up. Why did she always have to poke her nose in? She turned her attention to her dinner, but half watched Rhidian turn to a specific page in his notebook. On one side was a delicate pencil sketch of a woman's face in profile. The other side was blank, but the white paper was discoloured by the ghost of the orchid that had been pressed there for so long.

‘Is that your wife?’

‘She would never sit still and pose. For someone who was so beautiful she was actually quite shy. So I always had to catch her unawares. A quick sketch as she listened to a concert or while she was concentrating on a crossword. Now that I only have my memories, I have to keep drawing her, but she’s still slipping from me more and more each day.’

Rhidian replaced the dried orchid and closed that page. Silence. Jones cut into her pie. Rhidian sipped his ale. Any stranger observing them might conclude that they were a couple whose marriage had gone stale some time ago.

*

On the other side of the city, the Café Bar Bar was one of the new, soulless drinking holes that had sprung up as part of the gentrification of the Cardiff docks. It didn’t know whether it was a wine bar, a nightclub or a restaurant and because of this, it failed in all three respects. While he waited, Alun Gunter absentmindedly sneered at the specials board. Today’s offerings included ‘*Squab breast in a red wine jus with crushed peas*’. Gunter could imagine the poncy food, served up on a slate or a plank of wood; the portions so small that you’d have to pop into the chippy on the way home to fill yourself up. Perhaps the place came alive later in the evening. At early doors it was dead, which was just how Gunter liked it. He didn’t want any witnesses.

Outside, Ginnie Lane paused on the threshold to look at her reflection in the window glass and undo another button on her blouse. Yes, she wanted to be treated as a serious journalist. That didn’t mean that she couldn’t use every weapon in her armoury, and she hadn’t met a policeman yet who didn’t like a bit of cleavage.

Gunter looked up as the door opened. He recognised the woman from the TV. As she slipped into the seat opposite him, Gunter didn’t bother hiding the lust in his eyes as he gave her the once-over. Good legs. Lovely long hair. He liked the flash of bra lace. Nice touch that. He concluded that he wouldn't kick her out of bed, but, if truth be told, he preferred his women to have a bit more meat on them.

'Okay. Here I am' said Ginnie. 'What have you got for me?'

'I said this was off the record,' said Gunter.

Ginnie held up her hands, all innocent. 'And it is.'

'You don't want me to go looking for it, love. Trust me.'

Ginnie considered bluffing, then thought better of it. There was no way she wanted to give this lech an excuse to put his hands all over her. Ginnie reluctantly reached for her knock-off-Gucci handbag and pulled out her digital recorder. The glowing red light showed that it was recording. Ginnie made a big show of turning it off, then dropped the recorder back into her bag and snapped it shut.

'Now can we start?' she said.

'You know the police conduct guidelines. I'm not supposed to have any unofficial meetings with journalists, and if I did, I'm definitely not supposed to let them ply me with drink.'

Ginnie got the message and signalled to the barman. When he approached, Gunter ordered.

'Jameson's. Double. No ice.'

Ginnie handed over a crisp twenty pound note and then had to wait for Gunter to savour his first sip of whisky before he would let her continue.

'So. Why am I here?' she asked.

'The tip about the doctor's boat paid off, didn't it?'

'I got there ten minutes before the rest of the pack.'

'They didn't know about what was done to her body, did they?'

'No. But a reporter's only as good as her last scoop.'

'Greedy girl aren't you?'

'Just ambitious.'

'Give me your hand.'

'What for?' Ginnie didn't hesitate for long. Gunter took her hand and wrote a number on the back.

'What's this?'

'Your nomination to the annual press awards.'

Ginnie couldn't help but smile at the thought. An image flashed into her head of champagne flutes and her strutting to receive her award in that yummy black dress she'd bought in Vivienne Westwood, but had never had a chance to wear. Even this exciting fantasy couldn't quench her natural journalist's cynicism. 'And what's in this for you?' she asked.

'Let's just say that we're both scratching each other's backs.'

Gunter grinned. It wasn't a pleasant sight. Ginnie Lane was reminded of the razor-edged grin of a great white shark just before it went in for the kill.

31

It seemed like the whole hospital was sleeping. The few staff on duty spoke to each other in whispers and crept around on thick-soled trainers, chosen for comfort rather than style. An hour ago there was a commotion down the corridor when a new admission couldn't settle in the unfamiliar surroundings, but since then Rhidian had been left alone, sitting next to Loretta Swann's bed, wrapped up in his duffle coat, hands pushed deep into the pockets. His tired body may have been there. His thoughts were elsewhere.

Rhidian and Bethan's wedding day was only weeks away when the Red Maids case started to reveal itself. At first it had been difficult to accept that such horrors could have been committed by teenage girls, but the more that Rhidian and DS Bryn Gough dug into their backgrounds, the clearer it became that the girls were raging against a society which they blamed for failing them so badly. It was institutionalised negligence which had led to both girls being so badly damaged. If they had never met they would probably have turned their anger inwards; self-harming, eating disorders, drug addiction. They would have remained two tragic victims of a care system that tried its hardest, but often fell short. But the girls had found each other and together they turned their shared pain into anger and, finally into a murderous rage.

When their crimes hit the front pages they became a cause célèbre. Soon, other young women were copycatting acts of revenge against their own persecutors; the abusive fathers, the online groomers, the older 'boyfriends' who pimped them out to strangers. A well- known grime artist went to number one with a song about them. Graffiti celebrating the Red Maids' cause sprung up around the city, sprayed on the skateboard park, the approach to the national stadium and Social Services offices.

Finally, Rhidian and Gough's hard work paid off and the Red Maids were tracked down to the abandoned care home they had been using as a hideout. In the chaos of the police raid, one of the pair escaped the net. The girls had created such a co-dependency that it was as if the police had cut them in half. The free girl's anger burned with a terrifying intensity.

Bryn was Rhidian's Best Man. He was supposed to be getting fitted for his suit. He never made it to the hire shop. The ransom note soon arrived on Rhidian Hook's desk. It was a simple demand: the release of her soulmate in exchange for the safe return of Rhidian's right-hand man. Having seen the results of their violence close up, Rhidian didn't need convincing of the seriousness of the repercussions if her demands weren't met. There was no need to send the first finger. Rhidian finally found the girl, but not soon enough to save his best friend. It was clear that the girl had taken out all of her rage on her chained, helpless prisoner.

That night, Rhidian sat at his kitchen table absently toying with his wine glass, lost in dark thoughts. He felt that he was being watched and turned, to see Bethan standing in the doorway. He had no idea how long she had been there. She had learnt the art of patience. When he was ready to talk, she would be there to listen. Rhidian filled a second glass. Bethan accepted the invitation and sat, waiting for him to start talking.

'I know that people are going to be disappointed,' he said, staring into his wine.

Although she had known this was coming, it was still upsetting to hear him put it into words.

'People?'

'You. You are going to be disappointed.'

'And you won't?'

'I don't see that there's any other option.'

'You want to call off the wedding?'

'I can't put you in danger.'

'I've always known who you are. What you do.'

'That was before…'

'Bryn changes nothing.'

'It changes everything.'

'Do you still love me?'

'You know I do.'

'And I love you, so we are getting married.'

'He was my best friend. It nearly broke me, Bethan.'

'I know.'

'If I lost you…' He couldn't finish his sentence, so he finished his wine. But now that he had started, he needed to get it all out. 'This darkness that I have to deal with, that's my choice, not yours.'

'Do you really think it's a choice?' she asked. 'Would you do this if there was anyone else who could do it better? The only reason you keep looking into the abyss is because somebody has to do it. I know how much it costs you and I won't let you do it alone. Oh I know I can't interview a suspect or follow clues, but I can be here when you come home; to listen or to stay out of your way if that's what's needed. I will always be here.'

Rhidian had never heard her sound so strong. It allowed him to finally release the tension that had been building inside for weeks. She moved to hold him, feeling his sobs vibrate through her body.

Sitting next to Loretta Swann's bed, Rhidian refocused on the people who needed him now. Even though it was over-warm in the hospital, he was still swaddled in his duffle coat. He reached into the coat, pulled out his notebook and opened it to a page that had been marked with the old 'Velma' photo of the pre-surgically enhanced Loretta Swann. He didn't know why, but each time he visited her, he noted down the readings from her monitor. Blood pressure, temperature, oxygen saturation, her heart and respiratory rate. As he added today's figures he was pleased to see that they all showed signs of improvement. He turned to a fresh page and absently started sketching.

'All the money you spent on transforming yourself. How much good did it do you?' he asked the sleeping woman. 'The only men in your life wanted to use you. Sumner saw you as a project. And what was going on with James Calder? Did you think that was love? Could you have been that desperate? Did you know that Trevor Cassidy was stalking you? If so, why didn't you report it?'

Loretta Swann's face remained impassive. Could she hear him? How would he ever know?

*

On the other side of the hospital, PC Ash Vowles shifted uneasily on the plastic chair in an otherwise empty corridor. The young constable was supposed to have gone off duty an hour ago. He'd been crossing his legs, but there was still no sign of his replacement and he couldn't hold it any longer. He wished he'd never had that second coffee. He had inherited his mother's delicate bladder and the caffeine had gone straight through him. Ash peeked into the private side room. Trevor Cassidy lay unconscious, wired up to a drip and a cardiac monitor, his head heavily bandaged. He hadn't stirred since the paramedics brought him in. Ash weighed up his options and came down on the side of his bloated bladder. He headed off down the corridor to find the nearest Gents. As the door gently closed behind the constable, Cassidy's eyes sprang open.

As Ash turned the corner, a nurse approached from the other direction, heading for the Ladies. Ash was so keen to relieve himself that he only took in a few details of the woman; mainly that she was young and blonde and filled her scrubs very nicely.

The nurse burst into the Ladies, resting her back against the door, needing a moment to recover from the shock of seeing a police officer coming towards her. She was relieved that her disguise had passed the test. All that the cop had seen were her nurse's scrubs. He hadn't noticed that her hospital ID was fake or that her face might have been familiar if he watched the local news. Looking in the mirror, Ginnie Lane agreed that she made a good Florence Nightingale. She had tied her long hair back in a ponytail and wiped off her usual bright red lippy.

She left the toilets and turned left, headed down the corridor. The only people she passed were a porter wheeling an empty trolley, and a cleaner mopping up some sticky spillage off the floor. Neither of them challenged her, so her confidence grew with every step. This confirmed Ginnie's theory that the best way to avoid being exposed was to act like she belonged here.

Coming to the security doors, Ginnie tapped in the four-digit number that Gunter had written on her hand. Seeing the light turn from red to green, Ginnie pushed through the doors into an empty corridor. Third on the left Gunter had said. Pausing at the door, Ginnie looked through the round glass window, to see Loretta Swann lying in her hospital bed. Just as she was about to push through the door, a figure crossed the bottom of the bed. Thinking it was a doctor, Ginnie was ready to flee, until she realised that the figure wasn't wearing hospital scrubs. Then she recognised the distinctive black duffle coat. Detective Inspector Hook. This was an even bigger scoop than she could have hoped for. She already had the camera setting on her phone ready, so she held the lens up to the window, her thumb poised to take a snap, but the lighting wasn't good enough to get a decent photo. The only way that this picture would be worth anything was if both its subjects were recognisable, not just grainy shapes. There was only one thing for it. Ginnie summoned up her courage and pushed through the door, just as Rhidian leant over to gently lift Loretta's head so that he could rearrange her pillows. Ginnie brought her phone up, caught the image, then slipped her phone back into her pocket, just as Rhidian turned to see who the new arrival was.

'Sorry. I'm in your way,' he said.

'Not at all,' said Ginnie who couldn't believe her luck. He hadn't even looked at her face. All he saw was the uniform. As Rhidian sat back onto the chair, Ginnie slipped a hand into her pocket to make sure that her digital recorder was on before she approached the bed. She kept one eye on the detective as she went through the motions of checking the monitor.

'Her sats have improved,' said Rhidian. 'That's got to be good.'

Caught off guard, Ginnie could only muster a 'Yes. It's very encouraging.'

She was relieved to see that Hook was distracted by writing something in his notebook. She edged closer, pretending to check that the raised sides of the bed were secure. All she could see was that he wasn't writing; he was drawing something. An inner voice was yelling at her to get out while she could, but Ginnie couldn't waste this opportunity for an exclusive.

'I've seen your picture in the papers,' she said. 'You're investigating those murders.' Just a grunt from Rhidian whose attention was focused on trying to get the shading of his sketch right. Ginnie brushed an invisible crease out of the bedding. She made sure that she kept her back to the detective and threw out an innocent question. 'Is she a friend of yours?' Rhidian looked up from his notebook. Ginnie tried again. 'Or is she connected to your investigation?' She had asked one question too many.

Rhidian's instincts kicked in. He studied the way she moved, and realised that she had none of the sense of purpose of the other staff, who hustled in and did what they needed to with the least fuss because they had other patients waiting.

'You're not the usual nurse.'

'I'm covering for her. She called in sick.'

'I'm sorry to hear that. Next time you see Kate, give her my best.'

'I will.'

Knowing it was time to leave, Ginnie edged towards the door. Rhidian was quickly out of his chair, blocking her way.

'Her name's Cindy,' he said, now seeing Ginnie's face clearly. 'It's a poor journalist who doesn't check her facts.' He took in her hospital scrubs. 'Are there no depths you won't sink to?'

'I'm only doing my job. What about you? Why is a detective inspector spending the night sitting at a stranger's bedside?'

Rhidian tried to cover how she had scored a direct hit. 'If you've got any relevant questions, you know the press office number.'

Ginnie Lane's bullshit meter was just as sensitive as the detective's, and she knew she was onto something. 'Why are you here? How is Loretta Swann connected to the deaths of four people?'

Rhidian saw her gaze shift to his notebook that he'd stupidly left open on the bed. He closed it, but not before she'd spotted the sketches of Loretta Swann; her slender neck, her delicate hands.

'What exactly is your relationship with her?'

Anger burned in Rhidian's eyes. 'Out. Now.'

'This is your opportunity to put the record straight.'

'You've been recording this?'

Ginnie's guilty reaction confirmed this. Rhidian held out his hand.

‘Give it up, or get arrested.’

‘For what? Asking awkward questions?’

‘For impersonating a member of the emergency services. If that gets into the tabloids you’ll be finished. Nobody gets to take advantage of the NHS, not even journalists.’

Ginnie reluctantly pulled her digital recorder from her pocket and slapped it into Rhidian’s palm. ‘I’m going to report this.’

‘Yeah. Good luck with that.’ Rhidian stepped aside to allow Ginnie to stomp out.

Once out in the corridor, Ginnie dropped the feigned outrage and pulled out her phone and quickly checked that it was still recording, before heading for the nearest exit. In her head she was already writing the story that was going to open so many doors. Her contact on the *Echo* couldn’t ignore this one, and once she’d got herself established as a serious news reporter, she’d be straight off to the nationals. She was too excited to notice that the door to the relatives’ waiting room was slightly ajar and that keen eyes were watching her through the crack.

Back at Loretta Swann’s bedside, Rhidian asked himself why Ginnie Lane’s accusation had stung so sharply. Looking at his notebook, he was appalled to realise that the sketched portrait that started out as a memory of his wife, had somehow metamorphosed into Loretta Swann. The eyes and nose were Bethan’s, but the mouth and the shape of the jaw were all Loretta Swann. He ripped out the page, screwed it into a ball and threw it across the room. It bounced off the wall and landed on the floor at the foot of the bed. He stooped to pick it up. Not wanting anyone else to find it, he put the ball of paper into his pocket.

As Rhidian recovered, he sensed that he wasn’t alone. Thinking that Ginnie Lane had returned with more questions, he spun on his heels, just in time to see a figure move away from the door. It was only a fleeting glimpse, but Rhidian was sure that it wasn't the reporter. Whoever it was, they weren't dressed in blue hospital scrubs but something blood-red.

Rhidian quickly exited the room, just in time to see the red figure turning the corner. He ran to try and catch up, but the next corridor was empty. Then he saw the fire door to the stairwell just closing. Rushing to the top of the stairs, he could hear distant running footfalls and the sound of another door being opened on the floor below.

Taking the stairs two at a time, Rhidian found himself on the basement level. Because it was off limits to the public there was less lighting here, just enough for him to catch the flash of red disappearing through double doors at the far end.

Rhidian burst through the doors to find himself standing on the side of a hydrotherapy swimming pool. The large space was in near darkness, the only light coming from the illuminated signs above the two doorways, highlighting the emergency exits.

Rhidian paused and caught his breath. There was no movement. No sound. He saw the exit on the other side of the pool and judged that his quarry wouldn't have had time to get to it before he arrived. They must still be here, somewhere. Two sides of the pool were lined with changing cubicles. All of the plastic curtains were drawn shut. A dozen perfect hiding places. Rhidian had no choice. He needed to clear them, one by one, even though he had nothing to defend himself with. His pupils were large as he sought out any shape that was out of place in the deep shadows. He couldn't resist the sensation that the darkness and silence were closing in on him, so he reached into his coat pocket, pulled out his torch and clicked it on. It only provided a small area of illumination, but it was better than nothing. He felt wetness spread under his arms and tried to dismiss it as a product of the heat coming off the pool, rather than his own fear.

Approaching the first cubicle, Rhidian's ears strained to pick up the tiniest of sounds that might warn him of danger. Summoning up his courage, he took a grip on the edge of the curtain then tugged it aside. Nothing. He only allowed himself a moment's relief before he had to move to the next one. Grasping the edge of the curtain, he pulled it back. Again, empty. Rhidian took two steps to his left and reached for the next curtain. Before he could pull it aside, something slashed through the plastic from inside. Rhidian stumbled back as another metre-long gash appeared in the curtain. Through the torn plastic Rhidian caught a flash of a red hood covering his attacker's head, hiding their features. Rhidian looked at the figure's hands to try and identify what kind of knife they were using, but there was no glint of any silver blade. All that Rhidian could see was something dark being held in one fist. Whatever it was, it was slashing for his throat. Rhidian put up an arm to defend his face and heard the rip as his coat was slashed. It took a moment before he felt the cold sting in his arm that told him he had been cut.

Already off balance, Rhidian slipped on the damp tiles and went down. Before he could scramble back to his feet to parry another attack, the figure was upon him, pulling the plastic cubicle curtain over his head and face.

Hopelessly entangled, Rhidian was dragged towards the edge of the pool, the curtain tearing from its rail. Disorientated, unable to get any traction on the wet tiles, Rhidian's head and shoulders were pushed under the warm water of the pool. With the weight of his assailant on top of him there was no way to escape. The more he struggled, the more his attacker twisted the plastic, tightening its grip around his face. Then the water started seeping in under the tightly stretched plastic, expelling what little air was trapped there. Whether it was by suffocation or drowning, Rhidian was in no doubt that he was going to die.

Rhidian could hear his own desperate gasping as he struggled to suck in enough oxygen to stay alive. He could feel his heartbeat slowing. As he felt his strength drain away, Rhidian stretched out one of his trapped hands, his fingers straining to reach into his coat pocket and pull out his fountain pen. He pushed the lid off with his thumb, then used all of his remaining strength to stab the pen deep into his attacker's thigh. The weight was instantly released from his back and Rhidian was able to pull his head out of the water and tear the plastic curtain away from his face. As he gasped for air, he felt strong arms grab him. He flailed blindly, desperate to defend himself from another attack, until he heard a welcome voice.

'Boss!'

Rhidian relaxed when he saw that it was Anwen Jones. He tried to speak between ragged breaths.

'Red… hoody.'

'Nobody passed me.'

Rhidian leaned on Jones in order to pull himself onto his feet.

'Get after them.'

'They're long gone,' said Jones. 'And you need to get that looked at.'

It was only then that Rhidian saw the drops of red splashing on the white tiles and saw the four-inch gash in his coat sleeve. Putting his hand over the wound to apply pressure, Jones led Rhidian towards the exit.

Rhidian sat in a chair in a treatment cubicle as Sister Cindy Campbell examined the wound to his bicep.

'An inch to the left and it could have severed an artery,' she said. 'It's lucky your colleague was there to disturb them.'

'Yes. Why were you there?' asked Rhidian.

'I was looking for Cassidy.'

'He's not in his room? But I put a watch on him.'

‘The constable was caught short. By the time he’d relieved himself, Cassidy’s bed was empty.’

‘I want his name.’

‘He’s had his bollocking.’

‘Not from me he hasn’t,’ said Rhidian.

‘Don’t you think we’re better off focusing on finding Cassidy? Do you think he was the one who assaulted you?’

‘It was too dark. Their head was covered by a red hood.’

Jones held up Rhidian’s fountain pen which was inside an evidence bag.

‘You never know. We might get DNA off it,’ she said. ‘And if it matches the samples we took from Trevor Cassidy, we’ve got our man.’

Rhidian had to concede her point.

‘Did you get a good look at the weapon?’ asked Jones.

‘Not a knife. At least it didn’t have a silver blade.’

‘There are plenty of hunting knives with dark blades. Even my kitchen set are like that,’ said Jones.

Cindy studied the wound.

‘Whatever it was, it cut clean and it cut deep. Must have been as sharp as a scalpel. Which is good news for you. A few stitches should close it up nicely.’

*

Mrs Cassidy was settling down to her favourite soap opera. She had a big glass of vodka and a Hobnob biscuit ready. She had earlier told her neighbour that of course she was worried about Trevor. That didn’t mean that she had to miss her little treat. What she could never put into words was how she needed the distraction of this precious half hour. Immersing herself in the scripted chaos of these familiar fictional characters helped her to forget the stresses of her own life.

The theme music started up. She was taking her first sip of ice-cold, throat-warming vodka, when the frame of her front door burst into splinters and half a dozen police officers in full body armour and helmets suddenly filled her living room, shouting for her to stay still. After the room had been deemed safe, the wall of officers parted and a woman wearing a stab vest approached Mrs Cassidy's armchair.

'Mrs Cassidy, I am DCI Liz Devlin. I have a warrant to search these premises.' Devlin nodded to the officers who dispersed to search the house. 'This will go much easier if you tell us where he is.'

'He's in the hospital, where one of you lot put him,' said Mrs Cassidy.

Mattresses were overturned, wardrobes emptied, even the loft and the garden shed were searched, but there was no sign of Trevor Cassidy. The search team retreated back to the vans that had delivered them. Liz Devlin made one last appeal to Mrs Cassidy to tell her son to give himself up, before she too left, just in time for the end credits to start rolling.

*

Cindy Campbell finished washing the wound out with saline.

'Why did Cassidy attack you?' asked Jones.

'Because I was trying to stop him?'

'Or was it something more personal?'

'What do you mean?' asked Rhidian.

'We've established that he's been visiting Loretta Swann in secret.'

'And?'

'And what if he's seen you sitting by her bed every night?'

'Not every night,' said Rhidian.

'It's been often enough that he could think you're a rival.'

'A rival for what…?'

Cindy Campbell gave a chuckle. 'You do spend more time here than most husbands.' Rhidian shut her down with a look. Cindy returned to her task.

'Any interest I have in Dr Swann is purely professional,' he said, but neither of the women was convinced. The pain in his arm was momentarily forgotten as he had to ask himself, was Jones right? Was he falling for Loretta Swann, or was the attraction just some echo of Bethan? Before he could come to any conclusion, Cindy paused in her work.

'What is this?'

Cindy reached for some tweezers then gently plucked something out of Rhidian's wound. Rhidian was about to ask Jones for an evidence bag, but she had anticipated his request and had one ready to receive the tiny splinter of jet black material. Jones held the bag up to the light.

'Is it metal? A chip off a knife blade?' asked Jones.

'Get it to forensics,' said Rhidian. 'Finally. This could be the breakthrough we've been looking for.'

32

'Why were you even there?' asked Devlin, slamming her office door. It was early the next morning, and Rhidian Hook had been summoned to the DCI's office.

'I can't sleep in hotel rooms,' said Rhidian.

'So your next logical thought was, I know, I'll go sleep next to the hospital bed of a total stranger. Only she's not just a stranger is she? She's at the centre of your murder case.'

'Exactly what are you accusing me of?'

'It's not me. It's Ginnie bloody Lane who's saying that you've got too close to this Swann woman.'

Devin pushed the latest edition of the *Echo* across the table. Rhidian didn't need to read the article, filed under Ginnie Lane's by-line with the headline: '*The Detective and the Sleeping Beauty*', illustrated with the snatched photo of Rhidian putting a pillow under Loretta Swann's head.

'I was only adjusting her pillow.'

'The taxpaying public don't care about nuances like that. They see what Ms Lane wants them to see; a senior police officer mixing duty with pleasure.'

'It's tabloid distortion.'

'Once you become the story, you're no longer any good to the investigation,' said Devlin.

'You've got to let me see this through.'

'I'm sorry, Rhidian. You give me no other choice. Alun Gunter's got his hands full, so I'll have to see who else is available. How could you be so stupid?'

Rhidian hadn't been ready to share this, but realised he had no choice. 'These last six months have been a living hell.'

'You don't need to tell me.'

'Then I met Loretta Swann, and I don't know why, but I knew that we hadn't been thrown together by accident.' He saw Devlin's disappointment before she could hide it. 'It's not a physical attraction. It's not a case of her being a substitute for Bethan. Nobody could ever replace her. It's about being drawn to a kindred spirit, someone who's also living in the shadows; neither alive nor dead. I don't know if that makes any sense to you. I'm not sure it makes much sense to me, but it's all I've got.'

Rhidian wasn't sure if Devlin would understand, until he saw the anger drain from her face.

'How's the arm?' she asked.

'A dozen stitches, but it was a clean cut.'

'I didn't bring you back just to lose you, Rhidian.'

'Dr Bloom hasn't got his hands on me yet, has he?'

'Thanks to Sergeant Jones.'

'Yes. She is coming in handy.'

'So. How is this security guard connected to Loretta Swann?' asked Devlin.

'Cassidy's been obsessing over her for months.'

'And you think he's out to avenge her? He's not exactly my idea of a knight in shining armour.'

'No. But he's fit. Strong. He could easily have overpowered all of the victims.'

'Who is this Loretta Swann? How does she have so much power over so many men?'

'I'm not sure that "power" is the right word. She seems to have craved affection, but who did she attract; a sexual blackmailer, a plastic surgeon with a God complex and an obsessive Peeping Tom. I'm not sure that any of them really knew her.'

'But you do?'

Rhidian knew that this was Liz Devlin the woman speaking, not his DCI, so he changed the subject. 'We're forgetting one vital question. How did Ginnie Lane find out that Loretta Swann was at the centre of the investigation?'

'Maybe we've underestimated her, and she is actually good at her job?' said Devlin.

'What about Constable Weakbladder? Could he have tipped her off?'

'No. He's an idiot, but he's not bent.'

'If he didn't tip her off, who did?'

They were interrupted by an urgent rapping on the door.

'Yes,' barked Devlin.

Jones stuck her head in.

'Ma'am. Boss. I've got an idea about how we can find Trevor Cassidy.'

*

The covered market at the heart of Cardiff's shopping area had originally been a gaol. Now the building's Victorian shell housed two floors of stalls selling everything from home-made bara brith to Thai street food. Locals say that if you can't find what you're looking for under its grand glass roof, it's not worth having.

Anwen Jones looked like any other shopper, strolling around the upper floor, pausing to browse through some old vinyl records before walking on a few yards to read the café menu chalked up on a blackboard. 'All day breakfast. £5.75.' The mere thought of it set her stomach rumbling. Moving away from the tempting aroma of cooking bacon and the sizzle of frying eggs, Jones glanced at her watch. Half past four. They were well overdue. Jones looked over the balcony's ironwork balustrade into the main body of the bustling market.

From her elevated position Jones could see anyone entering through the St Mary Street entrance. This was where the city gallows had once stood, and where coal miner Dic Penderyn had been hanged after being found guilty of stabbing a soldier with a bayonet during the Merthyr Rising in 1831. Anwen Jones was distracted by more present-day matters, namely the butcher's stall opposite. All afternoon she'd been watching their stock of Clark's pies going down, until now, only one meat-filled treat was left. This whole operation was her idea. She'd found out from one of the neighbours that Mrs Cassidy had a daily routine. Every afternoon she took the same bus into the city centre. She went to the newsagent's for her lottery ticket and fags, then called in at the market for fresh bread and something from the butcher's for Trevor's tea. His favourite was breast of lamb, or, for a special treat, some fat, juicy faggots; the ones wrapped in caul fat, the proper way. Jones's logic was that Trevor might not risk phoning his mum, but he knew her routine, so if he wanted to make contact, the busy market would surely be the best option.

Would Mrs Cassidy stick to her usual pattern after the shock of the police raid on her home and with her son on the run from the police? Jones knew it was a long shot, but it was all they had. But Mrs Cassidy was late. Jones tried to deflect her growing sense of disappointment. If the stakeout was a failure, maybe she could drown her sorrows with a Clarksie. Jones dragged her eyes away from the lone pie and looked for the familiar duffle coat, with the fresh gash crudely held together with black Gaffa tape. She saw that the DI was still in position at the second-hand bookstall, from where he could cover the main entrance.

Rhidian Hook had been browsing the dog-eared paperbacks for so long that the owner had told him, 'This ain't a library, mate. Buy something or bugger off.' A quick flash of Rhidian's warrant card had put him back in his box. Rhidian glanced up at Jones. He should have called this off an hour ago, but he wanted to give her a chance to prove herself. But the intel she had gathered said that their target always went shopping between three and half past. The customers were thinning out. The bakers were packing up, having sold every last loaf and iced bun. Rhidian reluctantly pulled out his police radio, ready to call the operation off, when his earpiece crackled into life.

‘Boss. Movement. St Mary Street entrance.’

Rhidian took a step back, so that he could look down the length of the market hall to the far side. Jones’s voice came through the earpiece again.

‘Badly dyed red hair. Wearing a black T-shirt with ‘*Welsh Babe*’ on the front.’

Rhidian spotted the woman, approaching a vintage clothing stall. He surreptitiously spoke into his radio. ‘I’ve got her.’

‘Don’t think she’s the sort to be shopping for denim hot pants or 1950s cocktail dresses,’ said Jones.

‘All units from DI Hook. Target one is on site. Nobody moves until target two has been positively identified.’

Jones was the first to spot him. ‘At your eleven o’clock. Sunglasses. Grey hoody and tracky bottoms.’

Rhidian picked out the man standing at the florist’s stall, but whose eyes were everywhere except on the arrays of roses and carnations.

‘Are you sure that’s him?’ asked Rhidian.

‘Not a hundred per cent,.’ said Jones. ‘Moving to a better position.’

Jones never took her eyes off the man as she moved further down the balcony. He was the same build as Trevor Cassidy, but with his hood up it was hard to see his features. As she moved closer, Jones was dismayed to hear a voice chirp up behind her.

‘You again!’

Jones turned to see Darren Powers sitting at a café table, tucking into a burger and chips, his arm still in plaster which his mates had decorated with an impressive collection of cartoon cocks.

‘Wasn’t breaking me arm bad enough? Now you’re following me around.’

‘Shut up and eat your burger,’ hissed Jones.

But this only made him raise his voice to anyone who would listen.

‘You’re all witnesses to this. Police harassment in action.’

‘Seriously, Darren. Shut it, or I will arrest you.’

Darren reluctantly returned his attention to his grub. Jones’s relief was short-lived as she felt that she was being watched. She refocused on the figure peering out from behind a newspaper at the table behind Darren Powers. It was Trevor Cassidy. They locked eyes and everything froze. Neither wanted to make the first move. And then Cassidy was out of his chair and running, Jones hard on his tail, talking into her radio as she ran. ‘Positive ID on Trevor Cassidy. Top level. Heading for the stairs. In pursuit.’

Cassidy clanged down the metal stairs. Jones was right behind him. He was running for the nearest exit until he saw the uniformed police officers emerging from their cover positions to cut him off. He changed direction, running past his puzzled mother at the vintage clothing stall, heading for the main entrance. Cassidy was quick, but Jones was no slouch. She was just getting into range for a rugby tackle when Cassidy pulled a pushchair into her path. Slamming on the anchors, Jones slowed enough so that when she hit the pushchair her momentum didn’t knock it over. It was only then that she saw it was empty, but the delay had gifted Cassidy five yards on her.

As she pushed off into a run, Jones questioned, where was the backup? Where was Hook? She could see the sunlight streaming in from the street. Cassidy only had to push through the queue at the fishmonger’s and he’d be free. It was at that moment that a black-coated figure spun away from the fishmonger’s counter and in one smooth movement, hit Trevor Cassidy smack in the face with a two-foot pollock. Cassidy smacked the floor with a thud that made Jones wince. His groan told them that he was still alive, but he would be picking fish scales out of his face for some time.

‘What are you waiting for? It’s your arrest, Sergeant,’ said Rhidian, handing a twenty pound note to the fishmonger in compensation.

‘Cheers,’ said Jones, pulling her handcuffs from the back pocket.

‘You were right,’ said Rhidian. ‘He couldn’t stay away from his mammy.’

Jones rolled the stunned Cassidy onto his front so that she could snap on the handcuffs and deliver the police caution.

As Rhidian led the way to the waiting police car, they passed the distraught Mrs Cassidy. All she could manage was, ‘What is it this time, Trevor?’

Her son kept his head bowed, even after Anwen had helped him into the back of the police car. She glowed with success; a tasty arrest under her belt and a Clark’s pie, still warm in her jacket pocket.

33

Mrs Cassidy looked nervously around the stark police interview room. She needed her 'medicine'. A big long glass of it. When the door opened she tried to sit up straighter and hide her unease. Rhidian sat opposite her and placed a laptop on the table between them.

'Mrs Cassidy, my name is—'

'Where's my son?'

'I can assure you that he's being looked after.'

'When's he going to be released?'

'That might be down to you.'

'How's that?'

*

In Interview Room 2, Jones started the digital recorder. A burly custody officer stood, arms crossed, by the door, just in case of trouble. A duty solicitor sat next to Trevor Cassidy. The room was cooled by the air con, but Trevor had a good sweat on.

'Interview resumed at seventeen oh three. So, Trevor, we were talking about what happened when you left the hospital.'

'I hate those places, so I discharged myself.'

'Why didn't you tell anyone you were leaving?'

'I just wanted out of there.'

'And it's just a coincidence that you chose the one moment when the officer stationed outside your room had to use the toilet?'

'I was out of it. How would I know there was even a copper there?'

Cassidy had asked for a break so he could have a drink, but now the takeaway cup of tea sat untouched, going cold.

'So. Where did you go?'

'How'd you mean?'

'You got out of bed. Put your clothes on. Then what?'

'Used the lift. Went down to the ground floor. Walked out the rear entrance.'

'Why not go out the front like anyone else?'

'I don't know my way around that place. I just followed the signs to the nearest exit. No one tried to stop me.'

'And if I said that a witness saw you in the basement?'

'They're lying.'

'So we won't find your fingerprints on the door handles to the hydrotherapy pool?'

'The what? I didn't go anywhere near no pool. I told you. I slipped out the back. Past all the ambulances. Nobody tried to stop me. I never saw your boss. I never touched him. Attempted murder, that's bullshit.'

*

Down the corridor, Rhidian told Mrs Cassidy, 'I need to ask you where Trevor was at certain times.'

'He was home with me.'

'I haven't given you the dates yet.'

'First thing in the morning he brings me tea in bed, then goes to work. When he clocks off, he comes straight home; has my dinner on the table by six thirty every night.'

'And he never goes to the pub, the gym? Out with friends?'

'He's a good boy. Looks after his mam.'

'What about girlfriends?'

'He's taken a fancy to a few, but none of them have ever stuck.'

'So there are no secrets between you?'

'He tells me everything.'

'Okay.'

Rhidian turned the laptop around, so she could see the screen.

'What's this?' she asked.

'This, is what Trevor gets up to when he's at work.'

*

'Look. I know you found my discs,' Trevor told Jones. 'I'll put my hand up to that, but that's all.'

'Okay. Let's talk about what's on those discs, Trevor,' said Jones. Cassidy reached for his cold tea and drained it in one.

'There's one person who featured more than any other.'

'It's not my fault that she's so hot.'

'So you know who I'm talking about?'

'Professor Swann, yeah. But you can't tell me she didn't know what she was doing. Always flashing her cleavage, wearing tight skirts.'

'Are you saying that she knew you were filming her?'

'That's how some women get their kicks, isn't it? They like the power of knowing you're looking at them. It gets them off. As long as we don't touch, no, because then they scream blue murder. But that's all I do. I watch. I never touch.'

*

Rhidian pressed *play* on his laptop and one of Trevor's DVDs started up. Mrs Cassidy reluctantly put her glasses on so that she could see the screen. The security camera was following a group of tourists who were being given a guided tour of an exhibition of traditional Welsh tapestry blankets by Huw Llewellyn.

'This is what he does. He's a security guard,' said Mrs Cassidy.

'Just wait.'

The camera picked out a young woman at the back of the party. It still looked innocent until the camera zoomed in on the woman's breasts and held its focus there.

'So? He was distracted by a pretty girl,' said Mrs Cassidy. 'He's only human.'

'And this?' asked Rhidian, fast forwarding to the viewpoint of a camera in the Natural History room. The camera concentrated in on a party of teenage schoolgirls sitting on a bench sketching the diorama of a taxidermied brown bear fighting a timber wolf. The camera zoomed in on one girl whose skirt had ridden up, exposing her bare thighs.

'This is how your "good boy" spends his time.'

'Turn it off.'

'There's plenty more. In fact, there are hours and hours of it.'

Mrs Cassidy reached over and slammed the laptop lid down. Rhidian gave her a moment to recover.

'About these dates,' said Rhidian.

'You think I'm covering up for him? Honest truth. I'd love you to give him a shock; get this... whatever it is, out of his system. But I can't lie. He is at home with me every night. I don't know what else you think he's been up to, but seeing that was enough for me. He'll be mending his ways or he'll be finding somewhere else to live.'

Rhidian nodded, his instincts confirmed.

*

Down the corridor, as Jones ratcheted up her questioning, Trevor Cassidy shredded the polystyrene cup into a hundred pieces that covered the table like confetti.

'What did you do with the weapon?'

'I told you. You've got the wrong man.'

'If you're straight with me now, maybe we can get the charge dropped to malicious wounding.'

'I have been straight. Watching pretty girls. That's all I ever do.'

Jones looked into Trevor Cassidy's pleading eyes and concluded that he was either telling the truth or he was the best liar she had ever come across.

The door opened. Jones spoke up for the recording. 'Detective Inspector Hook has entered the room.'

'Show me your thigh,' said Rhidian.

'What?'

'Right leg.'

'Are you serious?'

'Just do it, Trevor,' said Jones.

'If it will put an end to this.'

Trevor Cassidy stood, unbelted his trousers and tugged them down. He aimed his Y-fronted crotch at Jones, but she just sneered. 'I would tell you put it away, only I can't actually see anything.'

Rhidian examined the flesh of Cassidy's thigh. There was no sign of any wound from where he'd sunk his fountain pen, nib-deep.

*

'It's not him,' said Rhidian, entering their office.

'Yeah. He's a creep, but he's not a killer,' said Jones, firing up her computer. 'But there is something else.' She looked through the stack of DVDs taken from Trevor Cassidy's bedroom. She found the one she was looking for and slipped the disc into the machine.

'Haven't you already logged all of those?' asked Rhidian.

'Yeah, but we were only looking at Cassidy's pervy behaviour. And while we were doing that, I saw something; it only half registered. I just want to double check.'

Rhidian pulled up a chair to sit next to Jones. 'So what am I looking for?'

Jones played a recording of security camera footage of Loretta Swann heading for the museum's main entrance. She was wearing a long raincoat and had a bag slung over one shoulder.

'Time code says seventeen thirty. Must have been going home,' said Jones.

As Loretta went to push open the heavy oak and stained glass door, she dropped her museum ID badge. The camera zoomed in as she crouched to pick up the badge and lanyard. All that Cassidy was interested in was how Loretta Swann's skirt tightened over her thighs before she straightened, and exited through the door.

'Another bit of opportunistic voyeurism. So what?' said Rhidian.

'Yeah. I missed it too,' said Jones. 'Look again.'

Jones replayed the footage, this time slowed down. Loretta Swann approached the doors; dropped her ID; crouched down to retrieve it. Only this time Rhidian saw it, even before Jones froze the frame.

'Her bag,' said Rhidian. 'What is that?'

Rhidian tried to identify the object that was peeking out of Loretta's shoulder bag.

'Some kind of statue?' said Jones.

Rhidian pressed *play*. The footage continued. As she stood, Loretta Swann realised that the object had become visible and swiftly covered it with a scarf before leaving the building.

'Whatever it was, I don't think it was meant to be going home with her,' said Rhidian with more than a hint of disappointment.

‘Maybe your Sleeping Beauty isn’t so innocent after all,’ said Jones.

34

There was a real spring in her step as Ginnie Lane left her head office. The interview had gone better than she could have dreamed. The promotion was hers. From Monday morning, she would be leaving the local sports desk and joining the main news team. She would no longer have to spend her Saturday afternoons freezing her tits off at bitterly cold football matches. Yes, her editor was pissed off that she'd sold her exclusive to the print media, but he couldn't deny that she had balls, and in the end he'd rather that she was working for him than for the competition.

Heading through one of the covered arcades of shops that criss-cross Cardiff city centre, she paused to look in the window of her favourite delicatessen. They always had such a wonderful window display of tempting, imported goodies. She could rarely pass without slipping in for a jar of truffle oil or some continental charcuterie, and today it was time to push the boat out. Tonight she had a date with the handsome photographer. She hoped that he liked stuffed vine leaves. Of course it was a shame that a few people had had to die in order for her to further her career, but she wasn't going to let that spoil her celebrations.

*

Morris Palfrey unlocked the museum doors to reveal the clearly impatient DI Hook and DS Jones waiting on the threshold.

'Sorry. Had the floor polisher on. Didn't hear you.'

'Mr Llewellyn?' asked Rhidian.

'In his office. Do you need me to...?'

'We know the way. You can get back to your work,' said Rhidian, heading for the rear of the museum. Taking the stone steps to Llewellyn's office two at a time, they heard the thrum of the floor polisher start up again.

Huw Llewellyn seemed puzzled by the photograph that Jones showed him on her phone.

'Can you identify the object?' she asked.

'Of course. It's from ancient Mesopotamia. One of their priest kings. What I don't understand is, what is it doing in Professor Swann's bag?'

'I assume that it's not museum policy to allow artefacts to leave the premises?' asked Rhidian.

'Only in exceptional circumstances; if we're lending to another museum perhaps. It involves reams of paperwork, extra insurance and specialist antiquities transport.'

'So you wouldn't just bung it into your shoulder bag?' asked Jones.

'Definitely not.'

'And why would she feel the need to take any object home with her?' asked Rhidian.

'These are all very good questions that Professor Swann will have to answer, when she recovers,' said Llewellyn. Rhidian got the impression that the curator was relieved that his colleague was still some way away from having to answer any questions.

'Do we know that she actually returned the statue?' asked Rhidian.

'All of our collection is catalogued, Inspector. Any missing item would be noticed in our annual audit which we completed only last week.'

'Just to be sure. Can you show us the statue?'

'Of course,' said Llewellyn. His hesitation had only been slight, but it was still obvious to Hook and Jones.

Rhidian and Jones followed Llewellyn into the archive, where the curator headed straight for one of the far drawers; column 23, drawer D. The long, deep drawer opened silently. Spread out on the padded bed of green baize lay a dozen artefacts from ancient Iraq. Rhidian scanned the pieces of ceramic and metalwork, until his eyes rested on the ten-inch statue of the bearded priest king.

'There he is, Inspector. Safe and sound. Maybe Professor Swann just wanted to do some extra research in her own time. Unorthodox and probably worthy of a verbal warning, but considering her situation, I think we can let sleeping dogs lie.'

Llewellyn went to close the drawer.

'Two hundred and five,' said Rhidian.

'Sorry, what?'

'I've just counted them. There are two hundred and five drawers.'

'Yes, I suppose there are.'

'And how many items are in each?'

'That depends...'

'A rough estimate will do.'

'Ten, twelve.'

'Even I can do the maths on that one,' said Jones.

'Over two thousand artefacts in this room, and yet you knew exactly where to find the one item we were looking for. You didn't need to check your records first?' said Rhidian.

Knowing that the game was up, Llewellyn's head bowed. He was surprised by the wave of relief he experienced as the burden of the heavy secret was removed from his shoulders.

'When did you find out?' asked Rhidian.

'Only yesterday.' Llewellyn slumped into a chair. 'Have you seen the newspapers? "Murder Museum", that's what they're calling us. Don't get me wrong, that kind of publicity will bring many more visitors through the doors. But it's also going to draw the attention of the Board and they will need reassurance that there's no chance of any more scandal.'

'So, you thought that you had better check your inventory?'

'Where I was shocked to find several… anomalies.'

'What kind of anomalies?'

Llewellyn lifted the statue from the drawer.

'The weight is good. The stone is right. However, the carving, it's just too clean. It's very hard to mimic centuries of wear.'

'You're saying it's a knock-off?' asked Jones.

'Not a bad forgery, but I've got shoes that are older than this,' said Llewellyn.

'How many items do you think have been swapped?' asked Rhidian.

'So far I've found eight. All from the archives. And I have only got as far as the second century BCE. There might be more imposters yet to be discovered.'

'And the whereabouts of the missing objects? We didn't find anything suspicious in Loretta Swann's flat,' said Rhidian.

'I've checked the legitimate marketplaces for antiquities of this quality. None of our artefacts have turned up there. However, there are plenty of collectors who don't care about the provenance of an object, as long as they can add them to their private collections.'

'What kind of value are we talking about?'

'For all the missing items? Hundreds of thousands. Not that they would make the same money on the black market of course.'

'And when exactly were you going to tell us about this?'

'I'm sorry. I didn't know what to do.'

'You didn't want to be implicated, you mean?' said Jones.

‘I’m not worried about my position. I just want to protect the professional reputation of this wonderful facility. If word got out that there are fakes among the collection, we might never recover.’

Rhidian and Jones waited outside his office, while Llewellyn printed off details of all the missing artefacts that had been replaced by forgeries.

‘It would explain where she got all the money from,’ said Jones. ‘And if James Calder found out what she was doing...’

‘He would have the leverage to blackmail her into having sex with him.’

‘And all just to pay for plastic surgery? Was it worth it?’

‘Even after all those operations, all the painful recoveries, having to hide until the scars had healed, after all of that, when she looked in the mirror, who did she see? The beautiful goddess that she’d transformed herself into, or could she still only see the plain Jane beneath?’

‘If Cassidy had been less obsessed with perving over her and actually did his job, he could have nipped this in the bud ages ago,’ said Jones. ‘And maybe saved some lives.’

‘I’m not so sure. Yes, we’ve got a link between Loretta Swann and Calder, but we’ve not proved any connection between her thefts from the museum and the murders of Darius Gull or Rhys Pryce.’

‘She clearly had several men under her spell,’ said Jones.

‘But Gull was gay and there’s no evidence that Rhys Pryce ever met her before crashing into her car.’ Rhidian’s attention was drawn to the floor polisher, now silent, abandoned in the middle of the gallery. ‘There is one other person who was rather captivated by Professor Swann.’

Jones saw what he was looking at. 'Who? Whatshisname?'

'Yes. He's always been there, but we haven't really noticed him. And what did he say? Something about how she had been an inspiration to him.'

Morris Palfrey lived in several rooms at the back of the building. There was no answer to Jones's heavy knocks.

'This is very unusual. He leaves the museum so rarely,' said Llewellyn.

Rhidian gave Jones the nod. She tried the door. It was unlocked.

'Wait here please, Mr Llewellyn,' said Rhidian.

Jones led the way in, calling, 'Mr Palfrey, it's the police.'

No response.

At first everything looked like a normal flat occupied by a middle-aged bachelor; consisting of a small kitchen–diner, a lounge with a pleasant view over the museum's inner courtyard, and a sparsely-furnished bedroom. Rhidian noted the lack of personal decoration. There were no photos of loved ones, no sign of any hobbies. Everything was neat and tidy. Rhidian thought that it looked more like a monk's cell than a comfy home. Then Rhidian saw the door of the cupboard built into the kitchen wall that at one time might have served as a pantry. Scratched through the paint and deep into the wood were six-inch high letters spelling out the name *Felix*. Jones was at Rhidian's side as he opened the door, revealing what could only be described as a shrine.

Arranged on the bottom shelf were a dozen candles of various sizes, from nightlights to bulky church candles. Icicles of melted wax had solidified as they dripped down the shelf, a testament to their regular use. Their purpose was clear: to illuminate the items arranged on the back of the cupboard wall. At the centre of this reliquary was Loretta

Swann's museum ID card, hanging by its lanyard. Positioned around the smiling photo, as if at the points of a clock, were various everyday, personal items displayed as if they were religious relics. A balled-up tissue stained with red lipstick, a plastic bag containing a half-eaten biscuit, a takeaway coffee cup with the name 'Loretta' written on it in felt pen by a barista, a CD of Dido's first album, and a bottle of Midnight Mist.

'What's this "Felix?"' asked Jones. 'Some kind of pet name?'

'It's not a name.' Rhidian and Jones turned to see that Llewellyn had followed them in. 'It's a Roman term meaning one who is favoured by the gods.'

'And what's the connection to a red head covering?' asked Rhidian.

'At public rituals in ancient Rome, officiants prayed and made sacrifices to the Gods *capite velato*, "with the head covered" by a fold of the toga drawn up from the back. A red toga. How did you know?'

'I thought it was a hoody,' Rhidian said. He nodded to Jones. She went in search of the distinctive clothing.

Llewellyn was clearly disturbed by Palfrey's shrine. 'I had no idea.'

'I'd be surprised if even Loretta Swann realised that she was the object of such devotion,' said Rhidian.

'Morris might have cast himself in the role of one of the *fanatici*; men who dedicated their lives to those they worshipped.'

Jones returned. 'No sign of anything like a red hoody, but I did find this.' She produced a map of Cardiff and its surroundings and spread it open on Palfrey's kitchen table. There were several locations marked on it that were instantly familiar to Rhidian.

'That's Gull's apartment. And the marina where Dr Moore's boat is moored.'

‘And that’s the coast road where Rhys Pryce was found.’

Rhidian’s eye was drawn to an unfamiliar mark, on a mid-terrace house in Barry. ‘And this?’

‘No idea,’ said Jones.

‘We need to find out whose address this is.’

‘On it,’ said Jones, stepping back into the hallway, already dialling on her phone

Rhidian secured Palfrey’s flat, to await the arrival of the crime scene investigators. As he and the curator returned to the body of the museum, Rhidian felt sorry for Llewellyn, whose position was becoming more untenable with every revelation. Absently looking into the nearest glass cabinet, one object caught his eye. ‘What is that?’ he asked, pointing to the fist-sized lump of black glass mounted in a jade handle which had been carved into the shape of a mythical bird.

‘It’s obsidian.’

‘That’s a type of glass, isn’t it?’

‘A volcanic glass that can be fashioned into some of the sharpest blades ever made,’ said Llewellyn. ‘So sharp that they could reputedly cut off a horse’s head in one go. The ancient Aztecs called this a *macuahuitl*. It could be used as a weapon as well as a very efficient butchering tool.’

‘Yes, I can attest to that,’ said Rhidian, automatically putting a hand to the tightness of his arm where stitches still held the wound together.

Llewellyn didn’t understand what Rhidian was implying.

‘That damage looks fresh,’ said Rhidian.

‘Damage? What damage?’ Then Llewellyn saw the fresh chip taken out of one edge of the ancient weapon; the matching piece having recently been stuck in Rhidian’s arm. ‘I don’t understand. How—?’

Rhidian was too distracted to answer as he looked at the rest of the collection of some of the earliest examples of man's attempts to kill his fellow man. Flint spear heads, a highly decorated Maori battle club, and a vast array of ancient knives that still looked sharp enough to kill.

'No wonder our pathologist couldn't identify the weapons,' said Rhidian. 'He wouldn't have any of these in his database.'

'You're saying that Morris Palfrey used our artefacts to kill?' asked the stunned Llewellyn.

'And to remove body parts,' said Jones, rejoining them.

'Oh my God!'

Jones was surprised to see that Llewellyn's skin could become even paler than usual.

'Working at night, he could have had them cleaned and back on show before anyone had noticed they were missing,' said Rhidian. He pointed out a crude saw fashioned from a whale bone studded along its length with shark's teeth. 'That, for instance, still looks sharp enough to cut through an ankle bone.'

'Or a ribcage,' added Jones.

Llewellyn was too shocked to reply. His mind was already being overloaded by the implications. How long would his beloved museum have to be shut down for? What were the Trustees going to say?

'Sorry if I'm missing something here,' said Jones. 'What's wrong with a good old-fashioned kitchen knife or a claw hammer? Palfrey's got easy access to loads of stuff like that. Why complicate things?'

'Because he believes that only the right tools will make the sacrifices work,' said Llewellyn, distracted by a display in the next cabinet. Rhidian saw what Llewellyn was looking at: a collection of small tokens made of wax or silver. Each was in the shape of a body part; eyes, feet, hands, legs. 'What are these?' he asked.

'Roman artefacts found at sites all around South Wales.'

'And their purpose?'

'They're votive offerings.'

'Votive what?' asked Jones.

'It's a practice that actually predates the Roman Empire. If you, or a loved one were suffering from an illness, you would buy or fashion a token in the shape of the body part that was ailing you. So for gout - a clay foot, for blindness you would buy a glass eye. You prayed for the intercession of your favoured god, then threw the token into the nearest sacred pool.'

'Was water always used?'

'Oh yes, water was regarded as a sacred place of healing because it was considered to be not of this world or the next.'

'Morris Palfrey went one step further, using real body parts instead of tokens to try and restore Loretta Swann's health,' said Rhidian.

He pulled out his notebook and turned to the page where he had noted details from Loretta Swann's medical notes.

'On the fourteenth, Rhys Pryce's foot was sacrificed. The next day Loretta Swann was able to come off the oxygen mask. The day after Darius Gull lost his tongue, Dr Swann's brain activity improved. The same with Calder and Moore. Improvements each time. No wonder Palfrey thinks that his sacrifices are working.'

'You sound like you admire him,' said Jones.

'Not for his actions, but for his level of devotion.'

'Er, Inspector.' Llewellyn drew their attention back to the display cabinets. 'There's a gap here.'

Rhidian saw that an artefact was missing. He read the descriptive label: 'Medieval Indian katar. What is that?'

'A punching dagger with a triangular blade. The grip is in the shape of an H, allowing for extra stability. Instead of slashing as you would with a normal knife, you punch. The blade becomes an extension of your arm. It only has a short reach, but in close combat it was deadly and could easily penetrate chain mail armour.'

Rhidian's imagination was already working, creating Technicolor images of the sort of damage that such a deadly weapon could inflict upon a human body.

Jones's phone rang. She talked into it urgently then turned to Rhidian. 'That address in Barry. It's Ginnie Lane's.'

'Putting Loretta Swann on the front page put her on Palfrey's list.'

'But he must know that we're onto him.'

'I don't think he cares about getting caught, as long as we don't stop his sacred quest. He isn't going to stop killing until Loretta Swann has fully recovered,' said Rhidian.

35

The row of terraced houses offered a splash of colour against the gunmetal backdrop of increasingly threatening skies. Although the stone surrounds of the doors and windows were all picked out in plain white, the brickwork was another matter. One house had been painted a shocking salmon pink, the next was lime green. Ginnie Lane's home was a very pleasant powder blue.

As Jones banged on the front door, Rhidian was on his phone, talking to Ginnie Lane's editor, who confirmed that she had already left work and wasn't due back until Monday. As Rhidian terminated the call, an elderly neighbour poked his head out of his upstairs window to see what all the noise was about.

'Can I help you?'

Rhidian flashed his warrant card. 'Police. We're looking for Ginnie Lane?'

'You've got the right address, only you're too late. Saw her heading off in her car with an overnight bag what, half an hour ago.'

'Any idea where she was going?'

'To see one of her boyfriends I should think.'

'How many has she got?' asked Jones.

'Too many to keep track of.'

'Thank you,' said Rhidian, before turning to Jones. 'Sergeant.'

Jones needed no second invitation, and, with two great thumps from her size eight monkey boots, soon had the door in.

'I hope you're gonna fix that,' shouted the nosy neighbour as they entered the house.

Jones followed Rhidian down the short hallway, passing a row of shoes arranged in ascending heel size; from comfy black flatties to cherry-red, six-inch stilettos. They paused in the doorway to the lounge, alert for signs of anything that might be out of place, but the house was silent. There was no obvious sign of disturbance.

'Diary. Address book. Laptop. Anything that might tell us where she's gone,' said Rhidian.

'Boss.'

While Jones headed for the stairs, Rhidian stepped into the lounge. He was drawn to a set of white wooden shelves. It contained the usual tokens of someone's life: a medal for completing the Cardiff Marathon last year; a few framed photos of parties with friends, and some colourful shells picked up on some exotic beach – definitely not Swansea Bay. In pride of place in the centre of the shelves was a silver trophy in the shape of an old-fashioned quill pen. Rhidian picked it up to read the inscription: *'The Athena Junior Journalist of the Year 2016'*. Rhidian wondered what was going through Ginnie Lane's mind when she won that award. Did she see herself, six years on, grubbing around in the gutter for stories to further her career?

Jones appeared in the doorway. 'Bedroom and bathroom are clear. But I did find this.' Jones opened the laptop onto the Windows welcome page. 'Trouble is, it's password protected.'

'How are your IT skills?'

'I'm no Steve Jobs, but I'll give it a go,' said Jones.

'We're running out of time so I need to know. Can you do this, or should I call someone from the tech department?'

'And how long is it going to take for them to get their act together?'

Rhidian accepted her point. 'Okay. Do it.'

Jones settled in front of the computer. 'Let's start with the obvious. Birthday. Pets' names. Favourite colour.'

As Jones typed, Rhidian tried to console himself with the thought that if they didn't know where Ginnie Lane had gone, perhaps Palfrey was equally in the dark.

*

The gamekeeper's cottage had once been home to Ginnie Lane's uncle Ivor. He had worked for the Brecon Beacons National Park until his retirement, and because the park no longer had any need for his position, he was allowed to buy the humble, two-up two-down stone building at a reasonable discount. However, retirement didn't suit a man who was used to being active ten hours a day. He tended the small garden and took long walks in the forest, but this was a shadow of his former life. When he faded away to a quiet, rather sad death, the family decided to keep the cottage on. During the summer and at Christmas and Easter, it was rented as a holiday home. Any time that it didn't have paid guests, members of the family could use it, on a first come, first served basis. For some, it was a chance to get out of the city and enjoy the woodland walks or dinghy sailing on the nearby reservoir. For Ginnie, it was a venue for romantic weekends with whichever man was in her favour at the time. There was no phone line and she insisted that all of her guests left their mobiles locked in their cars. She demanded their full attention, at least for forty-eight hours.

As she collected her shopping from the back seat of her car, Ginnie was looking forward to the treats to come. She had enjoyed being the one who made the first move for a change. In the bedroom she usually had to accept being submissive, but from today onwards she was determined that there was a new Ginnie Lane in town. From now on, she was going to be the one on top.

Shouldering her overnight bag, she closed the car door, pulled the box of groceries off the roof and headed for the cottage. She often forgot to lock the car's doors here. There was no other living soul for three miles. As she pushed open the cottage door, she was so distracted by thoughts of the sweaty pleasures to come that she didn't notice the car boot spring open, and a man's hand emerge.

*

Twenty five miles away in Barry, Jones was running out of ideas. She had typed in Ginnie Lane's birthday, her place of birth and her mother's maiden name. No go. Rhidian paced the room, looking for clues. His eyes stopped on the writing award again.

'Try Athena.'

Jones typed and hit *enter*, but only got another '*Password not recognised*'.

'Maybe we should just take it to computer forensics,' said Jones, reluctant to admit defeat.

'Too late for that now,' said Rhidian. As he stared at the laptop screen, Rhidian was inspired. 'Are we missing the obvious?'

'Like what?'

'That image.'

'It'll just be a randomly selected screen saver.'

'I don't think so. I know that place.'

Jones looked closer at the dramatic image of a wooded valley surrounding a stretch of calm water. The setting sun was reflected in the surface, giving the illusion that both sky and water were on fire. Stretching out into the water was a metal bridge leading to a grey stone tower with a green copper roof that tapered into a sharp spire.

'A lake? Could be anywhere,' said Jones.

'No. I know that tower... It's a reservoir. I went there with Bethan. It's near Merthyr.'

'Pontsticill,' said Jones. 'Yeah. We had a school trip there.'

‘I can’t imagine that Ms Lane is into civil engineering, so if she chose to look at that image every day, it must have some personal connection,’ said Rhidian. ‘And it ticks Palfrey’s boxes. It’s remote, and there’s water.’

As they rushed to the car, Rhidian hoped they would be in time. He didn’t like the ambitious hack, but he had no wish for their next meeting to take place at Bloom’s dissecting table.

*

Ginnie Lane stepped out of the shower, wrapped in her favourite fluffy dressing gown. Not exactly sexy, but sometimes she needed the comfort of its fleecy hug. Everything was ready. She’d shaved her legs and made sure that she was tidy down there. The champagne was chilling, and the new lace underwear she’d bought specially for the weekend was laid out on the bed. She was scrolling through the music on her smart phone, selecting which tracks best suited her mood, when there was a knock on the door.

‘He’s keen,’ she thought. She wasn’t expecting him for another hour. She pressed *play*, docked her phone, checked her hair in the mirror and opened the door. Her welcoming smile froze when she saw the red-hooded figure and the strange weapon he was holding. He let her scream, knowing there was no one to hear.

36

Jones stayed in second gear to navigate the potholes of the rough lane. Her headlights picked out the grass growing down the centre of the track which showed how little traffic ever came this way. Jones switched on the wipers as drizzle speckled the windscreen.

As soon as they saw the lights of the gamekeeper's cottage through the trees, Rhidian told her to stop. They exited the car, closing the doors gently to avoid alerting anyone inside. Somewhere in the forest an owl screeched out a warning. Now they were close enough, they could see the registration of the mint-coloured Fiat 500 parked out front.

'That's Lane's car,' said Jones.

'You take the rear.'

'Shouldn't we wait for armed response?'

'We don't even know that Palfrey's in there.'

'And if he is? He's already attacked you once.'

'He's so close to completing his mission, he's not going to wait for our backup to arrive.'

'But—'

Rhidian cut off her protests by striding towards the cottage. Jones had no choice. She went back to the car to grab the heavy-duty Maglite torch from the glove compartment, then followed Rhidian Hook towards the cottage.

The front door of the cottage was unlocked. Rhidian cautiously entered, pausing on the threshold to listen. Marvin Gaye was playing over the speakers, encouraging any listeners to 'Get it on'. A log fire was crackling. A bottle of champagne was chilling in an ice bucket. Rhidian gestured for Jones to look upstairs. Jones went off to search. He could hear her upstairs, the floorboards creaking above his head as she moved from room to room. Rhidian checked the kitchen, noting that the fridge was full of cold meats, fancy cheeses and two more bottles of champagne.

Jones returned. 'No sign of her, but there are some sexy undies and a box of condoms all ready to go. Reckon the neighbour was right. She was expecting company.'

Rhidian was only half listening because something had caught his eye. He crouched to pluck a small object from where it had lodged between the floorboards; a perfect, bleached white tooth tipped at the root with blood.

'Palfrey's here. Let's hope we're not too late.'

*

At the Hopewell Infirmary Cindy Campbell ran down the corridor to answer the alarms going off in Loretta Swann's room. She burst through the side room door to find a junior nurse leaning over the patient's bed, giving chest compressions.

'I've got nothing,' said the nurse. 'No output at all.'

An urgent check of the monitor showed a flat line. No pulse. No resps. No heartbeat. Seeing that the junior was flagging under the effort of pumping Loretta Swann's chest, Cindy Campbell swapped places, taking over the chest compressions, knowing that the crash team were on their way, hoping they would get there in time.

By the time Rhidian and Jones reached the reservoir, the rain had turned from a light drizzle into a real bone-soaker, which made climbing up the slippery grass bank to the summit of the stone dam even more laborious. They did get some help from a nearly full moon, its blue light glinting off the wet rocks and the dark water ten feet below. Rhidian scooped the rain out of his eyes, searching for any movement. It was Jones who spotted them.

'There! On the bridge.'

Rhidian saw the iron walkway that stretched from one side of the dam and out into the middle of the artificial lake. The far end of the bridge terminated in the Gothic tower which rose from the water on an octagonal base and finished with a pointed copper spire, topped by a weathervane. Two dark shapes could just be discerned, twenty feet out on the walkway.

Jones followed Rhidian's lead as he headed for the bridge, moving as quickly as they dared over the slick, wet stones. Now they could see the figures more clearly. Ginnie Lane was only wearing a soaked dressing gown; her hands were tied in front of her and she was gagged by one of her own scarves. She was trying to hook her feet into the fretwork of the bridge, but her captor was too powerful and kept dragging her towards the middle of the walkway. The moonlight turned his red-hooded toga black. Rhidian knew that even with the noise of the rain splashing on the water, there was no way they could approach over the metal bridge without being heard. He raised his voice against the storm and shouted across the choppy waters.

'Palfrey!'

The taller figure stopped and turned, to see Rhidian and Jones stepping out onto the bridge. Morris Palfrey tugged the wet hood back, revealing the fire of total devotion burning in his eyes.

Loretta Swann was now being attended by the well-drilled crash team. A male nurse held an oxygen mask over her mouth and nose, and gave two pumps on the air bag every time the junior nurse reached thirty chest compressions. Cindy Campbell briefed the on-call doctor as they prepared the defibrillator.

'She's been down for three minutes. Continuous CPR. No output.'

Sister Campbell lifted Loretta's silk top and placed the two sticky-backed electro pads onto her chest, one above and one below her heart. Cindy knew the stark statistics of how few people ever recovered from a cardiac arrest, even in a hospital setting. She mouthed a silent prayer, and hoped that Loretta Swann would be one of the lucky ones.

'Let her go, Morris. It's not too late,' shouted Rhidian, taking another tentative step forward.

Palfrey stopped dragging Ginnie Lane. Rhidian thought this was a hopeful sign, until he realised that this was only because he had reached his destination, stopping directly over what looked like a large, flat funnel in the water. Rhidian remembered it from a visit when he was a child. His dad told him all about how the bell mouth spillway was one of only three examples in the UK. Fifty foot across, it looked like an inverted bell. The water rushed into it, then swirled down, entering a vortex. So this was where the final sacrifice was to be made. Rhidian glanced back at Jones who was quietly talking into her radio, relaying directions to the armed response unit. He knew that he needed to buy them more time.

'I understand what you've been trying to do,' he shouted.

'How could you?' shouted Palfrey, forcing Ginnie onto her knees. With her hands tied in front of her, it gave the impression that she was praying.

'The papers are calling you a killer,' said Rhidian. Palfrey ripped open Ginnie Lane's dressing gown to expose her naked chest. Rhidian had to risk taking another step forward. 'But I know that this is a sacred mission,' he called.

Surprised, Palfrey turned his attention away from the petrified journalist. Encouraged, Rhidian took another step forward. 'You've got to ask yourself, is this what Professor Swann would want? How will she feel when she recovers, only to find out that you took lives in order to save hers?'

'The blood is on my hands, not Hers.'

Rhidian was encouraged that Palfrey was willing to talk. He was now close enough to see Ginnie Lane's eyes, begging him for help. 'Did you ever tell her what she means to you?'

'Who needs words when I could show her through my acts of devotion.'

'What did she do to earn such adoration?'

'She's the only one who ever truly saw me. Before Her I was nothing. She filled my heart with so much beauty. She gave me a purpose.'

'You let her in when the museum was closed?' Rhidian narrowed the gap to ten feet.

'She liked to work when it was quiet. It was our special time,' said Palfrey. 'I watched her work and she answered every question I could think of. I didn't have much time for learning at school. The teachers said I had special needs, but I never felt very special, not till I met Her. So when She needed me, how could I not act?'

'And it worked. You brought her back from the brink. Every day she's getting stronger.' Rhidian was encouraged to see Palfrey loosen his grip on Ginnie Lane. 'You can stop now. No one else needs to get hurt.'

Palfrey looked down at the cowering journalist, as if seeing her as a human being for the first time. He pulled her dressing gown together to cover her nakedness. Rhidian was relieved that he seemed to have had got through to Palfrey. But just as the caretaker was helping the petrified woman to her feet, he was distracted by movement on the far side of the reservoir where blue lights strobed off the low clouds. Jones used her radio. 'I said no lights!'

The approaching police cars turned off their rooftop lights, but it was too late. With one hand, Palfrey grabbed a handful of Ginnie Lane's hair, forcing her head back, exposing the soft white of her throat. From inside his toga he produced the katar, with its deadly, six-inch triangular blade. He pulled his arm back, ready to punch the dagger straight through Ginnie Lane's ribcage and pierce her heart. Rhidian called: 'Morris!'

'My name is Felix and She will get her heart.'

Before Palfrey could strike, Rhidian tried one last gamble. 'It won't work.'

'What?'

'The offering has to be worthy.' Rhidian looked at the snivelling Ginnie Lane. 'Is she worthy? We've both seen that she'll do anything; sell out anyone to get ahead. And if her heart is such a withered, black thing, will it be a suitable sacrifice?'

Seeing Palfrey hesitate, Rhidian stepped forward. 'After everything you've done; everything you've worked so hard for, do you really want to risk it all now?'

Rhidian was relieved to see that he had got Palfrey thinking. Jones couldn't understand what DI Hook was doing.

'Boss?'

Rhidian ignored her, his eyes never breaking the lock on Palfrey's. 'I know what it's like to devote your heart to someone.' Rhidian took off his coat and let it hang from one hand. 'I know what it's like to want to die in someone else's place.' He tore open his shirt, exposing his chest.

'You can't do this,' said Jones, behind him.

Palfrey turned the ancient weapon over in his hand, watching the rain slide off the blade that was still keen after all these centuries. Then he looked Rhidian in the eyes and said, 'I accept your sacrifice.'

Palfrey pulled Ginnie Lane to her feet and pushed her towards Jones, who caught the woman before she stumbled and fell. 'It's okay. I've got you.' Jones shepherded Ginnie Lane away across the bridge towards safety, but the sergeant's heart sank when she saw that the armed response units had had to abandon their vehicles on the other side of a locked fence, and were having to make their way on foot. They would never get there in time.

At the Hopewell Infirmary, the doctor selected the charge of electricity to send through the pads. A long bleep told everyone that the machine was ready to fire.

'Clear,' called the doctor. Everyone stood back. He hit the button and a shock jolted Loretta Swann's body. They anxiously watched the monitor. There was no change.

'Okay. Going again. Charging to two-forty.' Cindy Campbell took over the chest compressions while the doctor adjusted the dial, and the defibrillator built to the required charge.

'Clear.' Sister Clark removed her hands and stepped back. The doctor hit the button. A second jolt. Another wait. Nothing but flat lines.

'Charging to three-sixty'.

Rhidian Hook stood on the iron walkway, ten feet above the swirling vortex of water. He lifted his face to the rain and closed his eyes. Palfrey moved to stand in front of him and braced both hands on the hilt of the dagger. As he drew the blade back, Rhidian threw his coat into Palfrey's face, then grappled for the knife. Palfrey clawed the coat away, twisted, and used the momentum to push Rhidian back against the parapet of the bridge. Rhidian grunted in pain as his lower back hit the unforgiving metal. Palfrey's obsession gave him extra strength. All that Rhidian could do was focus on holding the dagger at bay. He could feel his muscles weakening. The wound in his arm started to burn as the stitches burst and a trickle of warmth ran down his bicep. He knew that he wouldn't be able to hold on. Jones was too far away. Palfrey was fuelled by the power of the righteous. Rhidian knew there was only one way out of this.

With the parapet in the small of his back acting as a fulcrum, Rhidian braced his legs against the iron floor and pushed with the last of his remaining strength. Caught off guard, Palfrey had no time to react. As Rhidian started falling backwards off the walkway, he still had a firm grip on Palfrey's wrists. From the other end of the bridge, Jones watched the two men tumble backwards over the edge and into the black water.

The impact took Rhidian's breath away, forcing him to release his grip on Palfrey.

From the bank Jones saw both men go under the water, then, nothing. She aimed her torch, sending its beam over the reservoir, but the light only picked out the shallow waves being kicked up by the wind. The first of the armed backup arrived.

'Light!' shouted Jones.

The constable added his torch beam to Jones's. More officers arrived. More torch beams searched the water, but nothing broke the surface. Jones was giving up hope when a head burst from the water, gasping for air. She squinted through the rain as every torch beam focused on the head and shoulders. Jones was relieved to see that it was Rhidian Hook.

Arms and legs working to keep him afloat, Rhidian looked around. Everything was a uniform blackness and he couldn't find his bearings. Which way was the shore? Then he heard a voice. It was Jones calling to him. He twisted in the water until he saw the light of her torch being waved, out of the darkness. As his eyes adjusted he could make out the deeper black of the reservoir wall. Relieved, he started to swim towards it with heavy limbs, only for strong arms to grab him from behind. Rhidian sculled around to face Palfrey. The cold was quickly sapping what little strength he still had. Rhidian knew that he was in no shape for a second fight, but when he saw the look of peace and acceptance on Palfrey's face, Rhidian understood that their battle was over.

'Tell Her, I regret nothing,' said Palfrey, and before Rhidian could stop him, he pulled the katar clear of the water, and plunged it deep into his own chest. A plume of red fogged the water between them.

Rhidian reached for Palfrey, only for the caretaker to use the last of his strength to kick himself away. Palfrey looked at Rhidian and nodded an acceptance of his fate, then the irresistible undertow from the spillway caught the caretaker and pulled him away. He circled once, twice, before his body was sucked over the lip of the spillway, spiralling down into the cold blackness.

Everyone in the hospital room knew this was their final chance. Their patient had been without any measurable heartbeat for too long.

'Clear,' said the doctor. He hit the button. Another shock rocked Loretta Swann's body, but with the same, disappointing result. Cindy Campbell's arms and shoulders ached as she continued with the chest compressions.

'I think it's time,' said the doctor. 'Does everyone agree?' He looked around the room. Grim nods all around. 'Okay, you can stop now, Sister.'

Cindy reluctantly stepped away from the bed. The junior nurse removed the oxygen mask from Loretta Swann's face. The doctor looked at his watch.

'Time of death…'

'Wait!' Cindy Campbell moved back into position. Placing the heels of her hands over Loretta Swann's chest; she started pumping up and down, and breathlessly explained, 'There was an output.'

Everyone looked at the monitor. For a moment there was nothing, then the flat line jumped. Once, twice, then a continuing beat, weak, but constant. Cindy Campbell stopped the compressions. The numbers started climbing. Blood pressure, heart rate, resps all crept back towards normal. Everyone agreed that they had witnessed a minor miracle.

Rhidian was trying to swim for the shore, but his limbs felt leaden, his muscles were cramping. He could feel his heart pumping harder to keep his vital organs working, and his core temperature was dropping fast. His strokes became weaker. His legs would no longer follow his instructions to kick. He struggled to get any air into his lungs. His head fell forward, dipped under the water, and he started to sink.

Surrounded by darkness, embraced by the freezing cold, he couldn't tell how deep he was going. And then, in the murk, he saw something; a smudge of ivory, then a swirl of long blonde hair. He waited for the shape to come closer. He longed to see Bethan's face and to be welcomed into her arms, but his logic kicked in, forcing him to accept that this was an hallucination; a side effect of his brain shutting down through hypothermia. With this acceptance, the form solidified and he realised that it was just a clump of weed waving in the invisible force that was now plucking at his body, dragging him towards the overspill. It would be so easy to stop fighting; to let the undertow take him; to hope that he would soon see Bethan. All he had to do was let go. And yet, something inside wouldn't let him. A tiny flicker of light in the darkness, a flicker that became a flame; a flame that became a fire that would not go out. He wanted to live.

Rhidian willed his legs to kick and forced his arms to move. Half a dozen good strokes and he had broken free of the undertow. His head surfaced, and he was able to take in his bearings. Surely the safety of the shore was too far away? The surge of adrenaline which had helped him escape the dragging depths faded away, leaving his muscles like jelly. He couldn't stop his head from dipping below the surface again. He took in another mouthful of water. His body gave up working; it was just a dead weight that was beginning to pull him under, until there was a splash, a few feet in front of him. A life buoy had been thrown from the reservoir wall. He feebly stretched for it. His fingers slipped off the smooth surface. He tried again and was finally able to get a firm grip with both hands. Then the buoy was moving, and he was being pulled through the choppy water. All he could do was cling on. If his grip failed, he would be gone. Then he felt the buoy bang into the wall. He looked up to see Jones, legs braced, the rope wrapped around her body, heaving for all she was worth. Other officers raced to the wall, strong hands found a grip, and heaved Rhidian out of the water and onto dry land. He lay there, looking up at his sergeant's concerned face. He didn't even have the strength to say 'thank you', but Jones knew.

At the very moment that Morris Palfrey's light went out, Loretta Swann's eyes flickered open. She looked around, unsure where she was, until the smiling face of Cindy Campbell loomed into her vision.

'Welcome back, darling.'

*

Emerging groggily from another disturbed sleep, Liz Devlin wasn't sure what had woken her. She was hot. Burning up. She fumbled for the bedside light and switched it on. Sometime during the night she must have kicked the duvet off. Her T-shirt was clinging to her skin. Her pillow was soaked with sweat. Then her heart skipped a beat. There were voices. More than one. Downstairs. She automatically reached out for her mobile phone, but all she found was an empty space, and she remembered that she had left it in the kitchen, charging up. No help could be summoned. She needed to do this herself. She reached under the bed for the baseball bat that she always kept there, just in case, and cautiously headed for the door.

She stepped out onto the landing. The voices were louder now; two men, but she couldn't make out what they were saying. Gripping the bat tighter, she took one step down, then another. Risking a glance over the banister, she could see a flickering blue light coming from the lounge. Then she recognised one of the voices; it was Roger Moore. Feeling the stress drain from her body, Liz moved swiftly into the lounge. Switching on the main lights confirmed that the TV had switched itself on. Liz found the remote control and turned off the 1970s war movie. She checked the windows and doors. Everything was secure. There were no intruders.

Liz dropped onto the settee, the baseball bat across her knees. She knew she wasn't going mad, but it couldn't be a coincidence that all of the electronic devices in her home seemed to have a mind of their own. Then it hit her, like a punch in the guts. Of course. The smart TV, the entertainment system, the Wi-Fi-controlled central heating system; Peter had installed them. She thought that it was just his fascination with the latest gadgets, and maybe that's all it was at the beginning, only now he had found a way to control her life, even from the other side of the world. In a fury she stormed around the house, ripping batteries from remote controls, disabling the camera-doorbell system, turning the central heating back to manual.

Angry tears stung her eyes as she remembered some of the private moments that her ex could have remotely observed. Her emotions veered wildly, from feeling helpless and abused to burning with fury.

Liz had dealt with many victims of domestic abuse in her time. She sympathised with the women, and sometimes men, who had let abusers into their lives and then felt trapped, unable to escape. She knew what she would advise anyone to do if they were in her place: report the abuse to the police. But how could she do that without exposing herself to criticism? She could imagine the whispers in the canteen now. Her job was to protect the vulnerable, yet she couldn't even protect herself.

As she recovered, Liz tried to persuade herself that in some ways, Peter had done her a favour in exposing the depths of his obsession by controlling her, even after their marriage was dead. Whatever sympathy she had once felt for him was well and truly gone. From now on she would only see him as another abuser. But she was no victim. It was time to move forward with the next chapter of her life.

37

First light. The plaintive call of a curlew cut through the light mist that hung over the mirror-flat water of the reservoir. Last night's storm was just a memory. The tranquil scene was broken when a police diver emerged from the water, turned to his team waiting on a nearby inflatable boat, and gave a thumbs up. Moments later, two of his colleagues surfaced, supporting Morris Palfrey's body between them.

Well wrapped up in his coat, Rhidian watched the boat bring the body to the shore where Bloom was waiting to examine it. Rhidian had let the paramedics give him the once over and re-dress the cut on his arm, but he refused to go to hospital. He needed to be here for the final act. He turned to Jones.

'Call the hospital. Check on Loretta Swann.'

'Why?'

'Call it a hunch.'

Jones stepped away, taking out her mobile. Rhidian joined Bloom, watching the limp, broken corpse of Morris Palfrey being placed on top of a plastic body bag. It looked as if every bone in his body had been crushed by the force of the water smashing it against the iron sluice gates. But there was a look of peace on the caretaker's features.

'Hardly the face of a cold-blooded killer,' said Bloom.

'A killer, yes, but his blood was anything but cold.'

Jones joined them, putting her phone away. 'How did you know? She's awake and talking.'

'So what do we put that down to; a coincidence, or the power of true devotion?' asked Rhidian, watching Bloom zip up the body bag.

*

As Liz Devlin strode into the police station she knew that she was turning heads. Gone was her trademark black trouser suit and white blouse, replaced by a vivid crimson blouse, a hip-hugging skirt, and knee-length boots. Her hair had been restyled into a long, tousled bob and she had switched her lipstick to a brighter shade of red. She felt an extra couple of inches taller.

*

Back in their office, Jones stifled a yawn as she pressed *play* on the DVD player. She only had a couple of discs from the council's CCTV cameras left to look through. It was all pretty much irrelevant now. It hardly mattered whether they spotted Morris Palfrey lurking around Gull's apartment or Anna Moore's barge. There was no need for a trial now that the self-confessed killer was dead. Nevertheless, Jones liked to be thorough. She might not have graduated top of her class, but where she lacked the sharp intellect of some of her peers, she made up for it with her dogged determination. She was happy being a tortoise rather than a hare.

She was looking through footage of the roads leading to Darius Gull's apartment, hoping to find evidence of Morris Palfrey stalking the barrister. An hour in and Jones's mind was elsewhere. She had called in at home for a change of clothes, but Sam had already left for work. She was looking forward to seeing him later, so that she could tell him all about the dramatic night at the reservoir. Then her attention snapped back to the monitor screen. She had to rewind the footage to be sure, but yes... was it just a coincidence, or…?

Heart thumping, Jones reached for the last disc of footage taken in the streets leading to Rhys Pryce's faux mansion. Now she knew what she was looking for, she could scan in fast forward. Her eyes were glued to the grainy footage, dismissing every vehicle that didn't match. With every false alarm her confidence grew. Then she saw the same vehicle again. When it stopped at traffic lights there was a clear image of the registration plate and she could have no more doubts.

*

Rhidian returned to the hospital room where he had spent so much time, to find that the monitors were now silent and the woman he had spent so many hours standing guard over was sitting on the edge of the bed, dressed in a hospital gown, reading the local newspaper. The headline shouted '*Echo Reporter Helps Catch Killer'*.

'Professor Swann.'

She turned her jade-green eyes onto him. 'Yes?'

'Detective Inspector Hook.' Rhidian saw Loretta clock the familiar overnight bag he was carrying. 'I called at your flat. Thought you might need some clothes.'

Rhidian put the bag on the bed then fished her house keys out of his coat pocket and placed them on the bed next to the bag.

'Thank you, Inspector. That was very thoughtful.' She smiled. It was worth waiting for.

*

Anwen Jones had no memory of the journey home. One minute she was driving out of the police station car park, the next, she was pulling up outside her house. As she headed upstairs, Sam burst out of the bathroom.

'I wanted it to be a surprise,' he said.

'What?'

Sam opened the door to the bathroom and stepped back inside. Anwen followed, to see the stack of brochures for shower fittings on the closed toilet seat. On the floor were a sketchpad with rough drawings, and a series of measurements.

'My wet room?'

'I've got tile samples in the van, and I can get the fixtures and fittings at trade. That'll save us a few quid.'

She let him finish making the last few measurements.

'I thought you couldn't do bathrooms?'

'I can't. But I do know a good plumber and a tiler who'll do it for mate's rates.'

'Did you meet them through work?'

'Yeah. Done a couple of jobs with them.'

'Where?'

'Here and there, you know.'

'Not really.'

Sam looked up from his calculations. 'What do you mean?'

'You're always very interested in what I do, but I don't know who your clients are, or where you work.'

'Clients, I mostly get by word of mouth. And I take jobs anywhere, all over the city.'

'How about Cardiff Bay? The new penthouses?'

'No. Haven't had any work there. Wish I had. They must have money to burn.' Sam laughed, but was that a hint of sadness in his eyes? 'Let me clear this up, grab a shower, then you can ask me anything you want. Okay?'

Anwen backed out of the bathroom. Sam closed the door. Anwen waited until she heard the shower going, then went to where Sam's jacket was hanging up. She pulled out his keys, and slipped out of the house.

*

Rhidian stood in the doorway and watched Loretta Swann unpack the overnight bag, pulling out a blouse, skirt, then some plain, white underwear.

'I didn't know what you would need, so...'

'This will do fine,' said Loretta. 'I can't wait to get out of this hospital gown.'

'They're going to discharge you?'

'They want to keep me in for a few more days, but I just want to get back to my life, and I have to trust that they know best.'

Rhidian tried to read her. Did she really think she was going back to her flat, her job, her old life, as if nothing had happened? Loretta Swann turned away from his scrutiny to open the bedside locker and place her clothes inside. She paused when she found two sets of silk pyjamas already there. She pulled them out and laid them on the bed.

'These aren't mine. Did you…?'

'No. We think that Morris Palfrey brought them.'

'Oh.' Loretta put the pyjamas back into the locker. She could never wear them again. She picked up the newspaper. 'Is it true? Did Morris kill all of those people?'

'I'm afraid so, yes.'

'Why?'

'He was making votive offerings to save your life.'

For a moment Loretta was speechless.

'He was such a gentle man.'

'Who knows what we might be capable of for love?'

'*Love?*'

'He knew that there couldn't be any kind of romantic relationship.'

'Then what?'

'He worshipped you.'

'Me? But…' As she tried to absorb this, tears pricked Loretta's eyes. She wiped them away. 'I'm sorry. It's just… I suppose that every woman wants to be adored.'

'Which is why you set about transforming yourself?'

'I was tired of being invisible.'

'And it worked. You were seen. By Trevor Cassidy.'

'Cassidy? Yes, I suppose I did catch him looking at me a few times.'

'He didn't just look. He recorded you.'

'What?'

'You weren't the only one. He had hours of recordings of young women in his private collection.'

A shudder ran though Loretta's body.

'I'm sorry. It's best that you hear it from me, before you read it in the papers.'

'Yes. Thank you.'

'And then there was James Calder.'

Loretta tried, but couldn't hide her surprise. 'How much do you know?'

'We had to search your flat.'

'You found his letters?'

'Why didn't you destroy them?'

'I thought I could use them against him. Make him stop.'

'How did it start?'

'He asked me out several times. At first I was polite, made excuses, but he wouldn't take the hint. In the end, I had to spell out that he wasn't my type.'

'But then he found out what you were doing in the archives and he had something to hold over you?'

Loretta's eyes widened with shock.

'Yes. We know about the thefts. Professor Llewellyn is compiling a list of everything that's been replaced by your forgeries. At this point I should caution you.'

'I understand,' she said.

'You do not have to say anything, but it may harm your defence if you do not mention when questioned something which you later rely on in court. Anything you do say may be given in evidence. Do you understand?'

Loretta nodded. Rhidian sensed that the guilt of her inadvertent part in all the lost lives was starting to weigh down upon her. As her shoulders slumped, there was little evidence of the goddess who had been worshipped by one small man with a huge heart.

Anwen stood in the back of Sam's Transit van. She didn't touch anything. She just looked around and asked herself, 'What am I missing?' She could see that he had replaced the stolen tools. There were new saws hanging on pegs, a shiny new generator and a power drill, still in its box. Nothing looked as if it had been unpacked, let alone used. The old aluminium stepladders were in the same place. The same went for the half a dozen used pots of paint. The old dust sheets were in a pile in one corner. What was wrong with this picture?

Remembering Sam's reaction the morning he discovered the theft, Anwen went to the pots of paint. All were the same colour - Tuscan Cream. Lifting a pot, she could feel that it was about half full. The others were the same, but hadn't he said that they were needed for a job? Why hadn't it all been used up by now? Opening the brand new toolbox, Anwen selected a flat head screwdriver and used it to pry the lid off one of the paint pots. As she had estimated, it was about half full, but all her instincts still told her that something was wrong. She dipped the screwdriver into the paint, only for it to hit something solid, a centimetre below the surface. She had already spotted the box of unopened latex gloves. Once gloved up, she reached into the paint and pulled out the package hidden inside. She dropped it onto one of the dustsheets which she used to wipe the paint away. Once cleaned up, she could see that the clear ziplock bag contained tightly packed white powder. Roughly estimating the weight and multiplying that by today's street prices, Anwen was able to calculate that if the other tins contained similar loads, she was looking at nearly a hundred grand's worth of high quality cocaine. Normally she would feel elated at having made such a big find, but she just felt sick to her stomach. A voice from behind made her jump.

'Guess it was only a matter of time.'

Anwen got to her feet and turned to face Sam. His hair was dry. He hadn't been under the shower. She realised that asking too many questions must have given her away.

*

Rhidian Hook was in the same plastic chair where he'd spent so many hours. Loretta Swann sat on the edge of the hospital bed, telling him how it all started.

'I found it in a dusty old box in a forgotten drawer. An Egyptian scarab. Tiny, yet beautiful, beautiful and so very saleable on the black market. But I knew that everything was catalogued and that one day someone would notice that it was missing. I needed to replace it with something.'

'So you made a forgery?'

'I have a contact; a specialist who makes legitimate facsimiles for museums. And before you ask, no, I'm not going to give you his name.'

Rhidian nodded. That was something he would need to pursue in a formal interview. 'How soon before you were discovered?'

'I think he suspected from the start. I'd picked the wrong object. Egyptology was James Calder's speciality. He found my substitute and knew that it wasn't right. He said he wouldn't tell anyone, as long as I went for a meal with him. Only it didn't end when we paid the bill. He said it would just be one night, only he kept coming back for more. He said he was in love with me, but you don't do that to someone you love.'

'Morris Palfrey must have found out. Calder didn't realise that by abusing you, he had signed his own death warrant.' Rhidian realised that she was looking at him strangely.

'Your voice,' she said. 'You're the one who talked to me through the night.'

Anwen looked around the interior of the van.

'It's a good cover,' she told Sam. 'No one would think anything of seeing a builder going in and out of different properties. That's why you weren't bothered about your stolen tools. They were just part of the window dressing, weren't they?'

'I can't even use a hammer.' A typical Sam response, but there was no humour in his words this time.

'Darius Gull. Rhys Pryce. They were your clients?'

'I only sell to people who can control it. Never to kids, or addicts.'

'What do you want, a round of applause?'

'It was just business. Supply and demand. And my goods are safe. Guaranteed.' He could see that he wasn't getting through to Anwen. 'It was just a way to make big money, fast. Then I'm out, for good. That's why I suggested Scotland. I've made enough to set us up. Nice house. Anything you want.'

'So it's got nothing to do with it getting too hot in Cardiff, what with two of your clients dead and the cops closing in on you?'

'I want to be with you. I don't care where that is.'

'As long as you've got your tame copper to pump for information about how close we were to identifying you?'

'It wasn't like that.'

'Yeah, right.'

'You've got to believe me.'

'How can I trust anything that comes out of your mouth?'

'I didn't even know you were a cop. Remember? On our first date, you said you were a civil servant.'

'And on our second date, I told you everything.'

'And I was already in love with you.'

Sam never saw the punch coming. The force of it sent him stumbling back against the van wall. He rubbed his jaw and spat out a gob of bloody saliva. 'Do it again,' he said, knowing that her anger was justified, and wanting her to get it out of her system.

Anwen pulled back her fist, but couldn't do it. Instead she yelled into his face, letting all of her rage and the pain out, before she leant back against the van wall, letting her body slide down until she was sitting. Sam sat next to her.

'Now what?' he asked.

Anwen wished that she knew the answer.

*

Rhidian stood with his back turned as Loretta Swan slipped out of the hospital gown and into the clothes that he had brought. Although he could see nothing, he couldn't stop his imagination from taking the sound of silk slipping over skin and forming pictures in his head. He tried filling the silence.

'After the accident, when did you become aware of what was going on around you?'

'The crash, being cut out of my car, I don't remember any of that. Then it was like coming out of a long sleep. Eventually I started to hear things. Faint, but gradually becoming clearer. The sound of the monitor. People moving around, and then the voices. Your voice.'

Rhidian scanned through his memory. What had he said in those long, lonely hours in Loretta Swann's hospital room? He had only been so open because he felt safe in the knowledge that she couldn't register his words. Or had he unconsciously wanted her to hear?

'It was like when you can't sleep,' she said. 'So you end up lying there in the dark with the radio on, and it's like there's nobody else in the world, just you and that voice and he's talking only to you.'

Rhidian remembered the many nights at the cottage when he had put the radio on to try and drown out the sound of Bethan's voice in the wind as it blew around the house, sighing down the chimney and whispering through any crack in the windows.

'Sorry. Can you help me?' asked Loretta.

Rhidian hesitated before turning, to see that Loretta was fully dressed, but she was having trouble buttoning the sleeves of her blouse.

'My fingers aren't working properly. They've said that the feeling will come back, in time.' She held out her arms. Rhidian stepped closer to tackle the buttons. 'Before I could move or open my eyes, there was a time when it would have been easy to give up,' she said. 'I could have stopped fighting and there would have been no more worries. No more pain.'

Rhidian's reaction told her that he understood this only too well. 'Your voice gave me something to hold onto, your words helped to drag me towards the light.' Loretta's expression clouded over as she remembered the current situation. 'Why did I fight so hard when I'm probably going to swap one kind of prison for another? Are you going to arrest me?'

'Not now. But you will need to come in for a formal interview.'

'And then you'll charge me, and it will go to court, and if they find me guilty, how long will I get?'

'That depends on the judge and whether you plead guilty.' He could see that she needed more. 'Worst case. Three years? Out in half that time if you're lucky.'

'I suppose that will give me time to work out who I want to be; what I want to do with the rest of my life. Not everyone gets a second chance, do they?' She could see that Rhidian knew exactly what she meant. 'I wonder.'

'Yes?'

'My future. Could it include you?' Rhidian didn't instantly say no, and this encouraged her. 'The nurse said that you talked to me all night.'

'That's true. Only I was thinking about somebody else.'

Loretta saw the pain behind his sad smile and understood that his heart already belonged to someone else, someone who she could never compete with.

*

Anwen and Sam sat side by side in the back of his van.

'All the gifts; the meals out... You paid for everything with drug money,' said Anwen.

'I was doing it for us.'

'Fuck off! Don't you dare!'

'Six months and I would have turned my back on it.'

'And how were you going to explain where all the money came from?'

'An inheritance. A win on the Lotto. Does it matter?'

'Of course it matters. You can't build a future on lies.'

'I never lied about how I feel about you.'

'Don't!'

'Is there really no chance...?'

'Are you mad? You've broken my heart and probably fucked my career and you think we can just carry on playing happy families?'

Sam hung his head. 'I'm sorry.'

Anwen got to her feet, taking out her phone.

'I know I've got no right to ask,' said Sam, 'Can you give me forty-eight hours' head start?'

'And be guilty of assisting an offender?'

'Twenty-four. Please, Anwen.'

'Okay. Twenty-four. But you get out of Cardiff, and you never come back.'

Sam just nodded. Not wanting to look at his face anymore, Anwen turned away.

Six paint pots half filled with Class A drugs were lined up on the pavement outside her house. Anwen watched Sam's van drive away until he turned the corner and was out of sight, then she pulled out her phone and speed dialled. When the call was answered, she heard her own voice sounding stronger than she felt.

'Put me through to DI Gunter.'

38

In his office, Rhidian closed his notebook for the last time, uncapped a chisel-pointed permanent marker, and started writing down the spine when Jones arrived. Rhidian was surprised to see that she was carrying his coat.

'I got most of the blood out. Mended the tear.' She didn't like his silence. Had she overstepped the mark? 'I know my sewing's not up to much…'

'Thank you, Anwen. That was very thoughtful.'

It was the first time he had used her first name. She hoped that was a good sign. Rhidian took the coat from her, running his fingers over the new repair. Another battle scar to add to the ones repaired by his wife. Then he remembered that he wasn't the only one who had been left bruised.

'Any news?'

'Traffic boys boxed him in, making a break for the bridge. If he'd got to England he would have set up again, found some other mug to fall for his patter.'

'You did the right thing.'

'I'm a copper. How could I not see what he was?'

'We can all go a little mad when we're in love. Look at Morris Palfrey.'

'Next bloke I meet, he'll be getting a proper background check. I'll need full references and he'll have to pass a polygraph.'

Rhidian recognised the usual deflective techniques employed by cops. Make a joke out of it. Pretend it hasn't got through your defences. Deal with the real hurt when you get home. He knew that there would still be moments of self-doubt for Anwen Jones, but she was tough. She would shake it off, eventually. Rhidian stood and put the coat on, comforted by its familiar embrace. Jones wondered where he was going.

'Have we got another case?' she asked.

'No. Summons from the DCI.'

He was almost out through the door when Jones asked, 'Does that mean you're staying?'

Rhidian paused, but didn't turn back or answer. When he had gone, Jones saw that he had left his notebook on the table. She picked it up and read the words written down the spine: '*Venus Sleeping*'.

*

As Rhidian approached the DCI's office, Alun Gunter exited. He looked like someone whose chips had been well and truly pissed on, until he broke into a grin.

'Better luck next time, Hooky.'

Rhidian didn't bother knocking. He found Devlin behind her desk, tapping on her laptop keyboard.

'Tell me you've sacked him,' said Rhidian.

'After he's just cracked a major drugs case?'

'Which was handed to him on a plate by Sergeant Jones,' said Rhidian. 'And how does that wipe out how he tried to sabotage my investigation?'

'He denies leaking the stories to Ginnie Lane, and I've got no proof to the contrary.'

'What did she say about it?'

'Ms Lane said "I never reveal my sources." And I hear that she's signed a book deal for her inside story on how she survived a "maniac psycho killer".'

'You know this isn't the first time Gunter's crossed the line?'

'What I suspect, and what I can prove are two different things. Oh don't give me that scowl, Rhidian. He knows that one more false step and he's history.'

Rhidian had to content himself with the knowledge that Alun Gunter would never change his ways, so it was only be a matter of time before he got his just desserts.

Devlin was disappointed that Rhidian was the only person in the whole station who hadn't noticed her new look. How could somebody be such an astute detective, yet not see something right beneath his nose? A fleeting thought hit her. She bet that he would have noticed if Loretta Swann even changed the colour of her nail varnish. Devlin quickly shut down the flare of jealousy and changed the subject.

'The IOPC have launched an investigation into Palfrey's death,' she said.

'There are plenty of witnesses to what happened,' said Rhidian, confident that he had no option but to take Palfrey into the water to save Ginnie Lane's life.

'Sergeant Jones has already given a statement exonerating you.'

Rhidian expected nothing less, but was still pleased by her support.

'How did the interview with Loretta Swann go?' she asked.

'Her solicitor advised her to go "no comment", but she knows the quality of the evidence we've got against her. She told us everything, except for the name of her forger.'

'And you're sure that she knew nothing about Morris Palfrey's plans?'

'Positive. If she hadn't been in that car crash; if her life hadn't been in the balance, none of this would have happened. Maybe her thefts from the museum would eventually have come to light, but nobody would have died.'

Devlin changed the subject. 'And how are you?'

'I'm having the stitches out tomorrow.'

'I wasn't talking about your arm. Was I right to drag you down off that mountain?'

'Why did you? It nearly blew up in your face.'

'You're too valuable an asset to lose.'

'You were only thinking about the good of the Force?'

'Of course.'

Neither believed this, but that was a conversation for another time.

'So. Are you back for good?' asked Devlin.

'On one condition.'

'I've told you, I can't do anything about Alun Gunter—'

'Sergeant Jones. I want her assigned to me permanently.'

'No more Lone Ranger?'

'I just don't want Gunter ruining her career prospects.'

Devlin knew that it was too much for Rhidian to admit that he needed help.

'If Jones agrees, fine.'

Rhidian hoped that Jones wouldn't turn down the offer. He knew that he was an awkward, moody bastard to work for, but so far she had put up with everything he had thrown at her.

'And how are you?' asked Rhidian, catching Devlin unawares. 'You and Peter. I wasn't there for you when you needed me.'

'You were grieving.'

'I'm here now,' said Rhidian.

'I'm good, thanks,' said Devlin, and for once she actually meant it.

Rhidian stood and headed for the door.

'Where will you be staying?' asked Devlin.

'At the cottage.'

'I don't want you racking up the empties again.'

'Then you'd better find me another case.'

Rhidian smiled. It was a lovely smile and it had been too long since Devlin had seen it. Rhidian was halfway out when he called over his shoulder, 'I like the new look, by the way. Soft but strong.'

*

It took Augustus Bloom three days at the Mathias Museum to identify all of the ancient artefacts utilised by Morris Palfrey during his obsessive and deadly campaign. These were bagged up and sent to the forensic lab where they found Darius Gull's DNA on the 2nd century shears and one of Calder's hairs on the Maori battle club that had cracked his skull like an egg.

Huw Llewellyn watched the white-suited forensic team at work under the bright lights they had erected in the main gallery. He tried to convince himself that one day everything would get back to how it was. One of the reasons he was attracted to working in a museum was the stability it offered, the sense of permanence. Within the thick stone walls, surrounded by artefacts of the past, he could hide from an ever-changing world which he increasingly felt at odds with. But funding was always a struggle, so he wasn't surprised when some of the Trustees voiced a desire to cash in on the museum's new notoriety. Llewellyn tried to remind them about the museum's august reputation, but a steering group was set up to look into rebranding the facility. One suggestion was that a whole room should be dedicated to the murders, with a special section showcasing all of the murder weapons (facsimiles of course, as the actual objects were still being held by the police as evidence). There was talk of guided tours for the more ghoulish visitors, which would conclude with a visit to 'the killer's lair', once CSI had completed their forensic search of Morris Palfrey's flat.

Llewellyn tried to keep himself distracted from the Board's more lurid ideas by concentrating on the day-to-day running of the museum. Today he was busy writing the job specs for the replacements for Loretta Swann, James Calder and Trevor Cassidy, and of course, they needed a new live-in caretaker as well. As he put the finishing touches to the job adverts he decided that there was one more position that needed filling: that of Museum Curator. It was time that he moved on.

*

Loretta Swann's trial was scheduled for the following April at the Crown Court. By the time Huw Llewellyn had completed his search of the archives for more fakes, the final tally was beyond his greatest fears and led to Rhidian concluding that Loretta Swann must have squirrelled away much more money than the twenty-five thousand that they had traced. When he went to arrest her on the new charges, he discovered that she had moved on, without leaving any forwarding address. Looking around her flat, it looked as if she had just walked out in the clothes she was wearing, leaving her old life behind. She had left a message that he knew was for him, written in lipstick across the statue of Venus: *'You only live twice'.*

The police still had possession of her passport so how she had fled the country was a mystery. Her photograph was circulated via Interpol and there were various reported sightings of her from Istanbul, Verona and Angkor Wat, but none quite matched the description on the international warrant for her arrest. Some said her hair was a different colour, others her eyes. Rhidian Hook wondered, if their paths ever crossed again, would he even recognise her?

*

Upbeat '90s pop was playing loudly on the Bluetooth speakers in Anwen's bedroom. She had already gone around the house, on a mission to erase any sign that Sam had ever been there. A black bag full of his clothes and toiletries was sitting on the lid of her wheelie bin, waiting for the refuse collectors to remove it. Now she was working on the kitchen.

Keeping busy, filling the silence; that was Anwen's answer to try and plug the hole that Sam had left in her life. She had cleaned out the fridge, polished the hob and washed the floor tiles on her hands and knees. She was about to switch her efforts to the bathroom, when she saw the red light flashing on the washing machine, telling her that the programme had ended. She clicked open the door and pulled out the slightly damp pile of jeans and T-shirts. With the washing basket filled, she was about to head for the clothes rack in the spare bedroom, when something caught her eye, something white, stuck to the drum. She knew what it was immediately. He said it was missing. She reached in and pulled out one of Sam's lucky socks; white, with a red St George's flag on the heel.

After Craig Prosser she had sworn that she would never cry over another man. It was impossible to hold to that promise now. She sat back against the washing machine and let the tears flow.

*

Liz Devlin returned home with a bottle of good wine to celebrate the clearing of two cases and the return of Rhidian Hook. After kicking off her boots, she put the Chardonnay in the fridge and looked for something that would complement it. She hadn't had much of an appetite these last few days, but now she was ravenous. She found the remains of a veggie lasagne from a couple of days ago. While waiting for the pasta to warm through, she opened her laptop to check her emails.

Her Inbox was heaving with the usual mix of junk and a few personal messages. Her car insurance was coming up for renewal. The new mattress was due to be delivered tomorrow. Could she contact them if she wasn't going to be in to take delivery? There was a message from her sister. When was she going to book some time off and come and stay with them? The kids really miss her. Liz was wondering what excuse she could use to put her off, again, when a message popped up.

'Hi Liz.'

Peter had been sending her regular messages since they split. They veered between the begging and the bitter. He kept changing his email address so it was hard to block him. She was about to send this latest message to the junk box, when a new one popped up.

'I like the new look by the way. Soft but strong.'

She looked at her reflection in the laptop screen. How could he know that she'd changed her appearance? How could he have overheard Rhidian's comment? Then she saw the tiny black dot at the top of her laptop and her stomach churned, realising that Peter had been watching her through the camera. She slammed the lid shut with shaking hands, knowing that her nightmare was not over yet.

*

Rhidian stood on the banks of the river Taff. He knew that Morris Palfrey was deranged to have believed that his votive offerings would bring back his beloved; but what if he had been right? Rhidian opened his hand to look at the preserved orchid. He knew that he couldn't bring Bethan back, but if her remains could be recovered, he could at least say goodbye. He crouched, holding the orchid in his cupped hands, letting the water filter in through his fingers, before finally releasing the flower on its journey. He watched the flower bob on the water until it floated away, around the bend of the river and out of sight.

Two miles downstream, the gently twisting silver ribbon of water slowed as it turned around a wide bend. Safe behind its impenetrable tangle of ancient hedges, reinforced with the thorny briars of wild dog roses, the cottage was invisible from the road. Even approached from the river, all that could be seen were glimpses of the solid, whitewashed walls and one lead-latticed window, at which sat a solitary figure, gazing absently at the pale-blue flower that drifted past on the lazy water.

The cosy room was picture-postcard perfect, with its huge fireplace, oak beams and wood panelling. The remains of homemade scones and a pot of tea sat on the old oak table. A selection of books lay nearby. She hadn't decided what she liked yet. Historical romances? Biographies? The latest Booker winner? She had dipped into them all, but nothing was familiar; nothing sparked the memories that she was so desperate to regain.

The windows were nailed shut from the outside. She had given up on trying the door. She knew it would be locked. He never forgot. She knew that she was alone because the old floorboards creaked and groaned whenever he walked around. While she waited for him to return, her long, delicate fingers danced in the air, as if plucking invisible strings.

The End

Printed in Great Britain
by Amazon

80941419R00222